Dark ROCK

B Baskerville

HB
HYEM BOOKS

Hyem Books

CHAPTER 1

They call it *Costa da Morte* - the Coast of Death. A stretch of Spanish shoreline from A Coruña to Muros, where according to legend, the Galician winds carry the cries and terror of those lost at sea.

Theo Monroe cared not for myths and legends: they were nothing but stories. Locals might say they were plagued with nightmares, haunted by the restless spirits and unfulfilled destinies of sailors and fishermen. But Theo Monroe's nights were restful, spent in satin sheets and often in the embrace of a beautiful woman.

Monroe had grown accustomed to the luxuries that came with cosying up to men like Zhou: the parties, the five-star restaurants, the endless parade of leggy gold-diggers. As far as jobs went, this was a good one.

It was Zhou's yacht, White Dove, he was on now, and the superyacht was like everything in Zhou's life: opulent and polished.

Monroe checked his dive gear on the swim platform while Sun Li, Zhou's right-hand man, did the same. He was the same height as Monroe but about a foot wider, his muscles stretching the thick neoprene of his wetsuit.

Zhou stared down at the pair from the upper deck, his left hand resting on the brass guardrail, a crystal glass of amber liquid in his right. His silk housecoat in a vivid shade of red wafted playfully in the Atlantic breeze. "Have a good dive, gentlemen. Remember, if you find any treasure..."

"It's all yours," Monroe called back. "The least I can do for your generous hospitality."

Zhou raised his glass, turned away from the guardrail and disappeared from sight.

They wouldn't find any treasure. The wreck of HMS Serpent had sat on the seabed since 1890. Anything worth scavenging would be long gone. But that wasn't the point of their expedition. Li liked diving, which meant Monroe had to like diving. Li was apparently less interested in Michelin Star restaurants and easy women, so diving was the best way Monroe had found to bond with him.

Boating in this area was tricky enough, with the constant swell and fog, but diving here was another matter. Li had waited a week for a storm to blow through and for the sea state to settle. They had a test dive yesterday around the rocky shore and caught a few fish despite the wind and chop having kicked up the seabed. Silt would still be a problem today; it would cloud their vision worse than any fog, and the Serpent brought her own dangers: old fishing lines, netting, ammunition.

Monroe finished his pre-dive routine, checking weights, buckles and air. Li did the same, then they pulled their masks over their eyes and gave each other the OK before slipping into the gunmetal-grey water.

The cold hit Monroe in the chest. It was psychological, he told himself. Nothing his suit couldn't handle. He took a moment to acclimatise, then pushed his head down, kicked his feet upwards, and descended.

The water quickly grew murkier, visibility closing into a shadowy ten metres. Schools of mackerel darted through their torch beams like silver arrows. An octopus retreated into a rocky crevice, its colouring shifting from rust to slate.

An overgrown garden of laminaria engulfed them, a seaweed forest of long, leathery ribbons obscuring their view and slowing their search for the Serpent. Li and Monroe stuck closely together, working to keep each other in their sights at all times, but the flickering light that danced through the kelp in ghoulish beams played tricks on Monroe's mind.

It took them over twenty minutes, weaving and picking their way through the tangle of laminaria, to find their first glimpse of corroded metal. HMS Serpent materialised out of the gloom, a ghost ship stripped of all her glory. Monroe knew her history: a November storm, three survivors, 173 souls lost. Now she lay broken across the Spanish seabed, her wooden decks long since devoured by the sea, leaving only an oxidised iron skeleton draped in a cloak of green encrusting algae.

Monroe moved methodically, cautious of where he placed his hands. The decaying, rusting hull was littered with sharp, protruding parts which could cut or impale him if he wasn't careful.

He flattened his body, gliding horizontally through a narrowed section, one arm stretching forward, the other reaching back. His body then ceased moving how he expected; Monroe's rear arm held back while the rest of his body continued gliding forward, pivoting around his shoulder joint. At first, he thought he'd caught his hand on the wreck, but he soon dismissed that theory.

The attack was ruthless, though oddly, as if it were in slow motion, almost dreamlike. Li appeared through the green-blue haze, a glimmer of light glinting off his oxygen tank. Before Monroe could react, Li had him pinned against a rust-streaked beam.

The cord appeared in Li's hands, fast and yet not, like lethargic lightning. The fight was quiet, with the sound of bubbles and a desperate whoosh of expelled air replacing grunts and shouts, but despite Monroe's wild struggles, Li's superior strength made the outcome inevitable. It took him mere seconds to secure Monroe to the wreck's framework.

The mask obscured most of Li's face, the regulator hiding any trace of his mouth, but the creases around his eyes deepened. A smile. Not a friendly one.

Li drifted back, legs kicking lazily, before he twisted and swam away without looking back, his fins vanishing into the murky kelp.

Alone, panic flared through Monroe as he raged against the tether binding his hands behind his back. But as the cold, hard realisation kicked in and his air gauge ticked slowly downward, Monroe appreciated the irony. He'd been tasked with slithering into Zhou's world. His infiltration had taken months. Every conversation, every shared drink, every confidential document. He was the snake on Zhou's yacht. But someone had noticed.

And now he was one more lost soul on HMS Serpent. One more unfulfilled destiny on the Coast of Death.

CHAPTER 2

On the upper deck, Zhou watched the water, waiting for Li's head to break the surface. He turned to his drink, studying the whiskey in the crystal tumbler. Not a ripple disturbed its surface. It could have been carved from citrine, so still was the liquid, so steady was White Dove's position in the water. So steady was Zhou's hand. He lifted the glass to his lips, inhaling the peaty aroma before taking a slow, appreciative sip.

He finished the liquor, placing it on a mirrored table. Discretely, a slim gentleman in a sleek, black suit and earpiece materialised at his side.

"May I get you anything else, sir?"

Zhou dismissed him with a lazy wave of his hand. The suit wiped the table where the glass had left a ring and disappeared from view, walking backwards a few steps before turning away – as protocol demanded.

He returned to the horizon, watching the afternoon sun sparkle on the water. Within the next minute, Li's neoprene head surfaced, as dark and slick as a seal. He pulled himself onto the swim platform, salt water streaming off his wetsuit in shining rivulets.

Zhou leaned over the rail. Li removed his mask and breathing apparatus and stood to attention.

"The task is completed as you ordered."

"I take it Mr Monroe enjoyed the excursion?"

Li's face split into a cold smile. "He thought it was to die for."

Zhou laughed. Strong men like Li were easy enough to come by. Ones who followed orders and took such obvious pleasure in their work were far rarer commodities. He pictured Monroe abandoned under the waves, imagined his terror at being bound to the wreck, the thought of his air supply slowly running out. Would he panic and breathe faster, or conserve energy and try to make the tank last longer? Zhou didn't know, nor did he care. Monroe was a liability. A traitor. What was that old American saying from World War Two? Loose lips sink ships? Well, not his ship. Not White Dove.

***

On the seabed, Monroe slowly worked his bound hands up and down against the abrasive metal surface behind his back. He hoped the corroded metal was sharp enough to cut through the thick cord. It was sharp enough to cut his skin. He felt the biting sting of salt water in his wrists and wondered if sharks swam in these waters. Though sharks weren't the only creatures he had to worry about. Long, purple and blue tentacles trailed for fifteen, maybe twenty metres. He looked up and saw the pinkish, balloon-like body of a Portuguese man o' war.

Monroe started rubbing his binds faster and faster. Not caring that he was using more air. He had to get out of there. Had to get back to the yacht and— Do what? He was no match for Li. No, he had to get to shore, find a phone and tell someone what he knew.

A rumble pulsed through the water as the yacht started its twin engines. It was low, like distant thunder. Then he heard the rattling noise of the anchor chain lifting from the seabed. He trashed his hands faster, felt the metal slice into his wrists. What if it tore into his radial artery, and he bled out? At least death would come faster, Monroe concluded, watching the shadow of White Dove's bow turn and move swiftly away.

***

Any consideration Zhou had for Monroe's grim, aquatic end was fleeting. The torturous imagery evaporated under the Spanish sun as White Dove's engines fired up.

"What is for dinner?" he asked Li.

Li began stripping off his wet diving gear. "Our friend, Mr Monroe, caught an octopus during yesterday's dive. Chef wishes to slow cook it and serve it with truffle aioli, capers, saffron and gold leaf."

Zhou pictured the dish, artfully presented atop confit potatoes, adorned with micro greens and edible flowers.

"Very well," he said. "A fitting tribute. We shall toast our departed friend."

Li bundled his dive gear and rinsed himself and his equipment with fresh water from the hose. He pulled on a white dressing gown, tying it tightly.

"And tomorrow, sir? Shall I instruct the captain to head east to San Sebastián? I can secure you a table at Kokotxa."

He considered the offer. Tempting. His humble beginnings had largely tasted of whatever his mother could afford at the market. Now, he couldn't go a week without a tasting menu filled with decadent morsels in exclusive venues.

"No," Zhou answered. His eyes drifted south along the dramatic *Costa da Morte*. Despite what they'd suspected about Theo Monroe, the show, as they say, must go on. His plans remained unchanged. His clients were about to change the world. It would be a black swan event, Generation Alpha's 9/11. And in the aftermath, they'd make Zhou richer than he ever dreamed possible. "Tell the captain to set a course south. Porto for a few days, then perhaps Cádiz and dinner at Mantúa. Afterwards, Gibraltar."

Li bowed his head. "As you wish."

"There's going to be a rock show, Li." He smiled, relishing the double meaning. "And I'd like a front-row seat."

CHAPTER 3

It was early in the day, and the spring sun wasn't yet high enough to warm London's streets. High rises and skyscrapers obscured the morning light as Buddy Thompson walked towards Vauxhall Bridge, coat buttoned, hands warmed by an overpriced coffee in a paper cup. He paused near the bridge to stare at the ziggurat of green-tinted glass across the Thames that housed MI6. Legoland, he called it. Sir Terry Farrell's postmodernist fantasy of what a spy fortress should look like, all sharp angles and secret corners.

The coffee was from his regular place, where the new barista – Clarissa, according to her name tag – had held his gaze a moment too long while writing his name on his cup. She'd spelt it *Buddie*, adding a little heart over the intrusive 'i'. He'd noticed but pretended not to, the way men in their mid-to-late forties probably should when twenty-somethings flirt with them. The grey in his hair might be distinguished, but it was still grey.

He couldn't remember how he'd become Buddy. A childhood nickname that stuck around long enough to become more real than the original. His mother was the only one who still called him Charles, and then only when he'd disappointed her, which given his choice of career, was more often than he'd like. She was oh so proud of his brother, the accountant, and his sister, the neurosurgeon. But whenever she asked about Buddy's work, he could only give stock answers: *Work's fine, boss is a dick.* He could hardly go into details and give her classified information about terror plots and prisoner exchanges for the sake of sibling rivalry.

His phone buzzed. The display showed *Napoleon*, and Buddy grimaced.

"Leon. A bit early for you, isn't it?" Buddy answered, watching a tourist boat cut through the Thames' murky waters.

Unlike his own nickname, Buddy knew exactly why everyone referred to Leon Groves as Napoleon – not that they called him that to his face – but the man was five-five and wouldn't weigh nine stone if he was soaking wet and wearing lead underwear.

"Got something that needs your touch." Leon's voice had that particular tone Buddy had learned to dread, the one that meant unpaid overtime and missed dinners. "That arms dealer we've been watching..."

"Be more specific."

"The one with the taste for expensive suits and cheap women."

Buddy chuckled. Arms dealers were a homogenous bunch. "Be. More. Specific."

"Zhou."

Buddy took a sip of his coffee. It had cooled enough to drink but not enough to enjoy. He knew the name. "What about him?"

"We've been tracking his yacht for the past month. We had Theo Monroe on him, but he went dark two weeks ago. No word since. He suspected Zhou was arranging a sale to Iran. Something big, apparently. Something real big. Look, the G7 is approaching, and we'd like something solid to take to the table rather than rumours."

Buddy watched a pigeon land in the road in the middle of the bridge. It waddled a few steps, all plump and well-fed, and made it to the pavement without being hit by any of the north-going, rush-hour traffic.

"His yacht just moored up in Gibraltar," Leon continued. "Queensway Quay, to be precise. We need details of the sale. Who, what, when, how."

Buddy puffed his cheeks. *Crap.* "You know who the best person for this job is?"

"That's why I called you." A pause. "We both know who you need to call."

Buddy did know. His former protégé grew up in Gibraltar. Brilliant but unpredictable. Uncontrollable, some would say. The kind of agent who got results but on their terms.

The fat pigeon ruffled his feathers and took flight, depositing a creamy splatter of avian excrement across Buddy's path.

"I'll make the call," he said, instantly regretting it. He hung up on Leon and stared at his phone, thumb hovering over a number he thought he'd never dial again.

CHAPTER 4

T he bothy's stone walls and slate roof had faced over a century of Highland storms. While the exterior looked weathered and beaten, the interior remained relatively dry and surprisingly cosy. The cottage was basic, with a wooden table and bench on either side. A raised platform spanning the length of the room was big enough for a sleeping bag, and lanterns hanging from the walls could take tea lights. A fireplace was stained black from the soot of a million fires lit by cold hikers. It glowed now with the final embers of last night's blaze, filling the cottage with the pleasing smell of smoke. More modern bothies were appearing on Scotland's landscape these days, ones with wood burners, Ikea kitchenettes and sheepskin rugs. But this was how Spencer Bly liked it: no electricity, no hot water, no Wi-Fi. Heaven.

Unfortunately, there was, however, decent 4G coverage. An old-school Nokia buzzed on the wooden table, vibrating against the grooves in the aged oak. Assuming it was an impatient client who couldn't cope with an out-of-office auto-reply, Spencer ignored it and continued packing a rucksack for the lonesome, eight-hour hike to An Teallach. Compass, map, first aid kit, water.

The phone fell silent, but only for a second. When it rang again, it went ignored.

Spencer tied her long, dark hair back in a neat ponytail that wouldn't interfere with her peripheral vision: old habits died hard. Her hair was almost black, thick and glossy, the ends a little frizzy and in need of a trim. Still, she'd cut her ends herself rather than endure the small talk of a hairdresser's chair.

On a portable stove, water bubbled, ready to brew tea, while her phone continued to buzz. She relented, glancing at the table to see Buddy Thompson's name lighting up the screen. She snatched it when it rang for the third time, answering with, "I don't work for you anymore, Buddy."

She ended the call and threw the phone down before he could respond. The phone hit the pot on the stove. It slipped, spilling scalding water over the back of her hand. Spencer neither flinched nor cursed, simply watched her skin redden with curious detachment.

He rang again. Persistent bastard.

"You're needed back in the field." Buddy's voice had an unusual urgency. She hung up.

Fifth call. "You fancy a spot of sun? Gibraltar. There's a yacht—"

"Not interested." She had plenty of sun right there in Scotland. It might be bloody freezing, but the April sun shone brightly. Her finger moved to end the call.

"Please, Spencer."

She knew it killed him to beg her, especially in that same desperate tone he'd used when trying to rush her out of his bed before his wife came home from her uncle's funeral.

Spencer sat silently on the bothy's sole chair, watching sunlight crawl across the stone floor. Eventually, Buddy continued.

"Anyway, this yacht. There's an arms dealer thought to be on board. Name's Zhou—"

"Zhou what?"

"Just Zhou. Like Cher. He's a Beijinger who we suspect is selling weapons to Iran. We had an agent befriend Zhou and one of his associates, a man called Sun Li. Our man was posing as a broker between private mercenary groups. There was talk of a huge deal, a USB drive, state secrets. Something big. Something bad."

Spencer laced her walking boots tightly around strong calves. "So keep him on it. You don't need me."

"We lost contact. He's gone dark. Leon expects he's been made."

"So, Napoleon's got an asset missing, possibly brutally murdered, and he's tasked you with sweet-talking me into taking his place. Think I'll pass."

"Spencer."

"Why me?"

"You grew up in Gibraltar."

"I never told you that."

"This is Six, Spencer. We know everything about you."

"Not everything." Because if they knew everything, they would never have hired her. She ran a finger along the burn on the back of her hand.

The silence that followed was filled with unspoken history. Finally: "Fine. But I don't work for you, and I certainly don't work for Napoleon. I'm an independent contractor now."

She told him her daily fee. He tried to negotiate. She threatened to hang up again.

Outside the window, sunlight had painted the side of the mountain range in shades of orange and purple. A few small clouds peppered a brilliant blue sky. She sighed. An Teallach would have to wait. She had a plane to catch, a yacht to infiltrate and ghosts to confront.

"Do you still have family there? On the Rock?"

"This is Six," she answered, quoting his words back at him. "I think you already know the answer. But yes, my father's still there."

"You should see him. Once the mission's complete, of course. He'll be pleased to see you."

Her lips twitched coldly. "See, Buddy. You don't know everything about me."

CHAPTER 5

Two days later, Robin Grimm was riding high on a mix of sex-induced endorphins and a full English from The Feathers Hotel. He sang along to a pop song that would otherwise be too cheesy and youthful for his early-fifties sensibilities. His Vauxhall Insignia, a sturdy slate-grey model with a well-worn leather interior and an infotainment system wasted on him, cruised along at a steady fifty mph. Departing from Woodstock, he joined the A44, meandering through the picturesque villages of Oxfordshire, the verdant fields dotted with grazing sheep and playful lambs. The road was smooth, the Oxfordshire scenery lush and tranquil, and his fellow commuters drove unusually courteously.

Today was a good day.

The pop song faded to news of famine in some God-forsaken country, the war in another, the G7 and a new strain of Covid. Boring, sensible stories for boring, sensible people. Robin had no time for current events and stories of death, not when he felt this alive.

As he turned off the A4095 onto the perimeter road, the imposing gates of the base loomed ahead. He pulled up to the security barricade, flashing his pass at the scanner. A surly guard eyed his ID before lifting the barrier. Robin eased into first gear and rolled towards the car park, choosing a space in the sunshine. Killing the engine, he reclined his seat slightly and exhaled.

God, she was stunning. Legs up to her armpits and an arse you could bounce a two-quid coin off. In short, she was way out of his league.

He was more what they called dad-bod. His physique was decent for his years, but it wasn't what it used to be. His hair was more salt than pepper, and his eyes wrinkled from squinting. His 20/20 vision was long gone, but he couldn't admit to needing glasses.

Robin considered sitting there longer, lost in his dirty thoughts and the sleepy warmth of the car, but work beckoned. He'd be useless on the base today, driven to distraction by that body, those cat-like eyes and fiery hair. He got out, bending over to stretch his lower back, allowing the breeze to cool his skin and wake him up. His thighs ached. Not that he was surprised. He'd put in quite the performance last night to keep her satisfied. He'd never hear from her again; he was sure of that. But the memory of her flat stomach and her tongue... goodness, that would keep him going for a lifetime.

A phone call, one to prove him wrong.

It was her: Cara.

He shouldn't have doubted himself. Clearly, Robin
Grimm still had it. Of course, he knew he shouldn't have
given her his number, but he was drunk and bursting with
hormones. No good could come from it. Still, he knew
if Cara snapped her pretty little fingers, he'd go running.
What man in his right mind wouldn't? Buoyed with the
thought of another hook-up – turning a one-night stand
into a two-night stand – Robin took the call.

***

Heathrow Terminal 3 at nine a.m., and Spencer already
wished she was back in the isolated Scottish bothy. She
stood in the baggage drop line, listening to a couple
ahead of her hiss accusations about forgotten passports.
Ahead of them, a baby screamed, its mother bouncing it
desperately while the father argued with a British Airways
representative about their seating allocation. Behind her, a
child was allowed to pull his own wheelie case, nudging it
into Spencer's ankles every time the queue edged forward.
She breathed in the recycled air filled with summer flu,
Covid, and God knows what else and tried to block out
the noise of stressed passengers. The Highlands seemed a
million miles away and a million times better.

Zoning out, Spencer mentally reviewed the dossiers Buddy
had provided: Zhou, his entourage, the boat, its crew. He'd
given her an estimated layout of White Dove based on its sister
ship, a charter boat currently in the Caribbean. She walked
around it in her mind, moving through the crew quarters, up

the various decks and cabins to the very top, where a hot tub bubbled temptingly.

Her bag was already weighed and tagged using the self-service machine. She just had to hand it to the assistant and present her passport. Behind her, another baby took over where the other had let off, screaming with righteous indignation about the torture that was air travel.

Her new passport declared her Angela Smith, thirty-two. Angela was a marketing executive, wore sensible blazers and court shoes and carried a Kindle loaded with business books. Angela wore her raven hair tied back in a practical bun. If Angela were real, Spencer didn't think she would have much in common with her.

Through security. Shoes off. Belt off. Liquids inspected. Welcome to the departure lounge; please enter through the gift shop. The flight was delayed by forty minutes. Of course. Something about strikes in France that had a knock-on effect. She filed through the perfume and make-up section, passed the endless bottles of liquor and Champagne and made a beeline for Starbucks.

"Just hot water," she ordered. "To take away."

The barista poured boiling water into the classic green and white cup. "Twenty-five pence, love. Just for the cup."

Spencer nodded and paid with loose change from her handbag. Angela's handbag. Spencer didn't carry a handbag. She added her own tea bag, not because she was cheap or skint, but because she was very particular when it came to tea. She added a splash of milk and headed for the gate. She'd be early, but at least it should be quieter there.

Finding a seat, Spencer watched families heading for Dubai, businessmen in crumpled suits off to New York or Hong Kong. The arguing couple from check-in had followed her here, their whispered accusations growing louder with each passing minute. A mother struggled with two young children while her husband slept, and Spencer caught herself cataloguing faces, exits, and potential threats. Old habits.

When it was time to board, Angela Smith's passport was studied with uncomfortable thoroughness. Still, Spencer maintained the slightly bored expression of a frequent business traveller. Finally, a nod and a "Have a good flight."

Just under three hours to Gibraltar, plus the delay, minus the time difference. She did the maths, settling into her window seat. Eleven a.m. departure, delayed to eleven-forty. Two hours and fifty minutes flight time. Arrival two-thirty. Change of time zone: three-thirty. Just in time for tapas.

Her seatmate was a broad-shouldered businessman who claimed the armrest and half her legroom as his sovereign territory. She cowered further towards the window with the first two touches of his thigh against hers, faking interest in Angela Smith's ebooks, but on the third invasion of her personal space, she employed her three-strikes-and-you're-out rule.

She looked him dead in the eye, refusing to move her leg. "Stop touching me."

He looked put out that she dared. "Sorry—" He didn't mean it. "—But these seats are far too small." He tried to spread his knees wider.

Spencer's long lashes and big brown eyes gave her a deceptively soft look, like the sort of woman who might move away in silence or nervously laugh off any awkward encounter.

"Not my problem," she said. "If you want half my legroom, pay for half my flight."

He smirked, glancing down at her chest. "How about I pay for a drink instead?" He raised a hand, trying to hail an air steward."

"How about you move your leg off mine before I start yelling about non-consensual touching?"

He sighed, rolling his eyes in a dramatic arc, before closing his legs and calling her a bitch.

CHapTer 6

Cara's voice was like honey, Robin Grimm thought. Or medicine. An antidote to middle-aged monotony and morning commutes. She spoke the Queen's English. Or was it the King's English now? Still, a slight accent broke through when she spoke quickly, a little hint of something else when she was excited. Was she hiding a working-class background? A secret northerner? With a body like hers, she could talk like Jimmy Cranky for all Robin cared.

Warmth spread through his cheeks as she told him how much she missed him already, how she wished to kiss him one more time.

"I have a surprise for you, handsome," she said before his phone pinged three, four, five times.

Robin opened WhatsApp. "Bloody hell," he gasped. No one was there to see the images over his shoulder, but he covered the screen out of instinct. "How did you...?"

"I set my camera to take a picture every ten minutes. Fifty minutes, darling. You are a machine."

His pride swelled, looking at her on top of him, her back arched in pleasure. "Well, you look like a flipping goddess, that's for certain. I look like a—"

"You look like a god, Robin," Cara said. "You made love like one, too." She blew a kiss and ended the call.

He felt dizzy when she said his name. He rested a hand on the Insignia's roof, the cool metal grounding him as he smiled like a kid on Christmas day. He felt his laughter lines deepen as he scrolled through the erotic pictures. He hadn't seen breasts that perfect in a long time. His forehead felt dewy, his insides twisted and turned.

You can't keep these, he told himself. *You have to delete them.*

Or did he? Robin wondered if there was an app for storing photos disguised as something dull, like a budget planner or something. A plain logo, a password, a way to keep them all to himself.

He began walking towards the building, concluding that he'd save the pictures but delete her number as soon as Friday rolled around. He'd give it to the end of the week in case there was a chance at round two; then, he'd delete her number and choose a new hotel for next week's work.

The base was slowly coming to life as others arrived, the sound of his boots on the tarmac muffled by the hum of vehicles snaking into the car park.

His phone pinged again. What delicious words or images did this vixen have for him this time?

Please pay attention, Robin. I am deadly serious. You are to do as I ask, or I will forward our little photoshoot to your lovely wife.

Robin stopped mid-stride. His heart seemed to slow. Blood drained from his face to his limbs, making him momentarily light-headed and weak.

His wife? How did she—? Then adrenaline flooded his system like he was being attacked. He readied for war, clenching his jaw and his fists.

Words he would never usually use filled Robin's head: Bitch. Cow. Whore. Slut.

Another ping.

I will call later, handsome. Be sure to answer.

***

Spencer spent the next two and a half hours of the flight watching the scenery change from green to shades of yellow. Eventually, the Mediterranean appeared, turquoise and inviting. Then, there it was in all its majestic glory: the Rock. Almost twenty years collapsed into memory: she was fourteen again, angry and scared. Very scared. Her father sat silently beside her on that first flight into Gibraltar, where she'd stayed until she turned nineteen. The same runway stretched across the peninsula's width, built on reclaimed land that still bore the scars of the Great Siege.

They landed with a bump that rattled the overhead compartments. The cabin turned into a greenhouse,

Gibraltar's heat seeping in before the engines had time to quieten.

Leg Spreader was up and out of his seat before the seatbelt sign had been switched off. He unloaded Spencer's carry-on from the overhead and looked expectantly at her for a thank you that never came.

Outside on the tarmac, Spencer removed Angela's blazer and let the sun warm her shoulders and neck. The Rock towered above the runway, its sheer north face peppered with tunnel mouths: old artillery positions once aimed at La Línea, just beyond the border.

Back inside, the baggage carousel turned with maddening slowness. A mix of languages floated around her: English tourists already complaining about the heat, rapid-fire Spanish from a group of businessmen, and the unique blend of both that was Llanito, Gibraltar's linguistic fingerprint. Spencer caught fragments about someone's cousin's wedding, a business deal in Fuengirola, the price of cigarettes at the airport shop. Leg Spreader was on the phone, talking loudly about how important he was. The arguing couple had made up and were engaged in a seriously public display of affection: his hand on her flat arse, her fingers in his thinning hair.

"First time in Gib?"

She pulled her eyes away from the amorous couple. The voice belonged to a man in his thirties, an airport security badge hanging from a lanyard around his neck. Ethan, it read.

"Yes," she lied. "Always wanted to come and see the monkeys."

"Apes," he corrected incorrectly.

He was about her age. She tried to place him, rattling through her old memories of the boys from Bayside. She wondered if they'd ever met in her previous life here. Had they moved in the same circles or hung out at Rosia Bay?

"They're Barbary macaques. Also called Barbary apes," he continued.

He was quite handsome, she thought, with his sandy hair and strong jaw. He clearly worked out but was no gym hound. Lean but strong. Defined muscles and tendons flexing under his thin shirt. She decided to test him. A red flag test. See how he handled being corrected.

"They're apes in name only. Barbary macaques don't have tails but are true old-world monkeys."

He raised his brows, but nothing in his body language suggested he was offended. "Is that right? I did not know that. I might have to head up to the reserve and apologise to each of them for mis— What's the species equivalent of misgendering?"

Spencer laughed. "Probably misclassifying? Are they as playful as I hear?"

"Playful? Yes. But also vicious when they want to be."

He could have been describing her.

"I'm Ethan, by the way." He extended a hand just as Spencer's luggage rolled by. She grabbed it from the carousel and pulled the handle up.

"I know," she said, pointing to his badge. "I'm Angela."

They shook hands. His palms were rough, but his grip was gentle.

"Well, Angela. If you fancy accompanying me up the Rock to help me say sorry to our primate friends... They are primates, aren't they?" He handed her his card: Ethan Campbell.

She tucked it in Angela's handbag. "Do you offer private tours to every woman landing in Gibraltar for the first time?"

"Only the ones who entertain me with monkey facts."

"I might take you up on that," she lied, tipping her luggage so it balanced on its two wheels. She gave him a coy wave and headed for the exit.

"Enjoy your stay," he called after her.

The automatic doors parted, and Mediterranean heat rolled in like a wave. She stepped out and looked at the Rock. It was iconic from every angle, but it was the sheer north face that took a person's breath away. 430m of cold, off-white Jurassic limestone that glowed orange in the low sun and narrowed to a striking peak. Spencer could smell jet fuel, hot tarmac, and the salty tang of the bay.

Welcome home, she thought.

CHAPTER 7

The 5/10 bus was waiting at the stop, its doors open to the heat and humidity. Spencer dropped £1.20 into the driver's hand and chose a seat near the front next to a woman with plum hair and a wheeled shopping case full of wine. The driver waited for the bus to fill, then pulled into the road and performed a U-turn before heading towards the Kingsway tunnel. Spencer watched Gibraltar's streets roll past the window for the six stops to Market Place, noting new highrises that had still been under construction when she'd left. She alighted and walked down Fishmarket Lane, where the scent of olive oil and garlic floated in the afternoon air.

Having no intention of starting work on an empty stomach and wanting some fresh air after the airport and the plane, Spencer chose a tapas bar nestled into the arches of Chatham Counterguard. The old fortification's thick grey walls formed part of Gibraltar's first line of defence, protecting the taller Orange Bastion, which loomed high on the other side of the alley. Any attack that breached the Counterguard would expose the assailants to fire from the bastion, trapping them in a lethal gauntlet. Today, the bastion's massive stone blocks, weathered smooth by onshore winds and salty air, were still impressive, though the cannons were now decorative and those patrolling them were tourists rather than riflemen and musketeers. Spencer had walked these bastions countless times as a teenager, choosing solitude over awkward attempts at friendship. Choosing anywhere over home.

"*Vino blanco seco, por favor,*" she ordered, then added, "*salmorejo con anchoas.*" The words felt familiar in her mouth despite not having spoken Spanish or Llanito for years.

The salmorejo arrived. It was typically served as a cold, creamy soup made from tomatoes, garlic, bread, vinegar, and olive oil. But, like today, it could also be thickened and served as a paste, a bright orange puree spread on a thin slice of toasted bread, topped with a couple of pickled anchovies. Spencer admired the colour. Orange, Gibraltar's true colour, she thought. It was everywhere: the salmorejo before her, the oranges that adorned the trees along Main Street, the sunset bleeding into the bay, the vivid monarch butterflies that danced through the parks, the bird of paradise flowers erupting from every garden. She'd tried to recreate salmorejo in London, but English tomatoes were pale imitations, watery impersonations of what a tomato should be.

Her phone buzzed as she signalled for the bill. Buddy's number.

She thought about hanging up for no reason other than to annoy him.

"Your accommodation's on Queensway Quay. The apartment's on the southern side of the marina. Take Queensway Road until you're almost at Ragged Staff—"

"I know where it is." She watched a tourist couple struggle with a map across the street. "Just tell me how to get in."

Buddy gave her instructions on how to access the apartment. He paused for a moment, then lowered his voice. "Zhou's a nasty piece of work, Spencer. And that Sun Li is ruthless by all accounts. Peter Tenby is in Cadiz. I can have him there in a few hours."

"Half-Pint Pete?" Spencer laughed, remembering the former SAS operator, his inability to handle his booze and his infamous hatred of his nickname. "Thanks, but I don't need muscle."

"I thought you'd say that." He sounded concerned. "Well, he's in the region if needed."

Spencer left a ten-pound note on the table and got to her feet. "This apartment," she began, extending the handle of her wheelie case. "It's properly provisioned this time?"

"I've been assured," Buddy answered quickly. "We don't want a repeat of the Bangor incident."

Ah, the notorious Bangor incident of 2023. One of the many reasons she no longer worked for Six.

Spencer headed south. She'd make the rest of the journey on foot. It would only take fifteen minutes. "No," she said. "No, we do not."

***

The entrance to Queensway was rather grand, with an ornate black and gold wrought-iron gate spanning the road. Above the gate, the words Queensway Quay were emblazoned in bold, capital letters in a stylish shade of grey. Atop the inscription, a regal crest of crown and shield. The impression was one of exclusivity; a gated residence for the elite and wealthy.

There were two pedestrian archways, one on either side of the gate. Spencer chose the one on the right, passing under its brief shade before approaching a memorial garden. The garden was a small, rectangular lawn lined with low white walls and plants that could cope with the intense summer heat: fan palms, yucca, a felt bush, and foxtail agave. There was a sign: no dogs, no games. A short, rusted chain guarded a short path of grey slabs with crooked edges that led to the garden's centrepiece – a giant black anchor.

She squatted next to the chain, lifted one of the slabs and retrieved the key. It was a predictable hiding place, but sometimes, the classics worked best.

The building was pale beige with turquoise shutters over the windows and a door marked *Moorland House 10-20*. Using the key, Spencer entered the communal hallway. She climbed to the top floor, breathing in the strong scent of pine disinfectant. A penthouse. She briefly found herself calculating the monthly rent on a place like this, wondering what it was costing British taxpayers. Then she remembered the daily fee she'd quoted Buddy.

The door to the penthouse looked like standard UPVC, but Spencer suspected that beneath that innocent white exterior lay reinforced steel. Anyone who tried kicking it down would break their leg before breaking the hinges. The small box masquerading as a doorbell was anything but. It was a neat piece of biometric technology that would make most security consultants salivate. Spencer pressed her thumb against it, waited for the fingerprint scan to complete, then leaned in for the retina check. Heavy locks whirred inside the door like mechanical insects.

Inside, the apartment was filled with clean lines and modern furniture. Nothing too flashy, and nothing that suggested this was ever a home for long. No framed memories, trinkets, or keepsakes. Everything was spotless and sterile. She found herself missing the bothy.

The kitchen gleamed with floor-to-ceiling glossy, grey cabinets. Spencer opened a large American-style fridge freezer. The refrigerator was stocked with a lone bottle of *leche semidesnatada* – semi-skimmed milk – and the freezer was big enough to hide a body in, not that she planned on needing that particular feature. Still, it was good to know. She filled the kettle and began opening cupboards. There were the usual basic staples: pasta, rice, tinned tuna, tinned tomatoes, jars of chickpeas. Bingo. An unopened box of Yorkshire Tea.

"Crisis averted," she murmured, preparing a proper brew.

Steam curled from the mug as she surveyed her new domain. The front balcony offered an unobstructed view of the marina, a bustling hub where sailing yachts and motorboats bobbed gently in their berths. The marina felt alive with activity. Sailors polished their pride and joys. A man hoisted halfway up his mast meticulously checked his rigging. Some looked to be preparing to go to sea, others were simply enjoying the day. A tall man with a black and tan terrier walked briskly along the pontoon, the dog eagerly pulling towards the gate, its tail wagging excitedly. Along the west side of the marina was a gated community of millionaire mansions. They hadn't existed when she moved to Gibraltar at fourteen, but over her time here, the land was reclaimed, houses built, and swimming pools dug. Across the water on the east side, a row of swanky bars and restaurants looked popular, their patrons basking in the sunlit terraces, glasses clinking in leisurely toasts.

Her eyes found White Dove easily. Moored at the end of pontoon A, it was larger than she had imagined, its white hull gleaming brilliantly. She laughed. White Dove. A symbol of peace owned by an arms dealer. The irony. She watched for a few minutes, waiting for her tea to cool, but there was no sign of Zhou, Li, or anyone else on board.

She moved to the other side of the apartment and looked out the window. A high fence topped with barbed wire guarded the naval base, home to both the Royal Navy and the Marine Unit of the Gibraltar Defence Police. A grey military craft named Cutlass was arriving back into its berth, and by the breakwater, a police boat with distinctive luminous yellow and deep blue checks patrolled the buoyed channel. She watched sniffer dogs working the perimeter and listened to the industrial creaks and groans of a working port: hoists, cranes, a cable-laying vessel out in the bay.

Spencer slipped off her court shoes and released her hair from the bun, shaking it free and finger-combing the lengths. She had ample supplies of Yorkshire Tea, so at least the priorities were sorted. Time to see what toys Six had left for her.

CHAPTER 8

Spencer unpacked her clothing into a walk-in wardrobe. A couple of outfits suitable for Angela Smith – smart enough for her businesswoman persona, light enough for the Gibraltar sun. A few more practical outfits – black trousers with numerous pockets, black vests and jackets, black cap, dark shades. Sneaky clothes for sneaky deeds. The wardrobe looked ordinary enough; a cleaner or overnight guest wouldn't notice anything amiss. Spencer opened the bottom drawer of a set of three and followed Buddy's earlier instructions, pressing the bottom panel in sequence: back right, front left, centre. The soft click was barely audible.

The panel lifted out to reveal a hidden compartment, no more than three inches deep, filled with blades: ceramic knives that wouldn't trigger metal detectors, some smaller knives with leg straps, and a set of Japanese tanto blades. Each had been sharpened recently. She picked up a tanto, feeling the rayon silk crisscrossing around the handle. Shorter than a katana at only ten inches, double-edged with a sharp-pointed tip, this was a tool that was built not for simply stabbing flesh but for piercing through armour.

Nice, Spencer thought. Very nice.

Another drawer, another shallow stash of goodies. Guns this time. She lifted a Heckler & Koch MP7 from the casing for examination. The weapon had been adequately maintained, its barrel clean, its moving parts lightly oiled. It weighed less than two kilos and could fire fifteen rounds per second. A bit overkill, Spencer thought. Guns were rarely her style. They drew attention and left a mess. Still, better to have one and not need it than to need one and not have it. She returned it to the drawer and pulled out a compact Glock 26 Gen 5. The Glock was more discreet. It weighed less than a kilo fully loaded and was only six and a half inches in length.

Surveillance gear and pharmaceuticals occupied another drawer. Two mini drones sat in protective cases alongside their controllers – a bit risky to use next to a naval base. There was a night vision monocular, some top-end binoculars, a thermal imaging scope, bugs, and other electronics. Spencer gave a cursory glance at the prescription painkillers and raised a brow at the others: modafinil, caffeine and amphetamine pills for staying awake, zolpidem and flunitrazepam for doing the opposite. She closed the drawer again; the only chemical assistance she required was tea.

Yorkshire Tea.

Spencer closed everything up, adding her shoes and underwear to the wardrobe. She returned to the kitchen and boiled the kettle again.

***

1100 miles north-northeast of Queensway Quay, Robin Grimm was a mess. All day, his work had been sloppy, and his supervisors dissatisfied. They hid their annoyance behind banter at first, but as the day went on, the barbs were increasingly obvious. Robin fobbed them off with a fictional migraine.

It was the middle of the afternoon, and Robin was on his way to the cafeteria for a break when his phone rang. Her. Cara.

His chest tightened. He was a reasonably healthy man, and he felt like he was on the verge of a heart attack. He ducked into the men's, checking the cubicles were unoccupied before answering.

"Listen," he growled into the phone, "I don't know who you think you are, but you're not getting a penny out of me, you blackmailing whore. I don't even have a wife."

"Yes, you do, Robin. Don't lie to me." Cara's voice was calm, far more measured than his.

He'd been careful, slipping his wedding ring off discreetly under the bar as they'd sat chatting the night before. It was during his second pint of real ale and her first glass of white. There'd been three more pints before she suggested they share something sparkling up in her room.

"I don't have a wife," he repeated, back to the wall, ready to leave the second anyone came in to use the bogs.

He heard Cara sigh, a long, drawn-out sigh as if he were boring her. "Ellen Morris," she purred. "Didn't take your surname when you married in 2000. Born on the third of August 1976. Graduated from the University of Gloucestershire in '97 with a 2:2. A kept woman."

Robin's blood turned icy. He moved to the sinks, the harsh fluorescent lights glinting off the chrome fixtures. He turned the cold water tap on, splashing his face with his free hand.

"Ellen describes herself as a full-time mother," Cara continued, "but your children are fully grown. How are Holly and Lance?"

"How dare you!" Robin grabbed the edge of the sink, his knuckles blanching. He wanted to rip the porcelain clean off the wall. Memories of family holidays, laughter-filled dinners, and tender moments with Ellen flashed through his mind, fuelling his rage. "You have no idea who you are dealing with, you dumb—"

"Hush now, of course I know who I'm dealing with. You are Robin Grimm, born on the fourteenth of October 1973. The second of three children born to Alice and Peter Grimm. Bee Gees fans, I assume. Barry came first, then you, Robin. Imagine Alice and Peter's disappointment that little Maurice turned out to be little Maureen."

Cara's voice seemed to morph as she spoke, the posh boarding school accent fading bit by bit into something else. Something eastern.

Ukrainian? Russian?

He'd heard enough. "Stop!" Robin's fist hit the mirror hard enough to shatter it. "Fuck," he said, grimacing as blood poured from his knuckles, dripping onto the reflective carpet of silver shards by his feet. He saw his fractured mirror image, saw the blind panic in his expression. What the hell was happening?

He grabbed paper towels from the dispenser, his boots crunching on fragments of broken glass. "Who are you? Is your name even Cara?"

"Of course not, silly bear." She let out a child-like giggle, the same giggle he'd found so captivating as they flirted in The Feathers. "Who am I? That is a long story. For now, all you need to know is that I am a problem."

Robin's mouth dried up completely before he asked the pertinent question. "What do you want?"

"A favour, darling. A tiny favour. Minuscule. After that, you'll never hear from me again."

CHAPTER 9

As the afternoon faded towards evening, Spencer pretended to read her Kindle while sitting under the shade of a giant yucca, its sword-shaped leaves casting sharp shadows. She was watching the gate to Pontoon A, slowly deciphering the code for the security lock. She watched three different people punch numbers into the security pad. Six digits. Two columns of buttons. On the left, numbers one to five and letters X and Y. On the right, numbers six to nine, followed by zero, Z and C. The codes for these types of locks always began with a C. C for cancel, resetting any incorrect entries. She'd watched long enough to know the C was followed by four numbers, then either an X or a Y. One from the left – probably the number one – and three from the right. If she watched long enough, she'd work it out.

She didn't have to watch much longer. A couple of men sauntered back to the pontoon, their voices slightly slurred from inebriation. The shorter typed in the code, turned the handle and tutted as it failed to open.

"No," said the taller. "Its one-nine-six-seven, you pressed one-nine-six-six."

Jackpot. 1967 – the year of the referendum when Gibraltar voted overwhelmingly in favour of staying British. Whoever programmed the lock was a proud Gibraltarian and the code was either C1967X or C1967Y. Spencer could live with that.

Beyond the gate, movement on White Dove's upper deck caught her attention. An older man emerged wearing a silk housecoat in deep burgundy. Zhou, she assumed, though it was hard to tell from her spot under the yucca. He looked to be on the phone, gesturing sharply with one hand. Even from this distance, his temper was clear. Two crew members polishing the stainless steel on the upper deck scattered at his approach, finding other tasks that needed their attention elsewhere on the vessel.

***

In the guest cabin he shared with James Wan, Sun Li slid his diving knife's edge across a whetstone in smooth strokes. The blade made a satisfying whisper against the stone. Sharpening helped him think. Usually.

Li was hunched on a queen-sized bed, his broad shoulders casting shadows over the quilt. He was shirtless and barefoot, wearing only a pair of khaki combat trousers.

"Monroe knew too much," Li said, testing the blade's edge with his thumb. Not sharp enough. Never sharp enough. "I should have killed him."

James looked up from his phone. He was lying on the other queen, half his face obscured by a mop of shoulder-length black hair. He wore a faded Ramones T-shirt and grey underpants, skinny legs stretching out across the bed like he didn't have a care in the world.

"You did kill him."

"I should have made certain."

"You left him chained to that wreck. He had what? Twenty minutes of air?"

"I should have cut his throat." The whetstone scraped against steel. "Should have watched the blood cloud the water."

"You were following orders. And since when do you doubt yourself?" James rolled onto his side and pushed his hair off his face. "The guy's fish food."

Li paused his sharpening. "He said he was a broker. Said he could help with future deals, but he was too interested in past deals for my liking." Another stroke of the blade. "What if he blabbed? If he survived..."

"He's dead. You don't need to be scared," James said, immediately regretting it.

Li moved with the speed of a striking snake. The newly sharpened blade pressed into the fleshy underside of James' jaw, drawing a single bead of blood.

"I am never scared," Li hissed. "Not of Monroe. Not of anyone."

The cabin's intercom crackled. "Li, Mr. Zhou wishes to see you in the lounge."

Li withdrew the blade. He wiped it carefully on James' bedspread, taking longer than necessary. Then he stood, pulled on a clean shirt, and tried to ignore the cold feeling in his stomach as he headed for the lounge.

**

As darkness draped itself across the Bay, Spencer changed into black leggings and a black hoodie. She tied her hair in a ponytail and pulled it out of the back of her baseball cap, pulling the peak low over her face. She looked like she was going out for an evening jog. Headphones on, no music.

Coming out of Moorland House, she turned right, heading for the end of the road where she could look out into the bay. It was peppered with the lights of vessels and across the water, the warm glow of Algeciras at night. To the south, Africa lurked in the blackness, the peak of Jebel Musa obscured by low clouds. To the east, the top of the Rock wore a crown of rubies: red warning lights, blinking steadily at any aircraft that might stray too close. Rounding the end of the block, she turned her back on the bay and walked along the marina side. The path was wide with a chain fence. Over the chain lay an eight to ten-foot drop to the pontoon below.

White Dove was on her left, its interior lit up with blue mood lighting. The windows on the middle deck were level with Spencer. She walked slowly, taking quick glances inside, putting faces to the profiles she'd read before flying down here. Sun Li was easy to spot, his triangular frame and moody posture apparent even in casual clothes. The captain was obvious, as was the chef in his whites. The former was an Italian by the name of Renato Santori, and the latter was a German called Peter Müller. According to her research, they came with the boat and weren't part of Zhou's inner circle. The man in a black suit and shirt was likely Mengze Dong, Zhou's butler for all intents and purposes. Still, he was also a childhood friend Zhou trusted very much and would accompany him and Li to meetings with potential clients. He was taller than Zhou and Li, but slim, his face long and serious.

Mengze moved to the lower deck. Spencer crouched to tie her shoelaces and paused to pretend to scroll through her music app. She watched him mix a cocktail and pour it into two highball glasses.

A woman's squeal caused Spencer to tense up. She stood and scanned the windows for the source, hoping the dark partially concealed her snooping. The crew shouldn't be able to see her very well from the illuminated interior. There was another scream, this time followed by raucous laughter.

She spotted him.

Zhou lounged like a man born into power, though anyone who knew his story would know better. He was sprawled across a pale leather sofa, the centre of the room's attention. His white silk shirt was open at the collar, shimmering faintly blue in the mood lighting. Thicker than Mengze but slimmer than Li, he had the build of a man who stayed in shape without obsessing over it. Next to him, a young woman in a flimsy spaghetti-strapped dress was curled into his side, laughing with her head tilted back, her throat exposed in careless delight.

Zhou's hand splayed across her bare shoulder, possessive and idle, as though she were some small exotic creature he'd decided to cage.

CHAPTER 10

Spencer left White Dove, continuing her walk past the apartments lining the length of Pontoon A. In her head, she catalogued those on board, or at least the ones she'd identified. The arms dealer, the muscle, the butler, the captain, the chef, two crew and the girl.

She discounted the girl, all six stone of her. Spencer had seen stronger stick insects. That left seven men. Doable. But it was the unknown that bugged her. Unknowns were trouble. Who else was hiding in there?

The pontoon was 170, maybe 180 metres from the gate to White Dove. A thirty-second sprint. Twenty-eight seconds after one of those caffeine pills from the drawer in the penthouse. Still too tight. Too risky. She needed to be stealthy.

Spencer reached the gate, punching C1967X into the keypad. Nothing. She tried again. C1967Y. It clicked open, and she followed the rickety ramp down to the pontoon.

Her heart didn't pound; it was steady. She walked like she ought to be there. Just another sailor returning home. She scanned the pontoon as she walked, searching for options that didn't involve a thirty-second sprint. She could jump on a random sailboat and hide in its cockpit, hoping no one was home. She ruled it out. Spencer didn't do *hope*.

Halfway along Pontoon A, a set of slippery stone steps led up the harbour wall to the path she'd just walked along. The only problem – they were a deathtrap.

It was only once Spencer had passed all the sailboats that her heartbeat increased. Only one boat left. She crouched in a deep squat, low enough so anyone looking out from the middle deck or the galley would struggle to see her. One crew member glancing the wrong way could put the entire mission in jeopardy.

She worked quickly to loosen the port mooring line off the cleat and lengthen it by a metre. She repeated the action on the starboard side, then turned and sprinted.

She ran hard and low for fifteen seconds, hoping it was enough time. She felt exposed and vulnerable, urging herself to run faster, pump her arms harder.

She spotted the deathtrap gap in the harbour wall ahead, and with a final burst of speed, Spencer leapt across the water. For a moment, she was airborne, dirty water beneath her. Her feet hit the algae-covered steps and slipped out from underneath her, arms windmilling.

"Not today," she hissed, regaining her balance by sheer force of will, scrambling up the steps, and rolling under the chain at the top of the harbour wall.

Phase one: complete.

Spencer kept her body pressed flat against the cold concrete, her heart hammering into the ground. Her knees were wet from damp algae, and she could picture green under her fingernails. She could smell it too.

With its mooring lines lengthened, White Dove began to sway left and right. Suddenly, a commotion erupted. Angry voices and heavy feet. Li and five men leapt from the yacht, hitting the pontoon with dull thuds.

Li's voice was loudest, yelling in English. He grabbed one of the crew by the throat, jabbing his finger in his face. "Incompetent fool!" he roared furiously. "How could you let this happen?"

"The lines were secure, I swear."

Spencer watched, her body relaxing but ready to jump up and run if needed. Movement on the middle deck caught her eye, so she crawled sideways, pushing herself away from the edge of the wall and pressing herself back against the apartment block, using the extra shadow for increased coverage.

Zhou stepped out, his white shirt billowing in the breeze, and looked at the scene below with cold disdain, like a king surveying unruly peasants. Li's grip loosened instantly. The crewman stumbled back, gasping, lunging for the lines to help his colleagues bring White Dove closer to the dock.

"My apologies, sir," Li said. "We'll have this sorted immediately."

Zhou didn't respond. Instead, he turned, leading the young woman up the stairs. Spencer strained to hear their conversation.

"...hot tub... private... enjoy ourselves..."

The woman came into clearer view. She had long dark hair, just like Spencer's, but unlike Spencer, she wasn't in her thirties. She wasn't even in her twenties.

"Christ," Spencer breathed. Was she even legal?

Spencer pushed a memory away, sliding around the corner and out of view. She let herself back into Moorland House and trotted up the stairs. Fingerprint, retina, kettle on.

She stripped out of her clothes and turned on the shower. She'd be washed before the water boiled. As she soaped herself, she counted the men again. Li she recognised as well as two of the others. Three were new faces.

"Ten," she said aloud, adjusting her tally.

At least ten men were on board. She sighed quietly as the warm water ran over her body. Sneaking on board was now out of the question. Even on a vessel as large as White Dove, there was no way she could get on there without being noticed. If she wanted that USB drive, she needed a new plan. A way to get on Zhou's yacht legitimately.

She needed to be invited.

CHAPTER 11

The next morning, Spencer fixed a simple breakfast from the supplies in the apartment's kitchen. Eggs, toast, tea. Depending on how long she stayed in Gibraltar, she'd have to go to the big Morrison's or Eroski to stock up. Planning on a morning run, she dressed in almost the same clothes as the night before: a black vest and black cap. Her leggings were dirty and smelled of bracken, so she switched them to a pair of shorts – black, of course. No need for a jacket, though. She smeared a film of SPF30 over her shoulders and the bridge of her nose and packed a small backpack with a water bottle and an empty Tupperware box that she found in the cupboard next to the fridge.

Headphones in place – no music – Spencer left the marina for the maze-like streets and alleys of the Upper Town. The labyrinth was one of steep, twisting staircases, narrow passages and sharp bends that mopeds and bikers took at high speed. She weaved through the streets, heading higher and higher until she left the air pollution and noise behind and found the green oasis of Devil's Gap Road. The trail was rocky and unstable, but the view was magnificent. She could see the entire western side of the territory; hell, she could see Africa.

She stopped by a pine tree to catch her breath, muscles in her thighs twitching after the long slog up what felt like hundreds of stairs. She took a few deep breaths, resting a shoulder against the trunk. She removed her backpack, unzipped it and took a long pull from her water bottle.

A line of hairy caterpillars crept along the bark in front of her, moving nose to tail, their bristly bodies rippling in perfect unison. The sight held her attention. They were oddly hypnotic.

"Well, hello there," she murmured, crouching down for a better look. "Just who I was looking for."

She reached into her backpack and pulled out the scratched Tupperware tub, placing it by the base of the tree. The soil felt cool and damp as she scooped it in her bare hands, packing a layer into the container. She reached for freshly fallen needles next, scattering them on top of the soil.

Spencer picked up the lid from the tub and used it like a scoop, gently coaxing the caterpillars into the container. They tumbled in, twitching and curling.

"Twenty-three... twenty-four. That should do it."

Snapping the lid shut, she brushed a smear of dirt from her thumb. A flicker of memory slipped through her guard: her teenage self up here on Devil's Gap or in the Northern Defences, the place they'd called the Jungle. Here she'd hide from the world, skipping school to track small mammals and sketch mushrooms in the margins of notebooks. Back then, nature made more sense than people. Still did, most days.

She slid the container back into her pack, pulled it over both shoulders and rose to her feet.

She descended the trail slower than she'd climbed it, trying to avoid disturbing her furry friends. By the time she returned to the apartment, the streets had awoken, and the bars around the marina were filling with those wanting a cooked breakfast. She rummaged through the kitchen drawers, finding some scrap mesh which she used to replace the Tupperware lid, ensuring the caterpillars had ample air circulation.

"There you go, little ones," she said, crouching to watch them, studying their movements.

After a quick shower, Spencer stood before the mirror, scrutinising her naked reflection. It was time to give Angela Smith a makeover, one a man like Zhou couldn't resist.

***

Spencer took the arched gateway through the thick, stone bastion at Wellington Front and zigzagged through the streets until she emerged on Main Street. On the surface, things looked British: recognisable shop names and familiar sights like red postboxes, but look up, and the architecture blended British, Spanish, Moorish and Genoese styles. Things were definitely less grey here than in London. Spencer took in the coloured wooden shutters that adorned white-washed walls, their slats tilted enough to let in the breeze but block out the sun. Wrought iron balconies embellished buildings with curved, decorative patterns. Geraniums dribbled over the top of them like pink and red paint.

Starting with Hilfiger and Next, Spencer couldn't quite find what she was after. As she left the latter, she almost bumped into a woman pushing a wheelchair. The man in it caught her eye, his gaze lingering quizzically on her.

"Angela!" someone called from behind, and it took Spencer a beat to register that she was Angela. She turned, seeing Ethan Campbell approach – the man she met at the airport. She turned back, but the woman had wheeled the man away.

"Fancy seeing you here." Ethan wore sandy cargo trousers and a black t-shirt that hugged his thick arms. He was carrying a motorbike helmet, swinging it gently in one hand by his side. His smile was easy and genuine, one Spencer couldn't help but return.

"Ethan?" she greeted. She nodded toward the helmet. "Out for a ride?"

He grinned, running a hand through his sandy hair and resting his weight against an orange tree, its branches heavy with fruit. "Just running some errands. I'm parked up near Casemates. Have you been?"

"Not yet," she said, lying because it was Angela's first time here.

"It's a big public square—" Spencer already knew that. "—Lots of restaurants—" She knew that too. "How about you? Doing some shopping?"

Spencer nodded. "Thought I'd treat myself to a new dress. Any recommendations?"

"Well, I usually only wear dresses on a weekend," he said playfully.

Spencer laughed. He pushed himself off the tree, and they walked north together.

"M&S, I'd guess. Or there's the Emporium, which used to be Debenhams. But with your figure, you'd probably make a bin bag look great— Sorry," he cringed. "That was meant to be a compliment, but it sounded creepy as hell. Cheesy too. Pretend I didn't say it."

"How about I just take it as the compliment it was intended to be?"

He looked relieved. "Listen," he continued, reassured, his tone hopeful, "That offer to show you the Rock still stands. Want to grab a coffee and head up?"

She hesitated. Part of her longed to accept, to spend a few hours up in the reserve with the trees, the monkeys, and yes, with Ethan. But Angela Smith had work to do.

"I appreciate the offer," she said, infusing regret into her voice. "But I have plans today. Rain check?"

Disappointment flashed briefly across Ethan's face, quickly replaced by understanding. "Of course. Another time, then."

Spencer said goodbye and promised to buy a bin bag if she couldn't find anything else. Then she slipped into M&S and headed for the women's wear department. Time to find Angela something eye-catching.

CHAPTER 12

H is hands were surprisingly steady, considering the gravity of what Robin Grimm was about to do. The bank of shared-use computers was empty; the usual buzz of activity had subsided as workers returned home. Most of his colleagues had already left the offices, hangars and workshops for the night. But the place was never entirely abandoned or unattended. This was a twenty-four-hour venue that employed thousands of individuals. Traffic came and went at any time of the day. There were refuelling activities, inspections, medical arrivals, and constant security.

The computer was an innocuous grey box that, for most, was a way of filing reports and receiving updates from the higher-ups. For Robin, it was now a grey gateway to potential ruin. He glanced around, ensuring that the remaining few people in the room were suitably far away. He could just make out their conversation about the footie over the hum of aircon and the distant drone of an engine being tested. Robin's hands felt clammy as he logged in using his own name and password. That was part of the plan. Everything had to look legitimate and go through official channels.

Cara had made it clear: she needed access, and Robin, as a trusted engo, could request temporary contractor credentials through the internal roster system. Dozens of civilian contractors passed through here each month. One more wouldn't raise alarms. Especially not one whose paperwork was already in the system, pre-verified, background-checked, and complete with an HR record and vetting approval.

All Robin had to do was issue a contractor request for Claire Gibson, Systems Technician, assigned to assist with scheduled diagnostics. He entered the departmental code, ticked the right boxes, and justified the request with vague comments about backlogs and tight deadlines. Her photo showed a pale woman in her thirties, with straight brown hair and glasses.

He wavered, looked over his shoulder and hit *submit*.

Robin stared at the screen as it loaded. A green tick confirmed the request had gone through. Claire Gibson's services were now required, and by morning, a temporary ID and security pass would be waiting at the east gate.

Robin sagged slightly in his seat. Still, he needed to send her proof. That was part of the deal. He pulled out his phone, snapped a picture of the screen confirming the contractor request, and sent it to her through WhatsApp.

No passwords. No confidential schematics. Just a single screenshot showing Claire Gibson listed in the system, scheduled to begin her contract as soon as possible.

Robin logged out of the system more frantically than he intended. His left eyelid twitched as he shut down the workstation. He stood and walked as calmly as he could from the room, down the corridor that stretched forever, to the double doors and out into the fresh air. He strode toward his car, checking his watch as he did so. She'd given him forty-eight hours to complete the task; he'd done it in twenty-nine.

Safely in his car, Robin locked the doors and wiped his brow. He opened WhatsApp, checked the double blue ticks. Delivered. Read.

He let out a long breath.

He'd done what she asked. Now, surely, it was over. The blackmail would end, and he could return to his normal, uneventful life. He started the Insignia's engine, vowing to be a better husband, a better dad. He deleted the conversation, deleted the photos, and blocked her number.

***

Spencer fastened her new lacy bra and checked her reflection in the full-length mirror in the apartment's bedroom. She wasn't usually the sort to pose in front of mirrors checking herself out, but she couldn't look like her usual, outdoorsy self tonight. She needed to look irresistible.

A sales assistant in one of Main Street's beauty stores had sold her some insanely expensive eye cream, promising it was liquid magic. In fairness to her, it had made the few lines she had disappear.

She'd already applied her perfume, nail varnish and makeup, opting for a glammed-up look of black eyeliner and bee-stung rosy lips. The dress she bought from a little boutique was just the right amount of figure-hugging. It was tight enough to show off her waist and chest but loose enough to disguise her strong thighs. She returned to the mirror, admiring how the fabric glistened slightly under the lights. Last but not least, a pair of stiletto heels and a chunky silver bracelet completed the look.

Spencer opened the middle drawer in the walk-in wardrobe, running her fingers over the various blades. She considered the small knife with the leg strap. Tempting. Deciding against it, she opened a different drawer and slipped something into her handbag.

Spencer paused in the kitchen, smiling at the tub of caterpillars. "How do I look, guys?" She curtseyed. "Why, thank you."

***

Monique's Bistro & Cafe was only a short walk from the apartment, but given Spencer hadn't worn heels this high in over a year, it took a few minutes longer than expected. The bar's trendy terrace was filled with fashionable people. Young, good-looking men and women in stylish outfits sipped cocktails and Champagne. Spencer chose a seat that still had evening sunshine and offered an unobstructed view of White Dove. She didn't pull her chair in, opting to leave her long, bare legs exposed to anyone passing by.

A server soon approached and took her order: a glass of non-alcoholic white wine. Spencer might have to drink on the job later, but there was no point starting early. When it arrived after a few minutes, she thanked the server in Spanish and took a small sip, listening to the sound of water lapping against the boats on the nearest quay.

Spencer was halfway through her drink when two men in impeccable suits walked by. One was Mengze Dong, Zhou's long-faced, serious butler. The other was one of the crew she'd spotted the previous evening. Spencer pretended to check her phone and read a message. She pouted, tossing her phone in her bag as if she'd just been stood up. Mengze lingered, his gaze travelling slowly from her stilettos to her face.

Subtle as a sledgehammer.

She fidgeted with her chunky bracelet, pulling the links through her fingers one by one until the two men continued walking, heading for the superyacht at the end of Pontoon A. Minutes ticked by. Ten, then fifteen. Just as Spencer was beginning to doubt herself, she spotted him: Zhou. He was headed her way, walking with the easy confidence of a man who thought he ruled the world. Her pulse quickened, but her expression remained the same.

He neither said a word nor asked permission, just slid into the seat opposite her, a predatory smile on his lips.

Spencer suppressed her own smile. It worked. *Show time.*

CHAPTER 13

Spencer lowered her shades a fraction to stare at Zhou. She adopted a confused expression. "May I help you?"

Up close, Zhou's face was smooth and square, with only a few lines traversing his forehead. His hair was black and shiny, showing no sign of his age. If he had any grey hairs, his stylist was covering them expertly. He was neat and clean and seemed to radiate wealth, but there was something ugly about him that Spencer couldn't put her finger on. Perhaps it was the arrogance in his expression, or maybe it was because she knew he sold guns and bombs for a living.

That was enterprise, she told herself. Governments all over the world were doing the same thing.

Zhou lowered his own glasses – Cartier. Mengze and Li had taken the table behind him. One eye on the boss at all times. "I can't stand seeing a girl as exquisite as you look so sad."

He offered his hand, making sure the cuff of his silk shirt didn't obscure his Rolex. "I am Zhou. Allow me to buy you a drink."

"Angela." Spencer offered a handshake, but he brought her hand to his lips instead and kissed the back of it. "And I have a drink, thank you."

He leaned back and spoke over his shoulder to Mengze, who in turn signalled for a server. Zhou turned back to Spencer, releasing her hand and gesturing at her glass. "We can do better."

The sun was lowering, the ripples on the water beginning to glow pink, reflecting on the hulls of sailboats moored in neat lines, their flags fluttering softly. A moment later, a bottle of Dom Pérignon arrived in an ice bucket with two glasses.

"So, Angela..." He sent the waitress away, popping and pouring the Champagne himself. It fizzed, filling the air with effervescent notes. "I like your name. Does it mean you are an Angel?"

Spencer pretended to check her phone again. "It means messenger of God."

"God? Well, that is interesting. You know, more than one person has called me the devil. Maybe you can be a good influence on me."

Angela giggled; Spencer thought he sounded like a prize tosser.

"Now tell me, what foolish boy stood you up?" He held up his flute to toast. Spencer met his glass with hers, the delicate clink echoing softly.

Spencer glanced at her phone again, rolled her eyes, tutted and played the part perfectly. "A very foolish one."

Zhou took a drink. "Forget him." His voice was as silky as his shirt.

She tossed her phone back into her bag and zipped it shut. "I already have," she said with a lazy smile and enough of a pout to make her lips look full and alluring. "So, why do they call you the devil?"

"Because either I am a very bad man, or because I lead people into temptation. How is the Champagne?"

She took another drink. "It's excellent."

He leant forward, holding her stare. The smell of his cologne wafted towards her, mingling with her own perfume and the zesty acidity of their drinks. "You see that yacht over there?" He gestured behind him, again showing off the Rolex. "It's mine."

"Which yacht?" she asked innocently.

"The biggest one in the marina."

She let her jaw drop as if this was new information. "No way? That's like the sort of boat a celebrity would have."

He shook his head with mock insult. "It's the sort of boat royalty would have. Join me for sundowners. Champagne on the bow." He held out his hand for her to take.

Spencer knew it was only a matter of time. Angela hesitated. "We haven't finished the bottle."

"Plenty more on board. Name a cocktail, and my private chef will make it for you."

Another fake jaw drop. "You have a chef?" She looked around for a waitress. "We need to pay."

He gave her a look that was half patronising, half charming. "It's already taken care of."

Zhou stood, revealing a designer belt. He was still holding out his hand to her. "Come on. Let me give you a tour of the yacht. You can take a sunset selfie by the hot tub. Post it on Instagram. Your foolish boy might see it. Might get jealous. Might see what a fool he is."

Spencer let her eyes flick to her handbag, to her phone within. She paused and pouted for a second, hesitating, then placed her hand in the devil's palm. "Lead the way."

***

White Dove's captain, Renato Santori, welcomed Spencer onboard, offering his hand as she stepped across the small gap between the boat and pontoon. He looked as if he wanted to ask her to remove her heels but knew better. Zhou's yacht. Zhou's teak. Zhou's repair bills. Santori held his white peaked hat to his chest, gave a small bow and made his excuses. She wondered how many women Zhou had invited on board before her. Santori certainly knew the routine. He was the captain but not the boss here. Just another employee. Another show of wealth. Window dressing.

Zhou placed his hand on the small of Spencer's back and guided her inside. The interior looked exactly how Spencer imagined. Cream leather, gleaming mahogany, brass fixtures glowing in the evening sunlight. It was beautiful, yes, but not her style at all. Angela, however, was very impressed, cooing and fawning at the sheer extravagance of it all. "Your TV is huge!" she gasped as the screen lowered from the ceiling. "Is that a *real* tiger?" she asked of the rug on the floor.

When she was handed another glass of Champagne, Spencer waited until Zhou's back was turned before stirring her index finger through the drink, feeling the bubbles against her fingertip. A minute later, her nail varnish still hadn't changed colour – the drink was clean.

He led her through the main living area, where designer sofas and armchairs surrounded a marble coffee table. Behind the couch, a ten-seater dining area was set up with a floral centrepiece. Around the room, sculptures of leopards and tigers prowled, bodies crouched, stalking their prey.

"The master suite is this way," he said. "Perhaps we will finish the tour there," he added with a wink.

She giggled playfully and was shown up a spiral staircase to a second lounge with a bar and office area. There was an expensive iMac, a Bluetooth keyboard and, most importantly, a safe. Spencer hid her smile by sipping Champagne. If evidence of arms deals stored on a USB drive were going to be anywhere, it would be in the safe.

Zhou took her through a sliding glass door to a sun deck, pointing out the sun loungers and discussing how he might take the boat to Capri or Monaco for the summer. Spencer glanced back at the lounge. The door was made of one-way glass. Potentially useful. Up another spiral staircase and they emerged on the upper deck. Mengze Dong was hunched over the rail, enjoying a cigarette and chatting to another of Zhou's men. They both straightened when he approached. Mengze put out his cigarette and offered to fetch either of them another drink. "Or I can ask Chef to make snacks."

Spencer declined. She'd had less than an inch of the drink in her hand, but Zhou told her to drink up and take advantage of his hospitality. "Two more glasses, Mengze."

Once Zhou's men had left, he pointed to the hot tub and raised his brows. "A dip?"

"But I don't have a swimsuit," she replied innocently.

"Oh, that won't matter once the sun goes down."

She blushed. Spencer didn't relish the thought of getting naked with Zhou, but she would. If all else failed.

"Erm..." A simpering little giggle. "And what time will it get dark?"

"See," Zhou grinned. "I knew I could lead my angel into temptation." He touched her chin. "It will be dark at twenty past nine. In about an hour. But... while we have the sunset, you should take a selfie. Actually, let me take it." He took Spencer's phone and directed her to sit by the hot tub. "Hold your glass up. A little more leg. Beautiful."

Zhou took the picture and handed her phone back. "Send it to your foolish boy. I dare you."

When the two flutes of Champagne arrived, Spencer tested the new drink again using her nail varnish and, once satisfied that it was safe to drink, took a long sip. It was creamy and delicious.

The photo was a good one. Long legs, shiny hair. She looked as Zhou said: Beautiful. Sexy even. Spencer barely recognised herself from her usual ponytail and cargo pants. She clicked *forward*, selected Buddy Thompson's name from her contacts, and sent him the picture with three kisses. Then she laughed out loud, turned *do-not-disturb* on and threw her phone back in her bag.

Foolish boy.

"Can we continue the tour?" she asked, batting her lashes. "It's all just so amazing."

Zhou shrugged. "The rest is behind the scenes. Boring."

"Oh, please." Pouting. "I've never been anywhere so glamorous before. I might never again."

Spencer considered what Zhou referred to as 'behind the scenes' to be the full picture. She needed to know every exit. The yacht was spread across four floors: the lower deck, main deck, upper deck, and the roof with its inviting hot tub. Each area came with its own set of challenges; sharp corners and hard edges could be both useful and hazardous in a fight. As Zhou led her through to the bridge, he couldn't resist showing off the captain's quarters and his collection of nautical charts. A heavy ornament by the captain's bed would be handy if blunt force trauma were required. In the galley, while Zhou pointed out dehydrators and rare ingredients, Spencer's attention was drawn to the knives arranged on a magnetic rail. The tour progressed past the guest rooms to the crew quarters, which featured cramped accommodation, a small kitchenette and a laundry room. Irons, steam, chemicals, hot surfaces.

"What do you do?" she asked innocently, admiring a bejewelled light fitting. "For work, I mean. You're obviously very successful."

"I buy things. I sell things."

You sell weapons, you creep.

"What kind of things?"

"Expensive things." He was being evasive. Not that Spencer was surprised.

"Like boats?" she asked, glancing around as they took another spiral staircase back to the main deck, counting the stairs, calculating the force needed to send someone tumbling down them.

Zhou chuckled as if she were a silly little girl. "Oh, White Dove wasn't expensive. Only fourteen million euros. Bargain, really."

Spencer wondered how many bombs and missiles someone would have to shift for fourteen million euros to be considered *not expensive*. But before she could do the sums, she realised the sightseeing was complete, and they were where Zhou promised to end the tour.

Alone with the devil. In his bedroom.

CHAPTER 14

Rain lashed against the kitchen windows as Buddy Thompson watched from the counter, sipping his coffee. Sarah bustled around the stove, her focus on the simmering pots. She smiled, humming along to the radio. It had been one of those days. Meetings that could have been emails. Meetings within meetings. Meetings that dragged on endlessly. The bloody G7. Ukraine. Israel. Syria. There was always bloody something.

Their kids were at the dining table, heads bent over homework, the scratch of pens and occasional sighs filling the room. It wasn't long after half-seven when Buddy's phone vibrated softly on the kitchen island, the screen lighting up with an incoming message. The name read: Stephen Blake. Stephen Blake did not exist. Well, there were probably many Stephen Blakes in the world, but Buddy didn't know anyone by that name. It was the alias he used for Spencer Bly in his contacts. He couldn't risk Sarah knowing he still had her number.

Muttering an excuse about needing to check something for work, Buddy slid his phone off the island and slipped into the hallway, heading towards the small office where he could lock the door and read the message in private.

He wasn't expecting an image. Certainly not one as seductive as this. Legs. Sunlight. Champagne. A hot tub on a gleaming yacht. Long hair wafting in a sea breeze. Three kisses at the end of her message. XXX. Buddy swallowed.

"Dinner's ready."

"I'll be right there," he called, not looking away from Spencer.

His body was frozen while he soaked in the image, but his mind was anything but. Why send it? What was she trying to tell him? Was the message just an update to show him she was on White Dove? A boast that she was getting somewhere with her mission? He ran a hand over his jaw, feeling his five o'clock shadow bristling against his palm.

"Dinner."

"I'll be right there."

Or was Spencer signalling for help? Letting him know her location in case something went wrong? She could handle herself. He knew that, but still, he worried.

"Buddy!" Sarah's voice was losing patience.

He stood and pushed his phone in his pocket, an uneasy feeling settling in his gut. The photo was provocative. Deliberately so. Her smile was coquettish and amused. Was she teasing him? Twisting the knife? Reminding him of what they'd been and what they could never be again?

Christ, Spencer. He took his phone back out, vaguely registering Sarah's shout that the food was getting cold and they were starting without him. He typed out a quick reply. Only two words: *Be careful.*

***

The bedroom was nothing short of palatial. When Spencer's family, what was left of it, up and left their home in northeast England in the middle of the night and relocated to Gibraltar, they moved into a small apartment. That entire apartment would have fit inside Zhou's floating bedroom.

She looked around at the super-king bed and silk sheets, spotting a poorly concealed panic button by the bed. There was a walk-in wardrobe, an en suite, and crappy abstract art.

Spencer's younger brother liked to draw on walls. His doodles were better than this sorry excuse for Cubism.

Zhou followed her eyes to the painting in question. "I appreciate the finer things in life." His fingers traced delicate circles on her back as he closed the door behind her. "A woman like you certainly qualifies."

God. Do you want some port with all that cheese?

He pressed a button on the wall, and the lighting dimmed. Warm ambient tones illuminated alcoves as the blinds drew by themselves, cutting Spencer off from the outside world. Zhou had the same predatory look in his eyes Spencer had seen on the stone leopard and tiger statues in White Dove's saloon. But, despite Zhou's impression of her, there was only one apex predator here.

He placed his hand on her bare shoulder, squeezing and massaging her flesh. "You seem tense. Nervous?"

"Not at all."

His fingers traced down her arm, taking with them the flimsy spaghetti strap of her dress. She didn't stop him, allowing the sparkly dress to slip to the floor like a serpent shedding its skin.

He leered over her underwear, feeling the lace with his fingertips. "One more glass?"

"I shouldn't."

"But you will." It wasn't a question. "The night is young, and I dare say you are not as angelic as your name suggests."

He had no idea.

Zhou brushed her cheek and left her momentarily to open a wine chiller, popping the cork on a bottle of vintage Ruinart. When his back was turned, Spencer wasted no time. She clicked a catch on the side of her chunky bracelet. The hidden compartment was tiny but afforded enough space to hide a pill – or two. She crushed them between her thumb and index finger and stirred them into his half-full glass of bubbly.

"You need to finish this glass first," she urged, slithering up behind him, pressing the flute into his hand. "Let's not be wasteful."

He didn't protest – how could he? – downing it in one before kissing her. Hard. Wet lips and fizzy tongue. Cold palms on her warm curves.

She untucked his silk shirt and pulled it over his head, revealing his lean but ageing torso. She caressed his flat stomach.

Minutes later, Zhou was naked, supine on the super-king. Spencer straddled his hips, smiling down at the devil as his eyes fought to stay open and his mind fought to stay awake.

CHAPTER 15

She slapped his cheeks to confirm he was asleep. Not hard – she wasn't a monster. Well, not right at that moment, anyway.

"Right, Sleeping Beauty, time for me to get to work." Spencer clambered off Zhou's comatose body, thankful the zolpidem kicked in when it did. She'd used a dose suitable for a man twice his size. He'd suffer no long-term effects but might wake up having had the best night's sleep of his life.

Bare feet silent on the wooden floor, Spencer took a condom from her purse, and trying not to look, slipped it on Zhou's rapidly disgorging penis. She removed it and dropped it in the bin in the ensuite along with the wrapper. Then she dropped her underwear and rubbed the gusset over his genitals, upper thighs and lower stomach. When he woke, his groin would smell of both natural and synthetic lube. All part of the charade. Zhou might not remember their night of passion, but would at least be convinced it happened.

After slipping her dress back on and tying her hair back, Spencer retrieved her phone and what appeared to be a phone charger from her handbag.

Zhou's breathing was deep and even. Spencer lifted his arm, floppy and heavy, and used his unconscious thumb to unlock his own device. She connected the two phones using the wire and waited as strings of encrypted data began flowing across her screen. The encryption would be heavy, but that was Six's problem. What mattered was getting everything.

While the download continued, Spencer slipped back into Zhou's ensuite. She relieved herself and took a clean white hand towel from the shelf. Returning to the bedroom, where Zhou was now snoring softly, she wrapped something of his carefully in the towel and placed it in her bag. It might prove useful later.

Next came a methodical sweep of the bedroom, starting with the obvious hiding spots: false drawer bottoms, the space behind the headboard, the ventilation panel near the floor. Nothing. In his wallet, Spencer found over £500 and €800. She fanned the notes in her fingers, counting out a few hundred and tucking them in her bra. She put the rest back, rationalising that a man of Zhou's habits wouldn't notice if some money had gone missing but might notice an empty wallet.

The sound of laughter drifted up from below – the crew in the galley, probably having their evening meal. Spencer checked her phone: download complete. Time to move.

She pressed a small button-like listening device on the back of a bedside table. They'd find it eventually, but by then, it would be out of battery anyway. She eased the bedroom door open, wincing at a faint creak. The corridor was clear. She visualised the boat's layout: galley, guest bedrooms, bridge, captain's quarters, second lounge, office, hot tub. Above her head, the sound of heavy footsteps, two swooshes, more footsteps. It was probably Li making his rounds, opening and closing a sliding door. She needed to get to that office.

Padding up the curved stairs, Spencer positioned her feet along the edges where the wood was less likely to protest. At the top, she pressed herself against the wall, listening. The burnt-orange glow of Li's cigarette was visible through the window, his back angled partly away as he gazed out at the darkening marina. He had his phone in his hand, scrolling through social media.

Spencer slipped inside the second lounge. As she crept across the plush carpet, the muffled sounds of the marina's nightlife filtered through the yacht's thick, panoramic windows. She turned right to the office area. When she'd watched White Dove and Zhou's entourage from the safety of the apartment, Li spent anything from five to ten minutes enjoying his cigarette. She hoped he erred towards ten minutes this evening. The safe was under the table. A solid, black, impenetrable box. Biometric to boot. She'd suspected as much, but it was still infuriating. *Damn it.* Thermite would do it, but she'd risk destroying its contents. Plus, thermite tended to draw too much attention. Hard to disguise a fierce white light that burned hotter than a magnesium flare and easily reached over 2500 degrees Celsius.

No thermite. For now, at least.

Spencer pressed a second bug down the side of the desk and plugged a drive disguised as a tube of mascara into the computer. Her eyes flicked between the progress bar and Li's silhouette while she waited for the data transfer.

A sudden movement – Li turning. Spencer dropped to the floor, using the safe as cover while his shadow passed by the window. The glass might be one-way, but no point in risking a silhouette. The computer whirred softly, files copying. Ninety per cent.

Footsteps approached the door.

Spencer's heart hammered as she squeezed beneath the desk. A swooshing noise as the door slid open, and Li's boots appeared in the doorway. The smell of salty marina water filled the room. Ninety-four per cent.

The intercom on the wall behind her crackled. Chinese – something about food. Li's boots turned away, his footsteps receding into the corridor. Ninety-six.

Spencer released her breath, crawling out from beneath the desk to watch the final files transfer. She almost had what she came for; the safe would be a problem for another day. She just had to get off White Dove without anyone realising their boss and his business had been compromised. Ninety-eight.

She planned on leaving via the main saloon, playing the tipsy party girl who'd had her fun. She'd blush, look embarrassed, let them think Zhou had simply drunk himself to sleep.

The data transfer was at ninety-nine per cent when Spencer realised her mistake: Li hadn't been alone on the deck. Mengze's slender frame in the doorway was a thin stripe of charcoal grey against the midnight blue sky. He stepped into the lounge and saw the woman in the sparkly dress hunched over his boss's computer.

The download hit one hundred per cent as Mengze slammed his bony palm on a panic button.

CHAPTER 16

U nfortunately for Spencer, she was female.

Most people are familiar with the fight-or-flight response. Walter B Cannon coined the term in the 1920s to describe the physiological response humans exhibit when faced with a threat. What most people don't know is that research on fight-or-flight was initially conducted solely on men. It took another seventy years before scientific attention was finally given to female stress responses.

This is why, when Mengze's eyes locked onto Spencer's, her primal instincts told her to freeze or appease.

Time seemed to halt, her muscles locking up in an ancient survival mechanism. Her brain told her to make excuses, say she was just curious, say Zhou had asked her to download something, say she simply got lost on the way out. The little voice in her head told her to smile.

That brief second of hesitation, when Spencer had to battle her biological instincts and shift from paralysis to action, meant that by the time she moved, Mengze was nearly upon her. She yanked the drive from the computer, threw it in her bag, and vaulted over the desk.

In a wild, desperate, barefoot dash, Spencer reached the spiral staircase, her hand on the metal bannister. Below, angry voices and quick feet were thundering up the stairs, leaving Spencer no choice. She ascended. Mengze was upon her, his skinny fingers clutching the flimsy fabric of her dress. She kicked back, her heel connecting solidly with his solar plexus, knocking the wind out of him. His arms flailed as he lost balance, tumbling out of sight.

Li soon replaced him, his broad frame bouncing off the stairwell walls as he gave chase, a razor-edged diving knife glinting in his hand. He reached out, almost snatching her bag from her shoulder. Spencer kicked again; it felt like kicking a wall. Li barely registered the impact. He seized her foot and yanked it back towards him. Spencer fell to the floor with a grunt. Li's right hand grabbed the back of her knee, crawling up the spiral staircase, inching his way up her body, knife raised. Spencer kicked her feet wildly, her heel connecting with Li's nose. He snarled, his head snapping back. Spencer was free. She scrambled up and burst onto the uppermost deck, the cool night air wrapping around her.

Li wasted no time. He and two of Zhou's men cornered Spencer near the bow. She was trapped like a caged animal awaiting the inevitable. But now that she had broken free from her freeze instinct, Spencer was not about to give up on her escape. The chase was on. And while she might not be able to outrun or outmuscle Li, she thought she could outsmart him.

Spencer leapt over the hot tub and collided with a metal railing. She somersaulted over it, landing on the roof of the bridge. Her feet slipped on glass as she slid down White Dove's windscreen, its large wiper blades snagging on her dress and tearing the fabric. Li was pursuing her, while the other two men dashed toward the side decks, attempting to flank her. She scrambled back to her feet, hurrying across the roof of the master suite and over another metal railing. She'd reached the pointed bow.

Spencer stopped and turned to look at Li, her damaged dress fluttering around her bare legs.

Li slowed, looking like a hunter ready to pull the trigger. "End of the road," he said, lips twitching into a smirk. "You are all out of boat."

"Not quite."

Spencer leapt backwards off the bow, arms and legs outstretched. Praying her calculations were correct, she reached in the darkness, her limbs finding the port mooring line. She grasped it hard, her fall coming to a jerky stop. She clung to it with both arms and legs like a sloth hanging under a branch, the cold, polluted marina water lapping three metres below. Her bag hung from her shoulder, swinging beneath her, its contents threatening to spill into the water. But unlike a sloth, Spencer moved quickly, heaving herself, hand over hand, across the rough hemp towards the harbour wall where the line snaked around a huge cleat.

Behind her, shouts echoed across the water – Li's voice cutting through the night as he barked orders for the other men to get to the quay. He gestured wildly before jumping into the darkness. Spencer felt the line jerk and tremble as Li gripped it, catching his weight with one hand.

Spencer hauled herself up the harbour wall, her fingers finding the cold chain fence. Her knees and elbows scraped against stone until her bare feet found purchase on the quay. She caught a glimpse of Li on the rope, his knife in his teeth. Untie the line and let him fall? Or run? She didn't have time to undo the complicated knot. Besides, the other men were running along the pontoon now. She bolted right toward the bay.

There were no street lamps, and the darkness here was nearly absolute, interrupted only by distant pinpricks of light from ships weaving through the Strait. Waves crashed against the rocks on the breakwater, their sound masking both footsteps and those of her pursuers.

The apartment was seconds away, but Spencer couldn't risk leading them to Moorland House. As she rounded the end of the block, she made a split-second decision, pulling her bag from her shoulder and hurling it into a landscaped area, trusting the thick leaves of a foxtail agave to hide the evidence she'd stolen.

Li's footsteps pounded behind her. Two more sets ran parallel along the pontoon – they were trying to cut her off before she reached the main road. Spencer's mind raced through the geography of Gibraltar's streets. If she was going to lose them, she needed the maze-like, tight, winding streets of Upper Town.

As she reached the memorial garden at the far end of the block, Li's voice echoed behind her. "I'll carve you up slowly for this!" His footsteps were too close, closing in rapidly.

Spencer didn't break stride as she grabbed a branch of a
Mexican fan palm from the border of the garden. She wrapped
the fanned fronds around her hand and pulled. The plant
resisted but then yielded with a sharp crack. She planted her
feet and pivoted, swinging the natural weapon in a wide arc.
The fan palm's stalk was lined with sharp, fang-like thorns
that pierced the skin on Li's cheek. As she pulled the plant
downwards, the thorns dug in, clawing and tearing through
his flesh. His scream echoed off the stone walls as he clutched
at the loosened skin around the gouge. Blood seeped between
his fingers while the diving knife clattered to the ground.

Spencer was already on the move, her bare feet slapping
against the pavement as she fled through one of the arches
flanking the gateway to Queensway Quay. The main road lay
before her, empty except for the sound of distant motorcycles.
She sprinted right, then turned left towards the gap in the
stone bastion at Ragged Staff, her lungs burning. The road
angled uphill at a steep incline. On the right, a wall too high to
clamber over. On the left, a car park and a giant mural of the
Battle of Trafalgar daubed in muted browns and sepia. In the
moonlight, the painted sails looked ghostly. No cover there.

The other two men were gaining ground as she continued
up the hill. Ahead, she could see Traflagar roundabout, and a
pub and a cemetery of the same name.

Headlights abruptly flooded the street. The roar of an
engine echoed as a motorcycle slingshot around Trafalgar
roundabout. The bike's brakes screamed as the rider spotted
her in the middle of the road and fought for control. It hurtled
down the hill, skidding, rubber burning against the asphalt.

Freeze or appease.

Primal fear immobilised Spencer in the middle of the road as she conducted a split-second risk assessment. What posed the greater danger: being run over or letting Zhou's men get their hands on her? The motorcycle's headlight bore down on her, growing blindingly bright. Unsure if she was dodging a bullet or rushing towards her death, Spencer tucked and rolled.

CHAPTER 17

S he was alive. The motorcycle's exposed engine screamed past her head, the bike falling onto its side, skidding sideways down the bank. Matt-black with fat tyres, it looked fast even lying on its side.

The rider groaned, lifting his visor.

"Angela?" His eyes were familiar. The airport. Main Street.

Ethan: her knight in scuffed leather.

He looked her up and down, seeing her bloody knees and torn dress. He saw the men chasing her in the dark.

"Jump on."

She didn't hesitate this time. Ethan pulled the bike upright, and she climbed on behind him, wrapping her arms around his waist. Zhou's men were closing in, crossing the road as Ethan revved the throttle. Their fingers grazed her torn dress as the motorcycle lurched forward, its engine roaring to life. The acceleration was instant, pushing her back. Feeling like she might be flung off the back, she tightened her grip, pressing her chest into his back.

Ethan took off down the bank, turned back onto the main road, and almost ran over Sun Li, who dove out of their way, blood still streaming from where the fan palm's thorns had shredded his face.

A crashing sound made Spencer whip her head around. Li had knocked a delivery rider off his motorbike, causing him to sprawl into a planter of bird of paradise flowers. Orange petals erupted like sparks from a flame as the stolen bike gunned after them, weaving through traffic.

The wind rushed through Spencer's ears and pulled hair free from her bobble. She chanced a glance ahead, seeing cars queuing at a red light. As her eyes began to water, she pressed closer into Ethan, using him as a shield.

"Mount the pavement!" she screamed in his ear. "Through Commonwealth Park."

They jumped as they hit the curb, veering right into a grassy garden, past a pond and fountain, and out the other end, back onto the road. Spencer looked over her shoulder: Li was still tailing them. "We need to get near Irish Town and John Mac Square," she shouted, referencing a pedestrianised, commercial area filled with lively bars and cafés. "Lose him in the alleyways."

The bike leaned hard as Ethan curved it to the right through another park, high-rise apartment blocks towering over them.

"We can't go that way," she yelled, picturing the streets ahead, seeing the flight of stairs leading up to the war memorial.

Ethan's reply was lost in the wind. "Hold on tight."

He turned hard, accelerating towards the stairs. Two thin ramps, only six inches wide, were integrated into the steps. They were intended for parents pushing buggies or dismounted cyclists pushing their bikes. They were not designed for motorcycle chases.

Ethan took the one on the left.

It was steep. Dangerous. Spencer squeezed her knees against Ethan's hips and clamped her arms around his chest. She thought Li would bottle it and give up the chase, but he stayed in hot pursuit, taking the right ramp. Spencer's teeth rattled as Ethan zigzagged through the backstreets between Irish Town and Main Street, stone walls pressing in on either side. She could feel every inch of the road. Each dip and bump shuddered through her body.

"Casemates Square ahead!" Spencer shouted. "Watch out!"

They fired into the plaza like a bullet from a gun. Late-night revellers dove for cover as Ethan weaved through tables and chairs. A waiter dropped his tray, glasses shattering across the cobblestones.

Li was gaining ground, his powerful bike eating up the distance. Ethan swerved into a tunnel beside the Lord Nelson pub and emerged on the other side before ducking into the next one. They exited onto a narrow street, made a few hairpin turns, and found themselves zipping along a road lined with palm trees and five-storey flats. The warm night air felt cold as it flowed across her bare arms and legs. She shivered.

"Right, then an immediate left!" Spencer directed.

Ethan cranked the throttle, ignoring her and taking an arch barely wider than the bike's handlebars. They were climbing, each turn tighter, each road steeper. Spencer's thighs filled with lactic acid as she pinned herself to Ethan's body. They made a sharp turn, approaching an ancient stone stairway. The bike's front wheel dropped onto the first step, the entire machine threatening to flip. Spencer shifted her weight back, helping Ethan maintain control as they bounced down. Halfway down the flight, he made a ninety-degree left turn onto another flight of stairs, one entirely in shadow. Even the moonlight couldn't find its way in between the tall buildings on either side. He braked and Spencer surged forward into his back. Ethan cut the engine; the motion, noise and cold wind abruptly stopped. All was still. He turned to face her, pressing a finger to his lips.

Li's bike drew near. She heard the bounce of his tyres and the growl of his engine. The growl intensified as it neared, but gradually, it faded again, leaving them in blissful silence as Li continued down the main flight of stairs.

They waited five minutes before Ethan dared turn the bike around and start his engine again. He rode slower now, calmer. He parked in a small courtyard next to two scooters, removed his helmet and nodded towards an apartment building where bougainvillaea dribbled over stone walls in a magenta waterfall.

"This is my place."

Spencer slid off the bike, legs shaking, adrenaline coursing through her veins. Her dress was in tatters, knees bloody from her roll across the pavement. But she was alive. The data from Zhou's computer was in her bag, hidden behind an agave plant. And now, apparently, she had an ally.

Ethan pulled a key from his pocket and opened his front door, pausing before allowing her entry. Spencer glanced back across the courtyard. The twisting streets of Upper Town were peaceful. No sign of Li. No revving engines.

"So, Angela," he said, rolling her name around his mouth as if he knew it was a pseudonym. "Want to tell me how, if this is your first time in Gibraltar, you apparently know every street in town, and more importantly, want to tell me why a man with half his face torn off is trying to kill you?"

CHAPTER 18

Spencer stepped inside Ethan's apartment. He turned on a lamp, illuminating a clean and organised living room. On the dining table, a model Spitfire rested on a sheet of the Gibraltar Chronicle. The aircraft was painted in a grey base coat, awaiting its camo-green and bullseye detailing. Tiny pots of colour and paintbrushes were lined up beside it.

Ethan closed the front door, the click sounding strangely loud in the silence.

"We should call the police," he said softly, brow furrowed. He picked up a retro telephone: red, spiral cord, circular dial. It was something from a different era.

Spencer shook her head. "No police."

"But they... Those men..." He stumbled over the words, his eyes sweeping over her dishevelled appearance. "Your dress is ripped to shreds. Did they...?"

"I'm fine. No police."

Ethan sighed, putting the phone back on its table. "At least let me take care of those wounds," he offered, glancing down at her knees.

In the bathroom, Spencer sat on the side of the tub next to a bottle of Head & Shoulders. Ethan fetched the first aid kit, popping it open to reveal its neatly arranged contents.

"Quite the Boy Scout, aren't you?"

"Always be prepared," he quipped back, kneeling before her, cotton wool in hand. "This might sting."

Spencer didn't flinch. For a man who could handle a bike the way he did, she was surprised at how gentle Ethan's touch was.

"You didn't even wince." He looked up at her with new curiosity, their proximity suddenly more pronounced. "Most people at least swear a bit."

"I'm not most people."

"Clearly."

He reached up to take her hand. Spencer's heart beat a little faster until she realised this wasn't a romantic gesture. He turned her hand over in his, revealing a deep cut across her palm and a bloody print on the side of the tub. "Oh."

"You didn't notice?"

"Adrenaline," she answered while Ethan cleaned the wound and applied a thin crepe bandage. "I... I hit that guy with a Mexican fan palm. It must have cut me, too."

He looked impressed. "You ripped his face open with a plant? That is... insane, actually."

Spencer laughed at the absurdity of it all, her guard momentarily dropping. "Yeah. And thank you, Ethan. For the first aid... and the ride. Your bike's not too bashed up, is it?"

He finished with the antiseptic and sat back on his heels. "Nothing a bit of paint won't fix. Yamaha MT07. Parallel twin cylinder, four stroke. Low and light. Perfect for zipping around Gibraltar. It doesn't have the biggest engine on the market, but..."

"But size isn't everything?"

He blushed. Laughed. "Exactly. You want some tea?"

"Yorkshire?"

"Tetley."

"No, thank you."

"Something stronger? I have at least eight kinds of whiskey."

Zhou's Champagne was still working its way through Spencer's system; she felt dehydrated. "Just water."

They returned to the living room, and while Ethan left to fetch her drink, Spencer studied his place more closely. The retro phone wasn't the only item harking back to the 60s: a vintage LP player, a colourful Bauhaus print. More meticulously detailed model aircraft were lined up on a floating shelf, alongside books on the Wright brothers, Concorde, and female pilot pioneers.

"Here you go." Ethan handed her a highball filled with ice water. She decided against the nail varnish test.

Spencer pointed at a tiny RAF Red Arrow Hawk. "Secret geek?"

"I prefer the term *aviation enthusiast*. And if either of us is a geek, it's the one who apparently memorised every alley in Gibraltar."

Spencer took a sip of her water, considering. "My name is Spencer," she confessed, the truth slipping out more easily than she expected.

"Spencer," he repeated slowly. "Suits you better than Angela. My sister went to school with a girl called Spencer. I saw her down Rosia Bay a couple of times."

"Was she cute?"

"She was weird."

Charming.

"Bit of a loner by all accounts. I heard she skipped half her classes."

She half smiled, sitting on one end of the sofa. "Wonder what she's doing now?"

Ethan sat too, leaving a respectful distance between them. Close enough for Spencer to feel the warmth radiating from him, far enough away to avoid their legs accidentally touching.

He chuckled. "She's probably on the run from the Chinese mafia."

Close.

As the evening wore on, the atmosphere in Ethan's apartment softened with the mellow strains of blues rock filtering through the crackly speakers of the vintage LP player. By the time one glass of water evolved into three, Spencer's torn dress slipped further up her thigh. Ethan fetched a small platter from the kitchen, laying it on the coffee table before them. Crisps, carrot sticks, sliced red peppers, and a bowl of garlicky hummus. They both reached for the snacks, their fingers brushing occasionally.

Eventually, Ethan yawned. "Will you stay?" he asked. "I mean— You take my room. I'll stay on the couch."

"Very gentlemanly."

"You sound disappointed." He helped her to her feet, her bandaged hand in his. He led her through to his room, waiting in the doorway. "Get some rest," he told her. "Whatever trouble you're in will still be there tomorrow."

CHAPTER 19

The ceiling fan cast strobing shadows across Ethan's walls. Spencer lay in his bed, his oversized Harley-Davidson T-shirt reaching halfway down her thighs; it was warm and smelled of tropical softener. Her torn dress lay crumpled in his bathroom bin. The bed was comfortable, maybe too comfortable. Every time she closed her eyes, she feared drifting off to sleep. Her mind replayed the evening's events in vivid detail: Zhou's hands caressing her bare skin, the rough friction of the mooring line, blood seeping from Li's shredded face.

She hoped they hadn't found the bag. The data she retrieved from Zhou's phone and computer potentially held the answers to Monroe's disappearance. What had he died for? Thoughts all beginning with *if* stabbed at her: if Six can crack the encryption, if the data revealed who bought what, if she'd risked her life for nothing more than Zhou's vacation photos.

Ethan's faint snoring drifted through the wall, steady and rhythmic. Her ego told her she'd have lost Li and his cronies on foot, leading them through a warren of passageways and tunnels. She had the stamina and knew Gibraltar's streets like the back of her injured hand. Still, Ethan had shown up at the critical moment, whisking her away on his Yamaha steed with no thought for his personal safety. He'd tended her wounds, given her a t-shirt to sleep in and kept his hands to himself. A gentleman.

The men at Six thought they were gentlemen because they wore smart suits and spoke with Received Pronunciation. But holding a door open and saying *ladies first* hardly counted if they leered at her arse as she walked through it.

The digital display clicked to 03:47. Spencer eased herself from the bed, goosebumps forming on her bare legs. She padded silently into the living room. Ethan's unfinished Spitfire glowed under a shaft of moonlight, its left wing dipping lower than its right.

She thought about writing a note. Something to thank him, to explain – not that she could tell him much. Better to remain a mystery. One day, she'd be nothing more than a story to tell his mates in the pub. *Did I tell you about the time I was in a motorbike chase with the Chinese mafia?*

The pavement felt rough under her feet, and the pre-dawn air was cool but not cold, a slight dew hanging to the glossy leaves of a Mediterranean buckthorn across the courtyard. She gently closed the door and slipped away wearing only Ethan's T-shirt.

A flicker of russet flashed in the underbrush, the red fox's presence marked only by the rustle of leaves and a fleeting shadow. Around the bay, Gibraltar never truly slept. There were always ships moving through the Strait, always early

crews preparing for departure. But at this hour, the streets of
Upper Town belonged to vixens and alley cats.

Victorian street lamps lined the street, guiding her back
towards the marina. Clean and elegant, with blackened metal
frames and bevelled edges, they spoke of a time long gone.
Spencer avoided their warm glow, tiptoeing through the cover
of palms and orange trees. It took her thirteen minutes to
navigate back to Queensway. Relief washed over her as she
found her bag still securely hidden behind the lush rosette
of the foxtail agave, untouched. She reached through the
silver-green leaves, slung it over her shoulder, and made her
way into Moorland House.

Wanting to wash the grime of Gibraltar's streets from her
feet, Spencer turned on the shower and removed Ethan's
t-shirt. She fished almost £400 in a mix of pounds and euros
from her bra and left it by the sink. As the water warmed,
she unwrapped the bandage on her hand. Fresh blood oozed,
forming a scarlet droplet that swelled and rolled across her
palm, dripping onto a pristine white towel. The scene before
her flickered, and for a brief moment, the bathroom in
Moorland House receded into the background, supplanted by
a memory long suppressed.

***

The bottle of formula cools while Spencer changes Liam's
nappy. Outside, the grey English morning presses against
the window, drizzle streaking the glass. Liam squirms as she
refastens the popper buttons on his sleep suit, somewhere

down the street, the number 1 bus rumbled past, bound for Newcastle city centre. She's only ten years old but has done this hundreds, maybe thousands of times. The first time, she'd been terrified of hurting her fragile newborn brother, but now, she could do it with her eyes closed. She shouldn't have these skills at her age; she knows that. It should be Mum's responsibility, but she died giving birth to Liam. It's not his fault.

Spencer remembers the night her dad, Harry, went to the hospital with Mum but returned without her. The sound of his uncontrolled sobs, a wild, primal cry of despair, is burned into her memory forever. She recalls her grandparents shooing her and Albie off to their rooms, telling them not to come out until morning.

"Everything's okay, Spencer. Go back to bed."

Adults lie.

Spencer washes her hands and then checks that the formula is at the right temperature. She holds Liam the way she has been shown and gives him the bottle. His tiny lips suck hungrily on the artificial teat. As she burps Liam, his little arms reach out, and his tiny fist strikes her nose. It doesn't hurt, but it catches her just right, causing a nosebleed. A ruby droplet balloons under her nostril and drips onto her white school shirt. Her shirt was already dirty, stained with baby food and mud. The washing never seems to be done enough these days. When she learns to use the washing machine, Spencer will do her own laundry.

Liam gurgles as Spencer places him back in the crib. She can hear shouting from downstairs. Her dad is arguing with Albie. Albie is six and incredibly annoying because he never stops talking. Liam can't speak yet, which makes him the best member of the family, as far as Spencer is concerned. Even when he cries, he's not as irritating as Albie.

She grabs some toilet paper from the bathroom and pinches her nose to stop the bleeding. It's Tuesday, swimming day, and she hasn't packed her things yet. She tickles Liam's feet to make him giggle, then races downstairs to the kitchen. One-handed, she puts the bottle in the sink, then takes a towel from the downstairs airing cupboard; it smells musty. Blood escapes the toilet paper and splashes onto the towel, staining it a dark pink. She knows the look her teachers will give her, but she has no choice. Spencer shoves the towel into her school bag.

Her dad is in the hallway. He's still yelling—not at Albie this time, but into the phone. He is angry. Spencer doesn't remember him ever being this angry when Mum was alive. He was always the more relaxed of the two. He is in his police uniform, which Spencer thinks makes him look very handsome and important. Still, his face is tired, pale, and lined.

"I don't care if they want custody," he hisses, "it's not happening."

He must be talking to his solic—, solicit—. She can never remember the word, but he's the man Dad says charges a fortune.

"Unfit? That's rich. I'm doing my best here."

"Dad!" Albie tugs at Dad's trousers. "I don't like the after-school club; it smells of beans. I want to go to football. Why can't I go to football?"

Harry ignores him, continuing to argue with the lawyer. "I don't care what you tell them."

"But Dad, James goes to football. I want to go to football with James."

Harry, pink in the face and close to tears, growls down at Albie. "Quiet! I told you we can't afford the kit and the fees, and there's no one to take you or pick you up."

Albie stamps his feet, scrubbing dirty footprints into the hallway carpet. Harry returns to his conversation. "No. They're my kids. They belong with me, not their grandparents."

He slams the phone down; the combined noise of the slamming handset, the shouting, and Albie's high-pitched whining sets Liam off. Spencer clamps her free hand over her right ear and tilts her head to the side, pressing her left ear against her shoulder, trying to dull the sound of crying. She begins to ask, "Do you want me to—"

"Dad!" Albie's face is far redder than Harry's. Spencer can sense his tantrums from three miles away. "I want to go to FOOTBALL!" He screams the words at the top of his voice, his mouth open so wide the skin around his face pulls taught. He scrunches his eyes, plonking his bottom on the carpet, banging his hands on the floor. Then the screams begin. One long, never-ending squeal, loud enough to make next door's dog start barking.

Harry looks like he could wrap his hands around Albie's throat and throttle the life out of him. Liam cries and cries. Albie screams. Harry yells, "Pack it in, so help me God, I will—"

"I. Want. FOOTBALL!"

Spencer shoves her finger deep in her ear, wanting to be anywhere but here. "Do we have to move to Nana's house?"

she asks, her words sounding weirdly echoey in her blocked ear.

Harry grabs Albie from the floor, roughly pulling him to his feet. He points a finger straight at Spencer, so close to her bloody nose that she goes cross-eyed. "No," he spits. "No one is going anywhere."

CHAPTER 20

B eads of water dripped from Spencer's long, dark hair. She placed her laptop on the dining table, ready to start work. Outside, the sky was inky. Quarter past four and the first pale light of dawn wouldn't creep across the horizon for another three hours. The marina seemed deceptively peaceful after the night she'd had. Halyards tinkled, flags flapped, but otherwise, all was calm. A copse of date palms wafted flimsily on the artificial island where mansions cost £6 million apiece. They were brand new when Spencer arrived as a teen, the talk of the town. Zhou could buy two and still call them a bargain. Speaking of Zhou, Spencer wondered if he was still sleeping soundly. There was certainly no sign of life on White Dove. The cabin lights were off, and the decks were empty, no silhouettes pacing, no flicker of a cigarette lighter in the dark.

Opening the laptop, Spencer entered her password, scanned her fingerprint, answered three security questions and activated the VPN. The mascara tube lay beside her mouse pad, its shiny black surface concealing the USB drive within. Zhou's data. Worth dying for, apparently, given how hard his men had tried to stop her from leaving with it.

The upload began, the progress bar creeping across infuriatingly slowly. The laptop hummed quietly, the only light in the room coming from its screen and a small lamp in the corner. Spencer pushed back from the table, walking across the hardwood floor to the kitchen. Her hands shook slightly as she filled the kettle: a delayed reaction to all the excitement, perfectly normal.

She crouched level with the countertop. Her caterpillars were busy munching on pine needles, oblivious to the night's drama.

"Morning, troublemakers."

One lifted its head as she spoke. She'd get them fresh needles soon.

Back at the dining table, cup of hot tea in hand, Spencer began sorting through the files. The encryption on some was familiar; standard codes she could crack. Others would need Six's expertise. But even the unencrypted files posed their own challenge. Her Mandarin had never been fluent, and what she once knew had grown rusty with disuse. She found herself frequently consulting translation software, cross-referencing characters she only half-remembered.

As dawn approached, the digital paper trail slowly revealed itself: financial transactions, damning emails, business proposals, some porn – naturally. A cold feeling started in Spencer's stomach, spreading to her limbs and forehead. She found evidence of weapons shipments, yes, but not to Iran. Plenty of action in Africa: semi-automatics to active terror groups in the Lake Chad Basin region, bombs to FLM in Mali's Mopti area, missiles to a jihadist group in Burkina Faso. The list went on.

She sat back in the chair and folded her arms across her chest. Buddy Thompson had specifically said Iran. *Something big. Something bad.*

But he'd also mentioned a drive. Just because Spencer didn't have the evidence yet, it didn't mean it didn't exist. Perhaps Zhou was keeping this deal offline. If it was big enough to have Six spooked, Zhou would be wise to cover his tracks.

Still, it wasn't what she couldn't see that troubled her; it was what she could. Business proposals to sell something to the Yanks, Canada, Germany, France, pretty much every Western nation, including the United Kingdom. And he wasn't planning on selling to terror cells and separatists. He wanted to sell to governments, militaries and defence contractors. Whatever he was peddling, it didn't come cheap. Zhou was planning on making an absolute killing. His €14 million yacht really would look like pennies after that.

Spencer unlocked her phone and brought up Buddy's number. It was 05:28. 04:28 in London. He'd be asleep, not that Spencer cared. She pressed the call button.

***

In London, Buddy's phone lit up beside him: Stephen Blake, aka Spencer Bly, aka Angela Smith. He glanced at Sarah, peacefully sleeping beside him, then eased himself out of their king bed. The wooden floor creaked beneath his feet as he slid into his slippers and crept to the living room, pulling the door quietly shut behind him.

"Spencer?" he whispered, sinking onto a sofa that was too expensive to ever be comfortable. "It's the middle of the night."

Even with the room unlit, he could make out the hideous cornflower blue wallpaper his wife had picked out. Sarah had spared no expense in making the room look like something out of a lifestyle magazine. Buddy, for his part, felt like a trespasser in his own home every time he sat down.

"I'm aware of that. Are we buying arms from China?"

"We?"

"The British Government. The Ministry of Defence. The British Armed Forces. We. Us. The UK."

"What? No, that's—" He lowered his voice further, conscious of the silence upstairs where his children slept. "I wouldn't have thought so. That can't be right; we have an arms embargo with them."

"What about the Americans? Are they buying from China?"

Buddy snorted softly. "They'd sooner use the metric system."

"Well, someone's lying to us." Paper rustled on Spencer's end. "I got into Zhou's phone and computer. There's still a safe I need to crack, but it's biometric, and I'm not exactly going to be invited back on board any time soon."

"How come?"

"I messed up. They caught me, and now they want me dead."

"Christ, Spencer—"

"I know, I know. But listen, Monroe was right about there being a huge deal, but it's not Iran. There's nothing here about Iran. Not a single reference. Zhou has business proposals to sell to us, the Americans, half the EU. We're talking tens of millions a pop. I'll send you everything. Maybe your tech wizards can find something I missed." She paused. "Any word on Monroe?"

Buddy adjusted one of the red velvet throw pillows Sarah insisted on fluffing every morning, more ornament than comfort. "Nothing. I'd like to think he's living it up in Tangier, but…"

"Yeah." The word carried weight. He wasn't the first agent to disappear. Wouldn't be the last.

"I'll make some calls to the MoD and see what I can dig up." Buddy rubbed his eyes.

"I'll get into that safe."

"Just… be careful, Spencer."

The line went dead, leaving him alone in the dark living room designed to impress people who didn't live there. He sat for a long moment, listening to his house settle around him. He opened her last message and stared at the photograph she'd sent him. He wished he'd kept her on the line. He should have asked about the photo and told her— What? That she looked hot? He was an idiot, but he wasn't that much of an idiot.

Buddy pulled Graham Reed's private number from his contacts. He'd worked with Digger back in Baghdad, and now he was the Deputy Director of Strategic Procurement at the MoD. So, if anyone knew if His Majesty's Government was making dubious arms deals, it would be him.

Reed answered on the second ring. "Buddy? You know I need my eight hours."

"I'll keep it quick, Digger, let you get back to your beauty sleep. Are we buying weapons from China?"

Silence, and then a bark of laughter. "Don't be daft."

"I'm not being daft. An agent found evidence of a potential deal between us and an arms dealer we've been keeping an eye on. It doesn't have to be from China specifically. Maybe this guy acts on their behalf, ships things around, makes it look like we're buying from elsewhere, somewhere independent."

"You think we buy weapons from some bloke down the pub?" Digger yawned. "We supply to them, Buddy, not the other way around."

"We sell arms to China? What about the embargo?"

"Buddy, the UK exported over eight and a half billion quid's worth of arms around the world last year. Granted, only thirty thousand of that went to China, but in years gone by, we'd flog millions a year to them. Forty mil. Sixty mil. We make. We sell. We don't buy any old rubbish at weapon jumble sales."

"Right. Just checking."

"Look, we import a shit tonne from the US and France, but we're ramping up production to cut down on that. And we get Heckler and Koch guns from Germany and C7s from Canada. But BAE, Raytheon and Lockheed Martin have got us covered."

Buddy let out a *hmm*. "Never mind. Might be faulty intel."

"Speaking of intel," Reed's voice dropped slightly, "heard you're on North Star duty for the G7."

"Yeah. Voyager detail."

"Well, try not to let anyone shoot the PM this time."

"That was one time, and it was a water gun." Buddy managed a weak smile.

"I'll see you there in that case. I seem to recall you owing me a bottle of Jameson's."

Buddy ended the call and stood in his dark living room, mind racing. If the Brits weren't buying from Zhou, and the Americans definitely weren't... He considered returning to bed, but he'd never switch off now. Besides, he couldn't face Sarah's questions if he accidentally woke her. He relocated to his study and pulled out his secure laptop; the sun would be up soon anyway.

CHAPTER 21

Z hou's used Champagne glass rested on Spencer's dining table beside a crumb-covered plate and a half-finished mug of tea. She had managed a few hours of sleep, and although she wasn't energised, she woke up somewhat rested and very hungry. Breakfast consisted of three slices of toast, a banana, and an orange. She had taken the Champagne glass from the arms dealer's bedroom after he passed out, wrapping it in one of his hand towels. Still, Spencer was pleasantly surprised that the glass survived her escape from the yacht.

She peered at the flute, the circular base and its delicate, slender stem. She angled her head this way and that and held it up to the light. She had taken it on a whim, anticipating its potential usefulness. However, turning her idea into reality wouldn't be easy and would require a ten-step process.

One step at a time.

Given that Sun Li wanted to torture and kill her, Spencer decided to disguise herself before leaving the apartment.

Zhou's men would be looking for an athletic woman with long dark hair; she would give them a blonde businesswoman instead. Angela Smith's boring blouse and pencil skirt were a decent start, but the wig and glasses made all the difference. Spencer studied her reflection in the bathroom mirror, adjusting the bobbed blonde wig: the face that looked back at her could have been Izzy's sister. Spencer pushed the thought away. Izzy belonged to another life, before MI6, before her teen years in Gibraltar.

The morning air was crisp as she left Moorland House and headed for the bus stop across the main road. Still no sign of drama on White Dove.

Morrisons was quiet at this hour. She filled her basket methodically: biscuits (because tea without biscuits should be a crime), orange juice, tomatoes, onions, period products, tortilla, a carton of salmorejo, three packets of gelatine, disposable gloves, and tinned tuna. The cashier barely glanced at her.

The pharmacy on Main Street was her next stop. There, she picked up some micellar water, cotton wool, and electrode gel, telling the pharmacist that the latter was for her husband's TENS machine.

Main Street was beginning to fill with mid-morning tourists buying toy monkeys and cheap booze. Spencer observed the throng drift from shop to shop from outside the pharmacy. Different groups seemed to form and reform, much like starlings in a murmuration, each individual moving independently yet still part of a coordinated whole. It was fascinating and a bit disorienting. A sudden stop by someone to admire tax-free jewellery in a shop window could cause a ripple effect, altering the path of those behind them.

Steps one and two of Spencer's ten-step plan for the Champagne glass were already complete. Time for step three: target selection. Across the thoroughfare, a café was serving breakfasts and strong coffee. A man in a cheap suit at one of the outdoor tables was smoking and making the young server's life hell.

"Love, sweetheart, darling." He punctuated each word with condescending smugness. "It's not difficult. I asked for the eggs to be sunny-side up. These—" He jabbed his knife at the plate. "Are over easy. Now be a good *chica* and get it right this time."

The server, still in her teens, flushed red as she took his plate. Spencer watched the girl's hands shake as she pushed through the door into the café.

Spencer looked at the man's smug smirk and thought, *Congratulations, you are the chosen one.*

She waited, watching him eat breakfast from a bench while she pretended to be busy on her phone. When the man finally stood to leave, she gave him a thirty-second head start before following. His walk reflected his character: entitled. He never changed course on the busy street, assuming everyone else should yield out of his way. He was an easy mark. Spencer timed her approach perfectly, stumbling into him as he checked his phone.

"Oh! I'm sorry!" Her hands shot out to steady herself, one grazing his jacket pocket. The wallet slipped out effortlessly. "I'm so clumsy."

"Watch where you're going," he snapped, brushing past her.

Spencer waited until he was gone before checking her prize. Colin Aynsley of Red Sands House. Forty pounds in cash. She pocketed twenty, then walked back to the café, where the young server was clearing tables, her eyes glassy and downcast. Spencer popped two ten-pound notes in her tip jar and dropped the wallet onto the floor beneath the table where he'd been sitting. Someone would hand it in. Or not. She didn't care.

The address was a six-storey, mustard-yellow block of flats nestled between the Botanical Gardens and Rosia Road. Spencer approached from the rear of the building, where older teens played basketball in a court that reminded Spencer of an exercise yard in a prison she'd once done fake time in. Black metal fencing surrounded the court, its hard surface painted green to mimic grass. The basketball hoops lacked nets, the goal posts too.

Spencer strolled casually into the block, unhurried, as if she lived there or were visiting a friend. Inside was a lovely internal courtyard with a tiled floor and a fountain that doubled as a shrine. Many of the tenants had brought the outside in, decorating their patch of communal space with potted plants and flowering shrubs.

Aynsley's place was on the second floor. She took the stairs, passing a few occupied flats. She could hear televisions, music, and discussions in Llanito all from within, but no one walked the corridors, no one saw her. Some doors had metal security bars over them; thankfully, Aynsley's did not. Spencer loitered, listened. No sounds came from indoors, but she knocked just to be sure. No answer.

The lock was basic: a standard Yale with a deadbolt. Child's play. Thirty seconds later, she was inside, closing the door quietly behind her. The hallway smelled of carpet cleaner and cat. Somewhere, a clock ticked. Step four: in progress.

Spencer took the disposable gloves she'd bought from Morrison's and moved through Aynsley's house like a poltergeist, careful to disturb everything while leaving nothing of herself. She toppled a lamp in the living room, yanked drawers half-open in the kitchen, and scattered papers across his home office floor. The art of creating chaos without leaving traces was a delicate one. The gloves would keep her prints out of there, and if she shed any hair, it would be blonde and belong to someone else.

In the bedroom, she knocked pillows askew and emptied the contents of his jewellery box onto the duvet. A quick scan revealed several knock-off watches and a heavy signet ring. She left them where they fell. She wasn't there to steal from him; this was about opportunity.

Spencer checked the communal hallway and left the way she'd come in, leaving his front door ajar. The only witnesses were the teenagers on the basketball court, and they were too engrossed in their game to notice a thirty-something in office attire. Out front, Spencer perched on a stone wall by the Botanical Gardens. To her left, a towering pine obscured a dragon tree, its leaves starbursts of shiny green, the ends singed sienna. To her right, two golden dewdrop saplings, small and delicate with tiny clusters of orange berries, looked like they would topple over in a thirty-knot wind. She shook her hair free of the wig, rolled up her skirt, tied her blouse around her waist and waited. If Aynsley saw her, he'd see a different person from the ditzy woman who bumped into him.

Aynsley returned within half an hour. She observed him approach, phone pressed to his ear, wearing that same irritating smug smile of superiority. He vanished into the building without so much as a second glance at her. A minute later, she heard his cursing from the second-storey window.

The police response was impressive, the patrol car arriving within minutes. A gesticulating Aynsley met them out the front, his face reddening as he explained the break-in. Spencer settled in to wait, checking her watch: the forensics team wouldn't be far behind.

Step five would prove trickier. She had to steal something right under the noses of the local law enforcement. Still, distraction was her friend: the police were here to investigate a theft, they weren't anticipating being robbed themselves.

A white Suzuki van drove two laps before finding somewhere to park. Blue decals read: Royal Gibraltar Police Force, Crime Scene Investigation Unit. Two investigators emerged: a tall man and a shorter woman. Spencer watched as they shook hands with the officer and offered sympathy to Aynsley. The woman opened the rear doors of the van and set a black canvas kit bag down on the ground while the man began unloading camera equipment.

Spencer stood, brushing dirt from her skirt. She began walking, her pace purposeful but not fast enough to draw attention. Timing was everything. The investigators started pulling on thin, white overalls. She was almost level with them now. While their eyes were down, attention focused on their zips and PPE equipment, Spencer reached down without

breaking stride, her fingers wrapping around the handle of
a black canvas bag. She continued down the street, turned
into the next building, exited through the courtyard and
back onto Rosia Road. One block, two blocks, three blocks.
No shouts of discovery, no running footsteps, just the
normal sounds of a Gibraltarian morning.

***

The garden is sunlit and warm. It's a summer's day in
Newcastle, and as Spencer's dad can't afford her school's
expensive holiday club or the local sports camp, she, Albie,
and Liam are at their Nana and Grandad's house. Albie is
kicking a tennis ball against a brick wall; Spencer lies on the
grass with her eyes closed, the sun warming her skin. Here,
there's a sense of calm. It's not as claustrophobic as home,
and eleven-year-old Spencer feels a rare moment of peace
settle on her young shoulders.

Inside the house, the washing machine spins loudly.
Nana is humming a tune to baby Liam while she prepares
lunch. Spencer twirls the ends of her long hair between her
fingers, listening to bird song and inhaling deep lungfuls
of a pleasant smell. Whatever Nana is cooking smells
nutritious and far better than the quick, ready meals she
gets during term time. The normalcy of it all makes Spencer
sad. The summer won't last forever, and soon, her days
will again be filled with school and her evenings filled with
playing mum.

It's not a game, though. Is it? she asks herself.

Albie's bare feet dash towards her. Spencer opens her eyes, catching a look of excitement flushing his face. He scampers straight to the living room, not noticing Spencer silently following. She waits in the shadow by the door. The living room is small and homely. A floral-patterned two-seater sofa. Two soft armchairs in matching prints. A wooden set of drawers doubles as a television stand. A rug, slightly stained but well-loved, rests under an old coffee table.

Nana's handbag is on the table – stylish, Italian. Albie peers in and removes her leather purse. His small hands fumble with the clasp, and before Spencer can say anything, he's removed two five-pound notes. Spencer's stomach drops as he stuffs them into his pocket. *Not again.*

"Albie!" she hisses, rushing over. Her brother jumps, guilt written all over his face.

"You were spying on me!"

"You can't do that," Spencer says, her voice a stern whisper. "That's stealing. We're not thieves."

"But I need more sticker packs for my sticker book. Dad said no last time, and I thought—"

"You'd steal instead? Dad's right. Stickers of footballers are a waste of money—"

"But everyone collects them. James has nearly finished his book."

"No, Albie. It doesn't matter." She thrusts her hand into his pocket, grabbing the two green five-pound notes. She picks up Nana's purse, her heart pounding as she scans around for Nana.

Too late. Nana stands in the doorway, a spoon in one hand, little Liam cradled in her other arm. She looks like she can't believe her eyes. She doesn't look angry; she looks sad. Spencer feels a sinking feeling in the pit of her stomach.

"Spencer, what's going on here?" Nana's voice trembles slightly.

"It's not what it looks like, Nana. I was just—" Spencer starts.

"I saw enough. I can't believe you would do this. You are old enough to know better."

"No, Nana. It wasn't me. I didn't." Spencer glances at Albie, wordlessly pleading with him to speak up. But Albie looks down at his shoes, silent. "I wasn't taking your money, Nana. It was—" she tries again, but Nana's expression hardens, the raised wooden spoon enough to silence her. The implied threat is understood.

"I think it's best if we have a little conversation with your father when he comes to pick you up." Nana turns and walks back into the kitchen, her steps heavy.

***

Spencer wondered, as she let herself into the apartment at Queensway Quay, whether Albie would appreciate the irony. His straight-laced sister had lectured him about raiding Nana's purse, stealing his friends' toys, and his teenage shoplifting habit. Now, she was twice the thief he ever was. Though technically, she supposed, it wasn't stealing if it was for King and country. Gibraltar was a British Overseas Territory, and as Spencer's fee as an independent contractor would be handled by His Majesty's Government, it wasn't really robbery – more like asset relocation.

She placed her bags on the dining table. It was time to begin stage six, but first things first: kettle on.

CHAPTER 22

A cup of tea later, Spencer's dopamine levels returned to homeostasis. She began unpacking her bags, moving her shopping from Morrison's to the kitchen and most of the items from the pharmacy to the bathroom. Unzipping the stolen forensics bag, Spencer hoped to see two things, and she wasn't disappointed. Laying the items on the table, she picked up a two-ounce tub of Sirchie Hi-Fi Volcano Latent Print Powder and unscrewed the lid. It was the good stuff, not the cheap knockoffs some departments used. A roll of clear lifting tape sported the same brand name. A bottle of cyanoacrylate was the icing on the cake. *Score.* The other items like tweezers, swabs, and stationery might come in useful later, but now, this was all she needed. Time to begin step six.

Spencer cleaned the kitchen, wiping down the counters with antibacterial spray and a fresh cloth. Next, she scrubbed and dried a shallow tray and placed it on the bottom shelf of the freezer. She opened a gelatin sachet, measured some water and checked its temperature carefully. Too hot, and the gelatin would lose its structural integrity; too cool, and it wouldn't dissolve properly. Stirring slowly to avoid creating bubbles, the clear liquid thickened gradually. Once it moved like honey but remained transparent, she knew she had the right consistency.

While the tray in the freezer cooled, Spencer checked on White Dove – still no drama, no panic, no guards patrolling the decks. Working quickly, she poured the mixture onto the chilled surface, using a spatula to spread it into a paper-thin layer. The cold surface caused the gelatin to set almost immediately, creating a sheet as clear as glass and nearly as delicate.

Spencer lifted the Champagne glass carefully by its base and examined it under a desk lamp. The Volcano print powder appeared almost blue-black in the light as she dusted it over the glass's surface with feather-light strokes. Gradually, like a photograph developing in a darkroom, the print emerged, whorls and ridges swirling over the clear glass.

"Hello, Zhou," she murmured, studying the pattern.

The lifting tape was next. Spencer cut a precise length, handling it by the edges to avoid contamination. She smoothed it over the dusted print and applied light, steady pressure, working from one side to the other to prevent air bubbles. The print lifted cleanly – textbook.

Transferring the print to the gelatin was more difficult. One mistake, one misaligned ridge, and the whole thing would be useless. Spencer positioned the tape and pressed down, holding her breath as she peeled it back. The print had transferred perfectly, each detail preserved in the fragile gelatinous sheet.

Step seven. Using a scalpel from the forensic kit, she cut a rectangle around the print. Three inches by two. The resulting patch was long enough to wrap around her index finger from tip to the proximal interphalangeal joint – the middle knuckle. She moulded it carefully over her finger, avoiding touching the print. The gelatine was warm and slightly tacky against her skin.

The cyanoacrylate spray would stabilise the gelatine without making it too rigid. Three light coats, allowing each to dry completely. Spencer flexed her finger, watching the fake print move naturally with her skin.

She held her hand up to the light, examining her handiwork. She wore Zhou's identity on her skin: the Devil's fingerprint.

Spencer knew she'd accomplished a lot already that day, but it was the final three steps that worried her far more than stealing from the Royal Gibraltar Police Force.

Step eight: Infiltrate White Dove.

Step nine: Open the safe and extract its contents.

Step ten: Vacate White Dove, ideally without being killed.

***

The late afternoon air carried the scent of salt and diesel to Spencer's balcony. It nearly, but not quite, masked the faint whiff of sewage from the overflow sewer that fed into the marina. A lunchtime power nap and a jamón ibérico bocadillo – ham in crusty bread – had helped stave off tiredness. Spencer was sitting in one chair, with her feet up on another, a glass of ice water on the table beside her. She wore headphones, tuning into the listening device she had placed in Zhou's bedroom. The muscles in her lower back tightened as she recalled his hands on her skin. Adjusting the volume, Spencer filtered through the ambient sound of the air conditioning and distant footsteps on the teak decking. After a moment, Zhou's voice came through clearly.

"Peter?" Zhou's voice held the warmth of a man addressing a valued employee. "Are you available to discuss tonight's menu?"

"Of course, Mr Zhou." The German chef's accent was subtle and refined, his voice somewhat tinny as it travelled through the intercom. "I've sourced some excellent trout. I thought we could begin with trout chuparquía and follow it with white asparagus, beurre blanc, and caviar."

"Excellent, excellent. And for the main?"

"Venison, perhaps? Accompanied by a foie gras and truffle terrine?"

Spencer could hear the smile in Zhou's voice. "You spoil me, Peter. Tell me, do you enjoy gambling?"

Spencer frowned. Zhou sounded relaxed and almost playful; it wasn't the demeanour of someone who had been drugged and had their security breached. He was either an exceptional actor or...

Li and Mengze stepped out onto the middle deck. The former had a bandage over one side of his face; the latter lit a cigarette.

The chef replied, "I've been known to play a hand or two."

"Join me at the casino tonight, assuming dinner meets your usual standards. My treat, of course. I'm feeling lucky."

"I'd be honoured, sir."

Spencer's heart rate increased. Zhou was leaving the yacht. Tonight. She opened Google Maps and located the casino at Ocean Village, at the northern end of Gibraltar.

***

Li's fingers found the bandage on his face again, tracing the edge where that bitch sliced his face with the palm. He had no idea palm trees had barbs like that. He looked forward to returning the favour, tying her to a chair and carving her pretty face and long legs until she begged for death. Beside him, Mengze's cigarette trembled slightly in his bony hand as he brought it to his lips, the ember glowing bright then fading with each anxious drag.

"We should have told him," Mengze said in Mandarin, his voice barely above a whisper.

Li watched a customs boat cruise past in the distance. "Should we have? Tell me, what would you have said? *Sorry, Boss, we found the woman at your computer, then lost her in the streets like amateurs?*"

"She couldn't have accessed anything important." Mengze's cigarette twitched again.

"She didn't access anything. She didn't know the password. The screen was locked." Li's wide jaw tightened, the bruise throbbing with the memory of the chase. He'd almost had her, could still see her silhouette disappearing on the back of the bike. The fact that she'd outmanoeuvred him ate his pride like acid.

Mengze crushed his cigarette into a glass ashtray, immediately reaching for another. "The safe was untouched. We checked. And Zhou woke up happy, relaxed—"

"Because he thinks she was just another pretty distraction." Li turned to face his colleague. "If we're wrong about this... If she knows... If she manages to stop—"

"He would kill us." Mengze's lighter clicked three times before catching.

"No." Li shook his head slowly. "He wouldn't kill *us*. Your daughter at university in Vancouver. My mother in her nursing home in Tiancun. My sister and her boys." He let the words hang in the salty air, watching a small Mediterranean house gecko scuttle across the guardrail. "Zhou is old school. He believes in making examples."

They stood in silence for a long moment, each lost in thoughts of distant loved ones who had no idea their lives hung on the decisions made on this deck.

"She was just a whore looking for payment. Snooping around for expensive trinkets." Mengze's words had the desperate edge of a man trying to convince himself. "She was just an opportunistic thief, a gold digger who got lucky with Zhou's attention."

Li forced a laugh. "Yes. Just a pretty thief." He touched his bandage one last time, then forced his hand down to his side. "Zhou's plan will go ahead, and we'll be rewarded handsomely. My mother's care isn't free."

Mengze swallowed. "We've come too far to fail now."

The door behind them slid open with a soft whoosh. Mengze jumped, while Li turned slowly. Zhou glanced over them from head to toe. "What on earth happened to you?" he asked. "Cut yourself shaving again?"

Li's wound throbbed. "I—"

"It was my fault," Mengze said quickly. "Li asked me to hand him his diving knife. I didn't realise he was standing so close when I turned around without looking first."

Zhou gave them both disparaging looks. "Come inside," he said. "We need to discuss this evening."

Li and Mengze exchanged glances, each seeing their own reservations reflected in the other's eyes. They had made their choice.

***

Spencer adjusted her headphones as the three men entered the study. The bug's placement provided her with a clear audio feed, although the Mandarin streaming through her earpiece made her wish she had spent more time on language refreshers between assignments. Weapons training and gadgets had always been more appealing than conjugating verbs.

She heard a whir and a crunch: the sound of the safe opening and money being fanned through fingers. There was the rustle of papers, the distinct sound of stacks of cash being counted.

Casino... she caught that word easily enough.

"Peter will join us," Zhou said in Mandarin, the chef's name standing out.

Li's voice came next, lower, grumpier. Zhou's response was immediate, something about a car. Laughter followed, the kind that comes at someone's expense. Spencer could picture the men mocking Li's bandaged face, the injury she'd given him becoming a source of humour.

More chatter, then someone – Mengze, she thought – said something that sounded like *hēiyán*, and the study erupted in raucous laughter. Spencer reached for her notebook, jotting down the phonetic spelling. Hēi... that meant dark or black, she was almost certain. The rest escaped her, but the way they'd laughed suggested an inside joke.

She sipped her water. The ice had melted now, and the afternoon had faded to evening. She was confused, less by the talk of the casino and more by what wasn't being said. No mention of a break-in, no security concerns, no hint of the chaos she'd caused the night before.

Had Li remained silent about their encounter? Why? Surely, a man like Zhou would not tolerate such an omission from his security team. The men's voices faded as they took the stairs to the main deck. Spencer made another note, underlining it twice. In her experience, people only kept secrets from their bosses when they had something, or someone, significant to lose.

CHAPTER 23

The stew smelled fantastic. Hints of beef, onion and herbs floated from the kitchen. Robin Grimm watched Ellen chop vegetables. She knew something was up since he returned home, his mind elsewhere, his nerves shot. He told her he was just grumpy and achy and made up stories about traffic jams and moody bosses. He hoped she bought it. Still, he fussed with his lanyard, pulling the fabric taught against his neck, letting the edges of his ID card dig into his wounded palm.

Jack barked. Robin released his lanyard and let the dog come back in from the overgrown back garden. They'd had two dogs once upon a time. Jack and Russell, the Jack Russells. Not the most original or wittiest of names, but the kids had found it hilarious at the time. Four years ago, Russell had a run-in with a Ford Focus; now, only Jack remained.

Jack ran to the dining table and rubbed his face against Holly's legs. She was home for a few days, typing away on her laptop and occasionally glancing at a textbook. Robin was so proud of his daughter. Of Lance, too. One training to be a doctor – must have got his brains from his mother – and the other a future engineer, just like her old dad. A chip off the old block.

After dinner, Holly planned on meeting her old school friends for a pint in the local boozer. Ellen suggested they nip down for one themselves, but Robin said he was tired. They'd stay in and see what was on Amazon Prime instead.

He pulled his phone from his pocket. He kept doing that. Habit now. Fear, too. He'd deleted and blocked Cara's number. Deleted the photographs. He was half tempted to bin the whole phone just in case. What good that would do, he had no idea. She already knew everything about him. He walked through the house, head down, shoulders slumped, up the stairs to the bathroom. He emptied his bladder and washed his hands, staring out the window at the country lane below. The lane, a quiet ribbon of crumbling tarmac edged by tall, wild hedges and the occasional gnarled oak, was bathed in the golden wash of the lowering sun.

That's when he saw her, Cara, resting lazily against a streetlamp, admiring her nails, her glossy red hair shining in the warm light from above. Beautiful.

Hastily, filled with fury, Robin dried his hands and stormed down the stairs, each step thudding against old wooden floorboards. How dare she. How dare that bitch come to his house. His family home. He'd show her.

Robin grabbed Jack's lead. "Taking the dog out before dinner," he said, barely managing to conceal the mood evident in his voice. Holly and Ellen watched them go but said nothing. Jack, an old dog now, struggled to keep up with

Robin's power walk. His gait didn't falter as he approached her. Eyes forward, just a man out walking his dog. He strode straight past her. She waited twenty seconds before following. Once he rounded the bend, confident he was out of sight of his home and those of his nosy neighbours, he stopped.

When Cara followed him around the bend, he was ready, reaching out to grab the fabric of her jumper, twisting it in his fist, pulling her closer. He snarled in her face. "What the fuck do you think you are doing coming here?"

Cara, unfazed, fluttered her lashes. "Oh, please. Don't play the tough man." She stroked the back of his fist. He let go of her, shoving her away.

"You came to my house! My wife could have seen you. I should kill you. Toss you in the river."

"Please, darling." Cara smoothed her jumper where he'd grabbed her. "Besides, if anything happens to me, much worse will happen to Holly. Understand?"

Robin's anger flared at the threat to his daughter. He gritted his teeth, breathed deeply.

"Listen, sweetheart," she continued. "You work for the government. Yes? I work for the Kremlin. Don't look so shocked, you already figured that out." Crouching down to pet Jack, she stroked him as she talked. "You carrying out my instructions means you have already committed treason, my darling. Me telling your wife about our night of passion is the least of your concerns."

She stood and stroked Robin now. Her hand caressed his neck and chest, her slender fingers playing with the ID card at the bottom of the lanyard.

"That won't work," Robin said. "You'll not get in with my ID."

"I don't need your ID, I have Claire Gibson's." She reached into her pocket and showed him a British Passport. One of the new ones with the dark blue, almost black, cover. The photo page showed the same woman for whom he'd issued a civilian contractor request: brown hair, glasses.

He swallowed. "So, you've blackmailed this Claire as well? Or was she always one of you? How the hell did she pass the vetting?"

Cara sighed, bored. "So many questions. Claire passed the vetting because she is a good girl. Genuine. Squeaky clean."

"Is that her real passport?"

She shrugged. "No idea. Not my concern."

"And what do I do with her when she signs in tomorrow?"

"My God, you are slow." Cara tapped her foot impatiently and looked at the sky. "Tomorrow, *I* will be Claire Gibson. Try to keep up. Now, as a civilian contractor, I assume I will need escorting at all times?"

Robin nodded. There was no way he could eat Ellen's stew after this. His stomach was in pieces.

"Then I shall see you at the security gate at seven-thirty."

"But—" Robin shook his head, trying to shift the cloud of confusion and terror. "But what about the real Claire? When she shows up for her scheduled assignment."

She smiled. "She won't."

What the shitting hell did that mean? Was she dead? Had Cara killed her or had her killed? He pressed a clammy hand to his forehead.

Jack barked, tugging to continue his walk. Robin just stood there, the air seeming to thin around him. He felt dizzy with rage.

"I'm done," he blurted out, pointing his finger at her. "I'm done. Whatever it is, I won't help you."

Cara gave him a condescending look as if he were a silly little boy. "You will. Unless, of course, you want Holly to find herself drugged, bundled in a van and delivered to some sadistic Moldavians. No? I didn't think so."

She moved closer, pressing her body against his. "I – Claire – will meet you at seven-thirty. Do not be late. It is... What shall we call it? Bring Your Mistress To Work Day."

She kissed him on the cheek, turned and walked away.

CHAPTER 24

It was a starless night, and clouds clung to the rock like a second skin. Spencer lurked by the roadside near a white bird of paradise plant. It stood taller than its orange cousins, and it seemed hardier too, with large, leathery leaves that reflected the glow of a nearby streetlamp. She was in her running gear again: black leggings, black jacket, black rucksack, her long, dark hair tucked under a black cap.

Two Bentleys arrived, their glossy black paint shining like an oil slick. Uniformed drivers stood by the rear doors, poised to open them for their guests. Both the drivers and cars were impeccably clean, the kind of service that screamed both wealth and meticulous attention to detail. Very Zhou indeed.

She counted them off as they emerged: Zhou in his perfectly tailored suit, Li with his bandaged face, Mengze chain-smoking as usual, Peter Müller looking uncomfortable in formal wear, James Wan with his hair slicked back, and the young one, Andy He, she thought his name was, checking his phone and bringing up the rear.

Four left on board, one being the captain who'd likely stay in his cabin monitoring weather reports and pretending not to notice anything else. Three potential problems.

As the cars pulled away, Spencer started her mental countdown. Six minutes to the casino. Ten with evening traffic. She forced herself to wait fifteen minutes, each second ticking slowly by. Long enough for them to arrive and for Zhou to order his first drink. Long enough for Li to let his guard down. But not too long. Every minute she waited was another minute Li could return if something went wrong.

If Li were a wise man, the yacht's security systems would be operational. Perhaps cameras, certainly motion sensors. One chance. One shot at this before Li raced back in one of those immaculate cars. Six to ten minutes of mounting fury when he realised what was unfolding.

Spencer approached from the shadowy side of the marina, staying low. She slipped under the chain fence and lowered herself down the harbour wall, its broad stones offering just enough purchase for her fingers. One slip and she'd hit the water. For a moment, she hung there, the dark water lapping below, then she pushed off. Her feet found the yacht's side deck with barely a sound.

Figuring she was safer outside than inside, Spencer used the external stairs to the upper deck. She crouched, crawling across the teak on all fours.

The door to the lounge/office was closed, and the glass was one-way. She waited and listened. No sound. If one of Zhou's crew were in there, the game would be over. She decided to risk it; the door slid open smoothly.

Inside, the safe waited, its biometric scanner glowing faintly in the darkness. Spencer tucked herself behind the desk and pulled on the gelatin fingerprint. She exhaled, then positioned it carefully over the scanner. Nothing. She tried again. Still, nothing.

The safe was a newer model, requiring proof of life to prevent exactly what she was attempting. Dead flesh wouldn't work. Severed fingers wouldn't work. It needed warmth and circulation, the subtle electrical signals of a living body.

Spencer reached into the backpack and pulled out the electrode gel she'd bought from the pharmacy. The medical-grade conductor would bridge the gap between her own bioelectrical signals and the fake print. She removed the mould and rubbed her finger vigorously against her thigh, generating friction heat, before putting it back on. She applied a thin layer of the gel and pressed her finger to the scanner, holding her breath. One second. Two seconds. The longest three seconds of her life.

A green light. The safe clicked open.

Spencer allowed herself two seconds to smile and punch the air before reaching inside. A velvet bag of precious stones and two wads of cash were tempting, but she shoved them to one side. Time was ticking. Spencer collected two paper files and a drive, shoving them in her backpack. She zipped it back up and checked her watch. She'd done it all in under two minutes. She had four minutes to get out of there. Eight if traffic was on her side.

The sensor on a camera in the corner of the room blinked. A pinprick of ruby red. Spencer emerged from the desk's shadow, pulled her backpack over both shoulders and approached the camera, blowing a kiss in its direction.

"Better luck next time, Li."

Spencer slid the door open and slipped out onto the deck and into the night.

***

Spencer's exit from White Dove was less graceful than her entrance. The contents of the safe weren't heavy. Still, it shifted her centre of gravity higher, throwing her balance off as she navigated the external stairs. She crept along the side decks, staying low in case any of Zhou's men happened to be looking. The harbour wall was seven feet above her, five feet above the metal guardrail. She climbed onto the rail, praying her core would hold strong. She didn't want to slip and fall between the boat and the quay. A sudden swell or gust of wind, and she'd be crushed.

Glancing down, Spencer caught sight of a zebra bream, its striped body shimmering in the rays of White Dove's underwater lights. Thick black lines traversed its pearlescent body. Its movements were elegant and effortless, unlike Spencer, who toppled forward, grabbing the top of the harbour wall and hauling one leg onto the concrete at a time. She felt the rough stone chafe against her Lycra leggings and pictured herself, sluggish and dressed entirely in black, like some giant, shiny leech.

She heard the shout just as she reached the top: Chinese, angry, urgent. They'd discovered her faster than expected. Spencer scrambled under the chain fence, the metal catching the backpack for a heart-stopping moment before she jerked free.

Spencer ran. She rounded the corner near the naval base at full sprint. The asphalt scraped her palms as she dropped and rolled beneath a parked Chelsea tractor in one fluid motion.

The pursuing footsteps skidded to a halt. Someone turned on their phone's torch feature, scanning it back and forth across Queensway. Through the gap beneath the car, Spencer saw their feet shuffle uncertainly. Then she heard something behind her, beyond the barbed wire, the distinctive click of canine claws on pavement and the measured stride of security boots.

"Evening, gentlemen." The guard's voice was low, gravelly and local. His accent wasn't quite Spanish; it wasn't quite anything. The Gibraltarians had an elocution and articulation all of their own. His German Shepherd, however, sounded exactly like every other *Deutscher Schäferhund* Spencer had met, with a growl capable of making men freeze, forgetting fight or flight.

Zhou's men tried to act casual, nodding a greeting back to the naval security guard. One uttered something about looking for a lost watch to explain the torch beam. Spencer stayed low, secure in the knowledge that even if they found her, they wouldn't try anything with His Majesty's Navy watching.

Tyres screeched at the end of the row. Car doors slammed. Li's voice was sharp and vicious. Amateur move, Spencer thought. Nothing drew attention like someone obviously losing their shit.

From her position beneath the 4x4, Spencer watched as Li grabbed one of his men by the collar and slammed him against the cream-coloured wall of Moorland House. The impact sent a dull thud through the night. Even without understanding the words, the intent was unmistakable. A warning. A promise. She felt a flicker of pity for the man; he might have a family waiting for him somewhere, a mother who still called to check if he was eating enough, a child who would never know what had happened.

The thought barely had time to settle. If one of them caught her, they wouldn't show mercy; there'd be no moment of reflection on who she might leave behind. And Li wouldn't just kill her, he'd take his time. Not a single, merciful slice to the throat, no clean severance of the carotid, no swift crimson flood. He'd use his diving knife. Small nicks first. Exsanguination by a thousand cuts.

The dog barked; the guard shouted. "Oi! Let go of him!"

Spencer watched Li reluctantly release his prey. He forced a smile and an apologetic nod to the man on the other side of the barbed wire.

"He... erm... slept with my wife."

Spencer rolled her eyes at Li's best effort at lying.

"Good for him," laughed the guard, not buying it. "Look, clear off and keep your hands to yourself. If I hear of even a hint of trouble tonight, I can identify every last one of you. *Entienden?*"

Li cleared his throat, released the man and patted him playfully on the arm. "Understood," he answered slowly, skulking east towards the main road. The others followed. Once out of sight of the guard, their torches flickered back to life. Spencer waited until the torch beams faded to black before rolling out from under the car. She stayed low and didn't look back.

CHAPTER 25

The lock on the apartment door clicked into place, and Spencer took a moment to catch her breath in the dark. Her legs trembled as she filled the kettle, the massive adrenaline dump making her limbs feel weak and heavy. She pulled a Yorkshire Tea bag from its box and dropped it into a plain white mug with a chip on the rim.

She dumped the backpack and the contents of Zhou's safe on the sofa, barely glancing at them. They could wait. Right now, she needed to calm down, slow her racing pulse, and breathe like a human again. The kettle began to rumble quietly, curls of ghostly steam rising above it.

In the bathroom, the intense LED lights flicked on with a blink and an audible hum. It was too bright. Spencer squinted against the glare as she peeled off her running gear, the gritty fabric clinging to her skin like newly formed scabs.

The harbour wall had left its mark. Angry red abrasions bloomed on her knees. But worse was the road rash down both forearms, raw and tingly from where she'd rolled under the car. She caught a glimpse of herself in the mirror, flushed, wide-eyed, looking like she didn't know if she made it back safely or just imagined it.

She froze, seeing the thick, dark blood on her inner thighs.

"Oh, for the love of..." she muttered, examining the burgundy sheen that was more than scuffs and grazes. Perfect timing. As if breaking into an arms dealer's yacht and being chased through the streets by his henchmen wasn't tough enough without adding this to the mix.

***

Twelve-year-old Spencer wakes up feeling strange and different. There's a heavy feeling in the pit of her stomach that she can't explain. She rolls out of bed, her young mind foggy with sleep. Her favourite summer pyjamas, the ones with the palm print that used to be vivid emerald but that are now a dull green, feel oddly sticky against her skin.

The floor is cold as she edges to the bathroom. It's winter in Newcastle, but the heating isn't on. Too expensive. A floorboard creaks under her step. She pulls the cord on the light; it makes a click-click noise as the lightbulb brightens the small room. The mirror above the sink is speckled with toothpaste splashes, and Albie's Batman toothbrush lies discarded by the tap. She looks down at a dark red stain covering her pyjama trousers. She is bleeding.

"What were you thinking?" Her dad's voice carries up the stairs. "You *knew* how important today was."

Dazed and unsure what to do about the blood, Spencer inches towards the noise, creeping down the stairs. Her trousers feel damp. It's unpleasant, like she's wet herself or sat in a puddle.

Below the bannister, thick pen marks in red and yellow swirl and zig-zag in unpredictable patterns over magnolia paint. The unmistakable artwork of a seven-year-old. One scrawl looks like a dinosaur, all teeth and spikes, drawn at kid-height along the wall. Another might be a footballer, arms raised in victory, though his head is oddly square. The felt-tip marks are still glistening in places, and the chemical smell clashes with the strong scent of their dad's aftershave, the one Mum bought him years ago.

Albie sniffles, but his chin is raised, his spine straight. His Spiderman pyjamas are rumpled from sleep, one leg pushed up to his knees. He clutches the marker pen like a sword, both guilty and defiant. A scruffy little warrior.

"I was bored," Albie says, his voice whiny. "I made it better. You never like anything I do!"

"That's because all you do is cost me money."

Spencer's legs feel heavy as she continues her way downstairs, the argument growing louder with each step, not that either her father or brother notices her. Her dad's dressed differently today: a shirt and tie. He'd look smart, like a businessman, if the shirt wasn't half-tucked and his face not flushed red with anger.

"I don't have time for this," he snaps, checking his watch. "I'm already late. Who do you think is going to clean this mess, Albie? Where is the money for new paint? Who do you think is going to have to spend hours repainting this?"

"I'll paint it."

Dad's mouth falls open. "Right. As if. Don't you think you've done enough damage as it is?"

Spencer has reached the bottom of the stairs. They're going to wake Liam. "Dad," she tries.

"Mum used to like my drawings," Albie protests, waving the pen dangerously close to his dad's clean shirt. Dad grabs the pen, wrenching it violently from his grip.

Albie screams. "I hate this stupid house! I hate this stupid family! I wish—" his voice cracks. "I wish *you* had died instead of Mum!"

The silence that follows feels fragile, like a glass balanced on a table's edge, a sneeze away from falling and shattering. Just when Spencer thinks her dad's face couldn't get any redder, it drains of all colour. He bends down, coming eye to eye with Albie.

"Sometimes," he says, his voice no more than a menacing whisper, "I wish that too."

"Dad," Spencer tries again. "I need help."

He turns, and his eyes drop to the stain on her pyjamas. All the fight seems to drain out of him at once. "Not today." His shoulders sag, and he presses his hands against his eyes.

"I can't do this," he says, the defeat in his voice worrying Spencer. "I'm sorry, Spencer. I can't." Without another word, he grabs his keys from the hook by the door and walks out. The door slams behind him, rattling happy family photos on the wall, nothing more than framed lies.

***

When Dad finally comes home, his eyes are red-rimmed and puffy. Spencer recognises that look; it's the same expression he wore at Mum's funeral, on Mother's Day, and on Mum's birthday. He's carrying a shopping bag from Boots and another from ASDA. His tie is undone, hanging loosely down either side of his shirt.

"I'm so sorry, sweetheart," he says, setting the bags down on the kitchen table. His voice is hoarse. "I shouldn't have walked out. Not today. Not when you needed me."

Spencer watches as he pulls items from the bags: packets of pads in various sizes, boxes of tampons, new cotton knickers still in their packaging, and soft flannel pyjamas adorned with floral prints. There's even a book with a pink cover: *Growing Up and Getting Your Period. Everything You Need to Know.*

She thinks about telling him about Nana, how Spencer had called her in tears after Dad had left that morning. How Nana rushed over to help her clean up, explained everything, and showed her how to use a pad. Nana took Liam back to her place, and Spencer walked Albie to school. They were both late, but his teacher understood when Spencer whispered what had happened. But looking at her nervous father arranging offerings on their scratched kitchen table, she can't bring herself to say it.

Spencer looks at all the items and sees pound signs flashing before her.

"Don't we need money for paint? For the hallway?"

"Albie's artwork can wait. I got some good news today," Dad says, attempting a smile as he pulls some pizzas from the ASDA bag to show that it was indeed a celebration. "They offered me the promotion."

Spencer's heart leaps. A promotion to sergeant? Finally, something good. Dad might not have to work such long hours. Perhaps they can have family film nights again, like they used to when Mum was alive. All the family cuddled on the sofa, under a double duvet with a bucket of popcorn. Maybe Albie will stop wrecking the place and throwing tantrums just to get attention.

"That's brilliant!" she says, meaning it. "Well done, Dad."

"Thank you, sweetheart." He puts one arm around her and hugs her.

"So you'll be home more?"

His attempt at a smile falters. "Actually, love, it means more hours and more responsibility. But—" he hurries on as her face falls, "—it means more money. We can get proper help. Someone to look after the three of you after school, assist with homework, and cook proper food instead of the ready meals we've been living on."

"A stranger?" The word sounds bitter; she doesn't mean to come across as ungrateful. She gazes at the book on the table, feeling sad. Mum should have been sitting here, explaining everything. Mum should have been the one to buy her first pads, to hug her and tell her it was all normal. Mum would have known what to do this morning, would have had supplies ready, would have made everything less frightening.

Everyone says getting your period means becoming a woman. The girls at school whisper about it in the bathrooms, treating it like some secret club, a milestone that separates the children from the grown-ups. But Spencer doesn't feel like she's crossed any magical threshold into adulthood. Besides, she stopped being a child a year ago, on that rain-soaked night when Dad came home from the hospital without Mum. That was the real dividing line, the moment that split her life into *before* and *after*. After that night, she learned to make Liam's bottles, to check that Albie had brushed his teeth, to be quiet when Dad's door was closed because that meant he was crying.

"They'll be professional," Dad says softly. "Qualified. Someone who knows what they're doing, unlike me."

Nana could have done all that if she hadn't tried to get custody, and Dad could have just forgiven her and moved on. Instead, Spencer took infant Liam over to Nana's every morning on her way to school and brought him home every day after school just so the grown-ups could avoid seeing each other. Spencer wants to tell him that she doesn't want *qualified*. She doesn't want *professional*. She wants burnt toast in the morning and off-key singing while doing the dishes. She wants someone who knows that Albie needs his socks inside out, or they feel wrong and that Spencer likes the light left on at night. She wants Mum.

But Dad's eyes are still red, and his shoulders are slumped from the weight of the effort, so she picks up the new pyjamas instead. "These are really nice," she says. "Thank you."

His smile this time is real, if small. "I got the flowers because..." He stops, swallows hard. "You like plants, right?"

Spencer nods. She does like plants, and she appreciates that Dad said plants and not flowers in a *girls-like-flowers* sort of way. She likes all the plants: the thorny ones, the ugly ones. She likes the plants that refuse to die, the ones that claw through cracks in concrete and thrive where they shouldn't, the ones people call weeds, but that are just as alive and just as beautiful, to anyone who knows beauty is more than petal-deep.

Spencer holds the soft flannel against her chest, breathing in its new clothes smell, wishing they'd smell like that forever and never go musty.

CHAPTER 26

T he kettle clicked off, pulling Spencer from her memories. She folded over the sink, momentarily resting her head on the cool bathroom mirror, feeling pensive and melancholic. Somewhere in the distance, a metal gangway groaned as the tide shifted beneath it. She tossed her clothes into the laundry bag and took a quick shower. Water that had boiled and then slightly cooled was better for tea anyway.

Hair piled on top of her head, and dressed in a soft cotton t-shirt and shorts, Spencer unlocked her laptop and inserted the USB drive. The moment of truth.

The folders appeared benign at first glance, camouflaged by corporate labels such as *Q4 Transactions*, *Performance Reports, and Operation Manual*. The kind of names that would typically make her eyes glaze over. Yet Spencer had been doing this long enough to recognise the patterns and the careful architecture of hidden information. She opened personnel files and found scanned passports and salary details.

She wondered if Sun Li, Zhou's muscle, was aware that his buddy, Mengze, the butler, was being paid more than he was. There were instructions to send thirty per cent of Li's wages to a nursing home in a residential district of Beijing. Another file indicated a substantial bonus for everyone on board for the coming summer. The captain's résumé detailed his various qualifications and the waters he had navigated.

The tea grew cold as Spencer moved through each file in turn. Outside, a pair of voices drifted past – low, clipped words in English, maybe a night-shift security patrol. She paused to rub her eyes, standing to stretch her legs. She paced, thinking about the data she'd found so far. The apartment was chilly overnight, but the crochet throw on the back of the sofa looked inviting. Spencer wrapped it around herself and sat back down.

She found the shipping logs next. Nothing that gave away what Zhou wanted to sell to the UK, USA, and other allies. No indication of a sale to Iran. Spencer sifted through the invoices. Smaller sums first, thirty grand here, forty grand there. Then larger sums, a cool two million invoiced to a business whose postal address was in Panama. Three and a half million coming from a bank account in Zurich. All US dollars. Shady? Yes. Worth killing a Six agent for? No. Then her eyes landed on a considerably bigger number: eighty-two million.

Eighty-two bloody million dollars from DVS Holdings Ltd. The description read *Specialised Industrial Equipment* but gave no further details.

There might as well be a flashing neon sign reading: *Nothing suspicious here. Honest, Guv.* A quick internet search led Spencer to a website that was so generic, it told her nothing about the company or its operations. A bit more digging gave her an address in the Cayman Islands. DVS Holdings was nothing more than a shell, a front. So, who had really paid such a ghastly sum to Zhou?

By two in the morning, Spencer's vision was beginning to blur. Too much screen time. A naval boat sounded its horn somewhere in the bay, while navigation lights from pilot boats cast a shifting pattern of red and green through the apartment window. She tip-tapped through email threads, trying to find who or what was hiding behind the shell company. The word *Hēiyán* made her pause. The same word that made Zhou's men laugh coldly. Her language skills were rudimentary. Still, she kept returning to dark something. Dark stone? Another nickname for Zhou? A code for a weapon?

The throw slipped from Spencer's shoulders as she sat up quickly, fatigue momentarily forgotten. An email from DVS to Zhou confirming the balancing payment:

> *>Do not worry about customs or importation. We have all the required FSB clearances. The delivery will be made without issue.*

Then, from Zhou to DVS:

> *>Good luck, comrade. A pleasure doing business with you.*

FSB: The Federal Security Service.
Russia.

Spencer typed the payment date and Russia into Google and clicked the News tab. Nothing at first. She adjusted the search parameters, trying dates in the days that followed. Still nothing. Switching to Russian and the Cyrillic alphabet using an online translator, she tried again. No mainstream news, but a political blogger named Elena Orlova had posted something on a site called *Uncensored*. A click on her profile told Spencer Elena was an independent journalist known for her sharp analysis of Kremlin defence spending and patriotic projects.

The post, dated two days after the payment, described a *strategic military acquisition aimed at reinforcing national power projection*. Elena called it *another step toward militarised isolation*. She claimed her source was deeply embedded and highly credible, warning that the development would not go unnoticed in Washington or Brussels. She signed off with:

Eighty million dollars, not for schools, hospitals or hungry mouths, but for the vanity project of a dying empire.

It was her final article on the site.

Spencer searched Elena Orlova's name. The top result: *Political Critic In Coma After Fall From Moscow Highrise.*

The correlation was too perfect to be mere coincidence.

Spencer picked up her phone and typed out a message to Buddy: *Call me.*

The sofa cushions were soft and inviting. Spencer told herself she'd rest her eyes for just a moment while she waited for Buddy's call. The laptop hummed softly beside her, its screen still glowing with the damning evidence of whatever game Zhou and Russia were playing.

***

A ringing phone cut through Spencer's dreams. She jerked awake, her neck stiff from sleeping at an awkward angle on the sofa. The laptop had gone into sleep mode, its screen dark. Morning light filtered through the shutters, painting stripes across her bare legs.

Buddy's name flashed on her phone. The clock said it was just after seven a.m. — six a.m. in London.

"Hey," she mumbled into the phone, orienting herself. Papers from Zhou's safe were still scattered across her coffee table.

"You sound rough," Buddy said. "Bad night?"

"Productive night."

Spencer stretched. Her body didn't feel sore, but it did feel awkward and sluggish, as if her legs hadn't been given enough blood supply while she'd slept. Once she got moving, she'd feel fine again. She looked longingly at the kettle and decided it could wait.

"Any news?" Spencer could hear the morning sounds of Buddy's family home coming to life: children being hurried to brush their teeth, breakfast radio playing in the background. She yawned, pulled the woollen throw around her like a cape.

"It's Russia," she told him. "Not Iran. At least, it's someone operating in Russia with contacts in the FSB. I wouldn't be surprised if it was state-sponsored."

"How do you know?"

"Hang on." She sent him a selection of links and attachments via email and heard his phone ping as the notifications came through. She waited while he scanned the first batch.

"You little beauty," he murmured. Then, louder, "You got the drive? You're saying you got into the safe? Did it go alright? You weren't hurt, were you?"

"I'm fine. Stop asking stupid questions, and I'll tell you all about it."

Buddy laughed; it sounded awkward. Spencer leaned forward and rested her elbows on her knees, her posture slouching as she relayed the information she'd acquired about DVS Holdings Ltd, the shell company in the Caymans and the eighty-two million price tag.

"Christ. What were they buying, a small country?"

She ignored him and continued with the details of the email trail, including how Zhou addressed the man as Comrade and how the mystery buyer stated that the FSB would ensure the shipment arrived without issue.

She stood up after telling him about Elena Orlova and her fall from a highrise. She stretched her legs and tiptoed over to the sliding door that opened to the balcony. She opened it just enough to let a breeze seep into the apartment. A grey-headed gull was perched on the quay in the dusky pink of the morning light. It stabbed at a mussel with its beak, pulling the contents out before tilting its grey-hooded head back and devouring it. Spencer smiled; it was unusual to spot a grey-head so far north. They rarely appeared in Spain and Italy. She considered it a positive omen: today would be a good day.

"Here's the weird thing," she said.

"Eight-two million wasn't the weird thing?"

"The weight on the shipping invoice is only listed as ten kilos. Not many munitions coming in at under ten kilos, not ones worth that price tag."

Buddy was quiet, presumably going over what Six knew about Zhou. "Zhou specialises in weapons: guns, missiles, grenade launchers. For that price, if he's not selling something that explodes, it must be something just as devastating."

Spencer agreed. It didn't add up. "Chemical weapons?" she suggested. "Say, for argument's sake, one litre comes in at one kilogram; imagine what you could do with ten kilos of novichok?"

"It's not worth thinking about. But the Russians don't need to buy that in."

"Another chemical then. VX, BZ, sarin, ricin?"

"Stockpiling any of those would violate the Chemical Weapons Convention, not that anyone purchasing quantities like that is likely to care."

Spencer yawned again. He was right. And what sort of chemical would come in at eight-two mill?

"Software," she said. "The email trail mentioned sending detailed instructions for installation and activation. What if it's a computer virus the likes of which we've never seen before? Imagine wiping half the world's internet. Taking out online banking or a power grid?"

Spencer watched the gull spread its black-tipped wings and take flight. She closed the sliding door, headed to the bathroom and rubbed her eyes, trying to focus. "There was something else," she said, sitting down on the toilet. "A term I kept hearing. Sounded like *Hēiyán*. I think it means dark stone in Mandarin."

"Dark stone?" She could hear the cogs turning, the slight tap-tap of his finger that always accompanied Buddy's deepest concentration. "Like jet? Obsidian?"

Spencer started to wee, didn't care if Buddy could hear. "Obsidian was traditionally used in weapons because it's so sharp. It's making a comeback. Surgeons prefer it over steel because cuts from obsidian scalpels don't scar. It's quite brittle, though. Tungsten's another option. That's used in armour-piercing ammo." She wiped and pulled a tampon from the box by the sink. "But I keep coming back to the ten-kilogram shipping weight."

"That's the thing. Maybe we're thinking too literally. It's probably just a random codename. But for what?"

"No idea. But it made Zhou's men laugh in a way I didn't like." She flushed, washed her hands and returned to the lounge. "What about a virus? An actual virus, not a computer one. A lot of people made a lot of money out of Covid. Eighty-two million might be a small price to pay if you can infect and lockdown the world, then flog them the antidote."

Buddy swallowed hard. "Yikes. Look, I'll dig through Theo Monroe's intel again, but I don't recall seeing anything linked to stones."

Longing for more sleep, Spencer felt exhaustion pressing heavily on her. Still, she switched on the kettle, returned to the sofa, and tapped a key on her laptop, bringing it back to life. She entered her password, answered the questions, and pressed her fingertip to the sensor. "I ought to return to these files..."

"You should get some rest," Buddy cut in. "A few hours won't change anything. Besides, the deal's already done. You sound dead on your feet."

"I'm sitting down, actually."

"Spencer."

"Fine," she said. "I'll get some more z's and go and be a tourist for a bit, get some vitamin D." But even as she said it, Spencer wondered why her gut disagreed with Buddy. If the deal was already done, why did she feel like she was running out of time?

CHapTer 27

His gaze never left the doors, hoping that, just as a watched pot never boils, a watched door wouldn't open. As Robin Grimm mechanically shuffled through his usual duties, the lanyard around his neck felt particularly burdensome, dragging his posture down, like weighted Rosary beads punishing a sinner.

Cara, now Claire Gibson, had arrived at the base at 07:30 as promised, driving a dark green Toyota. At the barrier, she presented her ID and was signed over into Robin's care without issue. No suspicion. No questions. The guard had smiled and said, "Have a nice day, ma'am."

No one ever told Robin to have a nice day.

At first glance, Robin had panicked, thinking the real Claire had arrived. Cara's fiery hair was now a soft brown, her face subtly contoured to alter her cheekbones and jawline, padded clothing made her appear a dress size larger. She wore plain, boxy trousers and an oversized cardigan in an unflattering shade of beige. The same glasses Claire wore in her passport photo were perched on Cara's nose. She looked dowdy. Plain. Entirely forgettable.

She'd introduced herself with professional politeness. "Claire Gibson. Systems technician. You must be Mr Grimm. It's good to meet you."

Robin had mumbled something in response, feeling like a man slowly walking into quicksand. He hated her for the charade, for the lie, for the ease with which she slipped into this new skin.

Now, behind him, Cara/Claire worked briskly. To any casual observer, she seemed merely another technician executing routine checks and maintenance. She knelt on the floor, her tools spread out neatly beside her. Quickly and quietly, she extracted a small, inconspicuous device and a thread picker from her tool belt. Gently, she unstitched the seam beneath one of the seats. Once the fabric flap was open, she wound a mechanical device no larger than a box of matches and embedded it deep into the seat's padding. From what Robin could see, there was no battery or electronics. It was entirely mechanical, like a wind-up toy. After inserting the device, she took a needle and thread, colour-matched to the seat fabric and restitched the opening with precise, invisible stitches. It took her no more than five minutes.

Moving to the adjacent seat, Cara/Claire began repeating the process. Robin, positioned strategically to obscure her actions from anyone else's view, tried to appear nonchalant. He inspected some nearby wiring and shuffled some papers, but his stomach churned with fear and questions. What was she planning? What was the device? He could see enough to understand that whatever she was planting in these seats was meant to be hidden and undetectable. Too small to be an effective explosive. It could be a tracker of some sort, but what would be the point of that?

***

Spencer woke to sunlight filling the apartment. Her phone showed 11:27. The rest had done her good. Her mind felt sharper, the anxiety about the evidence from Zhou's safe reduced to a manageable background murmur rather than the uneasy nagging that plagued her in the early hours. Buddy was right. The deal was already done. The mission was largely admin-based going forward, translating documents, deciphering encrypted files and digging further into DVS Holdings Ltd. Six would likely cut off her funding by the end of the day and send her a ticket for the first flight home tomorrow.

She made a breakfast that would double as lunch: two eggs, sourdough toast, yoghurt with fruit, orange juice, more tea. The routine felt weirdly normal after the past few days, as if she were growing accustomed to the sleek lines and minimalist modernity of the apartment. *Never.*

The weather report showed 26°C, clear skies, and barely a whisper of wind. Spencer chose her clothes carefully: high-waisted, tailored linen trousers that would cover her bruised knees, and a sleeveless silk top in deep navy. The outfit spoke of careful wealth – someone who shopped at the right stores but didn't need to show off about it. In other words, more Angela than Spencer. Perfect for a day blending in with the cruise ship tourists and Gibraltar's ladies-who-lunch.

Despite her duties coming to an end, Spencer had no desire to run into Zhou, or worse, Li. She decided wearing a wig was the safest option, even if it would feel hot and sticky in the heat of the midday sun. She chose the same bobbed blonde one she had worn to stage the break-in and steal forensic tools from the crime scene investigators.

The wig was expensive, made from real hair, in a shade they called old-money blonde. Classy. It was cut to fall just below her chin and settled into place over the cap easily. She secured it with a couple of hidden clips.

When Spencer looked in the mirror, someone else stared back at her. She didn't look like someone who crawled under cars or scaled harbour walls. Definitely didn't look like someone who had stolen incriminating documents from a Chinese arms dealer the night before. She looked like Izzy.

Working her fingers through the lengths of blonde didn't change things, nor did tucking one or both sides of the hair behind her ears. Izzy still stared back at her, holding her gaze, daring her to look away.

***

Suddenly, Spencer is thirteen again, slouching at the kitchen table with hair falling over her science homework like a veil of darkness.

She is home alone, blissfully enjoying the rare moment of peace. But silence never lasts long around here, and Spencer sighs as the front door clatters open. Liam toddles in first, clutching a painting of multicoloured handprints. Behind him, Izzy expertly manoeuvres around his slow little body while keeping one hand on Albie's schoolbag to prevent him from dropping it in the hallway like usual.

"Look what I made!" Liam announces, his cheeks still flushed from the cold walk home from nursery.

"That's going straight on the fridge," Izzy says, her dark blonde bob swinging as she heads to the kitchen. "Who wants a snack? Spencer, have you eaten?"

Spencer shakes her head, pretending to focus on her diagram while her stomach rumbles. She could have fixed herself a snack after she got in from secondary school, but she doesn't want to admit that she likes Izzy's snacks better. She can cook pancakes from scratch, and when she makes Nutella on toast, she makes it look like a cheeky monkey, spreading the chocolate in a circle and adding banana slices for ears and a mouth, adding blueberries for eyes. She knows how Liam likes his juice diluted and that Albie will only eat red grapes, not the green ones. Izzy always cuts the grapes in half because she says she had an entire lecture at college about how a child died choking on a grape. Spencer shuddered at that story: Albie thought it was cool.

"Your dad says you're good at science," Izzy says, peering over her shoulder to look at her work. "But if you need a hand, just say." She starts pulling ingredients from the cupboards and makes herself a coffee."

Spencer thinks she's okay at science. Not bad, but certainly not the best in her class. She half concentrates on her work, but from the corner of her eye, she keeps a watch on the rest of them. Izzy chops celery into short sticks and slathers cream cheese into the grooves. She turns it into a snail, adding a semicircle of cucumber for a shell and a cherry tomato for a head. Two slivers of carrot make antennas, and two small dabs of cream cheese become eyes. She does all this while calming Albie's brewing tantrum about something that happened at break time. She gently rests a hand on his shoulder and whispers a joke that makes him giggle despite his mood. It's the same soothing manner she uses at Liam's bedtime. She is a young and pretty ray of sunshine in their previously sad, dark home. Even Nana approves.

When Dad comes home that evening in his police uniform, his tired face breaks into the kind of smile Spencer hasn't seen in ages. It makes her stomach twist in a complicated way. She hopes Dad doesn't fancy Izzy. She's far too young for him. It would be gross; besides, they don't need a new mum. But as much as Spencer wants to resent Izzy and her perfect hair and her way of making everything seem manageable, she can't deny that the house feels warmer somehow. More like home again.

CHAPTER 28

Cara – or Claire – crouched low beside the panel housing the networking equipment. Robin watched her remove the cover, revealing wires and switches; blinking LED lights illuminated her flawless skin. He hated that he still found her beautiful. Despised himself. She pouted her plump little lips, examining the layout of the Ethernet ports, access points, and the neatly arranged patch panel that routed dozens of fibre optic cables.

She squinted, then said, "Hmm."

Robin didn't know if it was a good hmm or a bad hmm. He kept his mouth shut and eyes peeled.

She extracted a slender wire from the toolkit that lay open beside her. Its contents were carefully arranged, each piece of kit lying parallel to the next. The wire, thin and coated with a nondescript grey sheath, was nearly indistinguishable from the myriad of others that snaked through the system.

She noticed him watching, winked, and said, "Crossover adapter," as if that phrase clarified anything. Next, she chose a small, unassuming black box from her kit. It appeared custom-built, the size of a deck of cards, with blinking LEDs and a series of ports. She attached the grey wire to it and plugged the other end into a spare port on the panel.

"What does that do?" Robin finally asked, unable to suppress his curiosity.

She glanced at him, her lips curling into a faint smirk. "It's not a bomb, sweetheart. Don't look so worried."

He wanted to grab her by the throat and tell her to stop calling him sweetheart. He should squeeze the life out of her for what she'd done. But her words echoed in his head: *If you had a history of violence, we wouldn't have selected you.*

She inhaled deeply and let out a faint giggle. "It's just a little bridge, that's all."

She reached into the toolkit again, pulling out a slim, unbranded USB stick. Plugging it into a port on the module, she muttered under her breath as a small LED flickered red. She pulled a small flip phone from her trouser pocket and called someone.

"Uploading the protocol now."

The LED changed to green.

"Bridge active... Handshake established. I'll tidy up. Meet me at the extraction point in one hour."

The inaudible voice on the other end of the call said something. Cara looked at Robin, looked him up and down, then smiled. "He's been no bother... No. He won't talk. He knows the consequences... One hour."

She ended the call.

The place was silent for a moment, save for the faint hum of electronics. Robin watched as she zipped up her toolkit and screwed the panel back into position.

"Right," she said, standing and brushing a stray brown hair from her face. Her tone was commanding now, businesslike. The playful smirk was gone. She pressed a finger to Robin's lips. "You did good. Now keep these closed, and you'll never hear from me again."

He swallowed, not knowing who he wanted to kill more: Cara or himself.

"But one word," she continued, "one tiny little word and poor Holly will be..." She grimaced. "You won't even be able to identify the body, sweetheart."

***

Spencer spotted him halfway up the hill. The same elderly man in a wheelchair she'd seen on Main Street a few days earlier. The nurse, a stocky woman with coppery brown hair tied in a neat bun, struggled against the incline, her white uniform darkened with sweat patches. The wheels of the chair caught on a loose stone, and the nurse muttered something under her breath.

The old man sat rigid in the wheelchair. He wore a pressed linen suit despite the heat, his papery skin stretched taut over sharp cheekbones. A Panama hat shaded his weathered face and dark eyes. Those eyes, like orbs of jaspillite, locked onto Spencer's with unsettling intensity, as if he could see straight through her disguise, through the blonde wig and the carefully tailored outfit.

Three seconds passed. Four. Five.

Then, like a switch being flipped, it vanished. His eyes went vacant, staring through her like she were a shop window. The nurse, noticing the exchange, placed a protective hand on the old man's arm and quickened her pace.

Spencer continued north, passing through Casemates. The square was packed with midday activity: tourists queuing for fish and chips, groups of young men on their third pint of the day, locals rushing through lunch breaks. Still, Spencer barely registered them as she began the climb.

Hundreds of stairs stretched before her, the narrow alleys providing blessed shade, though the humidity still dappled her skin with moisture. By the time she reached Ethan's street, her lightweight sleeveless top was plastered to her back.

Through the ground-floor window, she saw him hunched over a laptop, completely absorbed in some form of flight simulator. He tapped the controls, his expression one of extreme concentration. The blue glow of the screen highlighted the angles of his square jaw.

She knocked sharply. Three raps.

He jumped, eyes narrowing as he peered at the unknown blonde through the window.

The door edged open, and Ethan's expression cycled rapidly from annoyance to recognition to confusion.

"Spencer?" He asked, opening the door fully, taking in the classy, dark blonde hair that reached just above her shoulders. "Almost didn't recognise you there."

"That's rather the point," she replied, adjusting the wig self-consciously.

"The mafia still after you?"

"Not the mafia. But, yes."

"Are you going to tell me who they really are and why they want to kill you?"

She smiled, shook her head, hair falling over her face.

Ethan's hand was tentative, reaching for the rogue strands, brushing them back. It felt nice, tender.

"I like your real hair, but this suits you too. Though, to be fair…" He grinned cheekily. "… You'd look good in a bin liner."

"So you've said."

Someone in a flat above opened their shutters. Guitar music floated down to the alley along with the smell of fried seafood, calamari perhaps.

Ethan leaned against his doorframe, arms folded over a lean chest.

"So, what can I do for you? Tea? Hummus?"

"I came to apologise," she told him. "I'm sorry for running out on you last time. Things are… complicated."

"I was beginning to think I'd hallucinated the whole thing." His posture softened, leaning further into the wooden frame. "It's not every day I get to ride my bike down Union Jack Stairs. You know, some might call fleeing from a madman a bonding experience."

"Some might, she laughed. I call it another day at the office." She bit her lip, took her shot. "Speaking of work, I have a few hours off, and you're not working today—"

"Beating my high score is extremely serious work."

She called him a geek again and asked, "I was wondering if your offer still stands. To go up the Rock?"

He tried to play it cool, but the corner of Ethan's mouth twitched upward. The guitar playing came to a sudden stop, plunging them into silence. "Well, I do have some interesting monkey facts to share with you," he said, pulling his motorcycle keys from his pocket. "Are you planning to run out on me again?"

"Not this time," she said. "Not if I can help it."

CHAPTER 29

The Yamaha MT07 wove through the narrow streets, braking and accelerating at each stop sign, traffic light, and jaywalker. Spencer sat behind Ethan, her arms wrapped around his chest, her silk top billowing playfully. The road twisted sharply, forcing them to lean into the curve as they climbed higher, past stone fortifications and whitewashed six-storey apartment blocks. The scent of exhaust faded with each metre of altitude until the smell of limestone heated by the fierce sun took over. The ride was slower than the last time she'd been on his bike, more controlled, pleasurable even. No impending sense of doom.

Ahead, the Moorish Castle came into view. Perched halfway up the Rock, its weathered stone walls bore battle scars and centuries of wear. The main tower's rectangular bulk dominated the landscape, a relic from when the Moors held power here. However, that power had changed hands more than once, and now the Gibraltarian flag fluttered from a flagpole on the ramparts.

The approach was steep, the road narrowing towards the toll booth. To their right, the Rock reared up, a vertiginous face of lichen-covered stone and hardy Mediterranean Pines jutting from yellow grass.

Ethan slowed the bike as they neared the barrier, glancing in his side mirror. A sudden blare of a horn cut through the noise of the motorbike's engine. A car surged forward from behind, its driver leaning on the wheel, his mouth already moving. Ethan twisted the throttle, slipping ahead just in time to avoid being clipped by the car's bumper. Spencer swore under her breath, tightening her grip around his torso as he brought the bike to a controlled stop.

The car, a Fiat, jerked to a halt beside them, the driver flinging his door open before he'd even finished braking. A stocky man with thinning hair and sweat-darkened armpits stormed towards Ethan, arms waving. Spencer lifted her visor to get a good look at him and his passengers: a skeletal woman with leathery skin in the front, and two teenage boys in the back, both wearing a *here-we-go-again* expression.

"You trying to get yourself killed?" His accent was from the south of England. Eastbourne or Brighton. "You cut across me like you own the bloody road!"

Ethan exhaled slowly and removed his helmet. He didn't rush. Didn't raise his voice. Just sat there, calmly meeting the driver's glare.

"You were in my blind spot," Ethan said. "Maybe don't try to overtake on a bend next time."

The driver scoffed. "Blind spot? Please, I saw you coming. You lot think you can just—"

Ethan tilted his head slightly. "My lot?"

The man hesitated

Ethan laughed. "You come to Gibraltar and think you own the place because you're British?"

"Listen, you'd be speaking Spanish if it weren't for my ancestors."

"*Hablo Español muy bien. Francés también.*"

The boys in the back of the car turned beetroot with second-hand embarrassment. The driver dithered, seeming torn between asking what the hell Ethan had just said or pursuing his argument further. The moment lingered until, at last, the driver let out a huff, threw his hands in the air, and stomped back to his Fiat.

Spencer, still seated on the back of the bike, patted his arm. "Impressive. You handled that well."

Ethan shrugged. "I'm guessing you'd have used a different approach."

"Diplomatic solutions aren't my speciality."

He turned and grinned at her. "You'll enjoy this then."

Private vehicles were not permitted in the national park. Visitors could take the cable car, book a private taxi, or park near the ticket booths and walk the rest of the way. Parking was limited, and outside the Moorish Castle, only one space remained. Ethan revved the throttle and lurched the bike forward, zipping right into the middle of the final space. He could have turned the bike sideways and left room for both vehicles, but that wouldn't have been as much fun.

The Fiat's engine growled aggressively as the driver realised what was happening. A moment later, the car screeched to a halt as the driver slammed the brakes, his rage bubbling over.

"You arrogant little—" he sputtered, jabbing his finger toward Ethan. "You did that on purpose!"

Spencer swung her leg over the bike, unhurried. She removed the helmet and finger-combed the wig.

Ethan followed, tussling his own sandy hair, utterly unfazed by the seething man. "Was that more your style?"

"Much more."

The horn sounded repeatedly as Ethan offered Spencer his hand. "May I?"

She linked her fingers with his, liking how it felt. "You may."

They headed towards the castle's arched entrance without a backwards glance, the sound of car horns and swear words following them.

CHAPTER 30

After the castle, they headed for the Great Siege Tunnels. The temperature dropped immediately, cloaking them in cool darkness. Spencer instinctively moved closer to Ethan, craving his body heat. The tunnels, carved into the limestone, varied from cavernous chambers to thin, claustrophobic passages.

At the end of one offshoot, she looked north, placing her hand on the cold stone wall. She could see the airport stretching across the peninsula and, beyond it, the border to La Línea – The Line. She imagined men in the tunnels in the late 1700s aiming cannons below, attempting to defend Gibraltar from land-based attacks while the battle also raged on the waves.

Spencer knew the story of the Great Siege, had it drilled into her repeatedly at school: Eighty thousand wealthy Spaniards moved to the hills across the bay, hoping to witness the destruction of the batteries. They thought it was a sure thing, a spectator sport. They wanted to see the fortress reduced to rubble and the British flag dragged through the dirt.

The blockade weakened Gibraltar. People were cold and hungry, malnutrition and smallpox were rife. Still, morale remained with faith that one day supplies would come.

It was a classic underdog tale. Spencer was surprised Hollywood hadn't adapted it into an epic blockbuster. The Brits were heavily outnumbered: sixty thousand Spanish and French versus just five thousand defenders. The besiegers had forty-nine ships of the line and ten floating batteries.

The Brits had twelve gunboats.

The floating batteries were meant to be unburnable, unsinkable. But, much like the classic underdog films of old, the defenders sent the vessels into Poseidon's grasp one by one.

Ethan switched on a torch as they moved off down another tunnel. "Mad how they honeycomb the entire Rock," he said, voice echoey.

Spencer ran her hand along the damp wall. "How far do they go?"

"Miles," Ethan replied. "They're longer than all the roads in Gibraltar. Some sections are still restricted. Military access only. They used to use them as ammunition caches. There are rumours they still do. Whenever a submarine comes in, some loon will start ranting on Facebook about how they're offloading nukes."

A distant rumble echoed through the tunnel, causing loose pebbles to skitter across the floor.

Spencer tensed. "What was that?"

"Just the Rock settling," Ethan said. Then, his expression grew more serious. "Or that's what we tell the tourists, anyway."

She slapped his chest. "I'm no tourist."

"And don't I know it."

Ethan led her further into a narrow passageway that twisted deeper into the Rock. The air was damp, thick with the odour of ancient stone. Spencer followed, her shoes slippery on the wet, uneven floor. Despite the chill, she felt warm. Whether it was from the thrill of exploration or feeling Ethan's hand in hers, she wasn't sure. She only knew that, for the first time in a long while, she wasn't thinking about the past.

She reached into her pocket, pulling out her phone on instinct. No signal. Not even a flicker of a bar. "We're off the grid," she said, showing him the screen.

***

Buddy Thompson's jaw tightened as the call failed to connect.

"Damn it, Spencer," he muttered, tossing his phone onto the polished desk. Though he was more angry at himself, he was the one who'd told her to take some time off.

Through the window of his office at Vauxhall Cross, London sprawled beneath a gathering layer of rain clouds. The Thames eased past the distinctive structure of MI6 headquarters. From certain angles, it resembled a Mayan temple of green glass and sand-coloured stone.

Buddy's office wasn't large, but its position on the eastern corner gave him views of both the river and Westminster beyond. Unlike the sleek, chrome-and-glass aesthetic of the building's public areas, his personal space was cluttered with the detritus of his years in intelligence. Framed maps of conflict zones covered one wall. A collection of foreign currency filled a glass paperweight. His desk, a solid oak affair, had survived three office relocations and was buried under stacks of classified folders.

On top of a pale blue binder was a slim, black laptop. Theo Monroe's laptop.

The office door opened without a knock. Felicity Weaver, from Cyber Operations, stood in the doorway. She was a tiny little thing with huge glasses that made her look like a praying mantis.

"You've seen it, then?" She nodded toward the printout in front of him.

"Just going through it now." Buddy gestured to the chair opposite his desk. "What's your read?"

"It's not conventional." Felicity remained standing, arms crossed.

A junior assistant appeared in the doorway, hovering uncertainly until Buddy waved him in. "Your itinerary," he said, handing Buddy a schedule. "Leon's called a meeting for three p.m."

"Thank you," Buddy replied, dismissing him with a nod. He picked up an email printed on a sheet of A4, circling a phrase with his red pen. "Bridge systems that are isolated for a reason," he read aloud. "What does that suggest to you?"

Felicity's expression darkened. "Air-gapped networks. Military command systems. Nuclear facilities."

"Precisely." Buddy leaned back in his chair, which creaked in protest.

He tapped the printout. The email to Theo was from an anonymous sender using a throwaway account.

> Not possible. Not the way you describe it anyway. They'd need to bridge systems that are isolated for a reason. It can't be done remotely. Would require physical access and a method to prevent manual override. This isn't like 2015. Different scale entirely.

"It's some form of technology or a cyber weapon," Buddy concluded. "But one that requires physical proximity to deploy."

"A Trojan horse," Felicity agreed. "Something that looks harmless until it's inside the walls."

Buddy reached for his phone again, trying Spencer's number one more time. The call failed to go through. It beeped twice and disconnected.

Through his window, he watched as rain began to fall on London, droplets racing down the glass.

"I'll try her again in an hour," Buddy said, more to himself than to Felicity. "Meanwhile, find where that email originated."

As Felicity left, Buddy turned his chair toward the window, watching the rain intensify over the city. He wondered what the weather was like in Gibraltar. He asked Google. The artificial female voice told him: "The temperature in Gibraltar is currently twenty-six degrees."

Not fair. He drummed his fingers on the desk, eagerly anticipating a change in scenery. And weather.

***

Squinting against the sudden sunlight, Spencer stepped out from the tunnels. Her phone remained forgotten in her left pocket as she and Ethan continued their adventure. They followed a narrow path, carving a route through hardy Mediterranean vegetation. Patches of Gibraltar candytuft clung to the rocks, their soft lilac petals trembling as a Spanish black bee buzzed industriously from flower to flower, never tiring. The air was infused with the scent of wild olive and pine. When Ethan wasn't looking, Spencer scooped up a handful of needles for the caterpillars, stashing them in her right pocket.

They continued south, walking in comfortable silence through patches of lush greenery, the canopy providing welcome shade on their approach to Apes Den.

"You know," Ethan said as they rounded a corner, "they really should call it Monkeys Den, not Apes Den."

Spencer raised an eyebrow. "Taxonomical inaccuracies bothering you?"

"Yes," he said, mimicking their initial encounter in the airport. "Did you know the Barbary macaques are Europe's only wild monkey population?"

"Yes."

"Of course you did. Okay, did you know the males help care for the young in the troop, even if they're not the father?"

"Yes."

"Okay, did you know legend says that as long as the monkeys remain on the Rock—"

"—Gibraltar will remain British."

Ethan stopped, folded his arms and rested against a stone wall. He frowned, "Right, I see I'm going to have to pull out the big guns. Did you know that macaques used to be under the official care of the military? If a monkey were ill or injured, it wouldn't be taken to the vets, it would be treated at the Royal Naval Hospital and would receive the same surgery or treatment as an enlisted serviceman."

Spencer did not know that. She told him as such.

Ethan adopted a satisfied expression, put his sunglasses on and said, "And on that note, let's go find the furry little buggers."

It didn't take long before they reached the main viewing area, where several macaques lounged on rocks and railings, sunbathing and eyeing visitors with calculated interest. A tour guide was handing out small crackers to his clients to feed to the monkeys. Ethan offered him two quid and came back with a handful.

"Palm flat, don't curl your fingers," he said, demonstrating. A medium-sized female approached cautiously, snatched the offered treat, and retreated to enjoy her prize.

Spencer mimicked his technique; a young monkey took the food directly from her hand. It was cute and gentle, its brownish-pink face full of curiosity.

"So sweet," she said, sighing. It felt like a long, long time since she'd seen them up close or watched them play. She missed them.

"Don't let them lure you into a false sense of security. They're clever crooks when they want to be."

As if summoned by his warning, a large male macaque leapt from a nearby tree branch and reached into Spencer's pocket, making a grab for her phone. Panic flashed through her. The phone was her connection to Six. If the monkey succeeded, the security breach would be catastrophic.

She flinched and grabbed the device back quickly. The monkey, shocked and annoyed by her sudden movements, bared its enormous teeth and lashed out with sharp claws.

Ethan was suddenly between her and the macaque. He raised his arms, making himself appear larger while producing a low, firm "NO!" Not aggressive, but authoritative. The monkey paused, then retreated several steps.

"Easy now," Ethan murmured, maintaining his inflated posture. The standoff lasted several seconds before the macaque lost interest, scampering away toward a family offering treats.

Spencer exhaled slowly. "Always the rescuer."

He shrugged. "You're like a magnet for trouble. Come on, there's something you should see."

He took her hand and led her to a clearing at the edge of the slope. From this vantage point, the sea stretched in a breathtaking panorama. The Mediterranean shimmered beneath the afternoon light, its waters a restless mosaic of sapphire and diamond. The mountains of North Africa rose high while ships floated in the Strait, appearing small and slow against the vast expanse of sea and sky.

"Worth the climb?" Ethan asked quietly.

Spencer turned to him, the agent in her eclipsed by the woman. "Absolutely."

Something shifted between them as they shared the beauty of the view. Spencer felt the warmth of his hand still in hers, the light breeze lifting strands of her blonde wig, the subtle scent of his skin.

Ethan turned to fully face her, his free hand gently brushing her cheek. The touch was questioning, leaving space for retreat. Spencer didn't retreat. She leaned forward, closing the distance, inviting him to do the same. Their lips met tentatively at first, then with growing certainty. The kiss deepened, Spencer's hand finding the nape of his neck, Ethan's arm encircling her waist.

For a moment, there was no mission, no Zhou, no Six. Just this connection under the dazzling Gibraltar sun.

When they finally broke apart, Spencer kept her eyes closed for an extra beat, memorising the sensation before reality rushed back in.

CHAPTER 31

S houlders stiff from three hours of strategic planning, Buddy Thompson emerged from the conference room at 6:17 p.m. The meeting had run long, but they had hammered out every detail: a three-day operation with precise objectives, contingency protocols, and, of course, the obligatory networking. He rolled his neck, feeling his vertebrae pop one by one.

"All set, sir?" The assistant appeared at his elbow with a fresh coffee, which Buddy no longer required.

"As we'll ever be." Buddy accepted the cup anyway. He took a tentative sip to gauge the temperature, then drained half of it in a single swallow. "Forward the final package to our friends at Number 10, send a polite but firm reminder to the delegation about the revised schedule, and call Digger back. Tell him, I told you to tell him he's a complete wazzock."

"Already done... apart from the call to Mr Reed. I've arranged your transportation. The car will be waiting at 0500 tomorrow."

Buddy nodded approvingly. The kid was efficient; he'd give him that. "Any word from Spencer Bly?"

"Still nothing. I can put a trace on her if you think it's necessary."

"No." Buddy frowned. "Not necessary. I'm sure she's busy."

***

By the time they returned to Ethan's apartment in Upper Town, the afternoon light was fading, washing the narrow streets in amber as Spencer followed him up the worn stone steps to his door. Neither spoke much on the journey back; the kiss at the viewpoint had created an electricity that made small talk impossible.

Ethan fumbled with his keys as he unlocked the front door. Inside the apartment, he opened the shutters to catch the evening breeze. He turned to say something, perhaps to offer a drink or give her an easy exit, but Spencer moved closer, pulling him to her. Their second kiss was nothing like the tentative one they shared overlooking the bay: this was heat and urgency.

His hands found her waist, thumbs tracing the curve of her hips through the thin fabric. Spencer reached up, fingers tangling in his hair, holding him close. When they broke apart, breathless, Ethan's eyes searched hers, questioning.

"Are you sure?" he asked, voice rough with restraint.

Spencer hesitated, just a beat, then gave a crooked smile. "Full disclosure," she said. "It's... *that* time."

Ethan blinked, then huffed a quiet laugh, kissing her neck. "You think a little biology scares me?"

She gave a breathless laugh of her own, relieved.

"So, I'll ask again... Are you sure?"

Spencer's answer was to reach up and remove the blonde wig she'd worn all day in case any of Zhou's men had seen her. Her natural hair fell loose, cascading down her back. A dark, wild waterfall.

"I'm sure," she whispered against his mouth.

***

Back in his office, Buddy tidied his desk, locking sensitive documents in the wall safe and signing out of his computer and tablet. Force of habit made him check that the Padstow file was securely locked in his bottom drawer. He opened the middle drawer and retrieved a bottle of Jameson in a gift bag. Eighteen years old and matured in ex-bourbon and Oloroso sherry casks, it had cost him over three hundred quid.

Digger would joke about liking his whiskey the way he likes his women: between eighteen and twenty-five, and completely out of his price range.

Buddy vowed to come up with a witty retort by the time they met up. He grinned. Working with Digger again would be the silver lining in this swiftly worsening situation. The old git had taken him under his wing back in Baghdad, and his tactical instincts remained unparalleled.

His phone buzzed. It was Sarah sending a pointed reminder about dinner at eight. *Don't be late.*

Buddy sighed, pocketing his phone without responding. Over the years, these work trip eve family dinners had become an excruciating ritual. Sarah would insist on them, claiming they were necessary "just in case," then radiating resentment the entire evening. He knew why—being left alone to handle the kids, the house, and every school emergency while he vanished into classified assignments without explanation. He could handle that guilt. But it was the other thing, the unspoken thing, that grated. She was convinced – *absolutely convinced* – that one day he'd exchange her for some bright-eyed intern or a sultry foreign asset seeking a British passport. He'd never given her a genuine reason to think it, none that she was aware of anyway. No scandals in the Daily Mail to be muttered about at the school gates. In the meantime, he'd clumsily praise her cooking, which he knew had been dropped off by a high-end catering company, and his children would provide monosyllabic replies when directly addressed. Otherwise, they'd be far too busy texting their friends under the table.

Fun times.

He gathered his coat, pausing to glance one last time at Theo Monroe's final message: an email to himself. Whatever technological warfare lay ahead, the transaction was already complete. They weren't trying to halt a sale; they were hunting a weapon already deployed. At least he could tell the Prime Minister that much tomorrow. Small comfort, but it showed progress.

Buddy locked his office and navigated the building's intricate security protocols, stepping out into a dim, gunmetal grey evening. London's traffic rumbled loudly across Vauxhall Bridge. Years had passed since the last major terror event had taken place in London. The city had moved on. People were getting on with their daily lives, scrimping and saving, grumbling about the Tube and ULEZ, unaware of the classified work transpiring each day behind the sand-coloured walls of the place they referred to as Legoland.

Buddy hailed a black cab, giving his Richmond address. As the taxi pulled away, he tried Spencer's number one last time. It rang out.

"Everything alright, mate?" the cabbie asked, eyeing him in the rearview mirror.

"Fine," Buddy replied automatically. "Just running late for dinner."

The taxi merged into traffic, carrying him toward the family obligation he dreaded.

***

They moved to the bedroom in stages, pausing against walls, exploring with hands and lips, shedding clothing piece by piece. By the time they reached his bed, Spencer had abandoned caution along with her disguise.

She straddled him, Ethan's hands gripping her hips, guiding, anchoring. She found the right angle, a slow, deliberate pull that brought him deeper, their movements syncing into a rhythm that built steadily, intensely. A sharp inhale, a half-caught moan. She pressed her hand into his chest, her short nails marking his muscles with half-moon imprints. Then he pulled her down, chest to chest, his breath warm against her throat. Short stubble grazed her skin as he whispered her name, a small intimacy that pushed her over the edge.

Afterwards, they lay in a tangle of limbs, sheets damp with heat and exertion. The night air sifted through the shutters, cooling their skin. Spencer rested her cheek against Ethan's chest, listening to his heartbeat slow from racing to steady. His fingers traced lethargic patterns along her spine, following the curve of each vertebra.

"You're thinking," he murmured, pressing his lips to her forehead.

"Occupational hazard."

"Looking for exit routes?"

"Not exactly," she said, reluctantly disentangling herself from his embrace. "But, I should go. I'm sorry." She sat up, letting the sheets fall away.

Ethan propped himself on one elbow, the moonlight painting his body in silver and shadow.

"Stay," he said simply, reaching for her hand.

Spencer paused, clothes in hand, ready to dress. "Maybe next time," she replied, squeezing his fingers before releasing them.

His eyes brightened, lips curving up into a roguish grin. "There's going to be a next time?"

No good could come of this. She knew that much. She'd be leaving Gibraltar in a day or two. And then what? They couldn't build anything real, not with the truth locked behind the Official Secrets Act. She wasn't about to invite him to move to the UK after just one night, nor was she foolish enough to remain here where paranoia still lingered in her teenage memories.

She liked Ethan. She would miss him. But she was a solitary creature. Always had been. Like a snowy owl watching from a distance. Like a tiger shark, forever moving, never lingering too long in one place.

Spencer leaned down to kiss him goodbye, intending to keep it brief. But the moment stretched, deepened, until she was back in bed, the cool sheets against her spine, Ethan above her, drawing her to him.

When she woke the next morning to sunlight and fresh orange juice, Spencer discovered she had seven missed calls from Buddy Thompson.

CHAPTER 32

The sliding door opened with a gentle swoosh. Spencer stepped out onto the balcony at Queensway while the kettle boiled and the bread toasted. The water in the marina was still and clear; she could see grey mullet feeding off algae-covered hulls, their scales flashing silver as they moved. A small egret perched on a yacht's mooring line. White and slender, with a long neck and stick-like legs, it watched the water intently, waiting for something small and delectable to swim by.

Zhou was on White Dove's upper deck, finishing breakfast. He wore a crimson housecoat and large sunglasses. Mengze, in his dark suit, lurked nearby, ready to fetch whatever his boss required, be it beverages, food, narcotics, or women. She remembered climbing on top of Zhou, his hands on her bare skin, praying the drugs would kick in quickly and knock him out cold. When she climbed on top of Ethan, she'd hoped the moment would last forever.

"He's still here," she said as the call to Buddy's mobile connected. "White Dove hasn't moved."

She heard someone ask if he wanted coffee, the distant tinkling sound of liquid hitting porcelain.

He thanked the server before addressing Spencer. "We found something in Theo's correspondence. Two things, actually. The first is an email from an unknown contact. We're working on tracing it. Listen to this."

He read the email about bridging isolated systems, manual overrides and the reference to 2015.

Spencer moved indoors, closing the door behind her. She poured the water from the kettle and buttered her toast. "New tech? A cyber weapon?" she asked. "What happened in 2015?"

"The Paris Terror Attacks and Charlie Hebdo. Volkswagen emissions scandal. Saudis intervening in Yemen. Russia intervening in Syria. UK general election."

Either Buddy was typing, or someone next to him was; she could hear fingers clicking on keys.

"Gets better," Buddy continued. "Or worse, depending on your perspective. Theo sent himself an email before he disappeared. Six dismissed it at first. They figured he'd sent it to himself by mistake, just an email showing off to a mate about his cushy gig on the yacht."

"But you're not so sure?"

The typing noise stopped, replaced by the sound of shuffling papers. "I think he feared Zhou was onto him. I think he'd hoped we'd find the message."

Spencer stirred milk into her tea. "Right. Let's see it then."

Her phone pinged.

Really enjoying this gig, mate. Opulent doesn't quite cover it. Beautiful views, champagne, caviar, the works. Easily the best yacht I've ever seen; White Dove is stunning. Relaxing, for the most part, though the ladies tire me out LOL.

Tried the chef's sea bass last night—unbelievable. Superb. Michelin quality! Impressive knife skills. Li's taking me scuba diving soon, hopefully we catch something. Lobster would be nice. Everyone's hoping we nab a tuna but think we need fishing rods for that rather than spear guns. Robaliza (European Sea Bass) is a better bet.

Very smooth sailing, barely a ripple at the moment. All I can see, for as far as I can see, is blue water and spectacular coastlines. Lately, though, the captain's been frowning at the weather forecast. A few weather fronts moving through soon. Swell's going to pick up, might be in for a rough ride. Expecting a bit of a storm on the horizon!

Kicking back until then though.

Theo

Spencer sat at the dining table and read the email once more. "...*Might be in for a rough ride. Expecting a bit of a storm on the horizon.* Certainly sounds like he knew something was up." She read it a third time, noting the short, often clipped sentences, and paused at the lowercase *c* in Champagne. Why use *robaliza* when sea bass would suffice?

She laughed when she saw it. "Clever Theo."

"What?" Buddy asked. "What did I miss?"

"First letter of every sentence. Predictable. Basic. Worked, though."

"Spencer."

"It spells out a name: Roberts Miller Valasek."

"Should I know that name?"

The background noise on Buddy's end of the phone increased. A tinny announcement and a rumbly sound as if a train was pulling into a station. She typed the name into Six's database. Nothing. "I don't think it's one person. I think it's three surnames."

She began with Valasek, the least common of the names. "According to Wikipedia, there are four notable Valaseks: a diplomat, a deceased physicist, a deceased footballer, and a computer security researcher." She clicked on the computer security researcher and nodded. "Right, here's your 2015 reference... Chris Valasek and Charlie Miller. They took remote control of a Jeep Cherokee via its Uconnect entertainment system. They demonstrated that they could control the air conditioning, turn on the radio, activate the windscreen wipers, and manipulate the steering, brakes, transmission, you name it."

Buddy was quiet, then let out a "Whoa."

"Fiat Chrysler ended up recalling 1.4 million vehicles to address the vulnerability. Maybe this is what the email meant about systems being isolated for a reason. It's possible that whatever Zhou has sold enables someone to reverse the efforts made since 2015 to prevent incidents like this from occurring."

"Jeep wasn't the only one," Buddy said, tapping away on his end of the call. "I might lose you in a minute. If I do, I'll call you back. Still there?"

She sipped her tea. "Yeah."

"2016. Keen Security Lab took control of a Tesla. But those hacks required individual access to specific vehicles. What if— I mean, for eighty-two million, they'd want to hack every car in a country. But for what end?"

Movement on the yacht caught her eye. Zhou was heading below deck, flanked by Li and James. "I'd imagine environmental reasons, but eco-terrorists don't have that sort of money. And there's no way someone could take control of that many cars; older models wouldn't respond."

"They wouldn't need to. Turn off enough cars at rush hour, and entire cities would grind to a halt. No one could get to or from work, or to or from school. Hospitals understaffed. Power plants all left unmanned... Spencer?"

But Spencer was preoccupied, her gut telling her she had missed a key piece of Theo's message. *A storm on the horizon.* Her fingers raced over her keyboard, frantically Googling and clicking on links. They had looked into Miller and Valasek, becoming wrapped up in the idea of hacking cars and trucks, but they had neglected Roberts. His name was the first one hidden in the email for a reason.

The line crackled with sudden static. Spencer checked her signal; it was still strong.

"Buddy?"

His voice came back, clearer now. "I'm here."

"I know who Roberts is," she said. "I know what storm is coming."

CHAPTER 33

"Surely, it's not possible," Spencer told herself, skimming news articles from ten years ago.

Static crackled down the line before Buddy pressed her for information, his voice tense. "Explain."

"Chris Roberts was another cybersecurity researcher, and like Miller and Valasek, he looked to demonstrate the vulnerabilities in vehicle entertainment and Wi-Fi systems. But where Miller and Valasek hacked a car, Roberts reportedly hacked... He hacked a plane, Buddy."

Buddy swore. "What?"

"Multiple times, apparently."

"But how?"

Spencer's eyes flickered to the north-facing balcony. An EasyJet plane was descending towards the airport. She shuddered involuntarily as orange streaked the sky.

"Roberts claimed he connected his laptop to the electronics box installed under his seat using an Ethernet cable. He was then able to access the plane's in-flight entertainment system. Once connected, he claimed he accessed the navigation systems and issued a climb command to one of the engines."

Spencer ran a hand over her face. She felt grimy, in need of a shower. *"Systems isolated for a reason."*

"You keep saying *claimed*," Buddy said. "Roberts *claimed* he connected his laptop. *Claimed* he accessed the navigation systems. Is there any proof?"

"The FBI believed him. Or, at least, they took him seriously enough to pull him off a plane and confiscate his laptop after he tweeted about messing with oxygen masks. It was 2015 as well. He was detained and grilled. Aviation experts and authorities seem highly sceptical of Roberts' claims. I'm reading that critical flight systems and in-flight entertainment systems are isolated from each other... There's that word again: isolated. They say it makes it highly unlikely someone could cross from the entertainment system to flight controls."

Buddy sounded like he was drinking his coffee. He paused before speaking. *"Highly unlikely* and *impossible* are worlds apart. I don't like this."

"Me neither."

Spencer looked out the window, past White Dove bobbing gently in the marina, past the people going about their days, enjoying a leisurely breakfast at The Lounge, Moniques or Rendezvous. She watched the EasyJet flight disappear behind rows of high rises and thought of the people she'd shared a plane with on the way here: the arguing couple who'd turned amorous by the time the flight landed, the struggling mother, her two children, her sleeping husband, even her flight neighbour, the leg spreader.

She exhaled sharply, turning from the window. "They're not interested in traffic jams, Buddy. Zhou's eighty-two-million-dollar payday wasn't for bringing a city to a standstill. He's sold a way to take remote control of aircraft, Buddy. Planes, drones, military transport, whatever. If what Theo uncovered is right, someone is about to buy themselves the ability to turn any commercial airliner into a goddamn missile."

Spencer put her phone on speaker so she could use both hands to steady herself on the kitchen counter. She watched the caterpillars munch through their pine needles, oblivious to her human worries. "We're talking 9/11 without anyone on board. No suicide bombers. No hostages. No risk of passenger heroics."

"Not possible," Buddy whispered. There was background chatter, someone discussing transport arrangements. "Like the email said, the systems are isolated. They'd need to physically bridge the systems. Even if they found a way to do that – built a device to do that – they'd need to compromise the pilots. If someone wanted to control the plane remotely, take over the autopilot, for instance, they'd need to prevent the actual pilots from disabling the autopilot system. As soon as they knew something was up, the pilots would take manual control."

Spencer swallowed hard and held a hand to her chest. "What if they already have?"

She looked north. No plume of smoke, no sirens. The EasyJet flight would have landed by now, and the landing gear deployed without issue. Safe. Controlled. As it should be. And yet, her skin prickled. The storm wasn't coming. It was already here, swirling in the skies over every major city.

***

He was always Richard at work. Never Rick or Ricky. Certainly not Dick. Still, today, Captain Richard Harmon had a different title. He flexed his fingers, felt the beginnings of arthritis crack in his knuckles, then ran his fingertips over the spotless control panel. Three decades of flying had created a certain pre-flight routine. Whether it was muscle memory or simple OCD and superstition, Richard didn't know, but he cracked those knuckles nonetheless.

He'd flown this route countless times, flown this particular Airbus A330 at least fifty times. Still, this flight was different. He wasn't Captain or Richard today. He was Dad. Today, First Officer Daniel Harmon – his son – was sitting next to him. Co-pilot.

"Copy that," Daniel said into the radio before turning to Richard. "ATC's cleared us. We're good to go." He flicked a switch. "Starting engine one." Then another. "Starting engine two. Fuel flow – normal. Setting flaps for take off."

The boy who had once sat on his lap in the simulator was now a fully qualified first officer on one of the most sophisticated aircraft in service. Daniel was Richard's carbon copy, only younger, healthier, and smarter. His chest swelled with pride as he watched his flesh and blood – his legacy – go through the pre-flight routine. He wanted to prompt him and tell him the next step, help the younger man out. It was all pointless, of course. Daniel knew exactly what he was doing. He wouldn't be here otherwise.

"Taxi lights on," Daniel said, flicking one of the numerous switches before him. "Releasing parking brake."

"Copy," Richard replied, fighting to keep his voice neutral. At thirty-two, Daniel had risen through the ranks faster than Richard had, and his natural aptitude for flying was evident from his first lesson at sixteen. He could still remember taking him to the airfield like other dads remembered taking their sons to their first football games. His own father had never seen him fly. Heart attack at fifty-four, gone before Richard had earned his captain's stripes. But here he was, flying with his son, the Harmon legacy continuing.

They moved through the checklist with the synchronised rhythm that only comes from years of training. Richard couldn't help but break protocol, reach over and cup Daniel's shoulder. "Love you, son."

Daniel sucked his lips in, looked like he was going to tell his old man to stop being so soft, but he broke into a wide smile, clapped his hand over Richard's and said, "Back at you, Dad." He glanced at the controls, followed with, "Thrust set."

Back to business. Richard's hand slipped back to the controls. No more father and son. Now, just *Pilot Flying* and *Pilot Monitoring*.

The engines roared as the Airbus accelerated down the runway.

"Eighty knots," Daniel said.

Richard felt the subtle shift in pressure as the heavy bird gained momentum, the wind whipping past the cockpit windows.

Daniel's focused voice came again. "V1."

Decision made. No going back.

"Positive rate. Gear up."

Daniel responded, "Gear up."

Richard pulled back gently on the stick. The nose lifted, and the ground fell away beneath them.

There was a familiar thunk-thunk as the landing gear retracted into the belly of the plane. Richard kept the climb smooth, hands steady. A few seconds later, the indicator lights flickered off.

At 400 feet, Richard gave the next command. "Autopilot one, on."

Daniel tapped the panel. The aircraft responded, holding its perfect climb angle.

At 1,500 feet, Richard adjusted the thrust levers. The engines eased slightly. He sat back, smiling at his son.

CHAPTER 34

He stood outside the maintenance hangar as the roar of jet engines faded to a distant purr. Tortured by the pain deep in his gut, Robin Grimm watched the Airbus climb higher, disappearing into the clouds. *Too late. Way too fucking late.*

Whatever Cara had done to the plane, it was done now. He'd helped her gain access; he'd watched the door while she worked. He wiped clammy hands on his trousers, leaving damp streaks across the fabric. They were shaking badly, and although he heard no explosion, saw no fireball, he felt an all-consuming sense of foreboding. He drew in a deep breath, feeling the air rattle in his throat, and stepped back into the hangar. Dim lighting buzzed overhead, flickering occasionally. His footsteps echoed as he moved between hulking steel skeletons of aircraft in various states of repair, like exhibits in an aeronautics museum.

It was quiet at this end of the base. Robin was alone, just him, his thoughts, and the tightness crushing his chest. He could hear Cara's voice in his head, telling him to relax, that it wasn't a bomb. He heard her threatening his daughter.

"You won't even be able to identify the body, sweetheart."

But the moment the plane's wheels left the tarmac, reality struck. In saving Holly, he had signed his own death warrant, along with that of everyone else on board. They'd never let him live.

Robin felt thoroughly helpless. He sank to the floor, back resting against a Dunlop tyre, his forehead on his knees. If he raised the alarm, Cara's bosses would have him killed, and Holly would be tortured, trafficked, sold, raped, and killed. If by some miracle they found the device and prevented whatever fate awaited them, they'd trace it back to him and his cowardice. These people didn't leave loose ends, and neither did his bosses. It would be jail: solitary, if he were lucky, shanked in the dinner queue if not. But if everything went according to Cara's plan, the end result would be the same, only with the crushing guilt of his involvement in all those innocent people's deaths. Robin squeezed his eyes shut. He was trapped in his own grave, waiting for someone to come and start shovelling dirt on top of him.

He opened his eyes. His hands had stopped shaking. He pushed himself to his feet. Beyond a Typhoon FGR4, a workbench stretched across the far side of the hangar, cluttered with storage boxes, rolls of electrical cable, and heavy-duty tool bags. He walked towards it, passing by spools of thin wire and neatly coiled hydraulic lines, searching for something more substantial. Kevlar-reinforced cable had the best strength-to-weight ratio of what the engineers had available to them. He measured out two and a half metres and severed it from the rest of the roll with a cable cutter. There was a metallic ping as the tool snipped through the fibres.

Robin wheeled a scaffold platform from the centre of the hangar to one of the longer walls, where the ceiling was at its lowest. It was a single-width alloy tower with three platforms. One wheel squeaked while another was stiff, struggling against the rough concrete floor. He secured the castors one by one, then positioned the stabilisers. There were four of them, Y-shaped tubular legs extending from partway up the tower to the floor, helping to balance the structure. Robin ascended the ladder built into the tower and pulled himself through the trapdoor to reach the first deck. He repeated this to access the second deck and then the third. His feet were over five and a half metres high; his head was seven metres and thirty centimetres from the ground.

Steel beams crisscrossed the hangar. From this position, he could access the lowest point. He looped the cable over the beam and tied it to itself, forming a double knot, then a triple. The material resisted initially; the new, reinforced fibres were stiff, but after a few sharp tugs, the knot seized tight. He wrapped the free end around his neck and repeated the process. One knot. Two. Three.

Robin pressed his boots against the wooden toerail of the trapdoor deck. He pushed the cable along the beam as far as he could reach. He didn't want his feet to find the scaffold again once his primal instincts kicked in and his body fought against his mind. He closed his eyes and thought of his family: the wife he had cheated on, the children he'd endangered. They were better off without him, he told himself.

Robin climbed over the guardrail.

***

Spencer paced the length of the safehouse balcony, phone pressed to her ear. Gibraltar was fully awake now, and the noise of motorbikes, scooters, buses, and cars braking and accelerating along Queensway Road and up Ragged Staff could be heard from the seaward side of the apartment block. People went about their daily lives, heading to school and work. A monarch butterfly fluttered by. It danced before Spencer for a moment before heading towards the memorial garden at the other end of the block. She barely noticed it.

"There must be over a hundred thousand commercial flights every day, Buddy," she said. "That's not counting military, private jets, cargo... If they're planning to target a flight, we need to narrow it down."

"If they've had this tech for a while now and haven't used it—"

"It means they're waiting for the right flight." The strain was evident in Buddy's voice. "The question is which one? We have the intel about the hack, but nothing specific about the target."

Spencer stopped at the edge of the balcony, looking north toward Spain. "Think about it. The Russians paid eighty million for this software. They're not going to waste it on some random commuter flight from Manchester to Málaga."

"We don't know for sure it's the Russians," Buddy countered. "Could be whoever they're funding. The next Al Qaeda."

"Same difference." Spencer's tone hardened. "It was bought for a reason. Whether they do it themselves or train someone else to do their dirty work, the end result is the same. They'll want a high-value target."

She turned away from the view, rested her back against the rail, tapped her bare foot against terracotta-coloured tiles. "They want to make a statement. Something symbolic. Twenty-five years ago, I'd say Concorde without hesitation. The prestige, the symbolism of Western technological superiority..."

"But Concorde's been grounded since 2003."

"I know that," she snapped. "That's why I said twenty-five years ago. Sorry. What I mean is, they'll want something equally significant. A target that shocks the world. Do you think Theo knew?"

"Theo would only know if Zhou knew. Is that a possibility?"

The line went quiet for a moment. Spencer sighed; her mouth felt dry. She moved to the kitchen and filled a glass with water from the tap. "It's possible. I can plant more bugs. Keep listening. But – I don't know – you don't buy a gun and then tell the seller who you're planning to kill."

"Air Force One?" Buddy suggested.

Spencer downed her drink and set the glass back on the counter with a thud. "The security they'd need to breach would be... If these guys can find a way to install it and physically bridge the networks, then they're also capable of finding a way to compromise the pilots. But Buddy, that would be more than sending a message; that would be World War Three."

CHAPTER 35

Cruising at 36,000 feet, the Airbus's autopilot maintained course with minimal deviation. In the cockpit, the sound of the twin Rolls-Royce engines hummed at a consistent seventy-eight decibels, just loud enough to mask the soft mechanical whir beneath First Officer Daniel Harmon's seat.

At precisely 07:30 BST, the countdown concluded. A miniature pressure sensor embedded in the cushion of Daniel's seat detected a subtle redistribution of weight as he leaned forward to adjust the air conditioning switch on the overhead panel. The device, no larger than a pack of chef's matches, registered this as confirmation that the seat was occupied, triggering a spring-loaded mechanism.

"We're running at optimal fuel consumption," Daniel said, tapping the glass display. "We're actually three per cent under the planned burn rate."

"Good news for the bean counters," Captain Richard Harmon replied, making a note on his electronic flight log.

Beneath Daniel's seat, a titanium needle measuring less than three centimetres long and less than a quarter of a millimetre in diameter thrust upwards at a velocity of thirty-five metres per second. It penetrated the fire-retardant fabric of the seat cushion, pushed through his uniform trousers, and pierced his right thigh through the biceps femoris muscle.

This instantaneously triggered a microscopic pump to inject 1.5 millilitres of colourless fluid into the muscle tissue. The compound, a synthetic tetrodotoxin akin to that found in pufferfish and a thousand times more potent than cyanide, began to circulate through Daniel's body.

The needle retracted at eighteen metres per second, vanishing back into the device's housing. The minuscule puncture site closed almost immediately, leaving only the tiniest speck of blood.

The entire procedure lasted less than half a second.

"Ouch!" Daniel flinched, his hand instinctively reaching beneath his leg.

"What's wrong?" Richard asked, glancing sideways while maintaining his watch.

"Nothing." Daniel shook his head, rubbing his thigh. "Just felt a weird twinge."

Richard frowned, the father in him overtaking the captain. The flight deck was designed for comfort during both short and long-haul flights, but muscle cramps were not uncommon, particularly if dehydration was a contributing factor.

"Stand up and stretch your legs for a minute," Richard suggested, checking the autopilot status. "Nothing on the radar. Perfect time for a quick stretch and a glass of water."

Daniel nodded as he unbuckled his restraint. The toxin was now circulating through his femoral vascular system, with molecules binding to nerve cell membranes and blocking sodium ions. His proprioception, the body's sense of position and movement, was already compromised, though he was not yet aware of it.

He pushed himself upright, stood, and took a step to the right. Daniel's pupils began to dilate, his pulse quickening to nearly double his resting heart rate.

"Dad, I feel—" But the words caught in his throat as his laryngeal muscles began to spasm.

Richard turned, startled by the sudden break in his son's voice and watched in horror as Daniel's knees gave way, sending him crashing against the back of his chair. His body slid downwards, collapsing onto the floor.

"Daniel!" Richard fumbled with his restraint. At the same time, an identical device propelled a needle upwards at the same velocity, delivering the same dose of neurotoxin. Richard didn't register it. Focused on his son, he unbuckled, dropped to his knees beside Daniel and pressed his fingers against his son's neck. The pulse was there, but rapid and weak.

For a moment, he stared at his son's unconscious body on the cockpit floor, his analytical mind evaluating response options even as the first molecules of toxin infiltrated his central nervous system.

Richard reached for the call button to summon the crew to his aid, but his hand froze halfway through the motion as he registered the sharp pain in the back of his right thigh. Older than Daniel, the synthetic toxin took hold of him even faster. His hand moved to his chest, then to his clammy forehead. He tried, fought as hard as he could, but the last thing Richard Harmon saw before his vision blurred to black was the dying face of his son.

The warning lights remained dark. No alarms sounded. The plane continued its programmed flight path, engines steady, airspeed constant, utterly unaware that both pilots were now incapacitated.

On the flight deck door, the reinforced locking mechanism designed after 9/11 to keep intruders out would now serve a different purpose: keeping help away from the dying pilots.

In the cabin, passengers talked shop, networked, read books, drank coffee, or in some cases, dozed peacefully, unaware that the aircraft carrying them was soaring through the stratosphere with no one at the controls.

CHAPTER 36

As Richard and Daniel Harmon's hearts beat their last, Spencer filled and boiled the kettle. "We should warn the aviation authorities. Tell them to be vigilant."

"I will," Buddy assured her. "Once I've discussed what we know with the PM.

"We should warn the Americans. Tell them what we know and what we suspect."

"I will," Buddy repeated.

"When?"

The phone connection crackled softly, the kettle began to hum as the water heated up, and two sailors bickered on the pontoon outside. The extra noise meant Spencer didn't hear Buddy's response clearly the first time.

"What did you just say?"

"I said, I'll discuss our fears with Leon. Then, if he gives me the green light, I'll call Washington as soon as I land."

Land.

Spencer stood still, teabag in hand, hovering it over an empty mug, waiting for the water to boil. "Buddy, where are you?"

"On my way to Marrakesh."

"Tell me it's a family holiday."

But Spencer knew the answer. There was no chance Buddy would be discussing MI6 dealings on a crowded EasyJet flight out of Gatwick.

"I wish. No, it's business rather than pleasure. Digger – you remember Digger – he's selling the Moroccans some kit to secure their southern border. North Star's working a trade deal before we head to Rome for the G7."

The casual drop of operational codenames made Spencer's pulse quicken. North Star. The Prime Minister. And if Buddy was travelling with the PM...

She threw the teabag on the counter. "You're on Vespina?" The question burst out of her, more statement than query.

If the UK had an equivalent of Air Force One, it would be Vespina. Part of the RAF Voyager fleet, Vespina was a modified Airbus A330 MRTT (Multi-Role Tanker Transport) specially configured for ministerial and royal transport. It featured radar warning receivers and missile approach warning systems. It was capable of confusing heat-seeking missiles and had enough range to reach almost any global destination without refuelling.

When Buddy replied, his tone was maddeningly relaxed. "Yeah," he said. "We haven't been in the air long."

She knew that what she was visualising was unlikely, but still, Spencer's insides turned to ice. She gazed at the sky through the balcony window, her eyes searching for aircraft.

The tech had been sold a year ago, she reminded herself, and they'd sat on it until now.

"Buddy..." Her voice trembled.

"Relax. We're alright. We took off from Brize Norton," he said to her. "Do you honestly think someone got into the UK's largest Royal Air Force base and tampered with the wiring? Not a chance."

Spencer remained silent, a feeling churning in her gut that she couldn't articulate. Her eyes were fixed on the horizon, searching – as if she could somehow see through miles of atmosphere to the aircraft transporting Buddy, Digger, the Prime Minister, and who knew how many others.

"Everything's fine," Buddy repeated.

The kettle clicked off. He was probably right. Spencer didn't like *probably*.

***

RAF Vespina could accommodate 160 people across three separate cabins. Journalists and TV crews were housed in the back in economy-style seating. The centre cabin featured comfortable business-class seats for trade delegates and those who weren't important enough to sit in the forward cabin with the VIPs. Up front, the seats were spacious and could fully recline. Each came with a table, light, and a curtain that could be drawn around to provide privacy. The trip to Morocco meant Vespina was not operating at full capacity. The rear two cabins were half full. Up front, though, it was packed.

Buddy Thompson pressed the button to his right, returning his seat from a lazy recline to its upright position. Phone still pressed to his ear, he looked around, taking in the familiar faces of government and security personnel. Digger – real name Graham Reed, the Deputy Director of Strategic Procurement at MoD – was inspecting the bottle of Jameson that Buddy had bought and presented to him upon boarding. As expected, he'd read the label and declared he liked his whiskey the way he liked his women: eighteen to twenty-five. Buddy was pleased with his retort, telling Digger he was the one who needed to be left to mature for a few decades.

Leon Groves was fast asleep in the row behind, fully reclined beneath a blanket. His short and slight frame made it appear, at first glance, as though a child had snuck into the VIP cabin. Only royalty or the Prime Minister's three children were afforded that luxury.

The man himself, Prime Minister Nicholas Selley, was sipping black coffee and was deep in conversation with the Foreign Secretary. Selley was a no-nonsense man from Cumbria. While many politicians boasted of faux working-class roots, Selley's were genuine. Born and raised on a council estate to parents who worked in Workington steelworks, there was no polished Oxbridge accent, no carefully crafted media persona, just the blunt, unvarnished pragmatism of a man who had fought his way to the top without favours or fortune. It was this absence of cronyism and nepotism that helped him secure the top job at a time when the public had grown weary of spin. His critics dared to challenge his education, mocking the fact that he hadn't attended university and making fun of his northern accent.

Big mistake. Selley wiped the floor with them in the House of Commons, pointing out that the more prestigious the education, the less they knew about the real world. He asked the outgoing PM if he knew how much a carton of eggs cost and how much the average family had to spend on childcare or gas bills. He even challenged the outgoing PM to a basic mental arithmetic quiz or spelling test. *Let's see who's really uneducated around here.* He made them look like the detached buffoons they were, and when election time came, it was a landslide.

Spencer was still on the line. Still worried.

She was a brilliant agent – former agent – Buddy reminded himself. As she'd made abundantly clear, she was an independent contractor, and Buddy was not her superior. His fault, really.

Spencer was inventive and tough. Resilient in ways few agents ever were. How she'd survived the Myanmar mishap, he would never know, but each time, she'd bounce back recalibrated, refocused. Still, Spencer had a tendency to race ten steps ahead, often catastrophising. Discovering that Vespina was in the air had immediately sent her mind racing to worst-case scenarios. It had flown at least twenty times since Zhou sold the mystery technology, and each trip had been without incident. As if the most sophisticated government aircraft in the RAF fleet could be randomly hijacked.

CHAPTER 37

"You're fretting over nothing," Buddy said, rolling his shoulders to relieve the morning stiffness in his joints. He glanced out of the window and saw blue skies and verdant fields. "Besides, you seem oddly concerned for my safety, considering you don't even like me."

Spencer's response was immediate. "There's a difference between wanting you to step barefoot on Lego bricks every morning for the rest of your life and hoping you die in a terror attack."

Buddy winced. The line fell silent, and Buddy found his thoughts drifting. Their history was complicated: a brief, intense connection years ago that had burned bright and fast. He had never felt for Sarah quite the same way he had for Spencer. But he loved his children more than either woman, so when push came to shove, he had chosen soul-destroying stability in suburbia. He chose not to disrupt his family's lives.

"Look," he said, trying to put her mind at ease, and his own, if he were honest. "Like we discussed, even if Russia wanted to remotely hijack a plane, and even if they managed to hack into the system via the plane's IP address like Miller and Valasek did with the Jeeps, they would still need to, first, physically bridge the systems to access the navigation controls, and second, somehow prevent the pilots from taking back manual control."

Buddy glanced around the cabin. Digger, sitting nearby, suddenly looked more attentive, eavesdropping on the technical discussion.

"Manual override is standard on modern aircraft," Buddy continued, keeping his voice low.

Digger lowered the whiskey bottle back into the gift bag, his eyebrow raised in quiet inquiry.

Buddy removed the phone from his ear and pressed it against his chest. "Former agent," he explained. "That thing I phoned you about."

He put the phone back to his ear and stood up, pressing his other hand against his lower back. "Still there?"

"Where else would I be?"

"Tell you what, I'll check on the pilots right now," he told her. "Would that help?"

"Tremendously. Tell them to disconnect the autopilot while you're at it."

He wasn't going to go that far, but he approached the cockpit door, ready to knock, when a cabin crew member intercepted him. "Sir, you can't—"

The man, though dressed impeccably, looked like a heavyweight boxer: wonky nose, shoulders wider than most doors and hands like frying pans. He was likely military and hired for more than offering coffee and helping with the overhead lockers.

"Just want a quick word," Buddy started, but the man firmly redirected him away from the door.

"Back to your seat, sir." It was an order, not a request. No question. No *please*.

Four rows away, Digger was waving at him to say, "What *are* you doing?"

"Tell you what," Buddy said while being ushered back one row at a time. "Would you mind popping in and—"

"We don't pop in. The door only opens from the inside."

"Right. Well, can you please call the pilot? You've heard how Russia sometimes jams GPS signals near their border, causing flights to divert? You must have; you work here. Well, we received intelligence about a new technology that can mess with navigation systems and autopilots. Can you give them a quick call and check everything is operating as it should?"

The crew member hesitated.

"Humour me," Buddy asked.

He nodded professionally. "Of course, sir." He then clamped his frying pan-sized hand down on Buddy's shoulder, unceremoniously dumping him back in his padded, fully reclining seat.

Buddy rubbed his shoulder, speaking again into the phone. "Happy now?"

"Ecstatic."

Digger watched him, the whiskey forgotten, a look of growing concern crossing his face.

***

Spencer stepped out of her apartment onto Queensway Quay, feeling the warmth of the sun on her shoulders and legs. Her phone was pressed to her ear as she made her way to the end of the block closest to the bay.

"Just let me know when you have proof of life," she said, ensuring that no one was close enough to hear her. The nearest person she could see was the security guard at the gate to The Island, and he was easily out of earshot. "Proof of life, and I'll stop pestering you."

She knew she seemed paranoid, but in her experience, paranoia kept people alive.

"The steward's checking now," Buddy replied, his voice tinny.

Resting her hands on a black railing, Spencer gazed out across the Bay of Gibraltar. Unusually, there was not a breath of wind, and the water lay before her like polished glass, unnaturally calm and devoid of whitecaps.

Spencer turned northward, facing Spain, her focus softening as if she could look straight through the towering date palms and millionaire mansions. She mentally traced Vespina's flight path from the UK to Morocco. A gentle arc across the Iberian Peninsula, passing somewhere in this vicinity – Cadiz, Seville perhaps – before banking southwest towards Marrakesh.

Pivoting slowly, she gazed south across the Strait towards Africa, which emerged from the azure waters. The distinctive peak of Jebel Musa – the Mountain of Moses – dominated the Moroccan coastline.

She turned her back to the sea, facing the imposing limestone monolith of the Rock. Two cable cars passed each other, one carrying tourists up to the summit and the other bringing them back to sea level. A steady stream of white taxis and tour buses wound their way up the narrow roads leading to the nature reserve. Only yesterday, she'd been there herself, holding Ethan's hand and exploring the tunnels.

The Rock of Gibraltar lay to the north of the Strait, and Jebel Musa to the south: the Pillars of Hercules. In ancient times, they marked the edge of the known world. The Greeks believed Heracles himself had split a mountain in two, creating the gateway between the Mediterranean and the vast, uncharted Atlantic.

"Anything yet?" she asked Buddy.

"Patience."

Her gaze drifted down to the marina, settling on the sleek, polished hull of White Dove, moored so that its stern faced directly towards the Rock, providing those on board with a perfect view.

Something clicked in Spencer's mind. A connection she should have made days ago.

"*Hēiyán*," she whispered, suddenly paralysed.

"What?" Buddy asked.

"*Hēiyán*," she repeated. The word that brought such laughter when Mengze uttered it. "I thought it meant black stone or dark stone."

"Doesn't it?"

"No," Spencer said, feeling suddenly nauseous. "It means dark rock. As in *the* Rock. Gibraltar."

Spencer's mind raced, pieces falling into place with terrifying clarity. "Zhou isn't hanging around Gibraltar because he likes cheap whiskey and cable car rides, Buddy. He's here to witness history. To see his technology in action."

Her eyes locked onto White Dove, looking pristine in the sunlight. She raised her gaze to the flawless cerulean sky above, a perfect cloudless blue as far as the eye could see. Just like Manhattan, September 2001.

"Spencer?" Buddy's voice had lost its casual edge.

"Vespina's the target, Buddy. The Prime Minister. All of you. And Zhou is here to watch it happen." She staggered, hand over her mouth, struggling to hold back bile as she stood on the quay. "But why? Why Gibraltar? Why the Voyager fleet? Why RAF Vespina?"

She was talking to herself, speaking quickly without pause, not registering Buddy's responses. "You're en route to the G7, right? It used to be the G8 until Russia was expelled. They're pissed at not being in the G8, pissed at us for arming Ukraine for so long. The Rock is a symbol of British colonialism, and striking Gibraltar would be an attack on British soil..."

Spencer's hands trembled as she gripped the railing for stability. Gibraltar had been a point of contention for centuries. To the UK, it's a vital strategic base, a last vestige of an empire that once ruled the seas. But to Spain, it's a stolen piece of land that should have been theirs all along. A strike here wouldn't just be an attack on British soil. It would rip open an old wound, reigniting territorial disputes and stirring nationalist fury on both sides.

Flying the British Prime Minister's plane, with the British Prime Minister on board, into a symbol of Britain would be more than a terror attack – it would be a declaration of war. And an attack on one NATO state is an attack on them all. The UK wouldn't stand alone. Canada, France, Germany—they'd all be drawn in. And Spain? Spain, a NATO member, might be caught in the crossfire of its own grievances. Would the price of supporting the UK be the return of Gibraltar?

"Spencer?"

Despite the fierce Mediterranean sun, she could feel a slow, icy horror creeping over her entire body. War was coming.

Her breath came fast and shallow. Christ, *Hēiyán*, why hadn't she seen it sooner?

"Spencer?" Buddy's voice was sharp now. Urgent. "The steward just hung up the cockpit phone." A beat. "The pilots didn't answer."

The world seemed to lurch beneath her feet.

Spencer doubled over, bile surging up her throat. She vomited over the harbour wall, watched it splash into the marina water below. She wiped her mouth and forced herself upright.

"Buddy, you need to get in the cockpit. Now."

CHAPTER 38

Buddy launched out of his seat, adrenaline flooding his veins. He tugged at his tie, the aircraft cabin feeling claustrophobic and airless.

"Thompson!" Digger caught up to him halfway down the aisle, clamping a hand around his elbow in a vice-like grip. "What the hell are you doing?"

"I need to talk to the pilots," Buddy said, ripping free of Digger's grasp, ignoring the warning in his old friend's expression.

"Talk to me. What's going on?" Digger stared him down, deep creases radiating from the corners of his narrowed eyes.

"They're not responding," Buddy said, looking through Digger.

Ahead of them, the guard stood at full height in front of the cockpit door, arms folded, feet planted wide. He looked like a human riot shield. His brow seemed lower than before, his shoulders higher. His gaze fixed on Buddy – cool, unreadable – but there was a new tension in his stance. Defensive now.

"Sir, I'm sure everything is fine. Perhaps they're busy with—"

"They need to answer that intercom right now," Buddy interrupted, pushing past him.

He reached for the wall-mounted unit beside the cockpit door and stabbed at the call button. "Flight deck, this is Buddy Thompson, MI6. Respond, please."

Nothing. Not even static.

He pressed it again, harder. "Captain, do you copy? Acknowledge."

Still nothing. This couldn't be happening.

Buddy raised his fist, began hammering on the reinforced door. "Captain! MI6! Open the door immediately!"

The impact of his knuckles against the bulletproof panel echoed through the forward cabin, drawing alarmed looks from ministers and cabinet members.

"Sir!" The steward grabbed his arm. "That's quite enough! You will be restrained if you do not return to your seat."

Digger moved to his side. "Buddy, mate, let's take a step back and—"

"The pilots are dead," Buddy hissed, just loudly enough for Digger to hear. He didn't want to believe it himself. Like Spencer, he'd calm down if the pilots answered. But they hadn't. So he didn't. "They're bloody dead, and this plane is being controlled remotely."

Digger's ruddy face drained of colour. "That's impossible."

"Not anymore."

Buddy pounded on the door again, harder, bone meeting steel. His knuckles split open, thin lines of blood streaking down his wrist, circles of red dappling the metal. He slammed his phone against it, a dull *thud* barely registering over the rising murmur behind him.

A ripple of movement: passengers twisting in their seats, mumbling to one another, some half-rising. The Prime Minister's wife unbuckled her seatbelt.

"Sir!" The steward wrapped his arms around him from behind, trying to grapple Buddy backwards.

Buddy drove an elbow back into the man's solar plexus. The steward staggered, coughing, but barely lost his grip. He was trained. Strong.

A deep voice cut through the chaos. "Thompson!"

Buddy's head snapped around.

Leon Groves was on his feet, flanked by North Star, the Prime Minister. They blocked the aisle, one face furious, the other concerned.

A half-second later, Buddy was slammed against the carpet. His head cracked off the floor, stars bursting in his vision. A knee crushed into his spine, pinning him down. He gasped, twisting, but the weight on his back was immovable. His wrist was locked in an unnatural bend, pain flaring up his arm.

His phone flew from his grip, skidding across the carpet. It hit a seat leg, bounced once, then vanished into the shadows beneath a row of reclined chairs.

A faint voice, tinny and distorted, seeped through the noise.

"Buddy? Buddy! What's happening?"

Spencer.

Buddy turned his head just enough to see Nicholas Selley's face. The Prime Minister looked down at him, security looming on either side.

Buddy fought for air. Fought for control.

"Prime Minister," he choked out. "I need to talk to you."

***

Spencer pulled the phone from her ear, staring at the screen in disbelief. The connection had dropped, leaving only dead air. She tried redialing, but the call went straight to voicemail.

"Damn it!" she hissed, shoving the phone into her pocket and heading north along Queensway Road. It was a brisk walk, threatening to break into a jog at any moment.

The morning sun was already high in the sky. It beat down on Gibraltar, casting short, sharp shadows under the red gum trees that lined the thoroughfare. The sky remained a perfect, uninterrupted blue, the kind of day tourists prayed for when booking their Mediterranean holidays.

She turned under the bastion, cutting through the arched tunnel at Wellington Front. She emerged from the cool darkness and headed towards Main Street, passing a group of sunburned Brits in floral shirts and cargo shorts, their faces flushed from too much sunshine and lager the day before. They staggered in search of a full English breakfast, talking about some footballer and a red card. A local shopkeeper rolled up the security gate on his tobacco shop, nodding politely as Spencer powered by. Outside Jury's Café and Wine Bar, two Spanish families argued good-naturedly about where to have dinner in rapid-fire Andalusian. They blocked the pavement, not bothering to move their buggies or shopping trolleys, seemingly unaware of all the people trying to squeeze by politely.

Spencer was less polite. "Move!" she shouted, jogging towards them now.

Reluctantly, they huddled slightly to one side of the narrow pavement, creating the smallest of gaps for Spencer to race through. She was prepared to shove the biggest man into a shop window had they not.

Her mind was moving just as fast as her feet. Zhou's business proposals suddenly made perfect, horrifying sense. The arms dealer was running the oldest con in the book: selling both the problem and the solution. She sidestepped a young couple heading towards a red phone box to take selfies. It was elegantly simple. Zhou sold the remote hijacking technology to the Russians or whoever else wanted to make a statement. Then, after Dark Rock succeeds, after RAF Vespina crashes full speed into The Rock with the Prime Minister and half the security services' leadership on board, who would the desperate Western nations turn to?

The very same man who had already developed the countermeasure.

Anti-hacking software. The antidote to the toxin he'd released. And at what price? £10 million per installation. In a world suddenly terrified of aircraft being hijacked by invisible enemies, governments would pay any amount.

A cyclist rang his bell as Spencer darted up Library Street towards Town Range. She wanted to grab Zhou by the throat, choke him until he told her how to stop this from happening.

Sun Li, too. He thought he was a tough guy with his big muscles and sharp diving knife. Spencer had knife skills of her own. She'd carve the truth out of him inch by inch if she had to, and she'd enjoy every goddamned second of it.

Right now, though, she had other priorities.

Spencer stopped running. Apartment blocks and shops largely obscured the view of The Rock, but as an alleyway to her right opened up, she could see it in all its monumental glory. A fortress. A target. Lush and green, pockmarked by dark scars where the tunnels emerged.

The tunnels.

Her heart hammered. As if the situation wasn't bad enough as it was.

CHAPTER 39

S pencer ducked into the narrow alley off Town Range, pulling her phone from her pocket. Her hands were shaking, making it difficult to unlock the device. She entered the code incorrectly twice, then opened a web browser and typed in *Flightradar24*.

A map of southern Spain and northern Africa appeared, the entire area dotted with small yellow planes. She swiped upwards until she reached Northern France. They hadn't been in the air long and were likely over Brittany or the Gulf of Saint-Malo.

"Where are you?" she muttered, searching for any sign of Buddy's plane.

There was nothing under Vespina, but that was to be expected. It was an unofficial name, not an actual callsign. She tried ZZ336 next: the RAF's official designation for the Voyager fleet's VIP-configured A330 MRTT.

Nothing.

Spencer's heart rate quickened again. Either the aircraft's transponder had been disabled for security reasons, or...

She dialled Buddy, continuing to walk through the labyrinthine streets. This time, the call connected.

"Buddy! What the hell's happening?"

The connection was poor, his voice cutting in and out. "Body slammed... got my phone back... can't get into... cockpit... not responding..."

Spencer continued to scan her surroundings as she wove through the narrow streets. Laundry hung from wrought iron balconies above her, vibrant shirts and sheets flapping like flags in the gentle breeze. The buildings pressed closely in on either side, their pastel paint flaking in the salty air, creating a canyon of faded blues, yellows, and pinks.

She was searching for one building in particular.

"Buddy, I can't hear you properly. Listen to me— Vespina isn't showing up on any flight trackers."

She stepped around an elderly woman sweeping the street outside an apartment block. She gave Spencer an unwelcoming stare, looking at the stranger with suspicion.

"What does that mean?" Buddy asked.

Realising she had taken a wrong turn, Spencer spun around. The streets here all looked so similar, cramped and winding, with unexpected steps and abrupt dead ends.

"It means either your transponder is disabled for operational security because North Star is on board, or this device, this software has done it."

In the background, Spencer could hear raised voices, the simmering of a security situation unfolding.

She ducked under a stone archway, emerging into a small plaza she didn't recognise. Pigeons scattered as she hurried past.

"How are you doing?" she inquired, taking a moment to get her bearings. This was no training drill. The aircraft was filled with real individuals, each with families, friends, and aspirations. She couldn't fathom what Buddy was going through on the flight.

"It's... quite tense. I've briefed the Prime Minister, and we're going through our options. I cut my head when they threw me down. The security detail is trying to breach the cockpit door, but those things are designed to withstand... Well, they're made to withstand us attempting just that."

Spencer spotted a street sign. "I need to speak to the PM," she said, turning sharply and heading east.

"I can pass on any message."

She stared up at the northern end of the Rock, eyes fixed on a dark hole in the limestone.

"No," she said. "Put him on."

***

Zhou stepped onto the immaculate teak deck of White Dove, his designer leather loafers making hardly a sound. The sun glinted off the gold Rolex Yacht-Master on his wrist, momentarily blinding him as he adjusted the collar of his Brioni shirt. His sand-coloured linen suit was light enough for the Mediterranean heat yet expertly tailored to retain its sharp lines. A crimson silk pocket square provided the only splash of colour in his ensemble, complementing the tint of his $5000 sunglasses.

A signet ring, inset with a black diamond, sparkled on his right hand as he reached for the glass of iced water awaiting him at his preferred table on the upper deck.

"Ah, good morning, Mr Zhou." Peter Müller gave a slight bow in greeting, then continued arranging ingredients on a plate. "I've prepared something special for your breakfast."

Zhou settled into his chair, surveying the marina with half-closed eyes. An enchanting hourglass of a blonde in a low-cut sundress strolled along the quay with a toy poodle.

Müller arranged the breakfast like an artist. A perfectly poached egg rested on a bed of saffron-infused rice, topped with Caspian caviar – not the inferior farmed variety. A small portion of Iberian ham lay beside it, sliced so thin it was translucent. The dish was completed with fresh figs, quartered and drizzled with aged balsamic vinegar. A basket of warm pastries – pain au chocolat and almond croissants – waited nearby, their buttery scent stronger than the stagnant marina air.

"The orange juice has been freshly squeezed, and your coffee is single-origin Arabica," Müller said, pouring the steaming black liquid into a bone china cup.

Zhou nodded his approval, taking a sip of the coffee. "Excellent as always, Peter." He cut into the egg, watching as the yolk melted over the rice in rivulets of liquid gold. "Please send the captain to me. We need to discuss our departure plans."

"Right away, Mr Zhou." Müller gave another bow. He retreated backwards a few steps, then turned for the stairs leading to the main deck.

Zhou savoured a bite of the egg and caviar. He gazed out at the marina where monohull sailboats, catamarans and motor cruisers of all sizes bobbed in the water. None as elegant as White Dove, of course. None as big. None as expensive.

He rechecked his watch, wondering if he had time to get acquainted with the blonde in the sundress before their excursion.

***

Unlike Zhou, Prime Minister Nicholas Selley wore an off-the-peg suit; his shoes were practical and reasonably priced. He cared little for ostentatious displays of wealth, finding them vulgar and crass. Of course, his image consultants urged him to upgrade his look, practically tripping over one another to offer a makeover. Still, it was his genuine persona that endeared him to voters weary of polished politicians.

Selley braced himself against the back of one of the plush chairs on the repurposed Voyager. A burst of turbulence shook the aircraft, sending a wave of fear through the passengers. Was this it – the moment they feared?

"Say that again?" Selley demanded, his northern accent thickening with stress.

Robert Rutherford, his security chief, repeated the unthinkable. "The pilots aren't responding, sir. Efforts have been made to communicate through all available channels. Six suspect that the flight controls may have been compromised."

Selley's weathered hands pressed into the fabric of the chair. Until ten minutes ago, he had never heard of remote hijacking. Now, he'd been told that the Russians, or whoever they were funding, not only had the technology but were implementing it right here, right now, on Vespina.

He glanced at Charlotte, seated three rows behind, trying to keep Emily, Mia, and Jackson calm. His youngest, Jackson, was prone to motion sickness. He'd clutched his mother's hand when they boarded, asking if he could sit by the window.

Selley had promised them this would be a simple diplomatic tour; Morocco, Italy, a few photos and a few flags, but plenty of family time and some sightseeing too. He'd even joked about letting them pick out tacky souvenirs.

Now the thought of them being here sent a surge of nausea rolling through him. His stomach turned over at the idea of Jackson's small body tumbling through fire, of Charlotte's hand reaching for the children as everything came apart.

He gripped the chair harder. *Not now*, he told himself. Right now, he had to be a leader, not a dad.

He straightened his posture as Buddy Thompson, face red with carpet burn, approached. His suit was rumpled, one side of his shirt untucked. There was semi-coagulated blood on his knuckles.

"Sir, someone on the line needs to speak with you." He extended the mobile phone towards him. "An asset, of sorts, on the ground in Gibraltar."

"Who?"

"Spencer Bly. Former MI6. Independent contractor now."

Selley took the phone, expecting the deep, authoritative voice of some ex-special forces operative.

"Prime Minister?" The voice was unmistakably female: crisp, not high-pitched as such, but contralto at least.

"I understand we have a situation," he said tersely.

"It's worse than you've been told, sir," Spencer said. "Aside from the danger to passengers and crew, and the potential casualties at the crash site, there's something we hadn't considered: The tunnels."

"Tunnels?" Selley glanced at his advisors, who appeared equally confused.

"Gibraltar is honeycombed with them, sir. Some date back to the Great Siege, others from the World Wars. They traverse the entire Rock."

Selley didn't understand. His lineage was steelwork, not mining. "What are you saying?"

"I'm saying that the plane you are on carries more than one hundred tonnes of fuel. If it impacts near any of the tunnel entrances, the resulting fireball will not only affect the crash site but will channel through the entire tunnel network."

He swallowed, visualising a fireball rampaging through a tunnel and obliterating anyone in its path.

He put the woman on loudspeaker just as she said, "Sir, some of those tunnels house active munitions stores."

He glanced at Rutherford and Thompson; both appeared unwell, some sort of morbid realisation passing over their expressions. Reed from the MoD nodded. "It's true. We have Tomahawk Block IV missiles in there. Strategic reserves. And..." His voice quivered. "Since the withdrawal from Afghanistan, two US MOABs."

Selley's mouth dried up; his legs felt unsteady.

"MOABs," Selley repeated, praying he would soon wake up from this awful nightmare. "MOABs. As in the Mother Of All Bombs?"

CHAPTER 40

Nicknamed the *Mother of All Bombs,* the Massive Ordnance Air Blast, or MOAB, was the largest non-nuclear bomb in the world. Developed for use in the Iraq War and first tested in 2003, the MOAB was never deployed in combat until 2017, when the U.S. used one to destroy an ISIS tunnel complex in Afghanistan's Nangarhar Province.

Prime Minister Selley took several deep breaths, recalling the chaotic withdrawal of Western troops from Afghanistan. In his mind's eye, he saw images of civilians cramming onto C-17 Globemasters after storming Hamid Karzai International Airport. He thought of the young Afghan women tearing up their diplomas, knowing their futures had been erased overnight; the Taliban press conference in the Afghan Presidential Palace; the Abbey Gate suicide bombing. In the blur of briefings and crisis meetings, he vaguely remembered the defence session where the UK agreed to evacuate two MOABs on behalf of the

United States. The Americans hadn't wanted them falling into Taliban hands, like so many abandoned vehicles, helicopters, and weapons caches already had.

Two MOABs, each with the explosive force of eleven tonnes of TNT and a blast radius of more than a mile, were now housed deep in Gibraltar's tunnel network.

Selley turned toward Reed. His voice was quiet but sharp.

"You're telling me we agreed to store two bombs *specifically designed to destroy bunkers and tunnels* inside the most extensive tunnel complex in Western Europe?"

Reed didn't answer. He didn't need to.

Across from Selley, Chief of the Defence Staff Admiral Bailey stood to attention. A greying buzzcut framed the Admiral's square, weathered face. In his sixties, he still cut a strong, imposing figure. No muscle wasting or curving of the spine; Bailey was still as much a serviceman as he ever was.

"It was supposed to be temporary, sir," Bailey said. "We agreed to hold them as a favour. The Americans haven't collected them yet because they haven't had cause to use them."

Selley clenched his jaw, closed his eyes. "And what happens if... When—"

Bailey didn't let him finish. "If a crash triggers a fireball that detonates the MOABs, the shockwave would level everything above ground. The town, the port, the naval and RAF bases will all be wiped out. Houses and hotels collapse. The Rock itself blows like a volcano but without the lava. Boulders flying through the air. Landslides. Fires. Total devastation."

Silence fell over their corner of the VIP cabin. Thompson had stopped breathing through his nose; his mouth hanging open. Rutherford sat stiffly, eyes locked on a fixed point somewhere just above the cockpit door. Someone stood, then immediately collapsed back into their seat.

Then Spencer's voice returned, still on speaker, tinny and urgent. "This isn't just a hijacking. Gibraltar is less than a mile wide. Only three miles long. If Vespina flies into the Rock, the whole thing goes with it. All of it. They'll blow up the entire territory. Everyone will die."

***

The soft clip-clop of Italian deck shoes on teak heralded the arrival of Captain Renato Santori. Squinting against the Mediterranean glare, he approached Zhou's table with a hint of reluctance. Dressed casually in faded chinos and a loose linen shirt with the sleeves rolled up, he looked like a man expecting a day off.

"You wanted to see me, Mr Zhou?"

Zhou liked Santori's Venetian accent, thought it sounded the way good food tasted – sweet and subtle. He didn't look up immediately, opting to finish his pastry first. Only after dabbing the corner of his mouth and folding his napkin did he acknowledge the captain.

"Captain Santori, I trust you slept well." It wasn't a question. Zhou pushed his plate aside and signalled for Mengze Dong, who was loitering by the stairs, to clear the table. "Whites on. We'll be departing within the hour."

Santori cleared his throat. "Departing? But sir, the engine service—"

"Can be rescheduled. Is there a problem?"

"No, no problem," Santori back-pedalled. "It's a beautiful day for it. May I ask our destination?"

Zhou gestured toward the west with his coffee cup. "Just into the Bay. Near Algeciras."

"Algeciras?" Santori pouted, looking confused. "There is not much there. Perhaps we cross to Tangier or head east to Cartagena?"

"Algeciras," Zhou repeated slowly, leaving no room for debate.

"Very well. Would you prefer to anchor overnight, or shall I inform the marina office that we will be back before nightfall?"

But the arms dealer wasn't listening. He was thinking back to his history lessons from school. They were interesting, sure, but they touched very little on European history.

"You know, I only learned about the Great Siege of Gibraltar two years ago," he said as Mengze refilled his coffee and stacked plates. "The Spaniards gathered in Algeciras. They came for entertainment, you see. They assembled on the hillsides as if it were a theatre, all eager to witness Gibraltar burn, as if the Spanish forces were matadors and the British were the bull."

Zhou's lips curled. He took off his sunglasses and handed them to Mengze to clean. "They were disappointed. The British proved... resilient."

Mengze returned the sunglasses to Zhou, who examined the lenses before putting them back on. Today would be different, he thought. Today, there would be fireworks.

Captain Santori shifted uncomfortably. "Sir?"

Zhou waved his hand dismissively. "Prepare the yacht, Captain. We depart at eleven hundred hours precisely."

"Yes, sir." Santori hesitated. "Will any guests be joining us?"

"No guests." Zhou's fingers tapped rhythmically on the table. "Just us. And a perfect view."

As Santori turned to leave, Zhou checked his bank balance. He relished watching the money tick up and reminiscing about his beginnings in a one-bedroom flat in a dreary tower block. He had come a long way. He was not the only dealer keen to sell the cyber lab's new toy. There had been competitors, men older than him, men with connections to powerful decision-makers. But when those same men all died in mysterious circumstances, the task naturally devolved to him. How unfortunate for their families. How serendipitous for him. For Zhou, money was not the only reward. There was power in watching something so solid, so eternal, crumble. Power in knowing you were the cause.

***

The yellow door to a ground-floor flat had seen better days. The paint was chipped, and one glass panel had a thick crack through it. The windows were clean, secured behind thick iron bars painted white. Crime was rare here; it was one of the safest places in Europe, particularly regarding violent crime. Still, burglaries did occur, and many ground-floor windows were protected in this manner.

Spencer paused, doing calculations in her head. The flight time from the south of England to Gibraltar was just under three hours. They had been in the air for twenty minutes. If she were orchestrating this attack, she would maintain the correct flight path toward Morocco until the last possible moment before executing the fatal turn. Maximum deception. Minimal warning. The flight path would take them further west, over Portugal. She reckoned the extra distance across the Iberian Peninsula and the sharp turn through the Strait would equal the time they had already been in the air.

Three hours and counting.

Spencer headed for the door. Her knuckles hesitated briefly before tapping against the wooden panel. She stepped back, waiting anxiously.

The door creaked open a couple of inches; a chain lock pulling taut on the opposite side. A woman's hazel eye peered back at her, then the door closed, and Spencer heard the swoosh of metal on metal as the chain lock was released. The woman was in her fifties, her coppery hair streaked with grey and pulled back in a tight bun. She wore floral scrubs beneath a plain green smock, stained with what appeared to be breakfast.

"Miss Spencer?" Recognition dawned on the woman's tired face. "Could it be?"

"Hello, Marisol," Spencer replied, forcing a smile. "May I come in?"

The apartment was musty but clean, frozen somewhere in the early 2000s: floral upholstery, doilies on the armrests, and a collection of porcelain animals arranged by size on the windowsill. Spencer recognised the smallest of them, a porcelain cat with a chip on its left ear. The place emitted a scent of air freshener, antiseptic, and squeezed oranges.

In the living room, a man in a wheelchair watched television with the sound turned low. His once-powerful frame had collapsed, with his shoulders hunched forward and his head dipping toward his chest. Thin strands of white hair fluttered in the soft breeze of an oscillating floor fan, like spider silk in the wind.

"Dad," Spencer said quietly.

Harry Bly's head snapped up, eyes scanning the room until they settled on her face. For a brief moment, there was nothing, then a flash of recognition and irritation, which vanished as quickly as it appeared.

"He's not doing so well this week," Marisol explained, adjusting a blanket across his knees. "Keeps asking to go to Chopwell Woods. I've told him that there's no such place here."

Spencer swallowed hard. "It's in England. Gateshead. Near Newcastle." She didn't elaborate further, picking up the porcelain cat she had bought her father for Christmas one year from one of the bazaars in Irish Town. She set it back down, glancing around, her eyes landing on the door to her old room. It was probably being used for storage now. Harry's police pension covered the flat. Spencer, Albie, and Liam all contributed towards Marisol. "He really wishes to go to this Chopwell place."

"It's too cold there," Spencer said. "Not good for his joints."

"Would you like some tea?" Marisol offered. "Juice?"

"No." Spencer's response came too quickly. She softened it with, "Thank you, but there's no time."

She turned to the nurse, decision made. "I need you to take my father to Spain. Today. Now."

"What?" Marisol's dark eyebrows shot up. "Miss Spencer, we can't just—"

"You can." Spencer opened her bag and pulled out a thick envelope. "You deserve a change of scenery. Some fresh air. This should cover expenses."

She pressed the envelope into Marisol's hands. The money she had stolen from Zhou – money he had earned supplying arms to terror groups and rogue states – finally put to good use.

"Take a taxi to the border, then catch a bus to Córdoba or Granada. It's lovely there: old towns, churches, museums. Dad always liked history."

Marisol looked inside the envelope and held it to her chest. "Miss Spencer, I don't understand. We have his doctor's appointments—"

Spencer's voice lowered. "I'm not asking, Marisol. Something... Something might happen today, and if it does, I don't want either of you near it. Please. Take him and go. Now."

Harry stirred in his chair. "Spencer? Is that you?"

Spencer turned towards her father. She knelt beside his chair and patted the papery skin on the back of his hand. He looked too old and too frail for his age. There were men his age out there still running triathlons, but severe arthritis, cigarettes, and alcohol had all taken their toll, along with stress and bad memories.

"Yes, Dad. It's me. You're going on a trip with Marisol. A holiday."

"Are you coming too?" Hope lifted his voice, making him sound younger.

Spencer's chest tightened. "Not this time. I have work."

She turned back to the nurse. Marisol looked concerned, biting her lower lip as she flipped through the money.

"How long do we need to be away?" she asked quietly.

"Just a few days. I'll call when it's safe to return."

Marisol nodded slowly. "I'll pack our things."

"No time," Spencer insisted. "Get the essentials and go. You can buy whatever else you need."

As Marisol hurried to gather medications and documents, Spencer returned to her father's side.

"Dad," she said softly. "I need you to go with Marisol. It's important."

He blinked his watery eyes. "The last time I had to run away, that was your doing as well."

She just wanted to keep him safe. "This isn't my doing, Dad," she said softly, hurt. "And it's just a holiday, you're not running anywhere."

Harry's face morphed again, this time to amusement. He let out a deep belly laugh; it caught in his throat and turned into a wheeze. He tapped his left hand against the wheel three times. "Couldn't if I tried."

Spencer laughed too, kissed his cheek, and told him to stay out of trouble. She called a taxi and informed Marisol that it would arrive in five minutes. During those five minutes, she helped Marisol gather two changes of clothes, medications, and toiletries – the essentials.

When the taxi drove off, taking her father and his nurse towards safety, Spencer gave herself five seconds to wipe away a tear and dispel the feeling of regret that had settled in her gut.

She checked her watch. She'd been in there for fifteen minutes.

Two hours and forty-five minutes.

Time was running out.

CHAPTER 41

Spencer watched the taxi vanish into the warren of streets and alleys. She broke into a run, heading south along Castle Road, past Sacred Heart Church. The Gothic structure had weathered two world wars and centuries of storms; by sunset, it might be rubble, its history reduced to dust.

Her boots pounded the pavement as she mentally ticked through her priorities. The walk from the church to Queensway Quay took twenty-two minutes. Spencer figured she could run it in under ten, probably closer to six or seven.

She wanted to get Zhou, show him he was far from untouchable.

It was time to dance with the devil.

As Castle Road blended into Lime Kiln Road, Spencer's breath came harder, not from exertion but from the pressure mounting in her chest. The timer in her head wouldn't stop counting down.

Pedestrians blurred past: tourists with cameras, locals with shopping bags, all oblivious to what might soon fall from the sky. Spencer dodged between them, earning irritated glances and muttered complaints.

Union Jack steps appeared ahead, their bold red, white, and blue stripes standing out against the weathered stone, forming a patriotic staircase that led down into the heart of the city. Spencer had navigated them countless times, but today, her focus was divided between too many critical variables.

She trotted down the uppermost steps, taking them two at a time when her foot slipped beneath her. The world buckled as she landed hard on her tailbone and slid down at least four stone steps before coming to a stop.

Spencer swore, remaining seated for a second, pressing her hands against the backs of her legs, her lower back and sacrum, assessing her body for potential injuries. Nothing broken. Bruised dignity, nothing more.

She pushed herself up, brushing grit from her palms and the seat of her trousers. Looking down at the steady descent that stretched before her, something about the perspective made her freeze... A different staircase. A different time. Spencer's hand searched for a bannister that wasn't there.

***

She's thirteen again, arms laden with dirty laundry that must go in the washer before Dad gets home.

The basket is too heavy for her young arms. She grips it at an awkward angle, the plastic rim leaving marks on her forearms as she cranes her neck to see over the mound of socks and school shirts. Behind her, Liam's high-pitched giggles echo through the hallway as Izzy makes monster noises, splashing through bathtime like it's the most important job in the world.

Then, *crunch*.

The unmistakable crackle of plastic underfoot. Spencer doesn't even have time to look down.

Albie's favourite toy car, the red one with flames on the side, fires out from under her heel like a bullet. Everything spins as the laundry basket launches from her arms. Her feet leave the ground.

The fall feels endless, like her brain is registering it in slow motion: the twist of her torso, the brief weightlessness, the moment her hip hits the stair edge first, then her shoulder. She somersaults, spiralling downwards until her right leg catches the bottom step with a sound like a branch snapping.

She lands in a heap, t-shirts and socks raining down around her like stale leaves in autumn.

Something feels off. She tries to stand, but her leg crumples with the strength of a wet cardboard straw. Spencer sits back down, blinking at her leg. It's bent, her shin jutting at an angle that's subtly unnatural. She touches it experimentally. There's heat, a growing lump, and a tingly feeling like a limb that's fallen asleep.

Instead of crying, Spencer begins methodically collecting the scattered laundry, smoothing creases and forming a neat pile beside her. It's only when Izzy comes out of the bathroom to investigate the noise of the fall that anyone realises something's wrong.

She appears on the landing, the ends of her bobbed hair damp and her cheeks flushed.

"Spencer?" Her voice catches, seeing her leg. "Oh my God."

For a moment, Izzy just stares, stunned. Frozen. Then her childminding training kicks in.

"Don't move, all right? Stay exactly where you are."

She disappears, then reappears seconds later, wrapping Liam in a towel, juggling him on one hip while she rushes down the stairs to grab the house phone. She thumbs 999, whispering into the receiver, voice taut.

Spencer watches from the floor, then reaches for a towel that has landed near her. She folds it neatly. Corner to corner. A perfect square.

***

Spencer started running again, this time slower, carefully watching her steps on the uneven, painted stairs. She had to concentrate. She would be of no use to anyone with a broken leg, and she needed to reach Zhou before his client turned Gibraltar into the world's largest bomb.

Focus, she told herself, putting her childhood aside. She had no time for history. Not when the future was about to go up in smoke.

CHAPTER 42

Prime Minister Nicholas Selley stood at a window in the forward VIP cabin aboard Vespina, the flagship and crown jewel of the RAF's Voyager fleet. He stared at nothing in particular. Below him, a few wisps of candyfloss clouds obscured the waters of Biscay, which rose and fell with a westerly swell. The first time Selley had been on a plane was when he was eighteen, when he and two mates had booked a cheap week in Corfu. He had spent the entire flight terrified but too proud to tell Keith and Jed. He wondered – if he had his time again – if that same eighteen-year-old would make the same decisions. Would he still find himself as the British Prime Minister? He'd spent his entire political career with his feet firmly on the ground, champion of the working class, a man who prided himself on straight talk and practical solutions.

Now, at 30,000 feet, that ground had been pulled from beneath him. He was still terrified and still too proud to tell anyone.

Emily, Mia, and Jackson had been moved to the middle cabin, along with his beloved wife, Charlotte, and anyone his Chief of Staff deemed non-essential. His children had been so excited about this trip. A rare chance to combine state business with pleasure. Morocco for three days, then Italy for the G7. Charlotte had planned excursions for the kids, and Emily was excited to see the Canadian PM's daughter again, after they had hit it off last year.

Holloway, the Chief of Staff, appeared at Selley's shoulder, pulling him from his thoughts. "The press corps in the rear cabin remains unaware of the situation. Foreign Office staff are creating a cover story in case they notice any adjustments to the flight path."

"Good," Selley managed. "The last thing we need is panic on board and the bloody Mail running live updates from their onboard source."

"Yes, sir. However, there is—"

A commotion erupted beyond the curtain dividing the cabins: a woman's voice, familiar and demanding.

"I don't care about protocol! I want to see my husband NOW!"

Charlotte.

"Sir, perhaps I should—"

"No," Selley said, finding his voice. "I'll handle this."

He stepped into the vestibule to find his wife of fifteen years facing down two security officers with the same furious expression she'd sported when confronting two home invaders back when they were newlyweds. Nerves of steel, that one.

"Nic!" She pushed past the guards when she saw him and lowered her voice. "What is going on? Nobody will tell me why we've been moved, and your security detail looks like they've seen a ghost."

Selley took her hands in his. They were cold.

"There's a situation unfolding," he said carefully, aware of the eyes and ears around them. "Everything's under control, but I need you to go back to the children."

"Bullshit," Charlotte hissed. "I've been married to you for fifteen years. I know when you're lying."

He didn't like lying to her; their marriage had been built on honesty. Still, he doubted the truth would help. If the worst were to happen... He'd rather their final hours weren't filled with crippling fear.

"There have been reports of unrest in Morocco; some groups object to our visit. Protests have erupted near the airport. We might need to divert."

She stared at her hands in his, then met his eye with a look that meant she knew he was full of it, but she'd let it go, for now. If Selley survived today, he'd be in deep shit tomorrow.

"Go and be with the children," he told her. "I have a meeting starting."

Her expression softened, and she reached up to straighten his crooked tie, a gesture so normal, so domestic, it nearly broke him.

Five minutes later, Selley was chairing only his second COBR meeting. Of course, COBR stood for Cabinet Office Briefing Rooms – the venue used to coordinate responses to national emergencies – but as only half the attendees were in the Cabinet Office, the name wasn't technically correct.

Seats in the forward VIP cabin had been hastily reconfigured so the PM and others could sit facing each other. The aura was tense, but at least it smelled of fresh coffee brewed by a suspicious member of the cabin crew.

Several laptops were open on a table. Seated around them were Chief of Staff Holloway, Secretary of State for Defence Randall, Chief of the Defence Staff Admiral Bailey, and Leon Groves and Buddy Thompson from MI6.

Via a secure video link from London, four faces appeared on the monitors: The Home Secretary, the Deputy PM, the Director General of MI5 and the head of GCHQ.

Selley took a slow, steadying breath, then took his seat. He cleared his throat and began.

"Ladies and gentlemen, we are facing an unprecedented situation."

He laid out the facts as he knew them: remote hijacking, both pilots unresponsive, Gibraltar, the missiles and bombs stored in the tunnels, estimated casualties, the implications of war.

"I want a strict media blackout," Selley told them. "We control any and all information released on this matter. For now, there is no statement. Nothing is wrong. There is to be no public panic or political hysteria about potential war with a nuclear power."

"Agreed." The Home Secretary leaned closer to his camera, his face red with anger. "If Vespina has indeed been remotely hijacked, we can *never* publicly admit it. This is a *colossal* intelligence failure."

The Director General of MI5 pursed her lips, looking slightly amused. This wasn't her failing; it was Six's.

Leon Groves opened his mouth, but Buddy Thompson interrupted, shifting in his seat. "We've been working this plot from the very second we heard rumours. We've already lost one agent, and another has risked her life to gather further intelligence. If it weren't for her, we wouldn't even know—"

MI5 interrupted, her voice cool and sharp. "As far as we are aware, Spencer Bly is not, in fact, an agent."

The Home Secretary reddened further; Admiral Bailey stared daggers at Buddy Thompson, a vein pulsing in the side of his big, square head.

Thompson coughed and tugged his collar. "True. She's off the books, but I can vouch for her capabilities. Like I said, she's the reason we can even have this conversation. I guarantee that right now, she's putting her life on the line to save ours."

Next to the Prime Minister, Randall clicked his pen. The sound was small but had the silencing effect of a gunshot. "You know Moscow will deny everything. They'll call it a Western fabrication, a false flag."

Selley exhaled slowly. He wanted to believe no one would be foolish enough to buy that narrative, but history told him otherwise. The tinfoil hat brigade would lap it up.

"Plenty of people still think 9/11 was an inside job," he muttered. "It won't matter how much evidence we have. Russia will claim we orchestrated this as an excuse for escalation."

"That's the issue," Randall said, rolling the pen between his fingers. "Look at how fast people swallowed the idea that MH17 was shot down by Ukraine. It doesn't need to be true, it just needs to be plausible enough for their allies to repeat it."

Admiral Bailey cut in, voice grim. "And if we fail to regain control of the plane, then what? A British military aircraft crashes into a British Overseas Territory, detonating NATO weapons on European soil? I, for one, welcome the chance to put an end to this posturing. Russia has got away with too much for too long. Article Five. Full-scale offensive. It's time for regime change."

The Deputy PM, silent until now, suddenly spoke. "Unfortunately, Admiral, the truth of the matter is, we can not afford it." She shrugged her shoulders with a deep sigh. "National debt is approaching one hundred per cent of GDP, interest rates are high, and public services are strained as it is. In my constituency alone—"

"So what do we do?" growled Admiral Bailey, his posture impeccable. "Let it happen? Accept the hit because your constituents want their bins emptying more often?" His fingers curled into a white-knuckled fist against the desk.

"Stop," commanded Selley, voice firm as silence thickened around the table. "I refuse to drag our nation and our allies into nuclear war. I will not allow thirty thousand people to die because I was too cowardly to make the hard choice. This job requires sacrifice. All our jobs do. We sacrifice sleep, our personal lives, our health. But never before in our history has a British Prime Minister had to contemplate sacrificing his life... or the lives of his own children." He blinked back a tear and looked at each face in turn before settling on Admiral Bailey. "Have the RAF scramble a fleet of Typhoon jets."

CHAPTER 43

The door to the apartment at Queensway Quay shut behind her, the heavy bolts whirring mechanically, automatically locking her in and the world out. She cast a cursory glance out of the front window. White Dove was still there, but not for much longer. Crew members filled the water tank with a hose connected to a tap on the pontoon, while others arranged the mooring lines for their departure. Water bubbled around the stern as the engine warmed up.

With her father safely on his way to Spain, Spencer could focus.

She headed straight for the bathroom to strip off all her clothes and use the toilet. She quickly washed her hands and face, noting the shadowy circles that had developed under her eyes.

In the bedroom, she removed tactical gear from the wardrobe: black combat trousers with reinforced knees and multiple pockets, a moisture-wicking compression shirt, and steel-capped boots that had saved her toes more than once. She pulled them on, lacing the boots tightly, double-knotting the ends and tucking them away. A lightweight tactical vest with ceramic plates would be ideal right now, especially when she thought of facing that knife-wielding maniac, Sun Li. Alas, she didn't have one and would have to make do.

Spencer raked a comb through her hair, gathering it into a middle ponytail. She threaded it through the back of her black cap and braided the ponytail into a tight plait. The hairstyle took thirty seconds. No points for fashion, but plenty for practicality.

Now for the tools of her trade.

She returned to the wardrobe and opened the top drawer in the dresser. She pressed three spots on the woodgrain panel in sequence, then popped open the false bottom.

Knives first. Her fingers traced over the collection before selecting a compact tactical knife with a four-inch blade. This went into a leg strap, which she secured to her right thigh. The angled tips of the tanto knives glistened under the apartment's LEDs. She slid one into a sheath with belt loops and clipped it horizontally to the rear of her own belt so it sat over her lower back.

Inside the second drawer lay her firearms: a Heckler & Koch MP7 compact submachine gun and the more discreet Glock 26 Gen 5.

Spencer lifted the MP7 from the drawer, checked it over, and loaded a magazine. Each magazine took forty 9mm rounds, bringing her ammo count to 120.

The time for discretion was over.

Into her pockets went cable ties, flash bangs, a bottle of potent sedatives, a pair of tweezers and a small box from the kitchen.

She checked her watch. Fifteen minutes had passed since she entered the apartment. She caught sight of her reflection in the floor-to-ceiling doors leading to the balcony. The woman looking back at her bore little resemblance to the one young Spencer hoped she'd grow up to become: a happily married botanist and mother of two.

She exhaled slowly before turning off the lights and heading for the door.

The stakes had never been higher; the consequences never graver.

No pressure.

***

Buddy Thompson was wiping his sweaty palms on his trousers when turbulence abruptly rocked the cabin. Some people gasped, others clutched their armrests. The fasten seatbelt sign, of course, remained unlit; no pilots were able to press the corresponding button in the cockpit. Buddy sat rigid in his seat, wondering how they'd done it. How they'd managed to incapacitate not one but two pilots on one of the world's most security-conscious aircraft. Brize Norton had a traitor in its ranks.

Bring back hanging, he thought.

The turbulence settled to a mild grumble but didn't fade completely. Opposite Buddy, Prime Minister Nicholas Selley's face was hard as stone, every muscle in his jaw and brow tensed.

Admiral Bailey leaned forward, muscular hands pressed into his knees. "No. No, sir. We can *not* have the British Royal Air Force shoot their own Prime Minister out of the sky."

"If it saves lives, then yes, we can."

"Sir—"

"We have no choice!" Selley growled. "Scramble the fleet. I want this aircraft ditched in the sea before it reaches Gibraltar. I command it."

The cabin fell silent. Randall flinched. He was a tall, pale man with thinning hair and an accountant's posture. He looked down, fiddling with the gold pen clipped to his folder. Chief of Staff Holloway stared at his hands. Digger turned his head to the window. No one made eye contact.

"With respect, Prime Minister," Buddy said, wiping his hands again, "that's premature. We need more time."

Selley glared at him. "Time, Thompson? We're on a hijacked aircraft heading for Gibraltar. If we crash there... the world changes forever."

"Give Spencer a chance," Buddy countered. "If we scramble jets now, we'll tip our hand. The hijackers will know we're onto them... They might move location... Change the target. We have to give her time."

"There *is* no time."

"We have *some* time." Why wouldn't his damn hands stop sweating? "Prime Minister, I recruited Spencer personally. If anyone can get the information out of Zhou and neutralise the threat, it's her. But she needs time, and we need to act like nothing is wrong."

"And if Spencer fails?"

The head of GCHQ cleared her throat in London. "We could jam the signal," she suggested. "It's technically straightforward. The Russians do it regularly near their airspace."

The Admiral grunted his approval, nodding his big square head. "It's true. They deny it, but it's true. Christmas 2023. Significant GPS disruptions were reported over the Baltic Sea. Poland, Lithuania, and southern Sweden were all hit with GPS signal interference."

"In Lithuania, there were 800 cases within three months alone," GCHQ added, removing her glasses and setting them aside somewhere off-camera.

Buddy raised his chin. "Jamming would prevent further commands to the autopilot... But—"

"Without regaining manual control, we'd be locked on our current course indefinitely," finished Admiral Bailey. "Until we run out of fuel or fly into hostile territory and get shot down regardless. We can't jam the signal without a clear plan to safely navigate or land this thing."

The PM's expression hardened as he absorbed the information. He lifted his coffee, holding it close to his chest. "Then we grant this Spencer time to work. However, we need to calculate a point of no return. A line in the sand. Once crossed, those jets take us down." He turned to Admiral Bailey. "How quickly can the Typhoons reach the south of Spain from their bases in the UK?"

The big man interlaced his fingers, resting them in his lap. "At Mach 2? Approximately one hour and twenty minutes, sir."

"What about Gibraltar?" Selley asked. "Do we have fighters stationed there?"

The Admiral shook his head. "Not permanently, sir. We've a squadron at RAF Akrotiri in Cyprus, but that's further away – two hours at Mach 2."

"There's Morón Air Base," offered Randall suddenly. "NATO facility in Spain, approximately eighty miles north of Gibraltar. We have assets there, as do our allies."

A flicker of hope ignited in Buddy's chest. "How long for those jets to launch and intercept?"

Randall looked to the ceiling, mouthing numbers. "Presuming authorisation from the relevant people... twenty minutes from scramble to intercept."

"Right." Selley sipped his drink, then stood. He didn't move straight away, standing like a statue for ten seconds before walking slowly to one of the windows on the port side. His shoulders rose with a deep breath, then dropped. "Who's good at sums?" he asked quietly, without turning.

"I am, sir," came a voice from the laptop: the GCHQ director again. "Vespina, an Airbus A330-243, cruises at 480 knots or 480 nautical miles per hour. Twenty minutes equates to one-third of an hour. One-third of 480 is 160."

She adjusted the angle of her camera. "I would assume our hijacker would want to keep us on our original course as long as possible, following the Portuguese coast south before making a sharp turn east."

Buddy nodded. As did Randall, Groves, and Admiral Bailey.

"160 nautical miles west of Gibraltar would place you in the Atlantic, south of the Algarve region." She shared her screen, bringing up a map of the region. Her cursor moved over the sea, then she clicked her mouse, bringing up the coordinates. "Eight degrees and thirty-five minutes west. That, Prime Minister, is your line in the sand."

She was good. Mathematics had never been Buddy's strongest subject.

"And when will we reach there?" Selley asked, back still turned to the group.

She paused, her lips moving a second before she spoke. "Two hours, sir."

Selley turned from the window. He looked impossibly tired, his eyes red in the corners.

"Well then, if you'll excuse me," he said, setting down his coffee and squaring his shoulders. "I'd like to see my children."

CHAPTER 44

The mercury was at twenty-six degrees, and it wasn't even mid-morning. A flawless blue sky made it a perfect day for tourism and a terrible one for stealthy operations. Spencer would usually wait for the sun to go down, but she lacked the luxury of time. She stood on the edge of the stone harbour wall, calculating the jump, eyeing the distance to the pontoon below.

The superyacht bobbed gently against its warps, light rippling on the polished hull where it reflected the water. Two men were tending to the mooring lines. On board were another eight men. Nine men between her and Zhou. Nine decisions. Nine chances to see who valued their life over Zhou's.

Spencer stepped over the chain fence, bent her knees, and jumped. She landed in a deep squat on the balls of her feet, her fingertips grazing the pontoon to stop her tipping forwards.

The first test came immediately. The two crew on the pontoon looked up from the cleats at the sound of her landing. They all stood quickly, Spencer closing the distance in three swift strides.

All men think they can beat a woman in a fight. Almost all of them would be correct. Most fancied their chances even if the woman was trained, even if she carried a knife. Most believed they could wrestle a blade from a woman's grip and sustain nothing worse than a little nick. A few of those men would be correct; the rest were idiots who thought their skin was made of Kevlar. Spencer had no time to deal with bravado or the potential two-on-one rumble, which is why she left her knives in their sheaths and pointed the MP7 at them instead.

Both men froze, their eyes widening. The first man dropped the thick, braided line he was carrying and turned his empty palms towards Spencer. The second clenched his fists but made no attempt to test her.

"You have a choice," Spencer said, aiming her gun at the more aggressive of the two. "Do as you are told, or die."

The younger man swallowed hard. His eyes darted towards the dock gate, but Spencer shook her head. "Not happening. On the boat."

He hesitated but obeyed, stepping onto the swim platform at the stern. The second man, the older of the two, stayed rooted to the spot, his hands still balled.

"Get on the boat," Spencer ordered. "Don't make a sound."

He exhaled sharply through his nose but stepped aboard, his jaw tight.

The main living area was as she remembered it: cream leather, rich mahogany, gleaming brass. The illegal tigerskin rug stretched across the floor, a marble coffee table pressing into its back. At the room's far end, a ten-seater dining table was topped with a crisp table runner and a red and yellow floral arrangement.

Spencer pulled the cable ties from her pocket and scattered them on the dining table. "You," she gestured to the younger man. "Tie him up. Legs to the chair legs. Arms behind. Tight."

The younger crew member nodded quickly and did as he was told, securing his colleague to one of the yacht's heavy wooden chairs. The older man tested the restraints, but Spencer pressed the muzzle of the MP7 against his temple.

"Don't be silly."

Once secure, she turned to the younger man. "Now you. Turn around, hands behind your back."

His breathing hitched, but he didn't resist as Spencer bound his wrists, forced him into a chair and tied his legs securely. She grabbed hold of the table runner and sliced a section off using the tanto blade. She gagged the pair of them before they could think to call for help.

"Time for a nap," she told them, taking the bottle of sedative from her pocket and using the dropper to squeeze a few droplets behind each of their gags.

Satisfied, she was about to leave the saloon when the door swung open and James Wan walked in. Shoulders hunched and eyes glued to his phone, he noticed neither Spencer nor her hostages. His black shirt was rumpled, his long hair loosely tied in a ponytail, errant strands dangling over his face. He looked bored and utterly oblivious to the fact his world was about to end.

Spencer shadowed his steps across the room, silently slipping the tanto blade from its sheath in the back of her belt. By the time James stopped in his tracks, took in the scene and spun around, Spencer was less than an arm's length from him, and by then, it was too late. She drove the tanto into his throat, the blade slicing effortlessly through muscle and cartilage, severing his trachea.

Blood arced across the saloon, coating the cream leather, the tiger, and the two crew. Spencer felt the warm liquid streak across her face, tasted wet metal. She watched dispassionately as James's phone clattered to the floor. His eyes glazed over as he collapsed forward, forehead thudding off the table before he hit the ground.

Two restrained. One dead.

Stepping into the hallway, she heard footsteps and rattling crockery approaching. Someone was coming up the stairs from the lower deck. Spencer hid around the bend as Andy, the youngest member of the ship's crew, continued up to the main deck, his serving tray laden with a cafetière and china cups. His eyes were lowered, watching the items clinking on his tray. He stopped suddenly when Spencer stepped into his path, the MP7's all-steel silencer pointing at his forehead.

"Don't scream," Spencer warned.

The young man's mouth trembled as the focus in his eyes shifted from the barrel of the gun to Spencer's blood-spattered face.

"In there," she told him, nodding towards the saloon. "If you scream, I'll kill you."

Andy edged through the door, his face drained of colour, the tray trembling more violently now. He gasped, eyes darting frantically between James's body and his two friends tied up at the dining table. The tray clattered to the floor, coffee splattering across the rug and Spencer's boots.

"Oh God—"

Spencer hit him around the head with the butt of the gun before his scream could fully form. He sank to his knees, stunned, his breath shallow and confused.

"I did warn you," she grunted, grabbing his collar and dragging him to the dining table. She tried to pull him up onto one of the remaining chairs, but he was too heavy for her.

"Fine," she conceded, pushing him face down on the floor to bind his hands behind him and tie his ankles to a table leg. China crunched underfoot as she moved to the serving tray and picked up a tea towel. She sliced it in half, using one piece to wipe the blood from her face and the other half to gag the third captive. And though he may be unconscious, a drop of sedative wouldn't do him any harm.

A clock ticked. He wasn't going anywhere. Time to move on.

Spencer took the stairs, descending quietly into the yacht's interior. The hallway was narrow and panelled in the same expensive mahogany. Following the scent of simmering vegetable stock, Spencer approached the galley. She hid behind the door, listening for voices. There were none, but she heard the sounds of a knife chopping on wood. A chef at work. Armed. Dangerous. Bringing up her memory of the kitchen space from her boat tour, Spencer pictured the layout. Once she turned into the room, she'd face a large, stainless steel island. Beyond it would be a ten-ring gas burner and knives hanging from magnetic strips. A fridge and chest freezer were to the right, sinks to the left. Spencer counted down from three and turned quickly into the galley.

Peter Müller, Zhou's personal chef, looked straight at her. He was standing on the far side of the central island, his white uniform spotless, a ten-inch chef's knife in his hand. Other assorted blades were laid out in front of him between cubed and sliced ingredients. Five chocolate millefeuilles, topped with gold-leaf raspberries and mini macarons, were on a tray, ready for refrigeration.

"Put the knife down," she ordered. "I'm not here to hurt you. Put the knife down and put your hands on the counter."

Müller stiffened, then slowly lowered the knife onto the island. His right hand twitched, fingers moving closer to his meat cleaver.

"I wouldn't," Spencer said.

Müller held more loyalty to Zhou than Spencer anticipated. His face twisted in sudden rage while his hand moved like lightning to the cleaver, his fingers curling around its handle.

Spencer squeezed the trigger as the blade left his hand. The cleaver whistled through the air as she fired, the silenced round striking Müller in the middle of his forehead, leaving a small, circular entry wound.

The chef stumbled back against the ten-ring burner before crumpling to the floor, taking the simmering pot of vegetable stock with him; the boiling liquid hissed as it hit the cold floor. An inch to Spencer's left, the cleaver thudded into the bulkhead, embedding itself in the wood with a solid thunk.

Close.

She stepped forward, her boots splashing in the brown, parsley-scented liquid. Müller was dead. No doubt about it.

No point wasting time checking his pulse or drugging him. The silencer had reduced the gunshot to about 130 decibels, roughly as loud as a slamming door. Not silent by any means, but she hoped the constant rumble from the engine room had masked the sound from the remaining crew.

Spencer stepped over Müller's body and turned the gas off. She considered her mental tally. There were nine men between her and Zhou. Three were restrained, two were dead, and four remained: The captain, another crew member, Mengze, and, most worrying, Li.

The element of surprise wouldn't last much longer; someone would discover James and Müller's bodies or notice the missing crew. Still, she was in no doubt. She would find Zhou, and she would make him talk.

But first, she'd eat a raspberry and macaron-topped chocolate millefeuille.

CHAPTER 45

P ressing herself against the wall at the bottom of the stairs, Spencer listened intently. The yacht seemed to gently vibrate in time with the engine's rumble. She waited, breathing silently, counting seconds. Delicious chocolate coated the inside of her mouth, the sugar providing a burst of energy.

She got to thirty seconds but heard no rush of footsteps or shouts of alarm. Spencer was confident no one had heard the gunshot that killed Müller in the galley.

Time to move. The captain would be next. Intelligence had identified that Renato Santori, like Müller, had come with the boat. They were mere employees rather than Zhou's inner circle. Still, that hadn't stopped Müller from putting up a fight.

Spencer retraced her steps, climbing to the main deck before continuing upwards towards the bridge. The sunlight grew brighter as she ascended, forcing her to squint against the glare reflecting off the lustrous brass handrail. The late morning heat felt stifling. Sweat formed on her temples and trickled down her spine.

The bridge door was slightly ajar, offering a partial view of the navigation equipment inside. Captain Santori sat in his chair, checking a chart plotter, his white polo shirt stretching across his shoulders. He was apparently unaware that three of his crew were tied up in the saloon or that the woman who put them there was now watching him.

Spencer pushed the door open with her foot, weapon already aimed.

The captain spun casually in his chair, leaping instinctively when he saw the gun. His hands automatically jerked up above his head.

"Don't move," Spencer ordered, closing the door behind her by kicking back with her foot.

"Please," Santori said. "*Per Favore*. I just drive the boat. What do you want? Money? I can get you money."

"Sit down," Spencer replied, gesturing with the weapon. "And shut up."

The captain lowered himself slowly back into his chair, eyes never leaving the gun. His legs were shaking, tears welling in his eyes. "I have a family," he pleaded. "Three children. Please."

Spencer trained her weapon on him while retrieving cable ties from her pocket. "They'll be fatherless if you don't stop talking." She threw a cable tie at him and told him to secure his feet to the base of his chair.

Santori complied, his shoulders trembling as he cinched the plastic tight.

"Hands behind your back."

"Please."

"Shut up."

She thrust the silencer towards him. Santori flinched, quickly putting his hands behind his back. Spencer spun the chair around, bound his wrists together and turned it back to face her. She put the gun down on a workspace and pulled the tanto blade from behind her back. Santori's eyes grew wide; he opened his mouth, ready to scream and plead.

Spencer put the blade to his lips as if it were a finger. "Shh. Stay nice and quiet, and your children will see you again."

As she grabbed his polo shirt in one hand, Santori squeezed his eyes shut, his stomach tensing away from her. Spencer sliced at the fabric, the tanto blade making easy work of the thin, breathable fabric.

"Open your mouth," she instructed. "Don't make me ask twice."

The captain didn't resist as Spencer drugged and gagged him. His body went limp long before the sedative would take hold, seemingly resigned to his captivity. Unlike Müller, Santori had chosen survival over employment. Clever man. He would live.

Leaving the captain secured, Spencer edged back towards the yacht's interior. She had yet to clear the crew and guest cabins on the lower deck, the lounge and office on the upper deck, or Zhou's master suite on the main deck. Considering what she knew of those remaining on board, Spencer guessed Zhou was either in his suite, in the office or on the sun deck. Li and Mengze would either be attending to Zhou on the sun deck or holed up in the guest cabins. As for the remaining crew member, he was likely to be... Spencer stopped in her tracks in the middle of the hall. A young man in a White Dove polo shirt stood in her path, his back to her as he headed for the stairs. He carried linen in his arms and spoke rapid French into a phone cradled between his ear and shoulder.

Spencer followed closely, blending into the shadows. She crept down the stairs, maintaining a distance of five steps behind him with her gun raised. From the main deck, he continued to descend before disappearing through a doorway into a laundry room. Spencer paused outside the room, adjusting her grip on the MP7 as she prepared to enter.

Air tickled the bare skin on the back of her neck, a gentle breeze that seemed out of place away from the port lights and hatches.

Not a breeze. A breath.

Spencer began to turn, but the arm was already snaking around her throat, yanking her backwards like a rag doll. The soles of her boots squeaked against the floor as she was dragged into the dark, her windpipe compressed under a thin forearm.

Mengze. It had to be. The arm was too slender to belong to Sun Li, and the longer the lever, the greater the torque. His lanky limbs granted him a disproportionate ability to crush her airway with minimal effort. The edges of her vision seemed to sparkle as her feet kicked uselessly against the floor, the MP7 skittering out of reach with a metallic clatter.

He didn't grunt or curse. He just breathed in her ear. Creepy.

With every second, his arm tightened. A fraction more and her windpipe would collapse like a rotting branch under a boot.

Spencer slammed her head back with all her strength, the impact sending shockwaves through her skull. She heard the sound of cartilage snapping as Mengze's nose crumbled. He growled but didn't release his grip.

The young Frenchman materialised in the doorway. His mouth opened, closed again, and reopened.

"I'll call you back," he told whoever was on the phone. He looked past Spencer towards the stairs and glanced at the MP7 on the floor.

With her vision blurring from oxygen deprivation, she reached blindly for the tactical knife strapped to her thigh, fingers scrambling until they found the handle and wrenched it free. With a twist of her hips, she drove the blade down and back into Mengze's thigh. He hissed, his grip loosening just enough for air to rush down her throat.

The crewman turned to flee, heading for the stairs.

No time to retrieve the gun. Spencer twisted the knife free and hurled it after him, the blade striking him between the shoulder blades. He stumbled, crying out as he collapsed face-first onto the staircase, his fingers searching desperately behind his back, unable to find the handle.

Mengze recovered quickly, surging forward. Spencer dropped to her knees, rolling sideways, scrambling toward her weapon. Her fingers closed on the grip as Mengze's hand clamped around her ankle, dragging her back towards him.

She twisted and flipped onto her back, raising the weapon just as Mengze pounced. He slapped the barrel aside, sending the shot wide, a silenced pop thudding into the yacht's expensive woodwork. He was on top of her, blood streaming from his shattered nose. He drove a fist toward her face, but Spencer jerked her head to the left, the punch grazing her cheek and smashing into the floor. She struck back, elbow to temple, hard enough to make him flinch.

Her free hand slipped behind her back, fingers closing on the tanto handle. She drew it quickly, driving it forward, slicing deep into the soft meat of his neck.

A wet gurgle. A rush of blood.

Spencer pulled the blade free and felt his body drain of both blood and life. He went limp, collapsing on top of her.

She sat up quickly, pushing Mengze's dead weight off her. She rolled him aside, his limbs folding awkwardly. Litres of his blood saturated her compression top. It was already cooling, thick and sticky against her skin.

The crewman was still moving, clawing his way weakly up the stairs, fingers desperately scrambling at the wood. Spencer stepped over Mengze's corpse, walked up behind him, and levelled the MP7. One shot to the back of the skull. A final twitch, then stillness.

She bent over, hands on her knees, catching her breath. The whole encounter had lasted seconds, but adrenaline burned through her limbs, leaving her lightheaded and winded.

Other than the engine, the yacht dropped into silence, but only for a moment. Somewhere above, heavy footsteps thundered.

Li.

Of all Zhou's men, Li was the greatest threat. He was ruthless, psychotic – and because she'd torn half his face off with a Mexican fan palm – vengeful.

Spencer licked her lips, the taste of copper spreading across her tongue. She smiled.

Li wasn't the only one with a taste for blood.

CHAPTER 46

When he heard the first bang, Li assumed it was a door slamming. He had warned the crew about being so careless. Zhou did not like loud noises or clumsy staff; he valued those who were poised, dignified, and in control. Not Li, however. Li could never be described as graceful or decorous, which was precisely why Zhou hired him. Subdued and elegant men were rarely capable of performing some of the tasks Zhou requested.

The pair of them, Zhou and Li, had grown up together. Born and raised in the same residential district in the north of Beijing, they both began their lives with very little, but it was Li who was the poorer of the pair. They were wildly different children and yet totally interdependent. Li was the reason Zhou didn't get beaten up by bullies daily, and Zhou was the reason Li scraped a passing grade. These days, their friendship had morphed from being two underdog kids up against the world into that of an employer and employee. Li resented it. Having to call his childhood friend *sir* was undignified.

He resented Zhou now as he sunned himself on the lounger in his designer suit. Still, would he rather be here in the sun, on a yacht, taking orders from an old friend, or back in the motherland working himself into an early grave? It was better to be miserable in Zhou's inner circle than not be in it at all.

"Mengze's not answering," Zhou barked, slamming his mobile on a small drinks table and waving his empty Champagne glass at Li.

Li wasn't a butler or a dog's body, but he forced himself to swallow his pride and take the glass from his boss. "I can fetch you another one, sir."

That was when they heard the second bang. Clearer this time. Definitely not a door slamming.

They looked at each other. Zhou sat up, his back ramrod straight. He removed his $5000 sunglasses and tilted his head so his left ear aimed towards the deck; the sound had come from below.

Li didn't need to be told to investigate; he was already running down the staircase, and by the time he reached the main deck, he could smell blood.

Down another set of stairs, more cautious now. He hardly needed to look, already sensing what he would find. Yet still, the sight ignited a wrath within that he could scarcely contain. Li's nostrils flared, inhaling the coppery scent of death. His shoulders tightened, his teeth clenching together, lips parting in a snarl.

The crewman lay in a heap on the stairs, his skull punched through with a bullet. A knife, one not too dissimilar to his, was lodged in the young man's back, protruding between his shoulder blades. Beyond him, Mengze's body was sprawled on the floor in a pool of viscous crimson, his long, lifeless limbs twisted under him at inelegant angles.

And in the centre of it all, that British bitch with the long, dark hair. The one who called herself Angela.

No sexy dress and heels today. Today, she looked like a soldier. But it was unmistakably the same woman. She stood with her gun lowered, chin raised, something small in her right hand. Blood – Mengze's, the crewman's, maybe even her own – soaked her black clothing, streaked her face and congealed in her hair. It dribbled off her boots.

Most people ran from Li, and when they couldn't run, they hid. But she just stood there. Waiting.

Li's pulse roared in his ears as he rushed toward her, fist already cocked. The punch was automatic, a natural consequence of seeing her still breathing while Mengze lay dead.

She half blocked it but went sprawling across the floor nevertheless, rolling helplessly onto her stomach as her gun clattered to the floor. She pushed herself to all fours, but as Li closed the distance, a sharp pain flared in his thigh. He glanced down, seeing a syringe dangling from his leg, its contents already injected. He growled, swatting it free.

Whatever she'd given him would take time to work. Time he intended to use enjoying himself. He would dismantle her piece by piece, one tiny cut at a time, until she begged to be put out of her misery.

Li's massive hands grabbed the intruder by her shoulders, dragging her to her feet. His fingers tightened around the long braid hanging from the back of her cap, tipping her head backwards, exposing her throat. She reached for her knife, but Li was too strong for her, wrapping his other meaty hand around her skinny wrist.

His face was an inch from hers, but still he moved closer, letting his lips graze her ear, feeling her body stiffen and try to squirm away from him. "You killed my friend," he snarled. "Now I'm going to kill you."

The bitch said nothing, then he felt the radiating nausea of her knee thrusting powerfully into his groin.

Li's knees buckled, but he remained standing. He felt sick, disoriented, bile creeping up his throat. It was enough for her to wriggle free. She raised her guard, slamming her elbow into his face, once, twice— Her strikes reopened his wound, stinging his ego as he remembered the thorns clawing and tearing through his skin.

Li's backhand caught her across the jaw, snapping her head sideways. She rolled with the impact but remained silent, no cry or plea for mercy. A woman should break after a blow like that, but she didn't; if anything, it made her come alive. The bitch smiled; she was more like Li than he'd given her credit for.

She reached for her knife again. She was fast, sprightly, but Li was faster. He grabbed her, his fingers closing around and twisting the fabric of the top she wore. With a grunt of effort, he lifted her off her feet, hurling her through the nearest doorway.

The bitch crashed into the small laundry room, skidding into the washing machine with a satisfying metallic clang. Steam billowed around her from an iron turned up high, the air thick and humid. A pile of freshly pressed sheets and pillowcases was folded neatly on the counter.

Li followed her into the laundry room, his bulk filling the doorway. "I'm going to enjoy making you beg," he said, running a finger along the weeping wound on his mutilated cheek. He lifted his knee high, ready to stamp on her, but she rolled sideways as his foot landed where her head had just been.

From the floor, she reached for a bottle of bleach, throwing it at his head. He dodged, but it gave her enough time to free the knife from behind her back. She held it in front of her, her eyes boring into his. It was a long blade, approximately ten inches, smeared with blood and sharpened to perfection; she thrust it defiantly towards him. Li backed off a few inches while she pressed her free hand to the floor, trying to get back to her feet.

As her weight shifted to her hand, he kicked it out from under her. The bitch toppled forward, but not before driving the knife through the top of his boot.

Pain lanced up Li's leg. He roared as she rushed him, wrapping her arms around his legs and toppling him to the floor. Knife still wedged in his instep, they wrestled, but only for a moment, Li easily overpowering her. His hand closed around her throat, lifting her until her feet barely touched the floor. He watched with satisfaction as her face began to redden.

Her fist connected with Li's solar plexus. He grunted but didn't release his grip, instead slamming her backwards into the wall. Li released her throat, letting her drop. Before she could recover, he spun her around, pressing her face-first against the wall. One massive hand pinned her in place while the other reached behind him.

The smell of heated metal and hot vapour filled the air as Li lifted the cordless iron from its station. Steam hissed. This would break her. This would make her beg.

He pressed the iron firmly into her back. He breathed in the acrid smell of burning fabric mixed with charred skin and waited for the scream, the pleading, the begging that always came when he applied his particular brand of persuasion.

Nothing. She didn't even flinch. Not a twitch, not a gasp, nothing.

This was wrong. This was all wrong. Li frowned behind her, his grip loosening in his confusion. He'd seen hard bastards take pain before, but never like this. She just waited there, like she hadn't even noticed what was happening. No human could take that. Not even Li.

"*Húli jīng*," he whispered, as a primal fear set deep in his gut. *Húli jīng:* The fox-demon that wears a woman's face but doesn't bleed, doesn't die. He shook the thought away just as she exploded into motion, her elbow driving backwards into Li's ribs with shocking force, using his momentary doubt to twist free. Her hand closed around the iron's handle, wrenching it from his grip before he could react.

In one fluid motion, she spun and swung the heated metal like a club. The iron caught Li across the temple, the impact sending stars exploding across his vision as he staggered sideways into the dryer.

Li's legs felt weak as she advanced on him. He tried to raise his arms, but his movements were unusually sluggish. Whatever had been in that syringe was beginning to take hold, his reflexes slowing with each heartbeat.

She pressed the iron's heated surface against Li's cheek - the opposite side from where she'd cut him with that fucking plant. The pain was immediate and excruciating, his skin blistering and burning as she held it there, her eyes boring into his. The smell of his own singed flesh filled the steamy air.

Li screamed, a raw, primal sound of agony that echoed off the laundry room's walls. The sound seemed to please her, her lips curling at the corners.

The drugs chose that moment to fully engage, his vision blurring as consciousness started to fade. Li's legs buckled beneath him, his massive frame crashing to the floor.

The last thing Li saw before the darkness took him was the fox-demon standing over him, the iron in her hand, no mercy in her eyes. She didn't double over in pain, didn't hold her wounds. He'd fought cartel enforcers, Chechen rebels who didn't want to pay what they owed, child soldiers hopped up on amphetamines and a fanatic in a suicide vest. But none of them had been this. None of them had been a demon.

"*Húli jīng,*" he said weakly, before closing his eyes.

***

The off-white, lumpy, woodchip wallpaper in the doctor's office reminds Spencer of porridge. She sits in the wheelchair, her broken leg propped up in a stirrup. The cast is day-glow pink, adorned with signatures in thick marker pen from Dad, Izzy, Liam, and Albie. Izzy added a heart, Albie dotted his 'I' with a star, and Liam's L is back to front. It's been a week since she fell down the stairs, and now she finds herself in

Dr Bennett's room, watching as a strip of fluorescent light flickers above. Her dad's hand rests on her shoulder, his thumb moving in small circles like he used to do when she was little and couldn't sleep.

Dr Bennett leans forward over her desk, her pale eyes serious behind gold-rimmed glasses. She looks very official in her white coat.

"Spencer, your father says you didn't cry when you broke your leg."

Spencer nods.

"You weren't in pain?"

"Well, I heard it snap. I felt it too. I could feel the bone moving around inside my leg…"

Dad flinches next to her.

"… but…" She shrugs, not really understanding the question.

"Spencer, I believe you have something called congenital insensitivity to pain," Dr Bennett says, removing her glasses to clean them with a microfibre cloth. "We've conducted several tests, and you possess a mutation in your SCN9A gene."

Both Spencer and Dad look at her blankly.

"This gene normally helps make something in your nerve cells called the Nav1.7 channel. These channels are like tiny gates that let signals travel in your nerves, signals that usually tell your brain if something hurts."

Spencer looks at her dad. "There's something wrong with me?"

"There's nothing wrong with you, sweetheart. You're perfect."

Dr Bennett holds her glasses up to the light and puts them back on. "Apart from your broken leg, you're a very healthy young woman, Spencer. This mutation stops the channels from functioning correctly, so the pain signals can't get through. From what you've told me about previous injuries and your medical history, you appear to have an unusually high tolerance. You feel pressure, touch, heat... but pain registers differently for you. It's like you're indifferent to it."

Dad straightens in his chair, leaning forward slightly. Spencer glances at him, sees excitement in his eyes. His thumb stops moving. "You hear that, Spencer? You've got a superpower."

Dr Bennett smiles. "You're picturing Spencer as a world-class athlete, aren't you?"

Dad shrugs guiltily. "Well, I mean, if she can run without her muscles burning, tackle someone without fear of her shins hurting..."

"Mr Bly," Dr Bennett's voice is gentle but firm. "I need you to understand something. Spencer's body still experiences damage exactly the same way anyone else's would. Her flesh still tears, her bones still break. In fact, she may heal more slowly because she won't instinctively protect an injury. She won't automatically shift weight off a sprained ankle or change position when muscles are strained."

The spark in Dad's eyes dims. Spencer watches his face fall like it did when Albie accidentally called Izzy *Mum*.

"Think of pain as an alarm system," Dr Bennett continues. "When most people touch a hot pan, they pull away instinctively – instantly. Spencer might not. She could suffer severe burns before realising something's wrong. Sunburn, frostbite, muscle tears, all these things could happen without the typical warning signals."

Spencer looks down at her cast, wondering about the broken bone beneath. How many other injuries has she walked around with, not knowing?

Dr Bennett clears her throat, and something in her tone makes Spencer look up. "There's something else we need to discuss." She glances at Spencer, then back to her dad. "About future relationships."

Spencer feels her father's fingers tighten on her shoulder.

"Some people," Dr Bennett says carefully, "might take advantage of this condition. A partner might... not be gentle. They might push boundaries, become physically aggressive."

Next to her, Dad swallows loudly.

"You understand what I'm saying, Mr Bly?"

He clears his throat and turns to Spencer. "That, like all superheroes, Spencer should keep her powers a secret."

CHAPTER 47

Li's head throbbed as he clawed his way back to consciousness. A dull, insistent pounding in his skull matched the fire in his cheek where the iron had seared his flesh. He tried to move, to touch the wound, but something bit into his wrists. His arms were wrenched behind him, bound tight, his ankles lashed to the legs of a chair. Fabric filled his mouth. It was wedged between his teeth, tied behind his head, irritating the gash on one cheek and the fresh blistering on the other. But the material itself was smooth; he could feel the softness of silk against his tongue and the delicate ripples of embroidered stitches. There was a chemical taste in his mouth – bitter, metallic. An antidote to the sedative, maybe? Li jerked his body twice, then told himself to relax: struggling was pointless, a waste of energy he might need later.

As his vision cleared, he registered his surroundings. Dark mahogany beneath him, a flash of red cushion under his thighs. It was one of the chairs from the dining room: Zhou's precious imports from a Shanghai master craftsman. But this wasn't the dining room – stainless steel, reflective surfaces, the smell of herbs and stewed vegetables – it was the galley. The door was closed.

A muffled sound beside him caused Li to turn. Zhou was in the same predicament, bound, gagged with the same red silk. His face was slack and unreadable, but Li knew Zhou well enough to sense the calculations ticking behind his dark eyes. When they got out of this, Zhou would ask Li to kill the woman in the most dehumanising way imaginable. He would do things to her that most people wouldn't wish on their enemies. But Li wasn't like most people. He would relish it.

Had Zhou fought? he wondered. Or had he complied, letting her do as she pleased?

The Brit moved into view. Angela, whoever she was, still wore Mengze's blood like makeup. Li tensed. He'd hit her hard, at least twice with his fists, thrown her through a doorway, slammed her into a wall, lifted her by the throat. He had pressed a white-hot iron into her back. And yet she stood there as if none of it had happened.

The flesh around her eye was faintly purple, her cheek swollen, but there was no weakness in her stance, no hesitation in her movements. No pain. *Húli jīng,* he thought again. Fox-demon. It was easier than believing she was human.

She reached for Zhou, pulling the gag from his mouth, the material cut from his pocket square.

Zhou cleared his throat. "That silk is worth more than your mortgage."

The woman rolled her eyes. "Then maybe you can trade it for something nice. A PlayStation for your cell. A box of strawberry vapes to keep your cellmate happy."

She turned to Li. He twisted away as she yanked the gag out of his mouth.

"You don't scare us," he spat, voice rough. It was a lie.

Her expression didn't shift, not even a flicker of amusement. She turned away, laying something on the galley island.

Li followed her movements as she set out items on the island's polished surface. A gun. At least two knives. Other shapes he couldn't quite make out.

She walked to the doorframe and gripped the handle of something lodged deep in the wood. Grunting, she used her entire weight to pull it free. The metal gleamed under the LED lights. A meat cleaver.

She studied it briefly before adding it to her collection. It was then that Li saw a pair of feet sticking out from behind the island. The chef.

"Is he dead?" Li asked.

She nodded. "Yes."

"How."

She lifted the submachine gun and placed it back down.

"Is everyone dead?"

The woman tilted her head slightly, then glanced at him. "No," she said coolly. "Just those who didn't do as I asked."

She moved toward Zhou, gripping his chin tightly and tilting his face up to hers. Zhou didn't fight it.

Her voice was almost gentle when she spoke.

"So the question, Mr International Arms Dealer, is... will *you* do as I ask?"

***

The arms dealer smirked but didn't answer the question, his mouth curling up on the left side, narrowed eyes surveying her. Neither man struggled against their restraints, but while Li seemed uncertain, looking at her like she was an alien, Zhou's expression was one of amused composure.

She could still smell the burn. She knew she'd taken damage. The oral sedatives had worked fine for the crew, but Li needed something stronger: a syringe straight into the bloodstream. In a clean fight, he'd have crushed her. But Spencer didn't need to win, only last long enough for the drugs to take hold. She'd managed it. Barely. She was standing, and he was not. Yes, he'd left his mark, but she'd returned the favour. They were both branded by the hot iron.

Spencer turned to the island. "I know about your $82 million payday," she said, running her finger along the smooth, black barrel of the MP7's silencer. "Congratulations."

Zhou's brows knitted a fraction. Li's shoulders tensed. Microexpressions that may as well have been neon signs.

She examined the ceramic knife. "I know you sold technology to DVS Holdings. I know DVS Holdings is a shell company in the Cayman Islands."

She put the ceramic knife down and chose Müller's cleaver instead. She liked the weight of it. The chef had taken good care of his tools, the metal's mirror finish reflecting Spencer's bruised, bloodied face. She tapped the pad of her finger gently against its razor-sharp blade.

"Question. Why would a shell company need contacts in the FSB? Never mind, I know why."

Zhou's dark brows performed another quick dance, upwards this time.

"You sold technology that allows a person to remotely hijack aircraft." She pulled the gag back over Zhou's mouth, forcing it between his teeth and shoving it back between his molars. Then she knelt before him, felt him flinch as she ran her fingers softly across his thighs and down his shins. She carefully removed the pair of expensive Italian loafers from his feet, the leather buttery-soft and worth God knows how much. She set them aside carefully, almost respectfully.

"Vespina," she whispered. "Did you know they were going to target the Prime Minister? Nevermind. It doesn't actually matter if you knew, and you can't answer anyway." She glanced at his gag. "What matters is that an old friend of mine is on that flight."

As if she'd ever let Buddy Thompson know she'd called him an old friend.

"This is for him."

In one swift movement, she pinned his foot, chopped the cleaver down and severed Zhou's little left toe.

Zhou's scream was primal, muffled somewhat, but still, it reverberated through the galley. Blood pulsed from the wound, spattering across the non-slip flooring. Li struggled against his restraints, the zip ties cutting into his wrists and ankles.

When his scream subsided, Spencer lowered the gag again. She asked three questions, moving the cleaver over three more toes in turn. "Who is at the controls? Where are they? And how do I stop them?"

Mahogany eyes rolled in their sockets until Zhou regained control. He breathed slowly through his nostrils, his head swaying slightly in time with the yacht. Spencer waited, but he said nothing.

"Fine." Spencer shoved the gag roughly back in his mouth and brought the cleaver down on the three toes, leaving only Zhou's big toe on his left foot. The toe curled and flexed, his leg trembling against the restraints.

Spencer waited for his scream to soften to ragged breaths, then removed the gag again. "Now, here's the thing. As much as I'd love to drag this out, taking each of your little piggies in turn, maybe your fingers too, definitely your ears, I don't have time. You know I don't. The clock is ticking. So you need to tell me how to stop the hijacker."

His lips curled into a tight smile. "Or what?"

"Or I kill you."

Zhou's breathing came in angry gasps through clenched teeth, his face twisted in agony. Blood continued to pool beneath his foot, seeping closer to Li by the second. Spencer watched him dispassionately, giving the pain time to become his entire world before she continued.

"Who controls the system?" she repeated.

Zhou spat at her feet. "You won't kill us."

Spencer tilted her head slightly, ignoring the spit. The amount of bodily fluids already over her boots, what difference would a globule of saliva make?

"You don't think I'll kill you? Really?" She wiped the blood from the cleaver with a clean tea towel. "Because I'm a woman? Because I'm predisposed to be nurturing and submissive?"

Li mumbled through his gag. Spencer yanked it from his lips, letting it hang around his neck. "Because we can't help you stop the hijacking if we are dead."

"If you won't help me..." She tapped his cheek playfully. "Then what use are you to me alive?"

Spencer stood before Li, moving slowly, allowing him to anticipate what was coming. Fear was a powerful motivator. She moved behind him, grabbing his left hand and levering his middle finger back until she heard it crack.

Li's scream was different from Zhou's, more of a controlled growl. She grabbed his thumb next. "You know, I heard thumbs never heal quite right. Start talking."

He didn't.

Spencer broke his thumb.

While Li snarled and thrashed in his chair, Zhou regained some composure. His face remained ashen, sweat beading on his forehead, tracing paths down his temples, but his eyes had ceased rolling.

"It's not your femininity that will stop you from killing me. It's your Britishness. The Brits will want me in a cell, not in the ground."

Spencer smiled thinly. "I think you underestimate the British."

She surveyed the two men, Zhou slumping in his chair, blood draining from his mutilated feet, Li rigid with pain, his fingers pointing in unnatural directions. Both men's faces had paled through pain and blood loss, a waxy, greyish undertone beneath their natural complexions.

Zhou licked his lips. "The British are not what they were in the days of the Great Siege."

The yacht's lines creaked around them as another vessel moved through the marina. In the distance, Spencer could hear a marinero's radio crackling.

"Then I think," Spencer said, opening a small plastic jar she'd placed on the galley island, "that you underestimate me."

CHAPTER 48

The house feels different after dark when Dad works the night shift. Without him and Albie butting heads, it's quieter, calmer. Albie still has his tantrums, but Izzy meets them with empathy rather than threats. Spencer can hear Albie's latest meltdown fading in the dining room, his sobs turning to hiccups as Izzy works her usual magic. There's no shouting or slamming doors, but the quiet isn't always comforting. Without a man in the house, a subtle eeriness creeps in with the night. For all his faults, Dad is still the one who'd stand between them and anything that goes bump in the night. Without him, Spencer feels the difference, as if the lock on the front door no longer works, and anyone could walk in.

"It's not fair!" Albie cries. "All the boys in my class go to football club. I'm the only one who can't go!"

Spencer, now fourteen years old and starting to grow into her adult body, rolls her eyes as she guides Liam up the stairs to bed. When she was ten, she was learning how to heat bottles to the right temperature and check nappy rashes. Albie's still acting like he's Liam's age.

"Story?" Liam asks while yawning.

"A short one," Spencer promises, tucking him in before selecting a book with cartoon bears on the cover. The room smells of a lavender spray Izzy bought that *keeps monsters away*.

Their lives have gotten better since Izzy arrived. Spencer's grades have improved now that she has time to study, and the place doesn't feel so empty these days. Dad smiles more often, though Spencer is pleased he never asked Izzy to be his girlfriend. That would be weird. And gross.

Liam falls asleep before the second page. Spencer stands to leave but pauses at the soft buzz of Izzy's phone on the dresser: an iPhone 3GS. She knows she shouldn't look; she knows she shouldn't. But when the screen lights up with another message, curiosity wins. Her friends, not that she has many, all have phones now. Dad won't let her have one. Not yet. When she was twelve, he said, "*When you're thirteen.*" When she was thirteen, he said, "*When you're fourteen.*" And now she's fourteen, the answer is still no.

The text preview makes her pause: *Any chance of more photos? I'll give you fifty quid.*

Is Izzy selling pictures of herself? She is very pretty. Maybe she has a second job as a model. It would make sense; babysitting her and her brothers can't pay that well. Or, and Spencer's brows lower as she considers it, is she selling naughty pictures of herself? Nudes? No way. Not Izzy.

She glances at the door. Albie's voice still carries up from downstairs, along with Izzy's soothing answer. "I'll speak to your dad about the football club, okay? But I can't promise anything."

Spencer picks up the phone. It's not locked.

The photo gallery opens with a quick tap. There are a few selfies, sure, but nothing rude. There's a picture of a bowl of pasta, Liam playing in the garden, a black cat, another selfie, a picture of Liam at the park, the sea. Then... Liam in the bath, Liam getting dressed, Liam sleeping in just his pants. Dozens of them.

Spencer's hands shake. She knows parents sometimes take photos of their children while they are undressed. There's a picture of her in the dresser downstairs from when she was two years old, running naked through the sprinklers in Nana's garden. But that was different; Mum took that picture. And Izzy is not their mum.

Spencer scrolls further, her vision blurring. Not with tears but with a fury so white-hot it makes her peripheral vision sparkle. There are close-ups. Intimate close-ups.

"This is wrong," she whispers.

The stranger-danger talks at school flash through her mind. Safe secrets. Bad secrets. *Bad secrets make your tummy feel funny.* Her stomach is doing more than feeling funny: it churns with acid and rage.

The message glows on the screen: *fifty quid.*

Spencer places Izzy's phone back where she found it. She stands frozen, hands on the dresser, taking deep breaths, one after another, until her hands stop shaking and her fury is channelled into something useful. She's fourteen, and once again, she has to be the grown-up.

Izzy and Albie's footsteps on the stairs snap her into action. She slips into the hallway, smoothing her hair and forcing her face into a neutral expression.

"Is he asleep?" Izzy asks, walking into Liam's room and reaching for her phone.

Spencer nods, watching Izzy's fingers close around the device before tucking it into her pocket. "Out like a light," she says.

She waits until Izzy has put Albie to bed and returned downstairs before allowing her fists to clench so tightly her nails draw blood.

Albie's door opens inwards. She can hear him sniffling in his room, probably clutching his favourite dinosaur toy. Moving calmly, Spencer secures a cord around Albie's doorknob, tying the other end to the rail at the top of the stairs. It will stop him from getting out and seeing what comes next. A simple precaution. She pauses at Liam's room. The nightlight radiates star-shaped patterns across his walls, and his stuffed animals watch over him from the foot of the bed. Silently, she closes the door, avoids the creaky floorboard on the landing and heads downstairs.

The kitchen light leaves a yellowish glow across their cheap countertops. The washing machine vibrates during a spin cycle. Izzy's cardigan hangs on the back of a chair, and her half-drunk cup of coffee sits on the bench, still warm.

"Izzy?" Spencer's voice sounds distant in her own ears. "Could you make me a hot chocolate?"

"Of course, sweetie."

Spencer clenches her jaw at the endearment. Spencer is more than capable of making hot chocolate. Izzy knows this.

Spencer knows this. Still, she makes her one anyway. She watches Izzy move toward the cupboard in the corner, the one by the old stainless steel oven, where they keep the tin of chocolate powder and Liam's sippy cups.

Behind Spencer is a spice rack full of out-of-date and barely used jars of cinnamon, turmeric, ground ginger and dried parsley. Above it is a shelf where they keep their knives out of reach of Albie and Liam. As Izzy bends down, Spencer takes hold of the wooden handle of their biggest knife. She doesn't hesitate. Doesn't pause to consider.

Spencer pulls Izzy's hair with her left hand and draws the blade across her neck with her right.

Blood arcs across the kitchen, splattering the walls and countertops. It drips down the tiles like runny, red paint.

It's over quickly. Less than ten seconds.

Spencer stands very still in the quiet kitchen, watching blood drip from the knife. She releases Izzy's hair, and their beloved childminder slumps to the floor, a dead weight, motionless in a growing pool of crimson. Spencer watches the blood spread across the faded linoleum floor that she had mopped just that morning.

CHaPTeR 49

Spencer rested her lower back against the stainless steel island in White Dove's galley. She held the plastic container in both hands, angling it so both men could see its contents. The box was the sort you'd get with a takeaway, roughly six inches long, four inches wide and three inches deep. Inside, two dozen caterpillars crawled over one another in a writhing mass.

Each caterpillar was about an inch long, with a bluish-black body marked by distinctive rusty-red spots along its back. They looked innocent – small, fuzzy creatures coated in fine, ghostly white hairs like the soft bristles of a brush. They moved slowly, undulatingly, their tiny heads occasionally rearing up as if sensing their surroundings.

Zhou and Li sat across from her, still bound to their chairs, hands lashed behind their backs, legs strapped to the thick mahogany legs of the dining furniture with cable ties. Zhou's severed toes left a viscous pool on the galley's non-slip flooring;

Li's arm and leg twitched occasionally as pain from his broken metacarpals and wounded foot radiated through his body.

Spencer glanced at the clock. Neither man had broken yet.

"Do you know what these are?" she asked.

Zhou stared impassively at the container. Li shrugged his broad, strong shoulders as best he could against his restraints, wincing as the movement aggravated his hand.

"Harmless little caterpillars, right?" Spencer continued. She reached for a pair of fine-tipped tweezers from her array of tools. "Wrong."

She extracted a single caterpillar from the mass. The creature wriggled momentarily before settling. Spencer extended her left hand, palm down, and deliberately placed the caterpillar on the back of her hand. Both men watched, transfixed, as it inched across her skin, leaving an almost imperceptible trail of translucent hairs.

She tipped the caterpillar back into the tub and ran her hand under the cold water tap for a few seconds.

"They won't do me any harm," she explained. "I have a... condition. A rare genetic disorder. But you two?" She let the question hang, smirking as she stepped closer to her captives.

"These are *thaumetopoea pityocampa* – pine processionary caterpillars. Their hairs are venomous, like hundreds of tiny hypodermic needles, primed to deliver a toxin called *thaumetopoein.* Upon skin contact, you'll experience immediate, intense burning and itching."

She took her ceramic knife and traced a gentle, wiggly line across Zhou's left cheek and down his neck.

"Next comes a rash that burns like acid. Angry red welts and hives that spread outward from the point of contact.

The affected skin develops blistering lesions as the venom penetrates deeper. The swelling can be... extensive."

Spencer extracted another caterpillar with the tweezers, holding it a few inches from Li's face. His eyes widened, tracking the wriggling creature.

"Inhaling the hairs can trigger your airways to close. Swallow one, and you could go into anaphylaxis. But my personal favourite? Necrosis of the tongue. Dead, rotting flesh inside your own mouth."

She grimaced and lowered the caterpillar until it dangled directly above Li's lips.

"Fancy necrosis of the tongue?"

Li pressed his lips together tightly, nostrils flaring as he tried not to breathe. She moved the tweezers towards Zhou and held his nose, threatening to drop the creature in his mouth as soon as his lips parted.

"No? Still not ready to tell me how to stop the hijacking?"

His jaw flexed, but he still didn't speak.

"Okay," Spencer said, withdrawing the tweezers slightly. They were still too calm and confident for her liking. The severed toes and broken fingers hadn't been enough. Time to escalate.

"Okay," Spencer repeated. "How about necrosis of the penis?"

Li blinked.

She grasped his belt, undoing the buckle and threading the leather strap through the loops in one quick flourish. The belt cracked like a whip as she tossed it aside. She tugged his waistband, creating a gap between his skin and the fabric, and tipped the container until three pine processionary caterpillars fell onto his crotch. She released the waistband, the elastic snapping back against his hard, toned stomach.

Li froze. Every muscle in his body locked.

When it came to fight or flight, Li was a fighter. An *offence-is-the-best-defence* sort of man. But tied up and with his manhood on the line, she'd left him with only the freeze option. He could fawn, of course, appeal to her, ask for mercy.

Not Li's style.

Spencer gave it a moment, let him sit rigidly in his best effort not to agitate the creatures crawling over his genitals. Then, she raised her free hand and delivered a stinging slap to his crotch with the back of her hand. It echoed through the galley. Li squealed as the microscopic hairs embedded themselves in his most sensitive flesh. It was a sharp, involuntary cry that tipped his head back and bucked his back. His scarred and blistering face contorted, breath coming in sharp, panicked pants.

Spencer turned to Zhou.

"You're next."

Zhou closed his eyes and turned his head away.

"A ladies' man like you..." she said, "... with necrosis of the dick? That's not sexy. Bit of a turn-off. I mean, there are some freaks out there who might be into it, but let's be honest, it's a hard sell. Bit of a niche fetish."

She pulled Zhou's waistband taut.

"Three seconds to talk."

Nothing.

Next to him, Li began to hyperventilate, sweat pouring down his temples. He started babbling in Chinese, incoherent phrases punctuated with pained whimpers. Spencer dropped the caterpillars into Zhou's trousers.

Then she waited – first for the stinging to progress to burning, for the hairs to penetrate his skin like microscopic needles, triggering violent histamine responses, and then the redness, the swelling and blistering.

Spencer filled a large pan with cold water from the tap and then carried it to the freezer. She pressed a button on the freezer door, and ice cubes tumbled out into the pan with plopping and cracking noises.

She knelt before Li, the pan by her side, as Zhou started squirming and grunting.

Li's eyes were wild now, bloodshot and streaming.

"I can make the pain go away," she said softly.

Li looked down at her, barely able to focus. His breathing was ragged.

"I know about your mother," Spencer added. "Thirty per cent of your pay goes to her nursing home, right? Private room, garden view, daily physical therapy. You're a good son."

His lips parted in a pained moan.

"I lost my mother when I was just a child," she continued, her voice quieter. "But you? Yours is still alive. Still waiting for you. What do you think will happen to her when the payments stop?"

Li shook, writhing in place.

"Do you think they'll keep her out of charity? Or do you think she'll end up in a miserable rat-infested state facility while a paying customer claims the bed? Think of her alone, confused, calling your name."

He broke. Words tumbled from clenched teeth in a frenzy of agony and fear.

"You can't stop the hijacking! Not unless you take over the controls! You need the remote! It's the only way!"

Spencer nodded slowly. She grasped his waistband in both hands, pulled his trousers down to his ankles, then tipped the entire pan of ice water over his lap. The caterpillars tumbled off him, some of their hairs floating in the runoff. She plucked the caterpillars from the pool of water and put them back in the tub.

Li sobbed with relief, shivering.

"The pain will return," Spencer said, standing. "So, option one, you talk, and I give you more ice, some anti-inflammatories and antihistamines. Or, option two, I choose two more furry friends from the box. One goes in your mouth, and one – poor little thing – goes up your arsehole." She grabbed his face hard, squeezing his cheeks where she'd torn one side open and burned the other. "The clock's ticking, and I have a box of caterpillars who'd love to meet your prostate. Now, where is the remote?"

CHAPTER 50

Pain.

Not the controlled pain Li had learned to master through the years. Not the bearable pain of a broken toe or cracked rib, injuries he'd endured without so much as a whimper. This was different. All-consuming.

The caterpillar toxin ravaged his genitals. Every microscopic barbed hair created a puncture wound of agony on his scrotum and foreskin. The ice water provided momentary relief before introducing a new torment. His nerve endings screamed contradictory messages as parts of him tried to shrivel and shrink in the cold while simultaneously swelling.

His broken fingers throbbed in rhythmic pulses, the dislocated knuckles radiating hell up his arm. The wounds on his face pulsated in time with his racing heart. Behind his eyes, pressure built, each throb feeling as if it would split his skull open.

Li had built his reputation on stoicism. All these years serving Zhou, he'd never shown weakness. Not when the Somali had stubbed out cigarettes on his arm at that Mogadishu hotel. Not when four men ambushed him in Caracas. But this? This was too much.

His body betrayed him utterly. Tears streamed freely down his face. The sounds escaping his throat weren't human; he sounded like a useless animal, an abandoned dog crying for its master. Worst of all was his shattered dignity. His pants bunched around his ankles, exposing him to the cold air of the air-conditioned galley. Sun Li, Zhou's feared enforcer, the man who had made hardened criminals weep, now sobbed openly, half-naked, helpless, broken by a woman half his weight.

Through the haze of pain, he heard the bitch's question again. The remote. She wanted to find it and stop it.

He didn't want to tell her. Zhou wouldn't kill him for betraying the Russians; they were merely clients, but he'd have him killed for betraying Zhou. But if he didn't talk, this psychotic fox-demon would kill him anyway. The caterpillars were just the beginning. He'd seen the array of tools on the galley island. She was far from finished.

"Li." Zhou's voice was ragged with pain. His boss sat restrained beside him, body slumped, skin ashen, caterpillars still crawling beneath his trousers. A mix of saliva and blood dripped from Zhou's slack mouth, where he'd bitten his tongue. His million-dollar smile now a grotesque and lop-sided grimace.

Li had never seen Zhou like this, stripped of his air of invincibility. In twenty years, he'd never seen Zhou sweat, let alone drool.

"Remember your bonus," Zhou managed. "Cash. Your mother... cared for... for life... Unless you talk. Then I'll kill her myself."

The woman waited, patient as a spider, her cold eyes moving between them.

Li's mother. Her thin, kind face appeared in his mind.

"He can't harm you or your mother," the woman said. "Look at him. Do you really think he's sailing off into the sunset after this? He leaves in cuffs or a body bag." She tilted her head at Zhou's slumped form. "I don't know why you're still afraid of him. He didn't even resist when I pointed my gun in his face and told him to tie himself to the chair."

The woman picked up a knife from the island, the one she'd stabbed his foot with in the laundry room. "He can't hurt you. But I can."

The blade shimmered as the bright Gibraltarian sun filtered through the lower deck's portlights.

"I can kill you," she continued. "Or, I can kill him. You'd like that, wouldn't you, Li? I can make him disappear. No more threats to you or your mother's life. You take over his business." She gestured at Zhou's custom Italian suit, now soiled with blood and sweat. "You take his contacts, his cash, his suits. No more being the attack dog. You'd eat in those same Michelin Star restaurants, only this time, you'd be at the head of the table, not begging for scraps."

The thought was appealing. A life without constantly looking over his shoulder for Zhou's disapproval. Freedom. Power.

Zhou spat blood. "You are not a traitor, Li," he hissed, squirming and bucking as the toxin tortured him.

The woman raised her eyebrows, waiting.

"It's not that simple," Li gasped. "It's more than just pushing a button."

"Explain," she demanded.

Zhou growled a warning.

The pain in Li's groin was rising again. Each throb seemed to emit discomfort down his legs and up his chest. "Only a pilot could operate it."

"That's my problem, not yours. Where is it?"

"Li," barked Zhou.

"I don't know exactly. I only know what they called the place. I don't think it's here," Li continued, measuring his words. "I don't think it's even in Spain."

Zhou lunged against his restraints, the chair legs squeaking against the rubber floor. "Don't you dare say a word!" he screamed, strings of bloody saliva spraying from his lips.

The woman simply placed a hand on Zhou's shoulder and pointed the tanto at his left eye.

"You'll kill him?" Li asked.

She nodded.

There was no going back now. He'd chosen betrayal over loyalty. "It might be over the Strait," Li said finally. "In Africa."

Her expression didn't change. She just stared into Zhou's eyes, the blade not even quivering. "Tell me," she said.

Zhou began cursing in rapid Chinese, invoking every imaginable fate upon Li's living relatives, but he'd made his decision, and Zhou's threats were now nothing but white noise.

"I overheard them," Li told her. "They said the pilot will be in the jungle."

***

Spencer repeated the words. "In the jungle..."

Not *a* jungle, *the* jungle.

She stepped back and played with the tanto knife – ten inches of double-edged, high-carbon steel. It wasn't new out of the box, but it had been cared for. She turned it back and forth, watching the galley lights glint on its blood-stained, mirrored surface. How many other agents had played with this toy? How many ghosts had it created?

Li was short of breath, his muscular chest fluttering, eyes closed tightly as he struggled with the toxin.

Zhou, still bound to the chair, twisted his head and spat at his right-hand man. Then he looked at Spencer as she stepped towards him.

"You won't—" Zhou began.

"You still underestimate me," Spencer said quietly.

She moved behind him, grabbing a fistful of his raven hair and jerking his head back to expose his throat, the same movement she'd used in another life.

Once upon a time, there was a childminder named Izzy. She did not live happily ever after.

His skin offered no resistance, the carbon steel slicing through his trachea and platysma as if it were nothing more than cream cheese. One pass of the knife was all that was needed to sever both the carotid artery and jugular vein.

It felt like, for a moment, nothing happened. The yacht rocked gently as a high-speed vessel sped across the bay, then

Zhou's eyes widened in shock, his mouth working soundlessly. The arterial spray began.

Blood erupted in a high-pressure arc, spattering across the yacht's stainless galley, crimson droplets peppering the appliances, the island, and Li's horrified face.

The arms dealer made a wet, gurgling sound as he tried to breathe through his severed windpipe. His body convulsed once, twice, then slumped forward as far as the restraints would allow. Blood continued to pump from the wound, the spray weakening with each failing heartbeat. Li stared at her while she wiped the tanto blade clean on the back of Zhou's sand-coloured suit jacket. She resheathed it in the holder on the back of her belt and tidied the rest of her tools.

CHAPTER 51

Dad's shift finishes at midnight. His key scrapes in the lock twenty-three minutes later. Spencer waits at the kitchen table, still in her blood-soaked clothes. Her school uniform is stiff now; the blood has turned brown and dried in hard patches. She hasn't washed. Her face is speckled red, and her hair is thick and sticky, clumping together.

The front door groans. Spencer hears him remove and hang up his coat. Then his footsteps pause in the hallway, noticing the light is still on.

"Izzy? How were the kids? Are they in bed?"

She doesn't answer. Just waits as his steps draw closer. Nine steps from door to kitchen. He freezes in the doorway, still in his police uniform. His lunch bag drops to the floor. His flask makes a thud, then rolls across the bloody tiles with a hollow sound. "Spencer?" His voice cracks with worry as he runs to her.

She stands, the kitchen chair scraping against the floor. "I'm okay. It's not my blood."

He stops. His eyes move past her to where Izzy lies by the oven, her blonde hair matted, a deep gash in her neck. He sees the sticky knife on the bench by the toastie maker. The colour drains from his confused face until his skin is an almost translucent grey under the kitchen spotlights. "My god. What have you done?"

He looks at his daughter, then at Izzy, then back at Spencer. He covers his mouth, leans over the sink and vomits beige and yellow sick.

Spencer picks up Izzy's phone from the table. Her fingers leave red smudges as she opens the gallery. She holds out the phone. "You'd have done the same."

Dad wipes his mouth. His entire body seems to shake as he takes the phone. She watches his face as he scrolls: confusion, disbelief, horror, rage. The muscles in his face and neck flex and twitch. He looks at Izzy again, but his stare is different this time: darker, colder. The phone clatters to the floor, the screen shattering completely.

"Liam," he whispers.

"Is asleep," Spencer says. "He never needs to know." She glances toward the ceiling. "Albie too. He's still in his room. He's safe."

She steps towards him, seeking reassurance, but he moves away, creating distance. Spencer blinks back tears. She can't cry now; she has to be brave. She extends her hands towards him. Crescents of crimson line her nails where blood has dried in her cuticles. Her father is a policeman. She presses her wrists together and awaits the cuffs.

***

Spencer washed her hands in the galley's sink, pale pink liquid spiralling down the drain. Her tactical shirt was soaked, the black fabric unable to hide the darker wetness. She caught her reflection in a polished splashback, her face stippled with scarlet freckles, hair matted with blood. She couldn't leave the yacht looking like the finale of *Carrie*. She turned the pressure up on the mixer tap, the flexible sort that could unhook and be used to spray dirty pans and trays. She removed her cap and ran it under the water, turning her head to wash her ponytail, cleaning at least some of the bloody mess from her hair. Spencer angled the tap at herself, spraying her face with cold water before angling the flexible pipe down the floor to spray her boots. It took under a minute; it would have to do.

Behind her, Li shifted in his restraints. Zhou's body had stopped twitching, the pool of blood beneath him expanding slowly now. She wrung her cap out, twisting it until it stopped dripping pink water. She replaced it on her head and pulled the peak low over her eyes. The wet material felt cool but rough against her forehead.

"Untie me," Li said, his voice hoarse. "I told you what you wanted to know."

Spencer glanced at him, water dripping from her chin. "Not a chance."

"But you promised."

"I did no such thing," she said, gathering her weapons.

"But how do I get free?"

"Not my problem." She slid the ceramic knife back into the strap on her leg. "But if you're still here in two hours, you'll have either blown up with the rest of Gibraltar, or I'll be back to deliver you to an MI6 phantom cell."

Decision made, Spencer ascended to the main deck, stepping over Mengze's body and ignoring Li's threats and insults that he shouted after her. She entered the main saloon, passing the subdued crew tied to the dining room chairs and stepped off the stern of White Dove onto the pontoon. Blinking in the sudden brightness of the sunshine, Spencer lifted the MP7's strap from her shoulder and let it slip into the murky marina water, where it disappeared, silencer first, with barely a splash. Grey mullet flashed silver as they flinched, darting out of the gun's way as it sank into the depths. The semiautomatic might have come in handy, but there was no way she could run through the sunlit streets of Gibraltar carrying it. Far too conspicuous. The knives could stay concealed in their black sheaths on her black clothing. Just small bulges that most people wouldn't notice.

The marina was busy with the usual activity as she opened the gate and stepped onto the quay: tourists strolling along the waterfront, enjoying chilled white wine at Moniques, yacht crews washing decks, harbour staff doing their rounds. Normal people living normal lives, all of them unaware of the bloodbath on pontoon A.

Spencer paused at the memorial garden, scanning for observers. Finding no one paying particular attention, she broke into a brisk walk, heading out of the marina under the arches and north on Queensway Road. The midday heat pressed against her skin, already drying her damp clothes.

Spencer merged into the pedestrian traffic, having to slow as a British couple argued over a map, taking up the entire pavement. As the lights changed from green to amber, Spencer took her chance and darted across the road to the sound of car and scooter horns. She tucked under the bastion, past a Manchester United supporters club and a boxing gym where athletic-looking individuals smashed medicine balls into the ground and flipped tractor tyres in the heat.

Spencer edged onto Secretary Lane, a narrow passage between old colonial buildings that provided momentary shade from the relentless sun. She emerged at M&S, almost falling over a woman pushing a buggy. An elderly local man sat on a bench, watching the world pass with sad, rheumy eyes. She thought of her father, wondering if Marisol had got him over the border yet and if he was still asking to go to Chopwell Woods.

A group of American cruise ship passengers with matching lanyards and oversized water bottles crowded around a tour guide who pointed toward the Upper Rock Nature Reserve.

"—and the cable car gets very busy this time of day," the guide was explaining as Spencer squeezed past. "If we don't hurry, we could wait up to an hour."

The tourists quickened their pace, as did Spencer, who broke into a jog, pulling out her phone and dialling the only number that mattered at that moment.

She rounded a corner, turning into an alley that led steeply uphill.

Please pick up.

The call connected on the fourth ring.

"Spencer?" His voice was pleased, excited. "I wasn't expecting—"

"You busy?" she interrupted, injecting false cheerfulness into her tone.

A young couple dodged to the left to avoid her, the woman laughing at something her partner had said. Above her, the massive limestone Rock of Gibraltar loomed. It was ancient, Jurassic. The Rock had seen centuries of violence. Today would be no different.

"I need you," she said. "Meet me in the Jungle."

CHAPTER 52

Not *a* jungle. *The* Jungle.

Spencer knew the words meant nothing to Li. To most, talk of jungles would conjure thoughts of the rainforests of the Congo or Boneo. Most MI6 agents would think the same. But Spencer wasn't most MI6 agents; to be fair, she wasn't even that, but she grew up here in Gibraltar, and the Jungle was a place etched into her adolescent memories.

The last wild place in Gibraltar.

Her clothes were almost dry now, stiff with the remnants of Zhou's blood. Her top moved strangely, the fabric on the back now fused to her skin. It pulled and tugged as she ran. She took a right onto the steep bank of *La Calera,* breathing heavily. She might not feel pain, but her muscles protested their fatigue, each muscular contraction slower and weaker as she pushed uphill. She felt the skin on the backs of her heels move loosely in her boots – blisters she'd take care of later. If there was a later.

The Northern Defences were a forgotten wasteland of overgrown vegetation and crumbling military installations nestled against the northern face of the Rock. Locals called it the Jungle for good reason. On weekends, it was the biggest playground in the country. A wild amusement park where children like Spencer's brothers chased metre-long horseshoe whip snakes through the undergrowth, returning home with scraped knees and torn clothes, talking of make-believe games that transformed the crumbling bunkers into pirate ships and alien spacecraft.

But during the week, the Jungle belonged to the teens. Not the well-behaved and well-to-do, but the rebels. The ones who bunked off to escape the suffocating structure of school. The ones who craved both fresh air and cigarette fumes. The ones who preferred muddy stones to plastic chairs.

Then, after dark, the smell of tobacco faded to the odour of weed and spray paint. This was a place where even a loner like Spencer could find her tribe. She remembered the tinny sound of Tupac or Bob Marley blasting from battery-powered speakers, the bass echoing off limestone as they passed bottles of cheap alcohol around. The tunnels were pitch-black passages that they navigated without torches, knowing every turn and drop by memory. Their fingers trailed along the cool, damp stone as they ventured deeper into the mountainside for a dare or a kiss.

Spencer slowed her pace, scanning the area as she approached Granada Gate, the entrance to the Northern Defences. She crossed the threshold, stepping out of suburbia and into the wild.

"Welcome to the Jungle," she whispered, only it wasn't.

His Majesty's Government had *improved* it. White gravel paths replaced dirt tracks that had once wound haphazardly through the vegetation. Rope fences cordoned off dangerous drops that kids had once leapt over for fun. Informational plaques. Picnic benches.

It looked almost... respectable, thought Spencer. Manicured and sanitised. The Jungle's wild spirit tamed by gentrification and health and safety regulations.

Spencer chose the path to her right and slowed to a walk, her senses heightened. The redevelopment meant less cover, and her footsteps crunched loudly on the gravel. She scanned around as she ventured deeper, noticing just how many vantage points there were in the terraced cliff face above. The dark hair on the back of Spencer's neck prickled as she took hold of a rope fence in her left hand and began the first climb. The terrorist controlling Vespina could be anywhere, watching her right now from any tunnel entrance or shadowy recess.

Visions of fireballs raging through the network of tunnels flashed violently in her mind. Any fire could burn out of control in the confined spaces and limited ventilation of the tunnels, but mix in aviation fuel, munitions, Tomahawk Block IV missiles and two bloody big MOABs, and the consequences were catastrophic.

Spencer prayed she was right about the Jungle, that she wasn't wasting precious time. She checked her watch, feeling the pressure of the ticking, flying bomb press down on her shoulders. It had to be the Jungle, she thought. If Spencer wanted to remotely control a hijacked plane, she'd want three things. A high vantage point, a quiet place free from interference and a clear line of sight.

The Jungle provided all three.

She paused at the first military ruins, their limestone blocks weathered smooth. Crouching beside the doorway, she drew her tanto blade and held it ready as she peered inside. The interior was empty save for an empty crisp packet and a broken bottle of Jack. Perhaps the place hadn't been completely sanitised after all.

Spencer moved on, approaching each structure with the same caution, checking former lookout positions, ammunition stores, and gun emplacements.

High elevation was the first advantage. These fortifications rose up the north face of the Rock and on a clear day like today, offered commanding views across the town and the Bay of Gibraltar to the west and the RAF base, Spanish border and La Línea to the north. Perfect if one needed an unobstructed signal between an aircraft and its controlling device.

Then there was the isolation. Despite the tourist improvements, the Northern Defences remained largely unoccupied compared to the Nature Reserve or Main Street. The ambient noise was minimal: just the distant hum of the traffic below, the ever-present Levante wind and the occasional cry of yellow-legged gulls. An ideal environment for maintaining stealthy concentration.

Spencer ducked into a dark tunnel. She could see the light at the other end, but still, she let her fingers trace the cool stone walls like she used to as she edged through, taking it one careful step at a time. She reemerged into the heat and dazzling sunlight, shading her eyes. An off-leash spaniel darted past, followed by its oblivious, phone-zombie owner. Spencer thought of stopping the woman, asking if she'd seen anything suspicious, but thought better of it.

The military infrastructure was another key asset. Suppose the terrorists didn't know about the munitions stores. In that case, they'd be under the belief that the tunnels would be a foolproof escape, a way to slip from one end of the Rock to another undetected. They may have even stored supplies in one in case of an extended hideout.

Most importantly, parts of the Jungle offered line-of-sight control. Maintaining visual contact with the target would be crucial for certain types of signals, especially if using a directional antenna or a laser-based system.

Spencer paused at a junction. The golden feathers of a pair of Barbary partridges glistened in the Mediterranean sun. She smiled, having not seen one since she left Gibraltar. The pair moved in sync across the scrubby roof of a low, abandoned lookout. The slightly larger male stood tall for a moment, grey chest puffed, then dipped his head to peck at the moss. The female followed. Now and then, they chirruped softly to one another. Spencer felt like she'd intruded on a private moment between two lovers.

A scuff of gravel sounded behind her.

The birds dashed for cover, their red legs disappearing into the shrubbery.

Spencer pivoted instantly, tanto raised. What adrenaline she had left flooded her system.

CHAPTER 53

B uddy tried not to stare, but his gaze constantly returned to the Prime Minister and his increasingly strained expression. The plane's engines hummed steadily beneath them, a constant drone reminding him of where they were and what was happening.

During the COBR meeting, after the Prime Minister had left to see his family, the remaining attendees had made the necessary calls to Madrid and Lisbon. Spain and Portugal had been warned that the Vespina would be entering their airspace without a transponder signal. They'd politely requested that the Iberians quietly keep track of the plane on their radar systems and relay their position back to London. Officially, it was "a minor fault, nothing to worry about."

Through the small window, Buddy could see the Portuguese coastline. How he longed to be on one of the golden beaches stretching beneath them. He could wade in the shallows of the Atlantic, feeling the water cool his feet while the sun warmed his shoulders. He could sit on a lounger, reading one of the many books he'd bought but never found time to read.

"Over an hour has passed, Prime Minister." The defence secretary's voice cut through the uneasy silence. "The fleet is ready to take definitive action. The Typhoons are awaiting your command."

The PM ran a hand through his thinning hair. "Christ."

He looked at Buddy. Buddy looked at his phone and jiggled it nervously. Still no word. *Definitive action.* The euphemism couldn't disguise what that meant. He pictured the Typhoons and the missiles mounted under their wings.

Nicholas Selley paced the cabin. His tie was undone, hanging loosely around his neck like a scarf. "This waiting is torture. We need to make a decision."

Buddy swallowed hard, trying to keep his voice steady and not reveal how terrified he was. "Not yet, sir. We don't need to make a decision yet. You said we'd give it two hours. We still have fifty minutes before we agreed to scramble the jets.

"Forty-five," corrected Admiral Bailey.

Buddy checked his watch. He'd been doing a lot of that. "Spencer's never let me down before."

"No one's ever hijacked the Prime Minister's aircraft before either," snapped Bailey.

The Admiral stood like a boxer, shoulders square, jaw working.

"Spencer is loyal to our country," Buddy insisted, his heart hammering against his ribs. "Whatever she's doing, it's time well spent. I know how she operates."

The PM turned to him, eyes narrowed beneath thick brows. "Your faith in your colleague is admirable, but I don't want to wait until the last second, Thompson. If I need to make this call, I'd rather do it sooner than later."

"Give her time," Buddy pleaded, not caring that desperation had crept into his voice. "Give her forty-five minutes. That's all I'm asking. Give us *all* forty-five minutes." Buddy glanced back towards the next cabin. "Give your children—"

Selley's hand was around Buddy's throat before he could finish the word. His steely eyes glowed with a fury Buddy had not seen in the usually stoic PM before.

"Do you think I'm unaware of where my children are? Do you think I don't understand the consequences of them being here with me?"

"I'm sorry," Buddy wheezed.

"Do not bring my children into this again, Thompson. Don't even look in their direction."

Robert Rutherford placed a calming hand on his boss's shoulder. "Let's all take a breath."

Selley's grip loosened, his arm dropping limply to his side. He pushed past the security chief, who was looking at Buddy as if he were an idiot, and stalked away toward the centre cabin.

Buddy slumped in his chair, rubbed his neck and tried not to think about his own family back home. He exhaled slowly, glancing again at the Portuguese coast.

Please, Spencer. Whatever you're doing, do it fast.

***

"Jesus, Spencer!" Ethan stumbled backwards on the white gravel, hands shooting up defensively. He wore dark cargo trousers and a grey t-shirt marked with grease stains. "Relax, it's me. Why the hell have you got a knife like that?"

The tanto quivered in Spencer's hand for a few seconds, then she exhaled and lowered the blade. She pushed strands of stray, sticky hair behind her ears and felt sweat trickle between her shoulder blades towards the burn.

Ethan kept his distance, palms still raised. His eyes widened as he properly looked at her face. "What happened to you?" He took a cautious step forward, ignoring the knife. "Your face—"

Spencer instinctively touched her cheek, feeling the tender swelling beneath her fingertips. She'd forgotten about the bruising.

"There's blood on your neck."

"It's nothing," she muttered. But Ethan was already reaching toward her, tipping the peak of her cap upwards, examining the damage with fingers that felt cool on her skin.

His jaw tightened, eyes sweeping over her face and body. "It's not nothing. You call me, saying you need me, and I find you beaten, hiding in the Jungle with a knife. Was it that guy? The one who was chasing you?"

"I don't have time for this, Ethan." She stepped back, needing distance. The knife hung awkwardly between them. She sheathed it behind her back.

He scanned the surrounding vegetation. "Are they here? Are you in danger?" He reached for her hand. "Come on, let's get out of here."

She pulled away, a bitter laugh escaping before she could stop it. "In danger? Yeah, you could say that."

"Let me help you, then." The concern in his voice made her want to run away with him and pretend today had never happened. But she knew she couldn't live with herself if she did.

A carefree butterfly, white and yellow, fluttered past, dancing between flowers.

"I do need your help, Ethan. But not how you think." She swallowed, looking at the cliff face towering above her. "You're an aeroplane geek, right? You work at the airport; your place is full of model aircraft. Have you heard of Vespina?"

He nodded. "Part of the RAF Voyager fleet. Our version of Air Force One."

"Right. It's been hijacked," she said, watching his expression shift from concern to confusion. "They're going to fly it into the Rock."

"What? That's—" He glanced to his right, following her eyes up the steep bank of plants and rocky staircases. His face paled. "A terror attack? Is this a joke?"

She shook her head. "No joke. I promise. The Prime Minister is on board, Ethan. This is more than terror. It's a declaration of war."

For a moment, he looked like he doubted her, questioning if what she was saying really was some sort of sick joke. "That's insane. Why would anyone—"

"Because Gibraltar is the perfect target," she said quickly. "Flying a British plane into such a contentious territory? One that's an emblem of the Empire? And killing our head of state at the same time? We'd have no option. You know what would happen after that."

She drew a deep breath, hands on hips.

"So we need to stop it," she said. "We find a way to stop it, or they'll scramble jets and dump Vespina and the Prime Minister in the Strait."

"Jesus, Spencer." Ethan ran a hand through his sandy hair. Dark sweat patches started to spread around his armpits. "You need to call... someone."

She stepped closer, lowering her voice. "I *am* the someone. You know I'm not Angela Smith, marketing executive. I'm MI6 – well, sort of – and I'm giving you an out, Ethan. You can walk away right now. Jump on your bike and pretend you never met me."

His eyebrows lifted. "You really think I'd do that?"

"It's what any rational person would do."

Spencer could see the internal struggle playing out. His body looked solid, but his eyes showed fear, flickering upwards, trying to spot the pride of the Voyager fleet in the cloudless sky.

"I'm not walking away." He folded his arms over his chest. "Whatever you're planning, I'm in. I just don't understand what I can do."

She searched his face for hesitation, finding none.

"Thank you," she said simply, touching his arm. "All will become clear. But first, we need to move. We're too exposed here."

CHAPTER 54

The fragrant scent of wildflowers wafted alongside the earthy aroma of moss-covered stonework. Prickly thistles and vibrant poppies leaned against the crumbling walls of squat wartime structures. Delicate daisies peeked out from a carpet of grass. It was pretty, Spencer thought. Not the Jungle that she remembered, but the Northern Defences still had an appeal now. It was just different.

Spencer took Ethan's hand and pulled him into one of the abandoned buildings she had already cleared. They ducked, minding their heads against the low ceiling. The darkness cooled her skin, and through a horizontal slit in the brickwork, she could see the border and, across it, Spain.

Explaining to Ethan why they were searching for a hijacker who was not actually on the flight was difficult, but Spencer did it as succinctly as she could.

"How do you know he'll be here?" Ethan asked, scratching nervously at his stubble.

"That man told me, the one you saved me from."

"Chinese mafia?"

"Not mafia," she said. "But yes, right before I slit his boss's throat as a thank you."

He twitched at her words. Half of his face was illuminated from the gap in the stone; the other fell into shadow. He tilted his head as if deciding if he believed her, steadying himself against the damp wall.

"He said the hijacker would be in the Jungle," Spencer continued before Ethan could ask her to repeat herself. "It meant nothing to him, but it makes sense to me. He'll be on the western side, wanting the plane to hit somewhere above the Moorish Castle."

"You're sure?"

"Yes. Think like the enemy. A clear line of sight and elevation are essential. Plus, striking here produces maximum impact, both in terms of damage and visual effect. Debris will scatter across the town, with the smoke and fireball visible from across the bay—"

She swallowed. Her throat felt dry. The image in her mind was as iconic, disturbing, and devastating as the Twin Towers on 9/11.

Her phone buzzed with a text message from Buddy: *forty minutes.*

Shit.

"We're wasting time," she whispered, pulling Ethan from the ruined defences and crouching near a tree. "We need to find him. Fast."

They pressed on, exploring the tunnels, abandoned stone batteries, and galleries. Clearing one building after another, they kept one eye on the cliffs above and another on the staggered drops below. They took forks in the path, doubling back once they reached a dead end, retracing their steps and feeling the tension mount with each passing minute.

"There," she whispered suddenly, dropping to one knee and pointing.

Rising from the tangle of foliage was a weathered stone staircase, ancient and crumbling, carving its way up the vertical face of the cliff. Vines and moss covered much of it, nature slowly reclaiming what humans had abandoned. At the summit, barely visible, the dark mouth of a tunnel opened into the rock.

Her eyes had seen something, a momentary flash in the tunnel entrance high above her. It was there and gone so quickly that it might have been nothing. But Spencer knew better. There was something up there for the sun to reflect off: a watch face, spectacles, a phone screen.

"Someone's up there," she said, pulling Ethan behind a large rock.

The stairs were dangerous for numerous reasons. At least two hundred of them stretched upwards, uneven and slippery. Some stairs were cracked, ready to break beneath the weight of an adult human. She'd scoffed at the rope fences and handholds earlier, but Spencer would have appreciated one now. Still, it was the exposure that worried her the most.

"He has the high ground and will see me coming a mile off."

Ethan's eyes widened. "There might be a way." He pointed toward a rocky outcrop about two hundred metres to their right. "I'm sure those passageways connect."

Spencer shaded her eyes and studied his face, wondering how confident he was. "How sure?"

"Ninety per cent."

Good enough. "Show me."

Ethan grabbed Spencer's hand tightly as they ran back along the gravel track before beginning their scrambling ascent up the precarious slope, grabbing tree roots and heavy rocks as they went. The loose soil slid beneath Spencer's boots, tumbling down the cliff face. She was slipping. Panic surged through her as gravity pulled her down. Ethan's hand shot out and grasped her wrist, his strong fingers digging into her skin. She could feel the strain in his muscles as he fought against her weight. With a resolute grunt, he managed to pull her back onto solid ground, their bodies pressed close together. Breathless and shaken, she clung to him, allowing herself ten seconds to catch her breath. *That'll do,* she thought. She pushed herself to her feet and continued climbing.

The tunnel entrance swallowed them whole, darkness pressing all around them until Ethan switched on the torch on his phone, casting ghostly shadows across the rough walls.

"Turn it off," Spencer whispered, her voice punctuated with sounds of dripping water. "Light travels far in places like this. We'll feel our way."

The tunnels were built for people smaller than Ethan. While Spencer could walk at her full height, Ethan had to stoop, his head bowed and knees slightly bent. He moved ahead with his right hand on the cool stone wall, feeling it curve to the west. Spencer followed with one hand on the same wall, her other hand gripping the back of Ethan's waistband. Getting separated in the dark would be a nightmare.

"How much further?" she asked, feeling the weight of the ceramic knife strapped to her leg. The tanto had had its fun; the smaller knife wanted its turn.

"Not far. Maybe fifty metres to where the tunnel branches."

"When we reach him," she whispered, "I need you to focus on one thing: whatever device he's carrying. It'll be a laptop, tablet, or some communication device. Nothing else matters." She tugged his waistband, forcing him to stop and look at her through the shadows. "Whatever happens, whatever you see or hear, grab that device."

Ethan breathed through his nose, the sound of his breath amplified in the confined space. "What are you going to do?"

She didn't answer.

The passage gradually widened, sloping upward. Ahead, a faint glow of daylight leaked through. Spencer drew her knife and signalled Ethan to switch positions and get behind her.

As they neared the final turn, she heard the soft clicking of computer keys. She raised the knife to her lips, then slowly eased toward the sound, stepping agonisingly slowly on the limestone floor. Eventually, the mouth of the tunnel appeared ahead. A man in dark clothing, his back turned to them, was silhouetted against the dazzling blue sky. He was hunched over a sleek laptop. Next to it sat a compact satellite dish positioned toward the open cliff face. Both the laptop and satellite dish were connected to a black power bank.

Under different circumstances, she'd ask Ethan if he was ready, if he remembered her instructions. She'd count him down from three to one. But now was the time for absolute stealth.

Spencer crept as close as she dared, as quickly as she dared, heart hammering so loud she was sure the hijacker would notice it.

He spun faster than she'd anticipated. The man kicked the satellite dish toward them, reaching for a weapon hidden beneath his jacket.

"The laptop!" Spencer shouted, diving forward.

The hijacker fired a wild shot that ricocheted off the stone, almost deafening them. Spencer lunged, knocking his gun hand into the wall. She crashed into him, driving the knife between his ribs three times in quick succession and bringing her knee up hard, connecting with soft tissue. The man howled but countered with an elbow strike that glanced off her temple, sending stars across her vision.

Through the chaos, she glimpsed Ethan scrambling for the computer, trying to pull it clear as the hijacker's boot almost swept it out of the tunnel and down the cliff.

Spencer ducked, but not in time. The butt of the gun missed her temple but hit her jaw. She bit into her tongue, tasting blood. As he lunged again, raising his weapon, she side-stepped, grabbed his outstretched arm, and used his momentum against him. One violent pivot, her muscles straining with the effort, and he was airborne, hurtling into the light.

His scream faded as he plummeted down those steep stairs that Spencer had refused to climb. He tumbled in a violent tangle of limbs, each roll soundtracked with sickening thuds and the noise of breaking bones.

Breathing hard, Spencer turned to find Ethan staring at her, the open laptop thankfully clutched against his chest, horror etched on his face.

"You just..." he whispered. "You just killed him."

Spencer spat blood from her mouth. Her gaze dropped to the computer in his hands.

"He had a gun," she said, voice emotionless. "And we have what we came for."

"But he could have told us—"

"Men like that don't talk," she cut him off. "They die first."

She took the computer from his trembling hands, already focusing on the next step. She swept her finger across the touchpad to stop the device from going to sleep. Having to crack a password would take up all her remaining time. She studied the screen, looking at the list of commands waiting to be issued to the autopilot.

The hijacker's death didn't even register for Spencer, but behind her, Ethan stood frozen.

CHAPTER 55

Ethan's face was slack, his eyes staring through the laptop screen rather than at it. It was the thousand-yard stare of someone whose brain had simply shut down in the face of overwhelming trauma.

"Ethan," Spencer said, reaching up to take his hand, feeling the cold clamminess of his palms. "I need you with me right now."

No response. Just the rapid, shallow breathing of encroaching hyperventilation.

"Look at me," she said, gently squeezing his hand. "Breathe with me, okay? In through the nose, out through the mouth."

His eyes finally met hers.

"That's it," she encouraged, guiding him down to the tunnel floor to kneel beside her. She pointed at the laptop. "Let's focus on the screen. See what's going on here."

Ethan pulled back, shaking his head. "I can't... I don't..." His voice cracked. "That man—"

The tenderness in Spencer's expression hardened. She didn't have time for kid gloves. Not with so many lives hanging in the balance.

"That man was a terrorist." She tugged his hand again. "A terrorist who remotely hijacked one of the RAF Voyager fleet. If we don't get control of Vespina, they will shoot it down, Ethan. They will shoot the Prime Minister out of the sky to save civilian casualties. Not that it matters, because tomorrow morning we'll go to war with Russia, and you know what that means? Civilian casualties. Thousands of them. So I need you to sit down next to me, look at the laptop and tell me what you see."

Something shifted in Ethan's expression. He took several deep, slow breaths, swallowed and flexed his hands to stop them from shaking. At long last, he knelt on the cool tunnel floor.

"There," Spencer said, relief washing over her. "Welcome back, geek. Time to shine."

He half smiled.

"You're all about aviation, right? The airport, the model aircraft, those flight simulator games. You're good at them?"

"Yes."

"Really good?"

Ethan paused, glancing up at her. "Yes. Eighteen thousand hours logged. Why?"

Spencer's shoulders relaxed slightly. If Malcom Gladwell's theory about ten thousand hours of dedicated practice leading to skill mastery was correct, then Ethan would surely be in the big leagues.

"Right, tell me what you see."

Ethan pulled the laptop towards him, fingers poised over the keyboard. Spencer watched, trying not to hover too closely, trying not to think about the countdown ticking away in her head. Nineteen minutes and counting. He frowned, vertical creases forming above his nose. After a moment, he ran his fingers through his hair, leaving it poking up at odd angles.

"I play Microsoft Flight Simulator X. Steam Edition, to be precise. This is not it. It's not even close. But I started coding my own game once. Some of the commands on here look similar to that. It's entirely based around the autopilot."

Spencer moved closer. She was competent with computers, but this was different to running encrypted files and emails through Six's programs. The laptop screen was black with white lines of code she couldn't decipher, its simplicity almost mocking her. "Meaning?"

"Meaning, it looks like I can issue commands to adjust altitude, speed and heading." He looked up at her, disappointment evident in his eyes. "That's it. Which is fine if you want to aim it at a giant rock, not if you want to bring it anywhere safely."

Eighteen minutes, Spencer thought, her anxiety building. A bead of cold sweat broke from her hairline, tracing her temple and jaw. Those people on the plane... Politicians, sure, but they were mothers and fathers, sons and daughters. All minutes from a very public death.

"We need to land the plane, Ethan."

He shook his head. "We can't. I'm sorry, Spencer."

Spencer's eyes darted to the brilliant sky visible through the narrow opening of the tunnel complex, glanced at the bay, and then back to Ethan. "A water landing?" she asked.

"It's an Airbus not a seaplane," he replied. "I know it's technically possible – US Airways, Sully Sullenberger – but the Strait of Gibraltar is not the Hudson. It's open sea and crosswinds. The amount of traffic."

He was right. If one wing clipped a container vessel or an oil tanker, they'd kill everyone on board both the plane and the ship. The fireball would destroy anything nearby, and the environmental implications would be catastrophic. They'd poison half the Western Med.

"Even if rescue craft were ready, I could only slow the plane down so much. If we hit the water at slightly the wrong angle, the wings or engines could shear off. Then the fuselage breaks up and the whole thing sinks before—"

"I get it," Spencer snapped, cutting him off. The images in her head were too much. "The water landing is out. Which leaves the airport. It's flat, it's clear—"

"No..." Ethan stood and approached the tunnel's mouth. "I only have access to the autopilot. I can't lower the landing gear. I can't use the brakes..."

"But can you land it? Can it be done?"

She knew what she was asking of him. The impossibly short runway stretched across her view, sea at either end, reclaimed land built using excavated rocks from the very tunnels they were standing in.

"That runway is less than two kilometres long," he muttered. "Commercial pilots consider it one of the most difficult approaches in the world, even in perfect conditions, even with full control systems..."

"We'll get help." She took his hands in hers, felt how cold they were. "The RAF base is down there. I know it's not the same as being in the cockpit, but between you and the pilots on the ground—"

"We have no landing gear," he repeated. "It'll be like belly-landing a passenger jet on a postage stamp."

Spencer grabbed his shoulder, turned him, forcing him to look her in the eyes. "Can. It. Be. Done?"

"Not safely," he finally said. "But, maybe."

***

The Atlantic waters off the Portuguese coast glistened. Buddy watched the northwesterly swell slowly roll towards the beaches almost on a diagonal. He shifted his focus to look at the glass instead of what was beyond it. His reflected face, usually serious, always slightly lined, appeared unnaturally serene. The plane's gentle vibration beneath his fingertips felt almost soothing.

He sat alone in row four, seat A, puzzled by his own equanimity. Around him, people coped in various ways. Digger made light of things and told jokes that earned hollow laughs at best. Secretary of State for Defence Randall had resorted to alcohol and had sunk half a bottle of rum in the past fifteen minutes. The PM busied himself moving between the cabins, hugging his wife and children in one before hurrying back to the other for updates. Of course, there were none. Most of the COBR team remained congregated around the laptop, sympathetic but helpless expressions staring back at them through the screen.

Perhaps Buddy's stoicism was shock. Or resignation. The mind's final gift before oblivion.

He traced the condensation patterns on the double-paned glass, watching a single cloud rush past. There was something beautiful about it all: the vast, perfect blue of the sky, the sea like sparkling ink. What a charming day to die

The phone in his lap vibrated.

Spencer.

A jolt ran through him, dismissing his relaxed resignation with it. His fingers shook slightly as he answered. "Spencer? Have you got anywhere?"

All the eyes in the cabin found him.

"I've got a dead terrorist and some sort of device." Her voice was breathless. "It's a laptop running a simple interface designed to send commands to Vespina's autopilot. There's a small satellite dish about the size of a dinner plate and a power bank."

Buddy straightened in his seat, picturing the setup, the fog of fatalism lifting. Hope, that dangerous emotion, flickered within him. "Do you understand the interface?"

"I'm good, but not that good," Spencer said. "I can hack someone's email and use encryption software, but cyber-aviation is out of my remit."

"You need to get the device to RAF Gibraltar." Buddy was on his feet now. He didn't remember standing up. Digger was mouthing something at him. *Speakerphone.*

"We'll need a pilot," he continued. "And someone with the right computer skills. We've got GCHQ on the line. Or we can get a hacker who understands—"

"All good," Spencer said, cutting him off. "But in the meantime, I've got something better."

Buddy could practically hear the smile in her voice.

"What could possibly be better than a pilot or a hacker right now?"

"A gamer."

He nearly dropped the phone. "Spencer, this isn't some virtual reality simulation."

"Trust me, Buddy."

Buddy pressed his fingertips into his temples, hearing a male voice in the background. The voice murmured something technical; Spencer responded with jargon. Who was this gamer? Someone she just happened to have on speed dial?

"We're going to try something," Spencer said. "Ethan thinks he's worked out which codes issue which commands."

Ethan. He pictured some hoodie-wearing twenty-something hunched over a laptop beside Spencer, their shoulders touching as they worked. The image bothered him more than it should.

Suddenly, the plane banked left, a gentle but unmistakable shift. Buddy's stomach dropped. Through his window, he saw the wing tip angling slightly upward. Groves shot to his feet. The Prime Minister rushed through from the adjacent cabin.

"Spencer, what the hell?"

"We turned you five degrees to port," she confirmed. "Just proving we have access. Hang on."

The plane straightened, returning to its previous heading.

Buddy looked around at the faces of his fellow passengers. Politicians, military personnel, civil servants, civilians. All united in helplessness.

"Put me on speaker," she told him.

He fumbled with the phone, his thumb shaking as he tried to find the right button. Prime Minister Selley, Admiral Bailey and the others gathered around, faces pale, eyes wide.

"Done," Buddy told her.

"Good news, everyone. The world's not ending. Not today, anyway."

Selley went to speak, but changed his mind.

"We have a plan, but we're going to need some help on the ground. Clear the air space. Every plane, every helicopter, every bloody pigeon if you can. Close the Spanish border and the pedestrian route that crosses the runway."

Spencer spoke quickly, succinctly outlining what she needed from the various British and Spanish authorities. Digger, Randall and Admiral Bailey brainstormed ideas and confirmed they would coordinate the arrangements.

"Then it's settled," Spencer said. "Ladies and gentlemen, please return to your seats and fasten your seat belts. Fold away your tray tables and ensure your seat backs are in the upright position. And brace. It's going to be a bumpy landing."

CHAPTER 56

Spencer's boots slid on loose rocks as she descended the steep staircase. The satellite dish and power bank bounced dangerously in her backpack while the laptop tucked under her arm threatened to catch on vegetation with each step.

Behind her, Ethan scrambled down less gracefully, his breathing coming as short, anxious gasps.

"This is insane!" he called after her. "We should head west, take the path to La Calera. My bike's parked there."

Spencer ignored him, calculating timelines. Doubling back to La Calera would eat precious minutes they didn't have. Yes, Ethan's bike was fast, and he could ride it like a pro, but traffic was already bad. It was peak tourist season, and taxis and buses full of sightseers would be clogging the roads. Once they closed the border, the traffic would back up and become impenetrable.

The dead man lay crumpled at the bottom of the stairs. Thirty-something and pale with a pointed chin, his untimely death would have been a tragedy if not for his terrorist leanings. A gaping head wound spewed crimson blood over sand-coloured stone. It pooled outwards, seeping into the dry soil on either side of the steps. No time to hide or cover the body, she left him to be found by some poor tourist or local. She could see the headlines: *Unidentified Man Discovered in Northern Defences*. Folk would blame the stairs, call them a death trap. The Gibraltarian government would act, closing the tunnel and installing more handrails. Then the headlines would read: *Health and Safety Gone Mad. Save our Wild Spaces.*

Not her problem.

Spencer stepped over his body and started jogging east. The Typhoons were still on standby; she had fourteen minutes to get the device to the airport and put her plan into action.

"Where are you going?" Ethan called from behind.

"Shortcut," she called back, breaking into a sprint now. She powered on, following the gravel track as far as she could, reaching an old lookout. She climbed over a rope fence, clambered onto a low stone wall and began sliding down the treacherous slopes of the Northern Defences.

"Christ," Ethan shouted after her. "You're actually mental."

Spencer's free hand grabbed at roots and stone outcroppings to steady herself. The loose terrain shifted unpredictably beneath her boots. Each step sent small avalanches of stones tumbling down the steep incline. She felt rocks dig into her back and tear into her trousers as she maintained a controlled descent on the precipitous drop.

Ethan's foot caught an exposed root halfway down. He pitched forward with a startled yell, momentum carrying him into a runaway slide.

"Spencer!"

He shot towards her, arms flailing, body picking up dangerous speed as he careened toward a sheer drop thirty feet below.

Spencer reacted instinctively. She lunged sideways, free hand shooting out to snag his wrist as he tumbled by. The sudden jolt of his weight nearly dislocated her shoulder, but she held firm, bracing her boots against a limestone outcropping.

"I've got you," she grunted, bicep tendons straining in her elbows. "Find your footing."

Ethan's feet scrambled against the slope until his trainers found purchase. He steadied himself, face ashen.

Below them, a concrete ribbon stretched across the artificial isthmus connecting Gibraltar to Spain: the runway. Already, Spencer could see vehicles positioning along its edges. Small figures in high-visibility vests scurried across the tarmac, clearing it of pedestrians and preparing for what was coming. In the distance, the border crossing was a mass of honking vehicles.

Twelve minutes.

"We'll never make it in time," Ethan said, eyeing the remaining descent.

"Yes, we will." Spencer pointed to a flat rooftop, perhaps a hundred feet below them.

Ethan shook his head. "You can't be serious."

She was already moving again, picking her way down the slope with composed haste. The five-story residential block was positioned perfectly: a stepping stone between them and street level.

They reached a point where the slope steepened dramatically. Beyond it lay a ten-foot drop, then another steep slide before the final plunge to the rooftop.

Ethan peered over the edge, swallowing hard. "I'm not exactly trained for this."

"Then follow my lead." She secured the laptop more firmly under her arm and checked that her backpack straps were tight. "Take it at a run, push off hard and bend your knees when you land. Don't think about it. Just do it."

Without waiting for his response, Spencer dropped over the edge, landing in a crouch on the narrow shelf below. The impact jarred her knees, but she kept moving, skidding down the next section. At the final ledge, she paused, looking back to ensure Ethan followed.

He landed beside her, intact but breathing hard.

"Last bit," she said, nodding toward the roof. "Ready?"

"Not remotely."

"Three, two, one..."

They ran and leapt together, sailing through empty air for a stomach-dropping moment. The rooftop rushed up to meet them. Spencer landed in a perfect roll, tucking the laptop close to protect it as she dispersed her momentum across her shoulder and back before springing to her feet.

Ethan's landing was an inelegant tumble that ended with him flat on his back, staring up at the cloudless sky.

"You alive?" Spencer asked, already checking the laptop.

He raised a shaky thumbs-up. "Technically."

She turned the laptop over, relieved it was not only in one piece but still awake. The command interface remained active, its simple display showing the last two instructions. She swiped the touchpad, preventing it from entering sleep mode for another few minutes.

Ten minutes.

"Come on," she urged, helping Ethan to his feet. "Fire escape."

They located the metal staircase on the building's eastern side. Spencer took the steps two at a time, the rhythmic clanging of their footfalls echoing through the narrow alley. Five flights down, they reached solid ground, took two side streets and emerged onto Devil's Tower Road.

The traffic situation was deteriorating rapidly. Cars inched forward bumper-to-bumper, horns blaring in futile protest. Drivers leaned out of windows, shouting in Spanish, English and Llanito. Police were visible at the junction ahead, trying to direct the growing chaos.

"This way," Spencer said, darting between vehicles.

They weaved through the gridlock, ignoring angry shouts from drivers. Spencer's focus narrowed to her to-do list: reach the airport, save the plane, prevent war. Simple. Just an average Tuesday.

In the Northern Defences, the vegetation and cool stone walls of ancient munition stores and tunnels had shaded them from the sun, but there was no escaping the heat here. It radiated off the tarmac and vehicles, shining at them from every angle.

They turned right onto Winston Churchill Avenue, the main road that bisected the runway. Ahead, the road was being sealed off entirely. Military vehicles formed a barricade while RAF personnel established a security perimeter.

The situation grew chaotic as rumours that the border was also closing spread quicker than warm butter. Hundreds of day-trippers who'd visited Gibraltar now found themselves stranded on the wrong side of the only route out. Tour groups clustered around harried guides. Elderly couples peered anxiously at their watches, calculating whether they'd make it back to their cruise ships before departure.

"Excuse us," Spencer called, pushing through the crowd. "Emergency!"

Few yielded willingly. She shouldered past a group of American tourists in matching red caps.

"What's happening?" one asked. "Is this some sort of drill?"

Spencer didn't answer, pressing forward. Ethan stayed close behind her, muttering apologies to those she shoved aside.

They reached the checkpoint where armed guards stood monitoring the growing crowd.

"Halt!" A guard raised his weapon as Spencer began climbing over the waist-high barrier. "Area's restricted."

"Spencer Bly," she announced breathlessly. "MI6." *Sort of.* "You're expecting me."

The guard hesitated, hand moving to his radio. "ID?"

"Look at me." Spencer gestured at her battered, bruised and bloody body. "Do I look like I stopped to pick up ID? *This* is my ID." She brandished the laptop just as his radio crackled.

"We're *waiting on an asset: Spencer Bly. Priority Alpha. Send her through immediately. Repeat: Immediately.*"

The guard's demeanour changed instantly, and he extended a hand to help her over the barrier. "This way, ma'am. Vehicle's waiting."

CHAPTER 57

The military jeep zipped across the tarmac, engine roaring. Spencer braced herself against the door frame, eyes fixed on the western end of the runway where a small group of uniformed personnel waited. Beyond them, the Bay of Gibraltar rippled under the relentless sunlight.

The jeep skidded to a halt. Spencer jumped from the vehicle before the dust settled, the open laptop still clutched securely to her chest. Ethan followed, his earlier hesitation replaced by duty and, as Spencer suspected, a little excitement.

Two figures stepped forward from the waiting group: a woman in an RAF flight suit and a man in civilian clothes with a military-issue laptop under his arm.

"Spencer Bly?" The woman extended her hand. "Wing Commander Heather Farraday." Farraday was a sturdy-looking woman with wide hips and stocky legs. An impressive shock of silver ran through her otherwise mahogany hair, which was secured in a bun at the nape of her neck. Her face was square, lined and tanned.

Farraday gestured left to the bespectacled man beside her, who wore jeans and a navy polo shirt. "This is Dr Jason Ramirez, head of our IT security team."

Ramirez removed his glasses, letting them hang from a lanyard around his neck; he was shorter than Farraday by an inch and thinner by a couple as well. Spencer shook their hands quickly, introducing Ethan as the one who established what commands they had access to within the device.

"Let's set up here." Farraday indicated a portable command station that had been established at the western edge of the runway. Like the terrorist in the Northern Defences, they wanted – needed – a direct line of sight.

Spencer set the laptop on a folding table while Ethan carefully extracted the satellite dish from her backpack. Ramirez examined the power bank, scratched his chin, and opted to connect the laptop to their own power outlet instead.

"What exactly are we working with?" Ramirez asked, putting his glasses on.

Ethan tilted the screen towards Ramirez, revealing the minimalist interface. "It's rudimentary but effective. Basically, we have access to the autopilot via a hacked Wi-Fi network. We can control heading, altitude, and airspeed. That's about it."

"No flaps? No landing gear?" Farraday asked, leaning over his shoulder.

"Nothing," Ethan confirmed. "We can point it and slow it down to a degree. That's all. No brakes."

Farraday straightened, her expression grave. "Belly landings are tough, but on our runway..." She left the sentence unfinished.

"Where's the aircraft now?" Spencer asked. "We estimated near Cape St Vincent."

Ramirez gestured to his own laptop and a radar screen next to it. "Vespina isn't transponding, as you already know. Spain and Portugal have been keeping tabs and pinging us the coordinates. HMS Duncan is positioned in the Atlantic, just west of the Strait. They have eyes on as of ten minutes ago. This display mirrors their radar."

Clicking the press-to-talk button on her radio, Farraday requested an update from the Naval ship.

"*Gibraltar Approach, this is HMS Duncan. We have visual on target bearing one-eight-six. Estimating current position of thirty-six degrees, twenty-three minutes north, nine degrees, thirty minutes west.*"

"Copy that, Duncan," Farraday responded. "Maintain visual contact."

Ethan studied the interface, fingers hovering over the keyboard. "We should make the turn soon."

Farraday nodded. "And we need to start bringing them down. Shallow descent, eighteen hundred feet per minute. Let's not leave it too late. When Vespina's nearer, we'll line it up at a heading of zero-nine-zero degrees to match the runway."

Ethan adjusted his grip on the keyboard. "We're at thirty-five thousand feet and closing."

"I need to make a call first," Spencer said, pulling out her phone. She dialled Buddy, who answered before the first ring had finished.

"Spencer? Sit. Rep."

"Western end of the runway with RAF personnel." She shaded her eyes and steadied her voice. "Ethan's going to adjust your heading soon. Warn everyone to expect a sharp turn to their left."

"Everyone's seated already, seat belts fastened," Buddy replied, his voice tight with tension. "The PM's asking for updates."

"Tell him we're doing everything possible." She turned to Ethan. "They're ready."

Ethan and Ramirez talked for a moment, then nodded in agreement. Ethan took a deep breath before his fingers began typing the command. "Executing ninety-degree port turn. Beginning descent profile. Vertical speed minus eighteen hundred."

On the radar screen, the blip representing Vespina began a slow, deliberate turn to the left.

"*Gibraltar Approach, Duncan here,*" the radio crackled. "*Target is banking to port. Repeat. Target is banking to port.*"

"It's working," Ethan said, sighing.

His relief was yet to reach Spencer. There were still many more things that could go wrong than could go right.

***

The plane banked sharply to port, causing several people to grab their armrests. Nervous laughter rippled from the cabin behind Buddy. He held his phone tight to his ear, aware of Prime Minister Selley observing him closely. Deep within his gut, a heavy feeling signalled a shift in gravity. They were going down.

Secretary for the Defence Randall raised a drunken eyebrow. "Well?"

"They're attempting the landing at Gibraltar."

Admiral Bailey inhaled deeply, leaning over Randall. "Without landing gear?"

"Without landing gear," Buddy confirmed, shifting in his seat.

"We need to brief the others," the PM said, glancing toward the press contingent and diplomatic staff in the rear section.

Leon Groves nodded. "Not the full story. Technical issue, diversion. Nothing about the hijacking."

Prime Minister Selley squared his shoulders. "I'll do it."

"No," Groves challenged, earning him a few questioning looks. "That message would usually come from the captain... We'll give one of the cabin crew a script to deliver through the intercom. It'll be more believable. I'll write it now."

Buddy twitched as a new voice started talking in his ear: a woman named Farraday. He listened, nodded, hung up.

"What was that?" Digger asked, arms folded high over his chest.

"They want everyone moved to the rear of the plane," Buddy replied. "Specifically, the middle and aisle seats." He unclipped his seatbelt.

"Christ," Digger muttered, unclipping as well. "That bad?"

"It's a belly landing on a runway designed for much smaller aircraft," Buddy said. "Bad, but better than the alternative."

Buddy stretched his neck from one side to the other before passing Farraday's instructions on to everyone in the VIP cabin. When he was finished, a message sounded throughout the aircraft.

"Ladies and gentlemen," the lead flight attendant announced, "due to an issue with our autopilot, we are diverting to Gibraltar and will be landing in approximately twenty-five minutes."

An issue with our autopilot? Short. To the point. Technically true.

The PM led the group as they collectively headed to the rear of the plane. Passing through the middle cabin, he spoke briefly with his wife and children, shepherding them towards the rear cabin. Charlotte Selley looked calm as her husband kissed her cheek and took young Emily by the hand, but her legs wobbled ever so slightly. She probably knew more was going on than the official story implied. How much had Selley told her?

A hand caught Buddy's arm as he moved into the rear cabin. He knew the man's face but not his name. A political reporter from the Telegraph. Trendy glasses, tidy facial hair, checked shirt and smart jeans.

"What's going on?" he asked. No pen hovering over a notepad, no dictaphone or mobile pushed into Buddy's face. He was asking for himself, not the scoop.

Buddy shrugged. "Something to do with the autopilot."

The journalist gave Buddy a pointed look. "They wouldn't move the likes of the PM to the safe seats at the back for a simple diversion. It's an emergency landing, isn't it? Not a regular one either."

Buddy shrugged free of the man's grip. "I'm sure it's all in hand."

He moved off, hearing whispered speculation flutter through the press pool. Some, sensing the gravity of the situation, stopped asking questions and began checking seat belts, tucking away laptops and phones. An aisle seat next to Digger was free. Buddy took it, tightening his belt until it dug into his hips.

"If we don't make it," Digger began.

"We'll make it," Buddy cut him off. Spencer was down there; she wouldn't let him down. She'd never let him down once. He, on the other hand—

Buddy leaned forward, arms crossed over the seat in front of him, head down, braced for impact. He closed his eyes, picturing the chaos on the ground. The image blurred and faded to a slow-motion, black-and-white movie of Vespina crash landing and bursting into flames.

The aircraft shuddered. Someone gasped. Buddy pressed his forehead against his forearms and waited for impact.

CHAPTER 58

The small blip representing Vespina edged outwards on the circular radar as it moved further from HMS Duncan. Wing Commander Farraday stood beside Spencer, speaking slowly and clearly into her radio.

"All units. Emergency Protocol zero-zero-seven-seven is now in effect. All crews to crash alert stations. Code Red inbound. Repeat, Code Red inbound."

A storm of activity erupted across the airfield. Jeeps, fire trucks, people running. Spencer turned to Farraday. "Zero-zero-seven-seven?"

"Our highest level of emergency landing protocol," she explained, donning mirrored aviators to shade her eyes. "We're prepping for the worst. I'm deploying everything we've got."

Ramirez pointed to a row of vehicles moving into position along the runway. They resembled space-age fire trucks, postbox-red with a bulbous glass front allowing the driver visibility in almost all directions. A ladder-mounted hose was fixed to its roof next to heavy-duty tubes. "Foam trucks," he told her.

Ethan turned from the laptop long enough to say, "They'll coat the runway with aqueous film-forming foam. AFFF for short."

He really was an aviation geek.

"Prevents fire," Ramirez continued. "When planes come in without landing gear, the fuselage scraping over concrete creates friction. Which creates heat. Lots of it. If even a drop of fuel leaks, we're talking immediate ignition."

The trucks got into position and began spraying a viscous white substance across the runway's surface, forming a glistening, fire-retardant layer.

"It's not great for the environment, but then neither is an aviation fuel fire."

Or World War Three, thought Spencer, looking behind her at the layout of Gibraltar's unique airport. The runway spanned the entire peninsula with nothing but water at either end.

"Won't that make it slippery? What if the plane doesn't stop in time?"

Farraday pointed east. "Hence, we're deploying arrestor nets. They're designed for fighter jets, not something Vespina's size, but they might help slow it down."

There was uncertainty in the way she said *might*.

"They're designed to absorb energy without snapping," she said. "If Vespina hits them, they'll stretch and slow it down. Assuming it doesn't plough straight through them."

Teams of men and women laid what looked like a rolled-up length of material across the runway, working to unravel and untangle it until it resembled an elastic ladder lying on its side. A supervisor signalled the team by thrusting his arms in a big V shape above his head. On his command, one length of the net was raised, supported by tall wedges that pivoted out of the tarmac.

"I didn't know we had those," Ethan said, eyes lighting up at what looked to Spencer like a giant badminton net.

Farraday sighed. "That's because we've never had to use them."

She was tense. They all were. Her broad shoulders were raised, her jaw flexing as she ground her teeth.

They were doing what they could, but there was still a risk of the plane skidding into the sea. "We need to clear the surrounding areas. If the plane overshoots..."

"Already underway," the Farraday told her. "Gibraltar Police are clearing Eastern Beach and Playa de Levante. A search and rescue vessel is being prepped as we speak. There's a no-sail order in place for all watercraft on either side of the runway. Nothing's allowed out of Ocean Village or Alcaidesa over the border."

Spencer felt little relief. The enormity of what they were attempting kept hitting her anew, like repeated slaps around the head. If they failed – if Vespina overshot the runway or skidded into personnel or burst into a fireball – the death toll would extend far beyond those on the plane.

Spencer's phone vibrated with a message from Buddy: *In position. Rear of plane. Crew ready to issue the brace command.*

"Ten minutes to initial approach," Ethan announced, making Spencer jump.

Farraday leaned over Ethan's shoulder, her eyes flicking across their data feed. "Speed's too high. Bring it down. Slowly."

Ethan's fingers hovered over the keyboard. "How slow?"

"Reduce to three hundred. And keep the descent shallow. Twelve hundred feet per minute, max."

Ethan typed *VS -1200* into the laptop and hit return. "Descending twelve hundred feet per minute."

Spencer glanced between them: Farraday calling the shots, Ethan translating them into code.

"Can we slow it down more?" Spencer asked.

Farraday shook her head. "Not too much too quickly. We can't risk a stall."

"There!" someone shouted.

Spencer squinted against the glare in the Bay of Gibraltar. An hazy shape appeared in the distance: a modified Airbus A330 MRTT descending fast over the hills of Algeciras. Vespina, carrying the Prime Minister, government officials, journalists, civilians... Buddy.

Ethan shuddered. "Okay, here we go. This is really happening."

Spencer placed a steadying hand on his shoulder. "You've got this. You have help."

Ramirez switched screens. "Got them on our radar now."

Around them, emergency vehicles positioned themselves along the runway's length. Fire crews in heat-resistant gear checked equipment. Medical teams stood by, hoping they wouldn't be needed.

"Altitude five thousand," Ethan said, voice trembling. "Drop the speed to two-fifty?"

Farraday nodded. "Affirmative."

The shape in the sky grew larger, its distinctive silhouette now clearly visible against the azure backdrop. Vespina, queen of the RAF Voyager fleet, was coming in hot and heading straight for them.

Spencer held her breath. They had one chance to get this right.

CHAPTER 59

"Ladies and gentlemen, this is your lead flight attendant speaking." Somehow, her voice remained calm, composed. "We are making our final approach to Gibraltar International Airport. Please ensure your seatbelts are securely fastened, and all loose items are stowed."

Buddy Thompson glanced around the cabin. The seating rearrangement had created a strange intimacy in the rear section. Ministers sat beside journalists, aides next to diplomatic staff, all personal and professional boundaries temporarily suspended.

"This will be an emergency landing without landing gear. At this time, we ask that you review the brace position illustrated in your safety card."

Behind him, Buddy heard fearful voices. Two rows ahead, the journalist from the Telegraph turned and caught his eye, fixed him with an *I-knew-it* stare. At the front of the cabin, a flight attendant demonstrated versions of the brace position, first, bending forward and hugging her knees, then cradling her head against the back of the seat in front of her. "When you hear the command '*Brace, brace*,' please assume this position and maintain it until the aircraft comes to a complete stop."

The plane banked again. Through his window, Buddy saw the coastline creeping larger. Low hills blurred past, roads crisscrossed Algeciras, and beyond the bay, the Rock of Gibraltar jutted into the sky. The aircraft was descending rapidly, the Strait now a gleaming blue sheet beneath them, peppered with ships and tankers.

Across the aisle, Prime Minister Nicholas Selley sat with his wife, son, and two daughters. His eldest daughter, Emily, was on one end of the row, followed by his wife, Charlotte, their middle child, Mia, Nicholas Selley, and finally, his son, Jackson. The three children were already in the brace position, small bodies folded over their knees. But Selley himself remained upright, one arm around Jackson and Mia's shoulders, hugging them closer to him, gently rubbing his weathered hands over their backs. His wife did the same with Emily, whispering comforting words to her daughter.

Behind Buddy, the Guardian's political correspondent whispered furiously into her phone. "I'm telling you, this isn't just a technical issue. The COBR team has been huddled the entire flight. First, they said it was the autopilot, now it's the landing gear. Something's going on. I think—" She noticed Buddy watching and lowered her voice further.

More passengers were making calls now. "Laura? It's Dad." An older trade delegate's voice cracked with emotion. "Just wanted to say I love you, sweetheart. No, everything's fine. We're landing in Gibraltar. Just... just wanted you to know."

A young aide from the Foreign Office typed rapidly on her phone, tears streaming silently down her face. Next to her, Admiral Bailey stared stoically ahead, his left leg jiggling up and down.

"Breaking news," one of the BBC reporters muttered into his phone. "Vespina diverted to Gibraltar. Emergency landing. Mechanical issues cited. Prime Minister and COBR team on board. Will update when possible."

The plane lurched, dropping again in a gut-wrenching jolt before stabilising. Someone squealed. The cabin lights flickered momentarily.

Buddy closed his eyes. He should call Sarah, tell her he was sorry. He should ask to speak to the kids and tell them he loved them. Instead, his thoughts turned to Spencer. Was she down there now, watching from the runway? The thought brought unanticipated comfort.

He almost laughed at himself. Minutes from possible death, and his mind wasn't on his family. It was on her: Spencer. Ridiculous.

Or was it?

The plane's vibrations grew more pronounced as they descended. They were low enough now to see cars moving along the coastal road. Around him, passengers were making final calls, sending last texts, exchanging meaningful glances with colleagues who had become friends. How many of them were thinking of missed opportunities? The choices they should have made, the paths they could have taken, and the ones who got away?

Digger nudged Buddy. "If we survive this, I'm retiring tomorrow and moving to the countryside. I never learned to paint, and I never told anyone this, but I always wanted to. Always made excuses about not having the time."

"You'll have plenty of time," Buddy assured him, patting his hand on the back of his friend's. "Spencer won't let us crash."

"You seem very confident in this girl's abilities."

"Woman," Buddy corrected. "And, yes I am."

But the truth was, this was out of Spencer's hands now. She'd risked her life to gather intel, uncovered a plot far worse and far more imminent than either of them had imagined and risked her life again to find the terrorist and the device. Now, it was all down to the team at RAF Gibraltar and some mysterious gamer called Ethan.

Out of the window, the runway snapped into view, dead ahead. The plane banked and straightened again, aligning with the concrete strip of land between Spain and the British Overseas Territory. Emergency vehicles were lined up along both sides of the tarmac. The runway itself shimmered strangely, covered in some kind of white coating.

"One minute to landing," came the lead cabin crew's voice. "Brace, brace."

The instruction was echoed by flight attendants throughout the cabin. "Brace, brace."

All around him, passengers folded forward into the protective position except for the Prime Minister, who crossed his chest, closed his eyes and tightened his embrace around his children.

Buddy assumed the position, forehead pressed against his forearms. His cheek was still sore from being tackled earlier. In the artificial darkness, his mind filled with black and white, slow-motion movies of Vespina breaking up on impact and bursting into flames.

The plane dropped sharply. Someone prayed aloud. The engines quietened.

"Brace, brace."

Then came the moment of truth.

CHAPTER 60

S pencer could feel her heartbeat in her teeth. She crouched beside Ethan, every muscle taut. They were at the very western end of the runway, aligned perfectly in the middle, looking due west. The dry heat of Gibraltar wrapped around her, her sticky clothes rubbing against her burned skin. Dust itched the corners of her eyes. Ethan, hunched over the laptop, checked something with the Wing Commander, then typed in another command. Sweat beaded on his brow. He looked utterly unlike the horrified man he'd been minutes earlier in the Jungle. He looked like someone born for this moment.

Spencer glanced skyward. She could feel it. The shift in the air. The electricity. The approach.

"Talk to me," she said.

Ethan didn't look up. "We're bleeding speed, but we're still coming in fast."

She checked her watch and looked behind her. Crash teams were braced behind foam trucks, ready to burst into action.

A kilometre away, the hastily rigged arrestor net fluttered gracefully.

Ethan cursed under his breath.

"What?"

"I think we're tracking too far north," he said, pointing into the bay.

Ramirez and Farraday agreed, having to eyeball the approach.

"Not by much," said the latter.

"I'm adjusting heading, turning five degrees to starboard."

Vespina, like a winged puppet, angled right.

Spencer bit her lip. It looked impossibly low.

"Correcting back to zero-nine-zero degrees," Ethan muttered, fingers tapping the keys. "Final heading locked. Altitude... dropping by eight hundred feet per minute."

They could see the curve of the fuselage now, the reflective glint of the sun off its nose. The heat shimmering on the tarmac made the image blur at the edges, like a mirage. It might not look real, but it was heading straight for them.

"Cut the throttle," Farraday instructed, removing her shades.

"Throttle to idle," Ethan said.

The scream of the engines softened as the plane coasted. It was gliding now, the landing gear still retracted, no trailing flaps to slow its descent.

Lower. Lower still.

It was going to hit them.

Spencer ducked instinctively, throwing her arm across Ethan's back, pressing him face-down into the tarmac. The laptop, having issued its final command, skidded away, clattering across the ground.

No engines, but Vespina roared overhead regardless. The sound was deafening, like it was tearing the sky apart. The shadow of its bulk engulfed them, plunging the four of them into darkness for a second before the belly of the aircraft skimmed overhead, terrifyingly close. They could see the panels, the rivets, the grimy underside.

Then—

Contact.

The fuselage hit the runway in a violent, metal-on-concrete grind, the impact echoing off the north face of the Rock. Sparks erupted, golden arches that fizzled into the foam. A shriek of friction filled the air. Spencer pressed her palms to her ears, trying to dull the high, metallic wail.

Panels along the belly peeled, folding and twisting as the aircraft slid, disintegrating in a spray of shrapnel. Vespina's wings flexed dangerously but held. Sheets of metal tore loose and cartwheeled away towards the ground crews. Sparks surged around the cockpit as it skewed slightly left, fire licking from its underside.

Spencer's body shook. Ethan sat frozen.

"Did it—?"

She didn't answer. Not yet. The plane was still sliding.

The arrestor net snapped taut, straining against the weight of the jet.

It slowed. Slower. Slower. Bands of the arrestor net started to break, pinging away like snapped elastic bands.

And then quiet.

A moment passed, then two, before a voice crackled over the radio.

"Tower to Ground Team. Vespina has stopped. I repeat. Vespina has stopped."

Spencer staggered to her feet, exhaling so hard she almost collapsed.

They weren't dead.

***

Buddy Thompson didn't realise the plane had stopped moving until he felt Digger plant a sloppy kiss on the back of his head. Spontaneous applause erupted a few rows back. Others were still crying, a few still praying.

The shock of sudden stillness was just as jarring as the skid. A heartbeat ago, Vespina had been squealing across the tarmac, cabin lights flickering, metal screaming beneath them as fiery sparks danced outside the windows. Now, it was still. The end had not come. Not yet.

Smoke billowed around the windows, the heat of scorched tarmac permeating through the cabin floor. Then, in a rush, the world outside sprang into action.

Red foam trucks tore across the airstrip toward them, their hoses spraying thick white arcs over the plane. Ground crew in fireproof suits sprinted alongside, waving signals, ducking low against the blowing foam.

In the aisle, a flight attendant struggled to unfasten her harness. "Doors to manual!" she stammered. "Prepare for evacuation!"

Buddy looked up toward the front of the aircraft and visualised the untouched, reinforced cockpit door and the two pilots who remained behind it. He swallowed hard.

The cabin crew yanked open the emergency exit at the rear. Sunlight and smoke flooded in with the sound of hissing foam and shouted commands. A blast of heat made several passengers recoil. Then, with a thump and whoosh, the slide deployed.

"Evacuate!" someone shouted. "Orderly fashion."

Another door opened mid-cabin, a second slide blossoming outward. Passengers were moving now, crowding the aisles, their panic kept barely in check by the calm, assertive voices of the flight crew.

"Leave your bags. Remove high heels. Step forward. One at a time. Arms crossed, slide down."

The slides on the opposite side in the middle didn't inflate.

"Slide three is out!" a crew member shouted, waving toward the opposite aisle. People began redirecting, surging toward the functioning exits. Buddy moved quickly, helping a young reporter with a tear-streaked face. She nodded her thanks as he gently pushed her forward.

Across the cabin, the PM urged his panicking son to go with Charlotte.

"I'll be with you in a minute. Please, son. Go!" He pried the young lad's fingers away, pushing the boy to his mother, who shepherded him towards the exit with his older sisters.

"Come on," Charlotte Selley said, wiping his eyes. "Brave faces now."

"Prime Minister," Buddy called. "You need to go with them."

Selley shook his head. "Not until every last one of you is off. I'll be the last man out."

Like a captain on a sinking ship. The last one to leave.

Buddy wanted to argue, but there was no time. He turned to help a junior aide who'd fallen, pulling him to his feet. The air inside the cabin was growing hotter now. Alarms still blared. Smoke was starting to creep in through the seams of the emergency doors. It reeked, clawing its way into Buddy's nose. Still, it was a different smell that made his nostrils twitch: Fuel.

At the forward exit, the flight attendants could smell it too. They caught each other's eyes, nodding silently. Their instructions became more frantic and commanding. "Move, please, move! One at a time! Quickly now."

A burst of fresh foam doused the side of the aircraft. Fire crews aimed directly beneath the fuselage to cool the hotspots along the belly. The cabin jolted slightly as the foam blast hit, and a few people screamed.

Buddy glanced back. The rear of the plane was emptying, the bottleneck easing. A final cluster of passengers surged forward. One by one, they jumped, slid, landed, and ran. Some crew followed.

Buddy turned again. Only a handful remained. The Admiral. Groves. Two crew. The PM.

The Admiral lowered his ageing body onto the slide, pushed himself forward and disappeared from view. Groves followed, as did the crew, slipping their court shoes off before bouncing onto the slide like they'd been taught.

Buddy grabbed Selley by the arm. "Time to go. We have to move."

Selley gave a single nod. Buddy jumped first. The slide caught him, sending him spinning fast. He hit the ground hard, tumbled, and came up on his knees. Behind him, Nicholas Selley slid to the bottom, his suit soaked with foam, his face ashen. Buddy grabbed his hand and pulled him to his feet. Together, they ran towards his waiting family and away from the smouldering wreck of Vespina.

Selley's children wrapped their arms around their father as he kissed their mother. It wasn't the usual staged and forced kiss politicians gave their poor wives – awkward pecks on doorsteps, shows of solidarity, blundering attempts to look like a caring family man – this was the kiss of a couple pleased to be alive. Selley was nothing but authentic.

Digger approached, remarkably still clutching the eighteen-year-old Jameson's. The glass bottle reflected the smoky plumes behind them. Digger took a swig and handed Buddy the bottle.

"Here's to your retirement," Buddy said, toasting his old friend. They stood together, taking alternating sips of the amber drink, both men blinking in the bright Gibraltar sun.

They were alive.

And now, they needed to figure out what came next.

CHAPTER 61

S pencer stood at the edge of the runway, hands on her hips, the heat hitting her from all angles. The adrenaline had faded now, replaced with the dull feeling of exertion. She wasn't sore. She didn't know what sore was, but she felt dizzy and fatigued. The pungent scent of foam mixed with singed metal infused the air. At the eastern end, Vespina sat like a crippled vulture, emergency crews swarming her like ants.

Ethan was beside her, bent over, hands on his knees. His sandy hair stuck to his tanned, clammy face.

Still, he was handsome, his eyes bright and clear, a layer of stubble coating his square jaw.

"You saved them," she said softly, taking his hand.

He turned. "*You* saved them."

She managed a smile, brief but genuine. Russia's eighty-two million dollar black op had gone up in smoke. World War Three was no longer a foregone conclusion. Gibraltar was still standing. The Rock hadn't exploded.

Spencer ran her thumb over the back of Ethan's hand, feeling his knuckles and tendons. The same hand had issued careful commands to guide the plane down to the exact position needed to save everyone on board. She imagined how the whole thing would be spun. Undoubtedly, the PM would give a statement that evening about how one of the RAF Voyager fleet had experienced a catastrophic technical failure. The pilots – father and son – would be described as heroes who'd managed to bring the plane down with extraordinary skill before succumbing to undisclosed injuries. They'd ask for privacy at this difficult time. Conspiracy theories would circle, all conveniently unprovable.

The world would never know the truth.

She wouldn't be named. Nor would Ethan.

Zhou's disappearance would be noted and speculated about. Sun Li would emerge as another player in the arms trade. All evidence of DVS Holdings would vanish. Russia would keep quiet, their failure to execute the greatest attack in a generation as much of an embarrassment to them as Vespina's infiltration was to the Brits.

Aviation authorities would receive confidential reports urging them to increase vetting and check that isolated systems hadn't been bridged.

Half a kilometre away, a man in charcoal trousers and a white shirt emerged from the smoke; half of his crumpled white shirt hung out of his waistband, and a striped tie swung loose from his neck like a scarf. His pace quickened, jogging towards her.

Buddy. Spencer stiffened slightly, letting go of Ethan's hand. There had been a time when she'd have run to him. That time had long since passed. As he neared, his eyes found hers.

"Jesus Christ, Spence," he said when he reached her. His hand hovered awkwardly, unsure whether to grab her or steady himself. He settled for a tight-lipped nod and cupped a hand on her upper arm. "You look like shit."

She was sure she did. A bloodied, bruised, burned, sweaty mess. Not that Buddy looked like a centrefold either. He was pale, apart from a red friction burn covering his cheek. His hair, greyer than she remembered, was ruffled. She pictured him raking his finger through it during the stress of the past few hours. A few new lines around his eyes, too, but he was still in shape, still a man of power who could turn heads.

Spencer recognised the remnants of what she once saw in him. Not that she'd ever say it. She looked him up and down, then said, "Back at ya."

He tucked the errant half of his shirt back into his trousers. "Seriously, though, are you okay?"

She wasn't about to open up to him about the memories being here had conjured up or the fear she'd felt for her father's safety. Nor would she tell him how much she enjoyed the sensation of the knife sliding smoothly through Zhou's throat. Instead, she nodded, said she was fine and told him there was a John Doe in the Jungle that someone would have to come up with a cover story for.

His eyes flicked to Ethan. He stood straight now, wiping his palms on his trousers.

"You must be the gamer," he said.

Ethan nodded, offered a hand. "Ethan Campbell."

Buddy shook it, then clapped him on the arm the same way he had Spencer, though she suspected he slapped him a little harder than he had her.

"You're a bloody hero, Ethan. Not that anyone will ever know."

Ethan blinked, unsure how to respond.

Spencer stepped slightly away, staring back at the smoking plane.

"You'll need to be debriefed," Buddy said, "Both of you." But she wasn't really listening. His voice seemed tinny and distant. "Then, maybe I can buy you a drink? I'm sure you need it."

Spencer shook her head. Whether he meant she and Ethan join him and the other crash-landing survivors in some Government bar, or the three of them sip gin and tonics on a hotel terrace, or just Spencer and Buddy alone in a dark corner of an Irish pub, she wasn't interested. She was pleased he was alive, but that was as far as it went.

"No drink," she said. "And no debrief either. I don't work for you, remember? I was never here."

Everything would be sanitised by the end of the day. A major news story, yes, but no black swan. And for now, it didn't matter. Because Vespina had landed, and almost everyone had walked away.

Which was precisely what Spencer wanted to do. She took Ethan's hand and walked away.

CHAPTER 62

The walk to Upper Town passed largely in silence. Ethan led the way, his hand never leaving Spencer's. Gibraltar's winding streets lay quiet under the shock of what had just happened. Whispered conversations about the belly landing at the airport carried over back walls and out of living room windows as residents huddled around televisions or checked social media.

Nicholas Selley was on board. And his children! Yes, really.

Is the border still closed? Gabriella might have to book a hotel.

People tuned into GBC to hear the latest, but so far, there was no statement from Downing Street or Gibraltar's Parliament Building on John Mackintosh Square.

They climbed the worn stone steps before reaching the courtyard where bougainvillaea poured down the walls like a magenta waterfall. Spencer had the vague sense that it should have been beautiful, that she should stop and smell them, savour being alive, but she felt detached, floating slightly above

herself. The splendour of the world didn't register right now.
But it would. Eventually.

Ethan unlocked the door and held it for her. She entered
without speaking. Inside, the apartment was just as she
remembered: clean, calm, organised. But there were signs of
him leaving in a hurry, dropping everything when she'd called
him: a half-drunk coffee on the dining table and an unwashed
paintbrush next to the model Spitfire and its little jars of paint
lined up beside it. He hadn't even paused to shake the brush
in water.

He lifted the handset from the red rotary phone, placed
it on the side table and turned his mobile to silent. Then
he disappeared into the kitchen, returned with ice water and
waited until she finished the whole glass before guiding her to
the bathroom, where he turned on the shower and adjusted
the temperature.

He unbuckled the strap around her leg that held the ceramic
knife and placed it in the sink. He unsheathed the tanto knife
from her lower back, pausing to look at the dried blood coating
the blade. Questions were in his eyes, but they went unasked.

"Jesus," he muttered, seeing the triangular burn branded
into her back. "You should be in the hospital."

"Six will pay for the plastic surgery," she assured him as he
cut the fabric of her top away, leaving only the parts now fused
to her blistered skin.

Undressed, he helped her into the shower. The water ran
cool, soothing her injuries as blood, dirt, and sweat rinsed off
her skin and swirled down the drain in a cloudy mess.

***

The water pools beneath her feet, rust-tinted like diluted Robinson's Summer Fruits. Teenage Spencer is in the shower, with the water set to maximum pressure. Steam fills her childhood bathroom, swirling above her head like wispy clouds. She scrubs her fingernails, the tough little bristles rubbing back and forth over her skin. She's unsure if the blood she sees is Izzy's or her own from scrubbing so hard.

Minutes earlier, Paddy arrived: another police sergeant and Dad's best friend. Unlike her dad's nervous fidgeting, Paddy was calm. He moved and talked like someone who'd handled worse situations than this. His grumpy face surveyed the scene, and the skin around his eyes tightened as he took in what had happened in his best mate's home. He opened a thick plastic bag and held it towards Spencer. "Strip down. All your clothes. Everything."

She looked at Dad, worried. Self-conscious.

"We won't look," he reassured her. "Just take off everything and put it in the bag. Put these over your feet and get in the shower. Don't touch anything. The shower is already on, and the door is open. Don't touch the bannister, the door handles, light switches, anything."

She did as she was told, shoving one stained item at a time into the bag until she was naked. She felt cold, dirty, exposed.

A knock on the bathroom door makes her jump; she drops the nailbrush.

"Wash your hair twice. Rinse until the water runs clear."
Dad's voice. Low, calm. "Don't forget your ears, neck,
between your fingers, even your nostrils."

She nods, not that he can see her behind the curtain.

"Your pyjamas are here," he says. "Fifteen minutes,
Spencer. Then we need to talk."

Spencer grabs the soap and scrubs every inch of her skin
until her body feels raw. Her hands and face prickle, her
shins tingle. She wonders what prison will be like. Or is it
called juvie? Young offenders? Whatever the name, it will
be horrible, for sure, but at least if they beat her up, she'll
not feel it. But the bullying, the isolation, the psychological
stuff, that can still hurt her. And she'll miss Liam. She's put
him to bed almost every night since he was born. What will
he think tomorrow when someone else does it?

New smells drift through the floor, and caustic chemicals
make her nose burn even over the coconut scent of the soap.
She hears furniture scraping against tile and the hollow
thud of something heavy being moved.

Through the pipes, deep male voices carry from the
kitchen below. "... I know a place... Chopwell."

Was that where they were sending her? Was Chopwell
a young offenders' home? "... it breaks down blood
proteins... Quick-dry paint, two coats minimum..."

***

Ethan undressed and climbed into the shower with her. He wrapped his arms around her, speaking gently in her ear. "Let me take care of you."

Eventually, the water ran clear, and Ethan soaped both their bodies from head to toe, his hands moving tenderly over her injuries, avoiding her back. He shampooed her long, tangled hair, massaging her scalp as she tipped her head back, closed her eyes and just breathed.

Ethan opened the window a fraction, allowing a breeze into the small space, cooling her further. Spencer felt the fine hairs on her arms prickle.

In the bedroom, they made love without urgency or adrenaline, his lips on her shoulder, neck, and collarbone, his fingers laced through hers. Afterwards, they lay entangled beneath the ceiling fan, the blades turning above like a falling sycamore seed caught in slow motion.

She thought he'd fallen asleep until he whispered, "Stay."

"The night?"

"Forever."

She stiffened but didn't move, letting her head remain resting on his chest. "I can't. This isn't my home."

"It was once," he said, staring at the ceiling. "You moved here once. Move here again."

Her toes twitched beneath the bedsheet.

***

Ten minutes later, when Spencer emerges in clean pyjamas with her wet hair pulled back in a plait, Dad's friend, Paddy, is standing in the dining room wearing blue plastic gloves. Dad nods while Paddy talks, his voice unflustered, as if he's working any other crime scene.

"My mate works for Royal Gibraltar. They have vacancies. I'm telling you, Harry, they'll snatch your hand off, mate. I'll make the call."

They see Spencer and stop talking. Paddy hands Izzy's phone to Dad. "You know what to do?"

Dad nods. He picks up his car keys and puts his own phone on the table. "Listen to Paddy, Spencer. Do everything he tells you." Then, to Paddy, he gives a sad, submissive bow of his head. "Thank you."

He leaves, and Paddy waits until he sees the car drive off before turning back to Spencer. The living room looks obscenely normal: Liam's toy dinosaur squashed under the coffee table, Spencer's half-finished English homework, the family photos on the wall. Only Paddy's latex gloves and her father's absence suggest anything has changed, that she murdered a woman in the next room.

"Izzy never knew her father, and her mother died when she was eighteen. Correct?"

"Yes," confirms Spencer. "That's why Dad chose her. He thought... with us both losing our mums, I don't know, maybe we'd bond or something."

"Boyfriend?"

"No. I don't think so."

"She never mentioned one?"

"No."

Paddy takes a deep breath and points to the sofa. Spencer sits down, wondering if he can question her without a parent. Shouldn't she have a lawyer?

"Listen carefully." He checks his watch. "Your dad's shift finished at twelve. He was home at twenty past. It was Izzy's last shift—"

"No—"

"Yes. Listen. I owe your dad one hell of a favour, so we're going to get this right. It was Izzy's last shift. Your father accepted a job with the Royal Gibraltar Police Force and starts next week. Izzy was sad that you kids were leaving, but she was going to try to find work in Manchester. When your dad got home, she was emailing recruitment agencies and giving her notice on her flat. Her email sent folder will confirm this."

Spencer's brows are lowered. She's confused. She picks up a cushion from the sofa, hugs it to her chest. Cold water drips from her plaited hair onto her back, between her shoulder blades.

"She stayed for a goodbye drink," Paddy continues. "You were allowed to stay up to say goodbye. Albie and Liam had to go to bed. Izzy's phone will show she went home at..." He checks his watch. "One thirty-seven. If anyone asks, you'll say she left at about half one. Tomorrow, Izzy will send a few texts and a few emails; she'll post a cryptic message on Facebook about a new start. Then she'll board a bus to Manchester and will leave her phone on the bus. Someone will either steal it, or it will be handed into lost property, but it won't be claimed."

It finally clicks. Paddy isn't here to arrest her. This isn't an interrogation; it's a rehearsal.

"It's going to be a long night, Spencer. Your dad and I will take care of the kitchen... and Izzy. You need to pack for everyone. One case each, no more. Passports, clothes, and a few toys. Gibraltar's a nice place. Sunny."

She's never heard of it.

Paddy looks her dead in the eyes. "You need to be clear on the timeline, Spencer. Start packing. Your dad will quiz you when he gets back."

CHAPTER 63

S pencer and Ethan sat curled together on the sofa, their naked bodies half-draped beneath a throw printed with retro LP covers. Ethan put his arm around her, holding her close, stroking her bare shoulder, carefully avoiding her wounds.

The ceiling fan turned lazily above them, shifting the warm air in gentle pulses. Outside, the sky was a dark navy blue, but a flickering streetlamp tinted the courtyard in strobes of soft amber. Somewhere in the building, someone was playing Oasis, Liam Gallagher's vocals bleeding faintly through the wall.

The television glowed in front of them in the otherwise unlit room. Ethan sipped Tetley from a chipped mug with a picture of a Barbary macaque on it; Spencer cradled a cup of hot water with lemon in both hands. The citrus-scented warmth did little to chase away the pressure of the day.

Onscreen, a polished GBC anchor sat poised, his face serious as he read from an autocue. A banner rolled beneath him: *BREAKING: Prime Minister's plane makes daring emergency landing.*

Footage rolled of the foam-slicked runway and charred tarmac, of emergency crews sprinting to the plane tangled in the elastic of the arrestor net. Cut to shaky phone footage of the landing from the perimeter fence, where four silhouetted figures at the western end of the runway ducked as the plane came into land.

Ethan nudged her. "Our fifteen minutes of fame."

"Fifteen minutes is right. Any trace of that footage will likely be wiped by then."

A correspondent on the ground began man-on-the-street interviews recorded earlier in the day when the light was still good.

"I was meant to be on a bus to Malaga," complained a red-faced man, gesturing angrily. His hands flew about, sunlight reflecting off garish sovereign rings. "But they closed the border, didn't they? I had an appointment. Bloody disgrace."

Spencer suppressed a chuckle. She recognised the man. Colin something. The condescending arse whose house she'd staged a break-in at. She bit her lower lip to keep from laughing. "He'll get over it," she murmured.

Ethan smiled, but his eyes were tired.

The footage changed again. Now, the British Prime Minister stood at a podium in a clean suit and new tie, his family behind him. His voice was flat, his words scripted by Six and heavily rehearsed:

"Earlier today, the plane I was travelling on, one of the RAF Voyager fleet, experienced a critical technical malfunction. Thanks to the calm professionalism of our flight crew and the swift response from emergency services, all passengers have been safely evacuated."

Spencer exhaled slowly through her nose. There it was. The official line. No mention of the pilots. No Russian-backed remote hijack, no war averted. Just a technical malfunction. Demeaning for the RAF but manageable.

"While investigations are ongoing, I wish to thank the authorities, both here in Gibraltar and those back home, for their seamless coordination in a time of crisis. My gratitude also extends to the emergency responders on the ground at RAF Gibraltar, whose courage and efficiency were instrumental in ensuring the safety of all on board, including my dear family."

Selley turned and smiled at his wife and children. Charlotte Selley returned his smile, adding a supportive dip of her chin and a loving look in her eye. His three children stood stiffly, unaccustomed to the cameras and still reeling from their experience.

"Our friends in Morocco have kindly rescheduled our visit for after the G7, which I am still very much looking forward to attending. Though I am happy to hear we will make the remainder of the journey to Italy by road rather than air."

Polite chuckles from the press.

"For now, let us be grateful for the lives saved, for the professionalism shown, and for the enduring friendship between Britain and Gibraltar. Thank you."

Spencer sipped her drink, let the lemon cleanse her throat. Ethan shifted, his arm tightening around her shoulders, drawing her in. She succumbed and let her head rest against his chest, where she listened to the slow thud of his heartbeat. He hadn't asked again if she'd stay. He didn't need to.

She felt it in the way he held her, in the way he watched her in silent sadness. It made her ache for him. Not because she didn't care. She did. But she couldn't settle. Not here. Not anywhere. London was too loud, too showy. Gibraltar was too claustrophobic. Newcastle... Newcastle didn't belong to her anymore.

She said she'd stay the night, and she'd honour that. But she would slip away soon, maybe before sunrise. First to Marbella, where a private clinic would take care of her back. Invoiced to Six, of course, the least they could do. Then she'd head west to Tarifa, spend a few weeks recuperating and watching the raptors finish their migration from Africa. She quite fancied sitting on a hilltop somewhere isolated from constant traffic and crowded thoroughfares. Somewhere where the only noise was the rushing thirty-knot wind. She'd point her binoculars to the sky and observe the vultures and eagles soaring overhead, effortlessly riding the thermals. There, she'd forget all about Zhou, Li, Buddy. Not Ethan, though. She had no reason to want to forget him.

She picked up her phone and tapped the screen to life. Brought up the BBC News app. The top headlines were all about Vespina. Statements from Brize Norton, RAF Gibraltar and Westminster, reassurances from the Civil Aviation Authority.

She scrolled through the thumbnails of the burned-out plane and stressed politicians to the next section: News from Tyne. A photo of police tape. Woodland. Mud.

HUMAN REMAINS DISCOVERED IN CHOPWELL WOOD.

Her stomach flipped.

Spencer had learned it here, in Gibraltar of all places, that secrets could be buried in caves, sealed in tunnels or wedged into the folds of the Rock, but with enough time, limestone eroded, and tectonic plates shifted. Sooner or later, all secrets were pushed to the surface.

Chopwell. Izzy.

Shit.

- AUTHOR'S NOTE -

As well as being an author, I am a sailor, a full-time liveaboard sailor who, after sailing around the UK with my husband and our little dog, decided to continue the adventure by cruising through France, Spain (including the Costa da Morte, or Coast of Death, mentioned in the opening chapter) and Portugal on our way to the Mediterranean.

We booked a winter berth in Gibraltar, where we would rest and plan the next sailing season. Arriving in Queensway Quay after what was rather a gruelling season left us with a huge feeling of achievement. Staring up at the iconic Rock of Gibraltar from pontoon A, my mind started racing: I *had* to write a thriller set here.

Writing what became Dark Rock helped me adjust to staying in one place after so long on the move; it gave me a sense of purpose when sailing was no longer my day-to-day routine, and it was a welcome challenge after writing police procedurals for so long. The Rock loomed over Queensway, so majestic and enduring, I wondered, *but what if it wasn't? What if I blew it up?* (Fictionally speaking, of course.) And thus began *a lot* of research.

The science behind Dark Rock:

Though Dark Rock is a work of fiction, several of the technologies and events mentioned are very real.

Chris Roberts, a cybersecurity expert, once claimed to have accessed a plane's autopilot system mid-flight using the in-flight entertainment console. He was questioned by the FBI but not charged.

A colour-changing nail varnish that detects date-rape drugs is not on the market, but in 2014, four students from North Carolina State University developed the concept. The idea gained a great deal of media attention; some praised it, others criticised it as a form of victim-blaming, placing the onus on potential victims to prevent their own assaults. Their company now produces discreet, single-use drug test kits instead.

In 2002, Tsutomu Matsumoto, a Japanese cryptographer, used gelatin to create a fake finger that could **fool fingerprint scanners** four times out of five. His research prompted security companies to strengthen biometric authentication.

The **pine processionary caterpillar** is a genuine threat in parts of southern Europe. The toxin in their hairs can cause severe allergic reactions in humans and, in dogs, necrosis of the tongue and even death. (Don't worry, no caterpillars were harmed in the making of this book, and none were placed down anyone's pants in the name of research.)

If you'd like to read more, please join my newsletter list at **betsybaskerville.com**. Newsletter subscribers have access to **The Classified Files**, a section of my website where I post exclusive stories and behind-the-scenes content, including Spencer's wildlife journal and my handwritten notes from researching Dark Rock.

Thank you

I want to take a moment to thank you, my readers. Many of you are here because you've read my DCI Cooper series, so thank you for venturing out of Cooper's world and into Spencer's. Don't fret, more Cooper is on the way. The rest of you may have only just discovered me and my books. Welcome!

If you've enjoyed *Dark Rock*, it would mean the world if you could pop over to Amazon, Goodreads, or wherever you purchased the book, and leave a review. It only takes a few minutes, but it makes a huge difference to authors and helps other readers discover new books.

Thank you to my husband, Rob, who was always willing to discuss ideas for this book. In fact, he was the one who insisted the caterpillars had to go down Li's pants. Sorry, Li.

My parents and my good friend Jane also read early drafts of the book, and I'm grateful for their suggestions, typo-spotting, and enthusiasm.

Cheers to my fellow sailors, Geoff and Karen; my fellow martial artist, Craig; and my fellow writer, Camilla. Geoff, a skilled clearance diver, helped add sensory and safety details to the initial underwater scenes. Karen, a gardener, joined me in exploring the Northern Defences and identified several plants that helped build Spencer's character as a wildlife expert. Having never ridden a motorbike before, I turned to Craig, who has several. His knowledge helped craft the motorbike chase scene, which became one of my favourites to write. Camilla has lived in Gibraltar for many years, and it meant a lot to have a friend outside of the sailing community who understood my need to write and create. Thankfully, she didn't report me to any authorities when I said I was planning to blow up Gibraltar.

- ALSO BY B BASKERVILLE -

The DCI Cooper Series:
Cut The Deck
Rock, Paper, Scissors
Roll The Dice
Northern Roulette
Hide & Seek
Finders Keepers
The House Always Wins
The Bridge

The Spencer Bly Series
Dark Rock

Stand Alones:
The Only Weapon In The Room
Dead In The Water

- ABOUT THE AUTHOR -

B was born and raised in Gosforth, Newcastle and is an alumnus of "Gossy High." Surprisingly, her academic journey led her to Sunderland University, where she studied sport and exercise development, a far cry from the creative writing path she would later tread.

Life took her to charming North Shields, a place that would become a source of inspiration for her writing. The local beaches and the bustling Fish Quay infused her work with a unique coastal flavour.

In a personal plot twist, in spring 2023, B and her husband embarked on an adventure by moving onto a boat, accompanied by their naughty Welsh terrier. Together, they sailed an impressive 1600 nautical miles, circumnavigating the UK's breathtaking coastline.

In 2024 they decided to continue the adventure by sailing south along the coasts of France, Spain, Portugal and Gibraltar.

Away from the keyboard, or the helm, B enjoys reading, weight training, exploring new places, yoga, walking said naughty Welsh terrier, and drinking copious amounts of tea.

- Be Sociable -

Newsletter: You can subscribe to the B Baskerville newsletter using the form on BetsyBaskerville.com. You'll mainly hear from me when I have something to share, such as a pre-order going live, a new book release or sale etc.

By joining my mailing list you will also gain access to The Classified Files, exclusive behind the scenes content.

Facebook: B Baskerville - Author

X: B__Baskerville

Instagram: B_Baskerville_Author

www.ingramcontent.com/pod-product-compliance
Ingram Content Group UK Ltd.
Pitfield, Milton Keynes, MK11 3LW, UK
UKHW041051021025
8186UKWH00041B/290